FUTURE POPES OF IRELAND

DARRAGH MARTIN

4th ESTATE • London

4th Estate
An imprint of HarperCollins*Publishers*
1 London Bridge Street
London SE1 9GF

www.4thEstate.co.uk

First published in Great Britain in 2018 by 4th Estate

1

A catalogue record for this book is
available from the British Library

ISBN 978-0-00-829539-4 (hardback)
ISBN 978-0-00-829540-0 (trade paperback)

This novel is entirely a work of fiction. The names, characters
and incidents portrayed in it are the work of the author's
imagination. Any resemblance to actual persons, living
or dead, events or localities is entirely coincidental.

Printed and bound in Great Britain by
CPI Group (UK) Ltd, Croydon, CRO 4YY

MIX
Paper from
responsible sources
FSC™ C007454

This book is produced from independently certified FSC paper
to ensure responsible forest management.

For more information visit: www.harpercollins.co.uk/green

For Aoife, Gillian, Caroline and Brendan

Contents

I.	Baptism	1
II.	Beatification	35
III.	Communion	79
IV.	Confirmation	147
V.	The Revolutions of Rosie Doyle	199
VI.	The Pride of Damien Doyle	245
VII.	The Tricks of John Paul Doyle	293
VIII.	Boom	341
IX.	Bust	381
X.	Last Rites	417
	Acknowledgements	438

Series I:
Baptism

(1979–1980)

1

Holy Water Bottle (1979)

It was September 1979 when Pope John Paul II brought sex to Ireland. Granny Doyle understood his secret message immediately. An unholy trinity of evils knocked on Ireland's door (divorce! abortion! contraception!) so an army of bright-eyed young things with Miraculous Medals was required. Phoenix Park was already crammed with kids listening to the Pope's speech – chubby legs dangling around the necks of daddys; tired heads drooping against mammys – but Granny Doyle knew that none of these sticky-handed Séans or yawning Eamons would be up for the task. No, the lad who would rise from the ranks of priests and bishops to assume the ultimate position in the Vatican would have to come from a new generation; the Popemobile had scarcely shut its doors before the race was on to conceive the first Irish Pope.

First in line was Granny Doyle, armed with a tiny bottle of papal-blessed holy water. The distance between Granny Doyle's upheld bottle and the drops flying from the Pope's aspergillum was no obstacle; this was not a day for doubt. Helicopters whirred above. The Popemobile cruised through the streets. A new papal cross stretched towards the sky, confident as any skyscraper, brilliantly white in the sun's surprise rays. All of Dublin packed into Phoenix Park in the early hours, equipped with folding chairs and flasks of tea. Joy fizzed through the air before the Pope even spoke. When he did, it was a wonder half a million people didn't levitate immediately from the pride. The Pope loved Ireland, the Pope loved the Irish, the Irish loved the Pope; *this* was a day when a drop of precious

3

holy water could catapult across a million unworthy heads and plop into its destined receptacle.

Granny Doyle replaced the pale blue lid on the bottle and turned to her daughter-in-law.

'Sprinkle a bit of this on the bed tonight, there's a good girl.'

A version of this sentence had been delivered to Granny Doyle on her wedding night, by some fool of a priest who was walking proof of why Ireland had yet to produce a pope. Father Whatever had given her defective goods, clearly, for no miracle emerged from the tangled sheets of 7 Dunluce Crescent that night or for a good year after, despite all the staying still and praying she did on that mattress. Then, all she had for her troubles was Danny Doyle, an insult of an only child, when all the other houses on Dunluce Crescent bulged with buggies. Ah, but she loved him. Even if he wasn't the type of son destined for greatness, the reserves of Shamrock Rovers as far as his ambitions roamed, he was good to her, especially since his father had passed. Nor was he the curious sort, so much the better for papal propagation; he didn't bat an eyelid as Granny Doyle transferred the bottle of water to her daughter-in-law's handbag. His wife was equally placid, offering Granny Doyle a benign smile, any questions about logistical challenges or theological precedent suppressed. Only Peg seemed to recognize the importance of the moment, that divil of a four-year-old with alert eyes that took in everything: Peg Doyle would need glasses soon, for all the staring she did, and Granny Doyle could summon few greater disappointments than a bespectacled grandchild.

In truth, it was her mother's handbag that had Peg's attention, not the bottle of holy water. After a long day of disappointment, when it became clearer that the Pope would not be throwing out free Lucky Dips into the crowd, Catherine Doyle's handbag was Peg's only hope. It might have a Curly Wurly hidden in its folds. Or Lego. Perhaps, if Peg was lucky, there might be a book with bright pictures, which her mother would read to her, squatted

4

down on the grass while meaner mammys kept their kids focused on the tiny man on the tiny stage. Peg knew it definitely wouldn't contain her copybook, which was the one treasure she really desired. Since she'd started school a few weeks ago, Peg had come to love her slim copybook, with its blank pages waiting for Peg's precise illustrations to match her teacher's instructions. *My Home* and *My Mother* and the gold star worthy *My Street* were lovingly rendered in crayon, letters carefully transcribed from the blackboard – *Very Good*, according to Peg's teacher. It would be weird to take homework on a day out, Peg's mother said, as if squishing into a field to squint at a man with a strange hat wasn't weird at all.

Peg sighed: the holy water bottle disappeared into the handbag, one quick zip cruelly thwarting Peg's happiness. Her mother didn't notice her gaze, looking instead in the direction of the stage, like all the other grown-ups. That was the way of Peg's parents: they looked where they were supposed to, straight ahead, at the green man, at the telly. Granny Doyle had different kinds of eyes, ones that explored all the angles of a room, eyes that glinted at her now. Peg avoided that gaze and focused on her new leather shoes, both consolation and source of deeper disappointment. On the one hand, the bright black school shoes were the nicest Peg had ever owned. She had endured multiple fittings in Clarks before they found a pair that were shiny enough to impress a pope and sensible enough not to suggest a toddler Jezebel. They were perfect. Except they would be better in the box. They looked so pretty there, Peg thought mournfully, remembering how nicely the tissue paper filled them, how brightly the shoes had shone, before the trek across tarmac and the muck of Phoenix Park had got to them. The morning had contained more walking than Peg could remember and not a bit of it had been pleasant: a blur of torsos that Peg was dragged through, the grass an obstacle course of dew and dirt. Only the thought of the shoebox – the smell of newness still clinging to the tissue, waiting for Peg's nose once she ever got home – kept Peg's spirits up; soon, she would be back in 4 Baldoyle Grove, in her room with its doll's house and shoebox and soft carpet.

'Come on, you come with me. We've a long drive ahead of us.'

The shoebox would have to wait; Granny Doyle had other plans for Peg. The grown-ups had been negotiating while Peg had been daydreaming and it suddenly became clear that Peg's feet would not be taking her back to 4 Baldoyle Grove that night. Peg looked forlornly up at Granny Doyle's handbag. She knew exactly what it contained: wooden rosary beads and bus timetables and certainly not a Curly Wurly; some musty old Macaroon bar, perhaps, which Peg would have to eat to prove she wasn't a brat or some divil sent to break Granny Doyle's heart, an organ that Peg had difficulty imagining. *It'll be a great adventure*, Peg heard Granny Doyle say, the slightest touch of honey in her voice before briskness took over with *Come on, now* and *Ah, don't be acting strange*. Acting strange was a popular pastime of Peg's, never mind that most of the grown-ups paraded in front of her deserved such treatment. Peg looked up at her parents. They were useless, of course; they couldn't refuse Granny Doyle anything.

'Come on, now,' Granny Doyle said, in a softer voice, feeling a stab of affection for her odd little grandchild. A calculating creature with far more brains than were good for her, perhaps, but Peg could be shaped into some Jane the Baptist for a future Pope. There was no doubt that such a child was coming – 29 September 1979 was not a day for doubt! – and Granny Doyle felt a similarly surprising wave of love for the crowds that only a few hours ago had been intolerable. Euphoria trailed in the air and Granny Doyle clung on, sure that this was the date when all the petty slights of her life could be shirked off, the superiority of Mrs Donnelly's rockery nothing to the woman who would grandmother Ireland's first Pope. Even the plod of the brainless crowd could be handled with tremendous patience, especially when she had her elbows at the ready.

'We're going to have a great weekend,' Granny Doyle said, cheeks flushed.

Peg had no choice but to follow, a long line of grown-ups to be pulled through as her shoes sighed at the injustices of outside.

Later, when Peg scoured photos of the Pope's visit to Phoenix Park, she found it difficult to remember the crowds or the stage or even the man. She had a nagging uncertainty about whether she could remember this moment at all; perhaps she had come to realize the significance of the event for her life and had furnished a memory shaped from fancy and photographs. Later, there would be the jolt that here was perhaps her first mistake; in her darker moments, Peg Doyle would wonder if everything might have uncoiled differently had she never taken her grandmother's hand.

But Granny Doyle's grip was not one to be resisted and Peg found herself pulled into the crowds before she could wish her parents goodbye. Something else that Peg would always wonder about: did she remember her parents extending their arms at the same time before she was whisked off? A gesture hard to read, half-way between a wave and an attempted grab, nothing that was strong enough to counteract the pull of Granny Doyle or the tug of the future.

2

Handbag (1979)

There is no record of what happened to the contents of the holy water bottle. As with many of the items in this history – the Blessed Shells of Erris; the Miraculous Condom; the Scarlet Communion Dress – no material evidence has remained.

Given the personalities involved, it seems likely that Catherine Doyle sprinkled the holy water on the bed-sheets as instructed. Both the angle of the holy water as it fell from the bottle and the arc of Catherine Doyle's eyebrows as she poured it have been lost to history. Did she do it with great ceremony, like a woman from the Bible pouring water from a jar? Was there instead a rueful roll of the eyes, an ironic dance routine? Can a more erotic encounter be discounted? Elbows propped on strong shoulders, legs curved around a supple frame, a conspiratorial glance between the two. Fingers dipped into a bottle, tracing the contours of a body, travelling across thighs, honing in on the source, the pump of future Popes ...

This history refrains from comment. It is enough to report that when Granny Doyle emptied her daughter-in-law's handbag nine months later and donated all of Catherine Doyle's things to the St Vincent de Paul, no bottle of holy water was found inside, empty or otherwise.

3

Folding Chairs (1979)

She could almost walk to Galway, Granny Doyle felt, still buzzing
from seeing the Pope that morning. Even Dunluce Crescent felt
fresh as she turned the corner, as if the glow from Phoenix Park was
contagious, no part of Dublin untouched. The quiet cul-de-sac
tingled with life, its unassuming brick houses suddenly resplendent
in this papal-endorsed sunlight. Her house was the finest, Granny
Doyle knew that: 7 Dunluce Crescent had a grand garden and a
large porch extension that gleamed in the sharp sun. Granny Doyle
felt a surge of pride for her son, for this was Danny's greatest
achievement. He could build things, had built the finest porch in
Killester; who cared if that upstart Mrs Donnelly had added a water
feature to her rockery?

The only emotion Peg felt at seeing Dunluce Crescent was relief
– which was misplaced, as her little legs had barely flopped onto
one of the porch's folding chairs before Granny Doyle was making
grand plans to leave again. 'We'll have to beat the traffic,' she called
out from the kitchen, as if any other Dubliners would be mad
enough to chase the Pope around the country. 'He'll be well on his
way,' Granny Doyle added, keen to share her radio updates with
her friends gathered in the porch. Glass was the great friend of
gossip and the porch served as the de facto community centre for
the other old biddies on the street. They had all moved into the
crescent within a few years of each other in the late Fifties and here
they were, families raised and husbands buried, their lives moving
in synch, morning Masses in Killester Church and the excitement

of Saturday's *Late Late Show* and Sunday roasts shared with disappointing children and glowing grandchildren and every event unpicked in Granny Doyle's porch, which contained a folding chair for each of the auld ones on Dublin's own Widows' Way.

Peg imagined Granny Doyle's neighbours as the fairies from *Sleeping Beauty*. Mrs McGinty was the tall, stern one and she mostly ignored Peg, which was far from the worst thing an adult could do. The McGintys had never had children and with her husband long gone, Mrs McGinty's life revolved around the Legion of Mary, the youth branch of which she chaired with zeal. Mrs McGinty stood poker-still in the porch, eager to get going, the boot of her car packed the night before.

Mrs Nugent was her opposite in almost every way. A tiny woman, full to the brim with mischief and gossip, Mrs Nugent had enough energy to power the road through a blackout. Hearing that Peg was joining them, Mrs Nugent unleashed a stream of chat – *isn't that brilliant, pet?* and *won't we have a great adventure, love?* – gabbling onwards as if she'd never met a silence she couldn't fill. Worse, she'd decided to bring one of her many grandchildren along for the trip, some ball of fury and flying limbs whose name Peg declined to remember, but who might as well have been called *Stop That!* for the number of times Mrs Nugent directed the sentence towards her.

Mrs Fay was the only one of Granny Doyle's neighbours who had the temperament of a Disney fairy. A large woman with a kind face and impeccably coiffed white hair, Mrs Fay's shoulders could easily have accommodated wings. Mrs Fay kept a basket of proper chocolate bars by her door for Halloween, not cheap penny sweets like Mrs Nugent or hard nuts and apples like Mrs McGinty. All sorts of other delights awaited beyond the threshold of 1 Dunluce Crescent, Peg imagined: freshly baked biscuits, shelves filled with books, curtains with tassels she could spend an afternoon admiring. Mrs Fay still had a Mr around, so she wouldn't be joining them – a shame, because Mrs Fay was the only one of them who had noticed her new shoes and Peg was sure she'd stash decent treats in her handbag.

'He's left Drogheda,' Granny Doyle shouted from the kitchen, information that seemed to add urgency to her clattering, even though the Youth Mass they were planning to catch in Galway wasn't until the next morning.

'He'll be lunching with the priests in Clonmacnoise next,' Mrs McGinty said.

'Isn't it a crying shame that Father Shaughnessy gets to meet him,' Mrs Nugent fumed. 'And him a slave to the drink.'

Mrs McGinty tutted, a sophisticated sound that conveyed both that *she* would never criticize the clergy so openly and that Father Shaughnessy was not the sort who should be lunching with the Pope.

'Oh dear!' Mrs Fay said.

Long ago, Mrs Fay had decided that most events could be met with an *oh dear!* or a *lovely!* and thus she was always ready to temper the world's delights or iniquities.

Meanwhile, Mrs Nugent had found a new topic to animate her.

'Did I tell you that Anita's Darren is going to be one of the altar boys at the Mass tomorrow?'

'So you said,' Mrs McGinty said in a thin tone.

'Lovely!' Mrs Fay offered.

Darren Nugent's proximity to a pope was enough to summon Granny Doyle from the kitchen. Before her brilliant holy water idea, she'd been tired of Dunluce Crescent's many connections to the Pope. Mrs McGinty had a fourth cousin who was concelebrating the Mass in Knock. Not only was Mrs Brennan's brother-in-law due to sing at the choir in Galway, but didn't he get his big break at her Fiona's christening, so she was basically responsible for his career. Even pagan Mrs O'Shea who could only be glimpsed at the church at Christmas, Easter at a pinch, had a shafter of a son who had helped clean the Popemobile. Now Granny Doyle could bear it all with fortitude, convinced that no Darren would ever develop a posterior suitable for a papal chair.

'I can get you all Darren's autograph tomorrow if you want,' Mrs Nugent offered.

'He'll have to learn how to write first,' Mrs McGinty tutted.

Granny Doyle was more magnanimous.

'That would be an honour,' she said, locking the inside door and scooping Peg up off her chair. 'And you'll have to get me yours as well: didn't you say that the Pope winked at you?'

This was a well-placed grenade, Mrs McGinty's fury at the blasphemy involved in a winking Pope strong enough to get them all out of the porch before it shattered. 'He did, looked at me right in the eye and winked,' Mrs Nugent insisted, chortling all the way down the footpath, displeasure the lubricant that kept them all together because Mrs McGinty lived to judge and Mrs Nugent lived to incite judgement. Granny Doyle beamed, loving the chat and her neighbours and her street and her granddaughter and even *Stop That!*, who at least had the wisdom to raid Mrs Donnelly's rockery when she was after missiles to launch at passing traffic.

Peg clambered into the back of Mrs McGinty's battered Fiat, beside *Stop That!*, who had abandoned her rocks to investigate the weaponry potential of seat belts. Mrs Nugent shuffled in beside them, *stop that!* and *are you all right, pet?* and *it was not a bit of dirt in his eye!* launched between the last few precious puffs of a cigarette. Peg wriggled away from *Stop That's* seat-belt attack to look out the back window. Mr Fay had joined his wife on the side of the road, the better to properly see off their car. Both Fays thought that attending the Pope's Youth Mass would be *lovely*, so there was slim chance they'd rush forward to rescue Peg. They stood there, smiling and waving, on the side of the quiet street in the afternoon sun. Peg gazed at the porch behind them, enticingly empty, the perfect place to spend the day, if Mrs McGinty hadn't pressed her shoe against the accelerator.

Dunluce Crescent was only a scrap of a street, so by the time Peg's head bobbed up again, they had already turned the corner and the kind smiles and waves of the Fays had disappeared from view, replaced with rows of other red-brick houses, indifferent to the motion of their car, waiting instead for fresh coats of paint and attic conversions and tarmac paving over gardens, the fortunes of the Doyles nothing to them.

4

Roll of Film (1979)

The next morning, something of a holiday spirit remained. They slept in, skipped the Sunday Mass, left the sheets in a tangle around their limbs. Danny Doyle still had some film left in the camera from the day before, so of course he clicked.

'You dirty pervert,' she called.

He smiled and wound the film again.

'You'll never be able to develop this.'

She fixed her hair, posing now, legs twined around each other in the air, no hand outstretched. Lying naked on their bed. Something between a smile and a smirk. It was the last shot. The film started to rewind as he pressed down, making him worry that it might not come out.

5

Plastic Spade (1979)

Peg woke up to the Pope's nose brushing her forehead.

'Isn't this brilliant? They were selling them two for a pound at Guineys.'

Mrs Nugent continued to wave the commemorative tea towel in her face while Mrs McGinty's expression conveyed the blasphemy involved in drying dishes with the Pope's face.

'You're not going to use that, are you?'

'Of course not,' Mrs Nugent said.

Granny Doyle snorted to show her displeasure with the ornamental display of a potentially useful object. Mrs Nugent ignored the pair of them.

'I'm going to get it autographed!'

'By your Darren?' Mrs McGinty asked slyly.

'By her winking boyfriend,' Granny Doyle said.

The titters that followed were too much for Mrs McGinty, who rounded on the slumbering Peg and *Stop That!*

'We'll never get anywhere if this lot don't get a move on,' she said.

Peg groaned. She'd hardly had a wink of sleep in the small folding bed she'd shared with *Stop That!*, who spent her dreams battling supernatural foes, limbs jagging towards Peg as she vanquished monsters. They'd arrived in Mayo late last night, the lot of them bundling into Granny Doyle's childhood home in Clougheally, at the edge of the Atlantic. It wasn't at all on the way to the Pope's Mass in Galway but it was a place to rest their heads and a chance to pick up further flock for their mad pilgrimage. A clatter of second cousins were coming with them, as well as Nanny Nelligan, Granny Doyle's mother. Peg couldn't help staring at her great-grandmother, whose many wrinkles announced that she'd been born in the nineteenth century and whose constant sour expression suggested that she might have been happier staying there. It was a shock to Peg that anybody could be older than Granny Doyle, yet here was this ancient creature, clad in dark shawls and muttering in Irish, roaming around her creaky house at the edge of the sea.

The house was haunted, Peg was sure of it, another reason she had hardly slept. They could definitely hear ghosts, *Stop That!* had agreed, in a rare moment of interest in something Peg said. 'That's just the wind,' Granny Doyle scolded, but Peg was sure she was lying; Peg caught the fear in Granny Doyle's eyes too. Even if it was the wind, it wasn't an earthly gust; Peg's window at home never rattled like this. It was the house, with its black-and-white photographs of people who had died, and its doors, which creaked with the ache of being opened, and its air, thick with secrets and sadness. Besides, Clougheally would be glad of the ghost, there wasn't much to the village otherwise: a few other houses, with scraps of farm; one newsagent's; two pubs.

'Will we have a quick trip to the strand before we head off?'

Aunty Mary, at least, knew that the only sensible thing to do in that house was to escape. Aunty Mary was Granny Doyle's younger sister, though Peg called her Aunty, because she seemed to belong to a different generation to the hair-curling ladies of Dunluce Crescent. Aunty Mary kept her hair grey and styled into a severe bob. The trousers she wore matched the *seen-it-all* stride of her legs and *say-what-you-like* set of her chin. Peg was sure that the students in the Galway secondary school where she taught were terrified of Mary Nelligan. Not Peg, though: Peg never saw a trace of this Scary Mary. Aunty Mary was the one to show Peg the spider plant where scraps from Nanny Nelligan's bone soup could be hidden, *sure that thing'll be glad of them*, or the rock on the strand where notes could be left for fairies, *we'll see what they say*, never a trace of harshness about her voice when she spoke to Peg.

Granny Doyle had gone off to get Nanny Nelligan ready for the day, so Aunty Mary seized her advantage.

'It'd be a crime not to say hello to the sun on a day like this.'

She had Peg and *Stop That!* dressed and marching down the path to the beach before Mrs McGinty could object; Aunty Mary had a way of getting what she wanted.

Seeing the dawn on Clougheally strand was something that everybody should want, Peg was sure of it. The Atlantic rushed towards them, bringing the news from New York, went the saying – not that anybody in Clougheally paid any mind to the sea's gossip, enough goings-on in Mayo to be busy with. Peg stared at the horizon, amazed at the sight of sky and sea for ever. A cluster of small fishing boats braved Broadhaven Bay and some bird swooped this way and that but otherwise the place was tremendously empty, a delight after all the bustle of Phoenix Park. Peg could easily imagine the Children of Lir soaring through a similar sky and settling on Clougheally's boulder, its claim to fame and name: *Cloch na n-ealaí*, the Stone of the Swans (an English error, Aunty Mary tutted, for *carraig* would have been the appropriate word for a boulder, though Peg liked the smallness of *stone*, as if the place was sized for her).

Peg made Aunty Mary tell her the story of the Children of Lir every time they visited. King Lir had four children, Fionnuala and her three brothers, who were as good as could be. Too good for their wicked stepmother, in fact: she had them turned into swans and sentenced the poor creatures to nine hundred years of exile around the loneliest places of Ireland. They cried and suffered and huddled in each other's wings but after nine hundred years they turned into wrinkly grown-ups, met Saint Patrick, and got baptized before they died. Clougheally appeared in the part with the suffering: three hundred of the Children of Lir's years of exile were spent in Erris, the borough in County Mayo where Clougheally was located. Local legend had it that they huddled together on a special stone and looked out at the Atlantic. It still stood there, so the story went, the Stone of the Swans, a boulder on the other edge of the beach, treacherously perched on a mound of rocks: a scary place to spend centuries.

'*Stop that!*'

Stop That! had a different interest in the Children of Lir's boulder: it was the most dangerous item to climb on the beach, so she made a beeline towards it.

'Would you not play a nice game or something?' Mrs Nugent huffed, her feet finally on the beach.

Stop That!'s idea of a game was scouring the sand for the ideal missile to fling at whatever poor bird was flapping its wings in the distance. Peg left her to it, guarding the treasures on her own corner of the beach. Aunty Mary had given her a plastic spade and the beach was hers to explore. There were all sorts of brilliant things to find: pennies that might come from different countries and brightly coloured pieces of glass and so many shells that Peg could have spent the day cataloguing them. Peg didn't rush, supremely content sifting sand from shells, arranging her little collection in order of size. She'd pick the prettiest to bring back to her windowsill in Dublin and she might even draw one in her copybook. Aunty Mary stood to the side, helping Peg spot a gem occasionally, mostly just watching her, quietly. Even Mrs Nugent kept her chat inside, enjoying her morning cigarette and cup of tea on the empty beach, that spectacular stretch of sand, where the flap of wings from across the bay could be heard on the right day. Organizing her collection of shells on the sand in the morning sun, Peg felt a surge of happiness.

But there was Granny Doyle, a cloud across the sky.

'What are the lot of ye doing? Mammy's waiting in the car and we'd want to get going if we're to miss the crowds.'

Aunty Mary braced herself and shot Peg a *such are the trials of life* glance.

Mrs Nugent stubbed out her cigarette on one of Peg's shells and turned towards her granddaughter.

'For the love of God, stop that, would you: you have your dress wet through! We *had* better get going: I'd say the Pope is only dying to get my autograph!'

6

Toast Rack (1979)

Catherine was the one to venture downstairs, eventually. She'd have to check the clock and phone Peg and deal with the day, though not yet. First, breakfast. She smiled as she caught a glimpse of her body in the kitchen window. Her bare toes drummed against the lino as she eyed the steel toast rack suspiciously; she wished the toast would pop faster, afraid the spell would break if she stayed away too long.

They'd eat the toast in bed, she decided, not waiting until it cooled to butter it.

7

Vatican Flag (1979)

Even the rain couldn't break the buzz in the air. Granny Doyle didn't even bother with her brolly. Nobody in Galway racecourse would have their spirits broken by a bit of drizzle. Pope John Paul II wasn't going to be dampened. If anything, he had more energy, as if Ireland had recharged him, not a problem for him to burst into song upon request. The crowd started it, tens of thousands of voices roaring out the song that had become his anthem.

> *He's got the whole world in his hands,*
> *He's got the whole wide world in his hands.*

Granny Doyle looked around the crowd and beamed. Galway racecourse was a sea of Vatican yellow flags, like an All Ireland where everybody was on the same team. Everybody was singing along: Mrs Nugent waving her tea towel and belting out the tune; Mrs McGinty thrilling in her best Church Lady voice designed to test stained glass; her mother bobbing her beshawled head in time with the beat; the Clougheally crowd of second cousins joining in, joyfully out of key.

The Pope stayed on the stage after the Mass, joy widening his face. When he spoke it was with the heart-heave of a teenage Romeo, a fallible and unscripted pronouncement, one all the more charming for it: 'Young People of Ireland: I Love You.'

The crowd erupted into a cheer that travelled like a Mexican wave.

Mrs Nugent chuckled.

'Didn't I tell you he's always talking to me?'

Even Mrs McGinty managed a laugh at this; it was impossible to frown. If she'd had a bottle large enough, Granny Doyle would have captured the happiness in the field and been a rich woman for years.

'Quick now, we'll take a photograph.'

Granny Doyle passed the camera to Mrs Nugent, scooped up Peg and marched over to her mother. Aunty Mary was left to the side; no harm, she'd only spoil it.

'Big smile for the camera, like a good girl,' Granny Doyle said to Peg.

Mrs Nugent fumbled for the button.

'All right now, one … two … three … cheese and onion!'

The photograph was a remarkable coup, heralding never-again-seen skills from Mrs Nugent. Peg, Granny Doyle, and Nanny Nelligan squinted at the camera in the foreground, Pope John Paul II was flanked by Bishop Casey and Father Cleary in the background, heroes all three. A special effect of the morning sun gave the appearance of halos, the smiles of all three women stretching to meet the light.

Months later, Peg clutched the photograph, thrilled at a memento she was allowed to keep. Granny Doyle had given it to her for Christmas, pleased that her plan had worked and that it was only a matter of months before some John Paul Doyle arrived into the world. Peg loved the photograph, even though her shoes were outside the frame. It was evidence that she was somebody who mattered, somebody who had once shared the sunlight with a pope. For years she clung to the sanctity of this snapshot, even when she might better have torn it in two. It captured the moment precisely: an island united, crowds of the devoted, everybody as happy as Heaven.

8

Bloody Tea Towel (1980)

The first miracle of John Paul Doyle was survival.

In other circumstances, the tea towel might have been kept for posterity, a version of Veronica's sweat-soaked shroud. A former nurse, Granny Doyle cleaned up the kitchen her son couldn't face. She picked up the chair that had fallen and scrubbed it down. She returned the phone to its table on the hall. She mopped the blood from the floor, decided it was best not to keep the mop. She scooped out the half-eaten breakfast cereal into the bin, washed and dried the bowl, returned it to the cupboard.

The tea towel was put in its own plastic bag and sealed in another bin-bag before it was thrown away.

9

Catherine Doyle Memorial Card (1980)

Danny Doyle lit another cigarette. He'd had to blow the smoke out the window, back when he was a teenager. Now it didn't matter if the little room filled with smoke, with his Da dead and Granny Doyle too worn out to shout at him. She was busy with the babbies, leaving Danny to his old box room and its sad yellow aura, the source of which it was hard to locate. It couldn't be the amber on the window from his smoking; the curtains were always drawn, especially in the day. The yellow of the curtains had faded to a pale primrose, hardly enough to explain the aura. So, it might just be the jaundice about his heart; what else was sad and yellow?

Another fag. Something to keep his hands busy. He wished there were cigarettes for the brain, something that his thoughts could wrap around and find distraction in. Brain cigarettes? He was going mad, he had to be. *Sure you're not high?* That's what she would have said, with an arch of her eyebrow – he could hear her voice clear as anything in the room – and Danny Doyle felt a sharp pain in his chest at the thought that the only place Catherine Doyle was in the room was trapped in a tiny rectangle.

There she was, smiling at him from a plastic memorial card. Her name (Catherine Doyle), her dates (1951–1979), some prayers and platitudes (May She Rest in Peace; Oh My Jesus, Forgive Us Our Sins and Save Us From the Fires of Hell). He'd let Granny Doyle pick the photo for the memorial card, and the sensible photo she'd chosen would not have been out of place in a Legion of Mary newsletter: this was not a Catherine Doyle he recognized. Surrounded by prayers and a pastel background, this woman was not the type to let toast crumbs fall onto a bed or push her face into silly shapes when Peg was taking a bath; this was not a woman who could quack. Staring at the memorial card, it was hard to remember the tone that she had used to tell the stories that put Peg to sleep or to admonish him when he'd forgotten to pick up milk, harder to imagine how 'Danny' might have sounded from her mouth, what shades of affection and exasperation might have coloured it.

Danny picked up the roll of film instead of another cigarette. Where could you take it? Not Brennan's chemist. Nowhere on the Northside. Maybe some shop in town, some alley off O'Connell Street. But then, the thought of it, a stranger staring at her naked body, looking at him like he was some sort of pervert: he couldn't do it.

Danny Doyle turned the capsule over and over in his hand, the single bed in his old box room already sagging with sadness underneath him.

10

Statue of the Sacred Heart (1980)

Peg stared at the holy water font in the hallway. It was one of the many features of 7 Dunluce Crescent that did not appear in her doll's house. It was a small ceramic thing, hanging precariously by a nail, a picture of the Virgin Mary on the front. Much too high for Peg to dip her finger into, which meant she relied upon Granny Doyle or her father to bless her as she passed the threshold. Neither was particularly diligent. Peg felt that she'd lost two parents for the price of one. Danny Doyle spent all his days in the box room with the curtains shut, all the Lego castles that they were going to build forgotten in Baldoyle, along with everything Peg had ever cared about (her doll's house; her shoebox; her life!). Granny Doyle was too busy charging about the house after the triplets to worry about the fate of Peg's soul. Peg almost felt as if she were becoming invisible.

'In or out, child, are you coming in or out?'

Granny Doyle still had eyes for Peg when she got in the way. Peg retreated down the dark hallway and left Granny Doyle to her chorus of old ladies. The triplets were asleep at the same time, so the chance to tell everybody just how busy she was could not be missed by Granny Doyle. Peg heard Mrs Fay's warm voice and suppressed the desire to rush into the porch and see if she'd brought any sweets in her handbag. It wasn't worth the fuss. Peg couldn't face Mrs Nugent telling her that *you're a brave girl, aren't you, love?* or Mrs McGinty trying to find some softness in her face or Granny Doyle losing patience and banishing her outside, where she hadn't a single friend to hopscotch beside. Besides, it wasn't sweets Peg was after; she'd lost her whole life, even a Curly Wurly wouldn't cut it.

Peg made her way into the empty sitting room, an eerie space with the telly turned off. The room had rules, invisible lines that demarcated territory as sharply as barbed wire. Granny Doyle sat in the armchair by the window, its cushions shaping themselves around her body, even in her absence. Danny Doyle took his father's spot in the armchair by the television, dinner tray propped on his knees when he watched the football. Guests took their pick of the chairs by the wall. Peg might have switched on the telly or clambered onto one of the forbidden armchairs but what would be the point? How could she care about cartoons? There hadn't been a television in her stately doll's house, only a library with walls of miniature books that Peg had arranged carefully. Peg squeezed her eyes shut and longed for some magic to make her small and safe and transported inside the doll's house but no, she was stuck in her stupid-sized body, too small to escape and too big to disappear.

Peg ambled past the dining room, with its mantelpiece filled with forbidden figurines, photos of people who Granny Doyle never saw, and postcards from places she had never been to. It was the nicest room in 7 Dunluce Crescent: sun streaming through the curtains and catching the dust in the afternoon. People hardly ever went inside, much less dined there.

Peg meandered towards the kitchen, the heart of the house. But what was here for her? No bright gingham tablecloth like in her doll's house, for starters, only some grubby thing splattered with stains. The smell of bone soup and burnt rashers clinging to the curtains. More pictures of the Virgin Mary than Peg could count, as if she were a family member. And Granny Doyle's wireless, the radio she kept on all day, so the patter of indignant listeners and reassuring men filled the room, no space for any thoughts.

27

If Aunty Mary had been visiting, Peg might have been able to escape to the back garden. Here at least was some quiet, the hedge nice and big to hide behind, a large stone where fairies could leave presents, so Aunty Mary said, her face gleeful when they overturned the slab and uncovered an old sixpence beside the scurrying wood-lice. Aunty Mary had the key to the shed, too, and here, beside the reek of petrol from the lawnmower and the jumble of abandoned possessions, were piles of books in cardboard boxes. Peg longed to put them on a shelf and move them about until they were arranged by colour or size or whatever took her fancy. She couldn't read them yet, but Aunty Mary left her be. No *aren't you a brave girl?* or *you'll be a good girl and help your gran, won't you?* Aunty Mary even gave Peg some books with pictures, to be getting on with, while Peg took 'a little break' from school to help out her granny with the triplets. But Aunty Mary was in Galway, teaching other children. The back door was locked and Peg didn't have the key, even if she could have reached the handle.

Aunty Mary might have understood why Peg was so upset at the loss of her copybook, another victim of the move. Peg had cried for a solid day when she realized her copybook was gone, her tears intensifying when Granny Doyle came home with a new one, its lines all the wrong size and none of Peg's pictures or attempts at the alphabet preserved inside.

'I want my copybook,' Peg dared to say, face red with the rage, fists clenched at such an unjust world.

'Ah love,' Danny Doyle sighed, patting her on the head and shuffling up the stairs, no use, as usual.

'I went to Nolans special for that,' Granny Doyle said, in a voice that was trying to be nice, even as she opened up the impostor copybook.

'I want my copybook,' Peg repeated, wishing that Aunty Mary or her mother or somebody sensible were there, but she only had

Granny Doyle, who turned to the counter and started to chop onions. Granny Doyle had a formidable back, which tensed to show just how much she wasn't listening, but Peg wouldn't let her win this fight. 'I want my copybook,' she howled, hoping that the words might smash windows or send the house tumbling down or right the ways of this wrong world. But all they did was send Granny Doyle's hands to her brow, onions abandoned as she turned around.

'Be quiet or you'll wake the triplets.'

This could not stop Peg, whose words had turned into wails.

'I want my copybook!'

'Listen, Missy, I won't tolerate this carry-on …'

Peg would carry on crying until she exploded, *I want my copybook* and *I want my old house* and *I want my mammy* clear in every scream and sob.

'Just shut up!'

'I want my copybook! I want—'

The slap pulled the air from Peg's lungs. A quick tap across the face, it only stung for a second, but Peg felt the air in the room shift in that instant. Granny Doyle's face reddened. She turned back to her onions as if nothing had happened, leaving Peg stock-still in the middle of the kitchen, her face turning white from the shock of it. Something her mother had never done. A violation. Peg knew then that her tears would be of no use here. She swallowed them inside, thinking that this was revenge of sorts. Fury filled her instead, a colder kind that kept her face pale. Her composure remained, even as Granny Doyle turned around in frustration – 'see, you're after waking the triplets' – Peg's mask fixed as Granny Doyle made a great show of taking away the new copybook and bringing it to 'somebody who'll appreciate all I do for them'. Lines had been drawn that day: there would be no more need for slaps or tears. Peg understood there was no out-wailing a baby; if she wanted her way in 7 Dunluce Crescent, she'd have to be inventive.

'Are you all right, love? Would you not want to go outside and get some fresh air?'

It was Mrs Nugent, in to heat up the kettle for a fresh round of tea. This was all grown-ups did: made tea and smoked and offered Peg things she didn't want.

'I can see if my Clare's ones are about? Tracey might even let you play with her new Barbie, though you're not allowed to give it a perm, the cheek of her, trying to make it out like me! Though, I says, you'd be paying a lot more for a doll with this quality hair, wouldn't you!'

Peg looked longingly out at the back garden, where the books Aunty Mary had brought were locked up in the shed. There wasn't a hope that Mrs Nugent would read her mind.

'Staying here to look after the young ones, are you, pet? Aren't you a brilliant help to your gran? Janey, I wish some of my lot were more like you!'

Peg left Mrs Nugent, who continued to chat to the radio, and trudged upstairs. She *would* look in on her siblings, cosied up in their cots in the biggest room in the house. They weren't even cute, like Peg's doll. All they did was sleep and cry and stare, the last action being apparently a great achievement. 'Isn't he a great one for looking at you?' the ladies in the porch said. 'Oh, he's a sharp one,' Granny Doyle agreed. *He* was John Paul Doyle, the only one of the triplets who warranted such attention. Granny Doyle had recognized her future Pope immediately in the runt of the litter, the one who had struggled to stay alive. Granny Doyle knew that cunning trumped primogeniture and here was the Jacob to Esau, a battler who could cut the queue to the head of the Vatican: Ireland's first Pope, John Paul Doyle!

A great one for his poos: that was how Peg saw John Paul. Helping Granny Doyle with the endless parade of cloth nappies through the house, Peg had excellent insight into the triplets' characters. While Damien produced nice little nuggets of poo that could be easily cleaned up, John Paul's explosive shits were messy and unpredictable. A testament to the luxury of riches that Granny Doyle piled upon him – for he would be the first to have a scoop of mashed potato; the baby who'd get the extra bit of bottle – but Peg knew that there was more to it than nurture: it was John Paul's nature to cause trouble, something he excelled at.

Any sensible person would have placed their bets for papal stardom on the other two babies, docile creatures who were happier sleeping than staring. Damien had the capacity to sit quietly in his high chair; unlike John Paul, he did not need to play 'food or missile?' with every object that crossed his path. He was as placid as could be; he was doomed from the get-go.

Rosie was a trickier character to get a handle on. The only one named by her father, Rosie somehow managed to wriggle away from the moniker of 'Catherine Rose Doyle' before she could talk. Even as a baby there was something vague and dreamy about Rosie Doyle; she had none of the solidity of a 'Rose' or a 'Catherine'. Against the perversity of John Paul and the purity of Damien, Rosie was a perpetual hoverer, a swirl of characteristics, none of them fussed enough to dominate. For the record, her poos, those reliable auguries of the future, were hard to classify, trickles that were neither solid nor liquid, not quite committing themselves to any shade of the spectrum.

One thing Peg was sure of: they were all united against her. If there were any magic to be found in 7 Dunluce Crescent, it was all concentrated in the triplets' room; eerie the ways in which they seemed to be connected, as if some elastic band that Peg could never see looped them together. How else to explain how they could all wake up at the same instant or wail as one? Or not quite as one, Peg realized, as she creaked open the door innocently and peered at her slumbering siblings. John Paul woke the second she looked at him; she was sure of it. His little face looked up at Peg, cunning glinting in his eyes before he opened his mouth. The elastic band snapped into place and there the three of them were, miraculously awake and immediately furious at the world. That was the way of the triplets: John Paul set the tune and the other two followed. 'Ssssh,' Peg tried but it was hopeless. She could hear the commotion in the porch below; she'd be murdered.

Peg had a second to decide: try and placate the triplets or run and hide? Her legs made the choice immediately; in 7 Dunluce Crescent, escape was always the answer. She shot past her father's closed door (as if he'd be any use) and dashed into her room. Well, Granny Doyle's room with a camp bed in the corner and a chest of drawers for Peg, no space even for a shoebox. Peg's heart raced as she heard Granny Doyle heave her way up the stairs. The triplets had only been down for the length of one cup of tea: she'd be mad. Peg examined the room for hiding places. There was the dusty wardrobe, no hope of Narnia behind Granny Doyle's rain macs and dry-cleaned skirts. The covers of Granny Doyle's big bed were an option, though the smell of Granny Doyle was enough to keep her away. Under the camp bed it was, a space Peg could just about crawl into. The walls were thin enough that Peg could hear Granny Doyle shush the triplets, John Paul cradled as she launched into some country lullaby.

Peg didn't dare move, as much as she hated the room and its statue of the Sacred Heart. It wasn't possible to switch it off, so Granny Doyle said, so Peg had to stare at the odd statue of Jesus, with his huge red heart, throbbing brightly in the dark. For some reason, it was the statue that made it hard for Peg to find sleep, not the restless triplets in the next room. Every night, she'd lie on the small camp bed, her body tight as a tin soldier, eyes fixed on the pulsating red candle. Granny Doyle had shared the room with the Sacred Heart since her wedding night. If the statue's light had bothered her once, it didn't now, and her snores always filled the room before Peg's sobs.

At least he wouldn't tell on her, Peg thought, peeping out from under the bed to stare at Jesus. He was too busy with his heart that never stopped beating, even after death: he wasn't bothered with the misdeeds of Peg Doyle. Nor were any of the statues or pictures of the Virgin Mary, when she thought of it. Whatever Peg did – spitting out Granny Doyle's soup or stealing a glimpse into the dining room – had no impact on the serene smiles of the Virgin Marys dotted throughout the house. She *could* become invisible, Peg decided; a thought to chew on. He'd keep her secret, this statue of the Sacred Heart, not a word out of him, even as Peg heard Granny Doyle cart the triplets downstairs, the hope of rocking them to sleep surrendered.

Peg would stay here until she was caught, she decided, settling into the carpet. She dug in her elbows, ready to wait Granny Doyle out. An hour passed. Two. Peg smelled the whiff of cabbage and pork chops from the kitchen: surely Granny Doyle would fetch her now. But no, Peg heard Granny Doyle's footsteps up and down the stairs as she delivered a tray to her father's room, no thought to check in on Peg. Tears welled up in Peg's eyes, their provenance unclear, as she probably wouldn't be in trouble now. Yet to be invisible had its own hardships, the statue of the Sacred Heart's expression unmoved by her tears, its heart continuing to flicker as night crept into the room.

It was as if the statue knew, Peg thought, years later: the statue understood that 7 Dunluce Crescent was impossibly small for all the people and feelings it was suddenly asked to contain. From the beginning, the house had been impatient to expel some of its new inhabitants, unable to contain the miracles that would push against its walls. The statue intuited this: perhaps it even anticipated the trouble that would come, the sights it would be forced to witness. Yet it kept beating on, even as dark filled every corner of the room, while Peg sobbed herself to sleep.

The statue saw what Peg didn't: the heave of relief when Granny Doyle found her, the sign of the cross, the kiss. Granny Doyle managed to shift Peg's floppy limbs into the camp bed. She pulled the covers around her, bewildered at the devilment that such a quiet thing could get up to.

Little do you know, the statue might have said, for surely it intuited everything that Granny Doyle and Peg would do and say to each other before their histories ran out. It kept quiet, its scarlet candle throbbing away, its lips frozen in a solemn smile, its hands outstretched in a gesture of compassion, though they were made of stone, and limited, ultimately, in their ability to provide aid.

Series II:
Beatification

(2007)

1

Rosemary and Mint Hotel Shampoo (2007)

Kiss to say, honey, I'm home.

'Hello, Mrs Sabharwal.'

Peg rolled her eyes.

'I've told you, I'm not changing my name.'

'I know, but today—'

'That's not how it works, you don't own me because a year has passed, I'm not a washing machine that you bought in Walmart.'

A smile from Devansh.

'You remembered!'

Kiss to say, of course you remembered.

Pause to savour the scent of New York City on an April evening: young love and fast food and the promise of heat.

Pause to detect something else.

'You smell nice!'

'Don't sound so surprised.'

'What is that smell?'

'I showered after swimming. Borrowed some lady's fancy shampoo.'

Kiss to avoid questions about rosemary and mint hotel shampoo.

Kiss to avoid questions about what Peg was doing in a hotel on a Tuesday afternoon.

Peg removed the wine and take-out containers and brandished a brown paper bag.

'One year: paper!'

Kiss to reward ingenuity.

'Sorry, I didn't know you were going to cook.'

'We can have a feast.'

'We can't have Chinese with pasta.'

'Why not?'

'I'll put some of this in the fridge …'

'Come here.'

Kiss to stop motion.

'You are looking sexy today!'

Peg opened the wine.

'*Today?*'

Kiss to demonstrate love in the face of provocation.

'You know I'd never be down on the librarian chic.'

'I know.'

Peg found a way to take a sip of wine.

'I had a meeting in the morning with a potential dissertation supervisor.'

'And you thought you'd seduce them into accepting you.'

'Exactly.'

A gulp of wine to wash down a lie.

'Let me know if you need a reference. I'm happy to vouch for your many attributes.'

'Generous.'

'I'll write a letter about your exceptional fingers which are excellent at typing …'

Kiss to demonstrate a relationship between word and thing.

'… and I can recommend your ears which can listen to lots of lectures …'

Kiss to tickle.

'… and these eyes …'

Kiss to touch.

'I'm starting to feel like Red Riding Hood.'

'Does that make me the wolf?'

'Mmmm, you're more of a bear.'

Kiss to say, fuck you, my love.

Kiss to say, Happy Wedding Anniversary.

Kiss to say, let's fuck across the counter amid knives and chopped peppers.

Kiss to say, yes.

Kiss to say, let's go.

Kiss to say, but not now, first, the dinner.

Pause to chop basil and let feelings settle.

'So, Ashima asked me to be Sara's godfather.'

'What?'

'They're having her baptized. You know what Gabriel's like and Ashima doesn't care but she thinks she can get Sara into some fancy-ass Catholic school, like she can't think of a worse fate for her child than public school.'

Shoulder-rub to comfort an underpaid, overworked public high school teacher.

'You think I'm godfather material?'

'Keep up that belly you'll be fat enough.'

'Whata ar'ya talkin' about?'

Kiss to stop impersonations.

'I couldn't go to the gym today; I was doing important research about this godfathering business.'

Peg walked over to Dev's laptop, knowing, before she looked, the site that would be open.

'Wikipedia is gymnastics of the mind.'

'Ha.'

'And I've been getting this sauce ready.'

Kiss to display gratitude.

Kiss to atone for judgement of Wikipedia reading and editing as an appropriate pastime.

Kiss to atone.

Pause to acknowledge the difficulty of approaching the topic of Peg Doyle's family.

'What were your godparents like?'

Peg's godmother was Aunty Mary.

'I'm not really in touch with them.'

But what was there to say about Aunty Mary?

'Were they relatives?'

Irish women disappeared from time to time and that was how it went.

'My godparents weren't really that important.'

And then they died and upturned your life in exile, but Dev couldn't possibly know about that; Peg had been careful not to show him the letter.

'Thanks.'

Kiss to acknowledge the appeal of pretend-hurt Devansh Sabharwal.

Kiss to avoid further questions.

'The main requirements are enough money to stuff a card, the ability to remember the kid's name, and, as far as I'm aware, being a Catholic.'

'Two out of three ain't bad? Ashima says they're being flexible about it. I guess it's silly. It's not like I'm going to start believing that dead dudes can make miracles.'

Tiny pause to tense at where the conversation was headed and search for any way to stop it.

'Did you see the news? Pope John Paul II is on his way to becoming a saint.'

A gulp of wine to wash down a lie.

'No.'

'Yeah! Mad isn't it, only two years since he's dead and already they've found some evidence of a miracle so he's halfway to being …'

She had the word in her head, despite everything.

'Beatified.'

'Right! I guess some guy in France claims that praying to the Pope cured his Parkinson's so now the Pope just needs one more miracle and he's Mr Beatified. Record time: it can take decades.'

'I guess men are working out their minds on Wikipedia across the world.'

'Ha! Yeah, I guess I got a bit distracted this afternoon … you know who else has a Wikipedia page?'

Pause to banish all conversation about the past.

'Pope John Paul III!'

Wine to wash away lies.

'I hadn't seen.'

'More than just a stub too, lots of links to YouTube and some interviews and …'

Move to the counter to banish all possibility of conversation about John Paul Doyle.

Pause to drain pasta and bitterness.

'So you're going to become a godfather?'

'I know, it's silly … I definitely can't provide spiritual guidance …'

Bite of lip to suppress knowledge of upcoming joke.

'Or *any* guidance, ha! And I don't want to be in the middle of one of Ashima's and Gabriel's fights. It's just, Sara is a great kid, you know? And it's nice to have that kind of official connection to a kid, especially if we're not …'

Pause to imagine children in subjunctive tenses.

Kiss to acknowledge vulnerability.
    'You'd be a brilliant godparent.'

Tiny pause to say farewell to children in subjunctive tenses.

'Well, it's not like I have to do it: you don't even remember yours.'
    Wine to wash down a lie.
    'No.'
    What was there to say about Aunty Mary? Fairy godmothers were for children, you couldn't ask them to stick around.
    'I'm still her uncle.'
    Irish women disappeared from time to time and that was how it went.
    'I'll still be part of her life.'
    That was the path of the Doyle women (Aunty Mary; her mother; Rosie; Peg): the only way to survive exile was to forget.
    'Peg?'
    Wine to wash away the past.
    'You okay?'
    Kiss to wash away lies.
    'Yeah.'

2

Box of Memorial Cards (2007)

Would the Pope be getting one too? Surely, he would, with the millions who'd want to be remembering him, and who could keep track of everybody who'd passed without the handy rectangles that memorialized people? Not Granny Doyle. The balance had tilted, so that she knew more who were dead than alive; she'd be lost without her little box of laminated lives. She sat in her porch and flicked through her box of memorial cards and wondered if the Vatican had ever made a memorial card for Pope John Paul II: he was two years gone, after all, they'd plenty of time. There might even be a special memorial card now that he was bound to be beatified: some poor crater cured of Parkinson's, already. She might have to start a new box; maybe she'd set up a special one for celebrities. *Daft thoughts*, she didn't know any celebrities and, in any case, there wouldn't be a special memorial card for the Pope – she had just checked, she hadn't any for poor John Paul I – and Granny Doyle would have to wait for somebody else to die before she'd start a new box.

'Daft,' Granny Doyle said, though the radio on the chair opposite her didn't respond. Some new yoke that John Paul had got her: Granny Doyle could swear that the news had got worse because of it. No mention of the Pope's miracle, never any good news, only some eejit jingling on about the upcoming election (as if she'd ever betray Fianna Fáil) and the nurses on strike (never in her day) and people killing each other from Mogadishu to Kabul while ads jittered on about things she didn't want: it was enough to send her to bed.

'It's a terrible world we live in,' Granny Doyle said, although the folding chairs were silent. Poor Mrs Nugent had settled into her box of memorial cards a long time ago and her daughters hadn't picked well at all; Mrs Nugent would have died a second death at the sight of the blotches and wrinkles in the photo. Mrs Fay hadn't been the same since Mr Fay passed a year ago, though she at least had done well enough to pick a picture where he still had a healthy batch of hair. Mrs McGinty was still going (she'd live to a hundred; indignation would power her that far) but they weren't talking to each other after the Pope John Paul III business. A shame, because the car outside Irene Hunter's had been parked there all night and the Polish crowd renting Mr Kehoe's house had received *three* packages in the space of an hour and all of that would have been enough to sustain the conversation for the morning.

'Daft,' Granny Doyle said, but the only occupants of her folding chairs were bits of plastic. Some new phone that John Paul had got her, with a camera on it, as if she wanted to be documenting her wrinkles. The new radio. And the Furby he'd got her, years ago, when she wanted company in the house but didn't want some yappy dog or cat conning her out of cream. A daft thing it was, gibberish spouting out of its beak most days, but she had let John Paul keep it stocked on batteries, had bought them herself when he forgot. It was nice to have a voice in the house, even if all it said was 'weeeeeee!' or 'me dance' or 'Furby sleep'. *Nice to have some intelligent conversation*, Granny Doyle would say, a joke between her and John Paul, something to be treasured, the thought that he was worried about her being lonely. And yet, if he were really worried about her being lonely, wouldn't he stay over some nights like she asked?

'Ah, well,' Granny Doyle said, looking over at the blob of purple and yellow plastic.

You can teach it to talk, John Paul had said, back when he visited.

That thing looks like a demon, Mrs McGinty said, back when they were still talking.

Isn't it lovely? Mrs Fay said, back when she still had some semblance of wits about her.

The Furby sat on the chair and slept. It spent most of the day sleeping, a sign of its intelligence. Granny Doyle stroked its fur but its eyes didn't open; probably for the best – it could scare the wits out of you with its laugh. She might have forgotten to put the batteries in. She could ask John Paul to get her some, but he'd just get them delivered, along with all her messages, which was a shame when the truth of it was she didn't mind about the milk – most of it ended up down the sink – it was her family she was starved of. Her fingers found her son's memorial card: a fine man he looked, there. Funny how photographs couldn't capture the size of a person. Mrs Nugent was diminished; no rectangle could capture the gossipy-eyed glory of the woman. Danny Doyle, on the other hand, looked bigger. A man who could build an empire, you might have thought. Well. She moved to the next one and there was Catherine Doyle, the dutiful daughter-in-law who'd left Granny Doyle three squalling terrors to rear instead of the one. And where were they now? Not in her box, thanks be to God, but the triplets had left her in an empty house, again. Not to mention Peg, a name like a paper-cut. Granny Doyle stiffened in her chair: no need to be remembering any of them. People made their beds; they lay in them. Except people never did make their beds properly any more, not the way her mother had taught her, not the way she had when she was a nurse, and this was a strange thing to be missing, to feel a pang for the house with all its perfectly made beds and nobody to lie in them.

'Daft thoughts,' Granny Doyle said, though the Furby stayed asleep.

She put the box of memorial cards under her folding chair; she couldn't remember why she'd picked it up in the first place. A dangerous thing to be doing, the past waiting to ambush you with each turn of the card, and the threat of tears too, *daft*, when Granny Doyle had never been a crier. Still, now she was, tears surprising her at strange times; it struck her that there might be a medical solution, some sort of hip replacement for the heart, or at least the eyes. In the meantime, she had banned onions from the kitchen.

The Pope! That was why she had fished out the box. Two years dead, the poor man, and her knees couldn't make it to the church to light a candle for him. She could have asked John Paul to drive her to the church, in a different life, where he hadn't torn the heart out of her. Would Pope John Paul II be getting a card? She couldn't remember what she had decided and she couldn't ask Mrs McGinty. She decided instead to root out the old photos from Phoenix Park; she'd battle the stairs if she had to.

Or, she could ask John Paul to bring down a box of old photos for her; he couldn't hire a company to do that. He was a good lad, despite everything that he'd done. He'd come if she called, if she could ever figure out which buttons on the phone to press. John Paul Doyle at least had turned out ... *well* caught in her mind, impossible to add, because whatever successes John Paul Doyle had achieved, she couldn't say that any of it had turned out as she'd planned, that giddy day when she'd practically conjured him into being. He might visit that weekend, yet, and the intensity of this desire – that John Paul sit beside her in the church for everybody to see – bowled her over, and she felt a hot liquid prick her eyes, and then somehow she was thinking about her other grandchildren, Damien and Rosie and Peg, taboo subjects, all of them.

The Furby opened its bright yellow eyes. Sometimes Granny Doyle wondered if Mrs McGinty was right: perhaps the creature was diabolical. Some dark nights, Granny Doyle wondered if the contraption had the voices of the disappeared trapped inside:

perhaps it was on this earth to judge her. *Daft thoughts* – John Paul had only bought it as a joke. Still, she kept the batteries in it. Still, she was glad of its gabble, happy to have any sound in the house. Still, she chanced the name.

'Peg?'

The sly old thing went back to sleep; if it had the voices of the disappeared inside, it wasn't sharing them.

3

Clerys Clock (2007)

You're a dirty pervert, Damien Doyle imagined Mark saying, once he arrived, feeling flushed at the thought of just how excited this sentence made him feel. He covered his blush with the *Irish Times*, sure that the O'Connell Street crowds were judging him, though they kept on walking. Damien stole another glance up at Clerys Clock, that grand structure that jutted out from the side of the department store and portioned out the city's time. The minute hand was closer to a quarter past; Mark was late. Mark was always late but Damien couldn't help his own punctuality; even the thought of turning up a few minutes late caused him distress. Besides, he didn't mind the wait; this was still novel, having somebody to wait for. A lover. Only lovers met under Clerys Clock, so the story went. Damien conjured visions of smartly dressed men waiting outside the grand department store, their hearts lifting at the sight of some pretty girl in a smock, rushing from some country train, stopping her step to a stroll, as Clerys' clockwork took over, sweethearts confidently tick-tocking towards each other for decades. Sweethearts who probably didn't call each other dirty perverts, Damien imagined, blushing again at this subversive meeting place: it was just possible that Clerys Clock might crash to the ground in protest.

Damien flicked through the *Irish Times* for distraction. He was the only eejit waiting under the clock – everybody had mobiles now, sure – and he wanted to project the impression of an upright citizen and not the kind of man waiting for the touch of his boyfriend's tongue in his ear. So, the news. More of the same: trouble in hospitals and protests against Shell in Mayo and the election in the air. The Greens had managed to nab a small piece about their education manifesto on page 4 but it was dwarfed by a story about the government's new climate change strategy, irritating when the Greens could use better coverage if they were going to gain seats, which they were: they had to! Damien skimmed the rest of the paper, only stopping once he found a picture of Brangelina, which sent his brain on a worried spiral about whether 'Marmien' was a worse couple name than 'Dark' until—

'Look at you, ogling Brad Pitt in broad daylight, you big pervert.'

Mark, surprising him as always, bounding up out of nowhere.

A quick kiss, the *Irish Times* and Brad Pitt quickly folded into Damien's satchel.

'You know only grannies and boggers meet under Clerys Clock?' Mark said.

And lovers, Damien almost said, though he held the words inside.

'I'm just appeasing your inner bogger—'

'I'm from half an hour out of Belfast!'

'"Bogger" just means "not from Dublin".'

'Sounds right. You, my love, are definitely an auld granny.'

'Feck off, you stupid bogger.'

Another kiss, right in the middle of O'Connell Street, grannies and boggers be damned.

This was new for Damien, all these actions that Mark could do so unconsciously – kissing a man in the street or holding hands with a man in town, not wondering whether Mrs McGinty or Jason Donnelly or who knew who would be turning off Talbot Street. Damien looked up at Clerys Clock ticking away; perhaps it had seen worse. Damien felt more self-conscious on the Northside, especially O'Connell Street; this, after all, was the home of religious nuts, where Damien himself, in his Legion of Mary days, had held up placards and bellowed chants against abortion alongside Mrs

McGinty. Though the fanatics had been moved along, exiled with the Floozy in the Jacuzzi, no sign of Granny Doyle, more space on the path for more types of people, and of course –

'That fucking yoke,' Mark said, weaving around the Spire and the circle of tourists. Mark couldn't walk past the Spire without a mini-rant; Damien could have set his watch by it.

'Wasn't Nelson's Phallic Pillar enough? Why did they need to build another giant penis? We keep shunting shite towards the sky, all part of the same problem – instead of making space to talk to each other we keep blocking the view.'

They had reached The Oval (Damien would have preferred the Front Lounge, but Mark only drank in old-man bars), Damien getting in the Guinness while Mark continued talking. 'The same problem' was the subject of the dissertation that Mark sometimes worked on: 'The Celtic Tiger Eats the Commons, 1973–2002'.

'It's the same shite as shopping centres. We used to have squares to discuss ideas in, now we have The Square. A great name, sounds like a place you'd want to visit and then it turns out to be an air-conditioned tomb full of stereos and shite. It's a smart trick, usurp the language of the thing you displaced: gouge out a valley and then call the monstrosity you plonk there Liffey Valley, brilliant really. But what we need is a square where we can share ideas instead of buy shite, you know?'

Damien did know; he'd heard this part of the dissertation before. Now that he was sure the bartender couldn't, in fact, be somebody from Dunluce Crescent, Damien relaxed and basked in Mark's monologue. Too many words, too many ideas to implement, but wasn't the Green Party the space for that and Mark was one of their best volunteers. Damien took another sup and admired everything about Mark: the frayed Aran jumper that he'd worn since the last millennium; the big hands that moved too much when he talked; the blue eyes that didn't move at all, lasered in on you, so that you could see every fleck of brown or grey in them, eyes that never seemed to need a blink or a break. Meanwhile, brightly coloured insects pirouetted in the region of Damien's diaphragm, the words fresh, even after a year: *my boyfriend.*

'... and *this* is why we need a space to freely debate ideas!'

Damien refocused. Mark had fished out the *Irish Times* to mop up some spilt beer and *this* was an article that Damien had missed: something about Pope John Paul II being beatified, not an election issue in Damien's opinion, though there was no telling what would get Mark going.

A thing to love about Mark: he could be so single-minded, wouldn't be swayed by any trivial distractions once he got going.

'Fuck all this hagiography shite! Nobody has the balls to say anything genuine when a famous person dies.'

'I suppose people need a period of mourning,' Damien dared.

'No,' Mark almost shouted. 'All this respect the dead stuff is just a way for the right wing to solidify their myths. It was the same with Reagan: the years after a public figure dies are the critical moment when their legacy is sculpted. You have to scrawl your graffiti before the concrete sets. Nobody has the balls to call the Pope out for some of his shite: preaching that condoms are a sin in Tanzania while people are dying of AIDS. It's fucked up that this is what makes saint material ...'

Damien took a sup of Guinness and nodded; it would be a while before Mark reached his pint or his point. He had to divert conversation from the Pope, away from any talk of Pope John Paul III. It had been years since he'd talked to his brother properly, not since *that business*, plenty of periods in Damien's past that he skipped over euphemistically. *That other business*, with Peg, who Damien definitely didn't want to think about. Damn the lot of the Doyles, Damien thought, nothing like family to stuck-in-the-mud you in the past, when Damien aspired to be all future. This focus on the future was what he loved about working for the Green Party, a political organization for the twenty-first century, not one rooted in the bogs of some civil war best forgotten, and here was the thing to steer them away from popes.

'Don't worry, babe, once I've got a new office in Leinster House, I'll keep you a section of wall to graffiti whatever you want.'

A thing to love about Mark: his eyes were only gorgeous, even mid-roll.

'Right,' Mark said. 'The whole country's going to change with this election.'

It was, though; Damien knew it.

'You won't be able to move with the paradigms shifting each other when the Greens get seven seats—'

'When we get ten seats,' Damien corrected him. 'And yes, it'll be all change. Catholic Ireland is dead and gone: it's with Pope J.P. in the grave!'

A thing to love about Mark: he was a great at impersonating radio talk-show hosts.

'The question is, how can we as a nation come up with ethical values that aren't tied to religion or nationalism? The question is, how do we become a people defined by the future rather than the past? Catholicism has been swept clear away, the question is how can we fill that gaping hole?'

'What was that you said about filling a hole?'

Mark laughed.

'Are you pissed already?'

'I am!' Damien announced, fizzy with the feeling; he felt drunk all the time now, even when he hadn't touched a drop.

4

Mitre (2007)

John Paul Doyle smiled. Smiling was his speciality: popes needed as many grins in their repertoire as politicians. A smile can take you further than a sentence, John Paul thought, something he'd write down, once he was reunited with his BlackBerry. It could be material for his biography. Or for a stand-alone stocking filler. Or, better, a self-help tome, paired with an exclusive seminar on smile-coaching. John Paul's fingers twitched; he was lost without his BlackBerry to record the thousand and one ideas that pinballed about his brain and he was on form that morning, odd as coke wasn't even involved: it must be the fresh air. Another idea: find something to bottle the fresh air here – a net? A bottle? – and ship it out to Dublin. Atlantic Air! John Paul was sure some eejits would drop a tenner for a sniff. He gulped in a lungful and let out a huge *nowhere I'd rather be than on the edge of the Atlantic in a pair of boxers and a pope hat!* beam.

In his few hours in Clougheally, John Paul had already trotted out several different smiles.

A *Pope John Paul III has arrived in Clougheally!* megawatt grin unleashed that morning.

A secret *yeah, this kip is Clougheally, nice eh?* smile flashed to the camera-guy.

A *so nothing's changed and here I am, back* half-smile all for himself.

A *fuck this fresh air!* grin and yelp for the benefit of the camera-guy, as he stripped to his boxers.

And a *let's get to work* smile and nod: he had to keep some of the smile power on reserve for the cameras.

John Paul couldn't help a grin at the thought of the video: it was going to be a good one. The Official Miracles of Pope John Paul III followed a certain formula. A familiar biblical reference (loaves and fishes; healing the sick) was revitalized with a contemporary twist (famine in Ethiopia solved; an escalator opened so no poor soul would have to miss five floors of shopping). Often, the video required that John Paul stripped to his boxers, useful for the controversy and the clicks. Today, Pope John Paul III would walk on water, miraculously buoyed by the powers of natural gas. He'd fall in, of course – that was how Pope John Paul III rolled, no gag too cheap – but he'd be back on his feet for the finale: standing on the gas rig and pulling out nets of money from the water. Nobody had hired him to perform this particular miracle, but as a cultural figure of some importance, Pope John Paul III had the obligation to wade into controversial topics and provide clarity. Some people didn't think that Erris was the right place for Shell's gas pipe; typical, for bedrudgers followed progress like flies to fresh shite. Pope John Paul III would banish the protesters. *Ignore the naysayers*, his smile would radiate. Didn't the Bishop of Kilcommon himself bless the gas rig a few years back? Believe in me and we'll walk on water; he'd write that one down too.

First, the video! John Paul made his way over to the fellas by the currachs and gave them Pope John Paul III's best *I'm freezing my bollix off here, let's get going lads, man among men* grin. Then, John Paul couldn't help it, even though the cameras weren't rolling yet: he made a show of searching for a sail, kerfuffling about for a second before he unleashed his catchphrase.

Ah now, I wouldn't know anything about that!

Coupled with one of Pope John Paul III's gormless smiles, of course, the one that suggested that the poor holy fool had got himself into another mess again. Together, the smile and the catchphrase had helped launch him towards YouTube stardom (well, in Ireland at least). He'd secured an upcoming feature on *Xposé* on TV3 and a mention in the *Sunday Independent*. He even had enough money to throw a few bob towards a camera-guy, an essential expense as his routine became more polished; he'd get an intern next! All tax-deductible, and if any prying eyes had questions about irregularities in his accounts, he had his catchphrase at the ready: *Ah now, I wouldn't know anything about that!*

The sentence proved reliably robust, especially when it was sheathed in irony. Most sentences these days had irony wrapped around them like a condom and so this one was a treat: an expression of not knowing that conveyed just how much you knew. He might keep it when he launched his political career, John Paul decided. Election season was on its way and he had a hunger to grace telegraph poles with his grin. Next time. Pope John Paul III was practically already a mascot for the government; he'd met half the Cabinet at the Galway Races. His grin at the end of the videos radiated optimism. Haven't we all done well, it said. Onwards and upwards. Don't let the begrudgers into government. Vote Fianna Fáil for five more bright years of prosperity. Vote John Paul Doyle for the best handshakes in town. He'd have to write some of this down, once he found his BlackBerry, and he'd have a real think about running in the next election, suss out some seat he could cruise easily through, a coy smirk and *ah now, I wouldn't know anything about that!* at the ready if some reporter got wind of his ambitions.

'Do I know you?'

John Paul turned. It was some auld one, weaving over to them before he could get in the currach. He shot the camera-guy a private smile: *here we go …*

It was hard to tell what views the auld one opposite might have about Pope John Paul III. If she were one of the 'it's a holy disgrace' brigade, he'd have a sober smile at the ready, one that

55

communicated respect and contrition and had 'May he rest in peace' hidden in its dimples. He even had an earnest, delighted, *yes I did hear about his miracle, isn't it great?* smile ready if she talked about the latest news, a *well, I have to be getting on* crisp grin to be unleashed if she suggested that his antics were demeaning the very concept of miracles. But she might only be after an autograph, so he had a bigger grin in reserve too, one that announced that it was the only dream of Pope John Paul III to pose with her and that he was delighted to sign a photograph for her granddaughter.

'You're Bridget Doyle's young one, aren't you?'

That wiped the smile clean from his face.

'Mary Nelligan's sister's grandson, isn't that yourself?'

A central part of being John Paul Doyle was learning to live with the black hole inside of him. He had strategies to keep the vortex under control. It was surprisingly easy, most of the time. The trick was to keep moving. The trick was to avoid the Doyles. The trick was to keep conversation light. Certain proper nouns were taboo (Peg; Damien; Rosie). Certain periods of time were to be avoided, large pockets of the 1990s not to be thought of. Smiles to be stretched; to breaking point, if it came to it. Don't dwell: that was a key one. The black hole liked nothing more than for you to stay still and dwell: that was when it grew, gulping away inside of you, reaching for internal organs.

The worst thing was that the black hole could surprise you. It could stay hidden away for a long while, hanging out beside an appendix or a gall bladder or whatever other useless things whiled time away inside a body. But then some small thing would activate it – some auld one asking if you were anything to the Nelligans – and there it was, pulling the heart and lungs towards it, swallowing everything, including whatever neurons sent messages to the mouth because even as John Paul searched for a smile he couldn't find the shape of one.

He should have seen it coming. Once he got Aunty Mary's letter, he should have realized: no avoiding the other Doyles now. Competing maxims had tumbled about in his head – *Don't Dwell* wrestling with *Seize Every Opportunity!* – until here he was, dipping his toe back in Clougheally after ten years; he should have known he'd be recognized. There was the shop where he'd pinched penny sweets and there was the boulder he'd climbed and there were the shells on the strand that he'd seen the Virgin Mary inside and here was the past, a rush of feelings twisting away inside, the murder of John Paul Doyle their only aim.

Relax, he tried to say, willing his knees to stay still. It had been ten years since he'd been to Clougheally. The auld one didn't know a thing. No need to get into the past. If he could stare down the sea without flinching, he could see her off too. After a moment, a smile found its way to his face: bemused, kind, *you must be mistaken*. He held out his hand, the master of all occasions.

'Sorry, I don't think we've met. I'm Pope John Paul III!'

The auld one looked suspicious.

'You're sure you're not Bridget Doyle's grandson?'

John Paul flashed his best smile, the one in tune with his catchphrase.

Ah now, I wouldn't know anything about that!

5

Rucksack (2007)

Of course, Rosie got onto the wrong subway and *of course* she ended up in the worst place in New York. Rosie wasn't prepared for the intensity of Times Square. That comforting pocket of Irish accents by the Aer Lingus bag carousel had disappeared and she was surrounded by American voices. Heat charged through the streets without bends and promised to knock her horizontal. Cheerful chains sold donuts that could blind you and coffee that was mostly whipped cream, and M&Ms in so many flavours and colours that you might die before you decided what to eat. Huge billboards flashed confidence and sold clothes and Broadway shows and screamed *Here You Are at the Centre of the Universe!* making Rosie want to lasso the first plane she saw and hitch her way back to Clougheally.

Breathe, Rosie reminded herself. She was on a mission. She had travelled an ocean to find a long-lost sister; she would not be deterred by a few flashing billboards. Tourists barged into her rucksack and cursed at her in a variety of languages but Rosie wasn't going to budge until she'd figured out how to get back inside the subway. She gazed up at the billboards, hoping that one of them might morph into a giant neon arrow; it was not too much to hope that the universe might be on her side. No space for directions in Times Square, though, only ads for H&M and news flickering across in an excited loop. Rosie felt even tinier. It was incredible that Peg lived in this city, which had no news about the election in Ireland or the protests in Clougheally. Not a peep about John Paul

Doyle. Just a stream of figures, stocks and shares going up and down, and whatever things Bush was ruining (the climate and Iraq, today) and then, a sentence to shock: POPE JOHN PAUL II TAKES FIRST STEP TOWARDS SAINTHOOD.

The sentence whizzed past before she could question it, not that Rosie cared about the details. She inhaled deeply and closed her eyes, practising radiating love towards her enemies. She did this, every morning, as part of her yoga routine, imagining turquoise rays of love that matched her hair emanating from her body and rippling towards her enemies. Usually she focused on the living – her family provided ample material – but if Pope John Paul II could be counted as a nemesis, then she should try to overcome her anger and send him love. Her eyes opened quickly: she couldn't picture it. And was nowhere safe from popes? Surely, here was a square that was safe from his reach, the home of *Saturday Night Live* – or its general vicinity, Rosie didn't care about the details. Hadn't Sinéad O'Connor stood in one of these buildings – or somewhere close; her aura remained, that was the important thing – and held up a photograph of the future saint, only to rip the picture into fragments. 'Fight the real enemy,' Sinéad O'Connor had said and twelve-year-old Rosie had known that the words were for her. *This is the man who stole away your sister*, Sinéad O'Connor might have said, as she ripped the photo into bits, while Rosie, curiously, had felt the opposite process, the formation of a solid identity, a core of steel inside the dreamy girl with her head in the clouds; in the aftermath of catastrophe, watching the Pope ripped to nothing on television, Rosie Doyle became a fighter.

Rosie stood mesmerized by the news ticking across the side of some building, but there was nothing more about the Pope. No sign of Sinéad O'Connor in Times Square: nobody to get upset about the news at all. The crowds around her showed no signs of perturbation: necks continued to crane upwards, fingers snapped at disposable cameras, voices squealed at the sight of women

59

dressed as candy or cowboys wearing nothing. She had to leave, Rosie realized. It had been a mistake to come, foolish to knock on Peg's door after all these years. Rosie started to walk. She didn't care which direction, abandoning her desire to descend underground, charging past tourists and *Sesame Street* characters and a military recruitment centre that made her want to spew a kaleidoscope of vomit.

After a couple of minutes, she realized where her legs were taking her. She was walking uptown on Broadway, billboards disappearing as the streets hit the fifties. As if her legs had their own agenda, Rosie thought with a rueful smile. Manhattan was difficult to get lost in, another general point against it for Rosie, who was a great meanderer, but a feature that was useful at this current moment in her life, with sweat on her brow and turmoil in her chest and a giant rucksack on her back. The friend she was staying with lived uptown off Broadway so she could probably walk it and then she wouldn't have to worry about taking an express train to the Bronx by accident. She was on a mission, after all; she couldn't forget Aunty Mary's letter.

Would Peg want to discuss Aunty Mary's letter? Would she even talk to her? These were questions that Rosie might better have asked before her flight across the Atlantic, ones to be brushed away now. They'd find the words, Rosie was sure of it. She imagined her aura: turquoise, loving, strong. She'd get the best of this city and her family. Rosie Doyle was a fighter (wasn't she?).

A breeze arrived as she reached Columbus Circle, some magic wind sent to ease her travels. Things would only get better from here. Soon the bodegas would outnumber offices and people would smile on stoops and the smell of green would rush across from parks and at the end of the path, waiting, would be Peg. They'd find the words, Rosie resolved, the soothing wind on her face a sign from the universe that everything might work out grand. The word sounded odd in her head – it had a different meaning on Broadway –

but Rosie clung to it, anyway, appreciating its solidity, the smell of Ireland off it. *Yes*, Rosie thought, marching down Broadway towards a long-lost sister, everything might turn out *grand*.

6

Rosemary and Mint
Shampoo (2007)

'What's the worst thing you've ever done?'

Peg added a giggle as punctuation; Gina, she figured, was a giggler. Nate pretended to take the matter into serious consideration, his head rattling from side to side.

'The worst thing I've ever done?' Nate repeated.

His name was not Nate though, no more than he was actually forty-nine. Peg did not mind. He knew what he was doing, something Peg loved about older men: he didn't require reassurance or cheerleading, could swipe a credit card or roll his tongue across a buttock with the certainty that nothing would ever be found insufficient. If he wanted to be called Nate, so be it. This was how she liked things: names as temporary as hotel bed-sheets.

'Yeah,' Peg said, draping herself across the length of the bed.

It was a question she liked to ask in hotel rooms, where white walls were blank enough to absorb all sorts of misdeeds.

Nate knelt over Peg, knees knuckling into her sides, large hands firm on her chest.

'Worst thing I've ever done?'

His hands moved towards Peg's throat.

'Yeah.'

He started to squeeze.

'Haven't done it yet, babe.'

*

After, Nate turned to Peg and smiled:

'How 'bout you, babe? What's the worst thing you've done?'

Killed a man, Gina should have said, perhaps a giggle afterwards.

Wait till you see, Gina should have said, flipping him over roughly: *your turn now*.

Wouldn't you like to know, Gina should have said, turning onto her side.

Peg said nothing, tensed on the bed, the question ricocheting back to her, demanding to be answered.

She'd leave it be. Plenty of other things to entertain in hotels. Gina, Peg was sure, was a fan of miniature things. Little bottles of vodka, clear and fiery and amazing. Adorable bottles of shampoo with ridiculous ingredients. Rosemary and mint, a scent to banish all trace of the past. Ironic, when rosemary signified remembrance, Peg thought, though Gina kept her mouth shut. Each bottle to be replaced within the hour once they'd left, all part of the deal in hotels, which were brilliant at acting as if nothing had ever happened there before, every day a new start, anonymity the aim and amnesia the game; brilliant, really, that a whole industry could be built on the importance of forgetting.

Bored, Nate switched on the TV.

Gina was not married to Nate so she would not, Peg decided, object to the turning on of the television; Gina was not a nagger.

'Wow!'

Peg rolled over and looked at the images of Pope John Paul II.

Nate sat up, suddenly alert. The kind of kink he was into, he could certainly be Catholic.

'Holy shit, he's already performed a miracle – that was fast!'

Peg watched Rome reel by, starting when she noticed the date on the screen.

'Fuck!'

Nate turned around.

Peg could have asked Nate about the logistics of forgetting wedding anniversaries – he had a well-worn groove on his finger – but Gina was more of a giggler than a talker.

Nate put his arm around her.

'You okay, darl?'

'I'm fine,' Peg said, certain that Gina was not a Catholic.

7

Archival Box (2007)

Peg removed the lid slowly. No surprises inside: sheets of loose correspondence, waiting to be sorted. Nothing that could be construed as an emergency. Nonetheless, the urge to dive in and escape into work overwhelmed her; she had to steady her hands against the box.

In the archive, at least, things were simple. Collections arrived smelling of garages and neglect, objects perilously stored in regular boxes. A survey was commissioned. Items were rehoused. Staples and paper clips, those perfidious collaborators with rust, were replaced with plasticlips. Carefully labelled acid-free folders were organized in archival boxes. Finding aids were written. Series were designed to guide the intrepid researchers of the future. Eventually, rows of archival boxes were lined up, awaiting transferral to an off-site warehouse in New Jersey, neat labels announcing the triumph of order over entropy.

'What's the strangest thing you've ever found?'

But here was Rosie, meandering through the stacks and haphazardly inspecting boxes, chaos trailing after her, as usual.

Dev answered, when Peg didn't.

'You've found lots of mad stuff here, right? One time, you found a bloody glove, right?'

Wrong, Peg thought, though she nodded. She sometimes worried that she had outsourced affability to Dev, but now, with a long-lost sister to be dealt with, she was glad of his chatter. If Rosie insisted on barging back into her life, then she would keep things on her terms, conversation kept on a leash, *how did you like downtown?* and *what are you up to tomorrow?* and *this is where I work!* enough for the evening, no need for *why did you come back?* or *how is John Paul?* or *and Damien?* or *what on earth can you want from me?*

'You found a colony of cockroaches once too, yeah?' Dev prompted.

He had quizzed her about her work too, early on, when question marks curved at the prospect of unexplored histories. Every archivist had a story. Strange hairs, found at the bottom of a box. A poem scribbled on the back of an envelope. An unsent love letter.

'It's mostly files,' Peg said, pointing to the row of records she was working on.

Rosie nodded, clearly doing her best to feign interest. They might leave, yet.

'Do you have any government documents?'

But here was Rosie, poking around as if she might find the folder to topple the Bush administration.

'You'd have to go to DC for that,' Peg said, half hoping she would.

'Or Guantanamo,' Dev said. 'Wouldn't be surprised if they've installed some room to bury documents there.'

Peg was about to say something about archival standards but then Rosie made a dark joke about the slender space required to hold the government's proof of Iraqi weapons of mass destruction and then they were off, the pair of them congratulating each other's condemnations, while Peg stood by her desk, like some fool of a child eager to show her parents her homework. Rosie and Dev had only known each other a week, but they were already fast friends, protesting against Iraq that afternoon and sharing spliffs and debating whether Obama had any hope of beating Clinton. Of course they got on: the two of them were like dogs, so eager and affectionate, so ready to please, while Peg was some mean old cat, sleeking away from their weed-fuzzed observations and longing to do a line

66

of coke in a hotel room with some man who'd never be vulgar enough to disclose who he voted for.

It had been a mistake to bring them to her workplace, an illusion that she could retain control. Or, the mistake had been having Rosie for dinner and introducing her to Dev. Or, perhaps, answering the phone at all. They were too different. Rosie liked tea, pot after pot, while Peg craved espresso. Peg was a Libra while Rosie was 'technically a Gemini, but really I'm more of a cuckoo Aquarius'. Peg was doing a Master's; Rosie couldn't even decide what to order for lunch. Such a sister! Who else would come to New York unannounced after twelve years apart? Peg stared at her mess of a sister, with her bright blue hair and her indifference to nail polish remover – twenty shades visible on each nail, like some primary-coloured palimpsest! – and her insistence upon earnest conversation about the state of the world. Peg felt the need to shake her – *such a sister* – and yet shouldn't she hug her, because she was looking back at her so sweetly, the way she always had.

'Dev is showing me his dissertation materials,' Rosie called across, tenderness softening her amusement.

'The History of Mathematical Notation!' Dev proclaimed, in the voice he used now to discuss academic matters. 'You can see why I dropped out!'

Peg resisted the urge to stop Dev opening drawers.

'Where are the stones, Peg? Cuneiform is the oldest form of writing here: thousand-year-old etchings on stones! And you know the best part, it's not even poetry or the names of kings that gets recorded, just transactions of debt. As if thousands of years from now, all that remains of our lives is a receipt from Walmart!'

'Here,' Peg said, finding the box on her cart.

Dev removed the stone from its box and glowed with gratitude.

'Amazing, isn't it? How old are they again?' he asked, already taking his phone out to check Wikipedia. 'Peg introduced these to me, back when we were eyeing each other up across a crowded reading room …'

Dev left space for her scoff; Peg bristled at complying so reliably.

'My dissertation was about the history of parentheticals, even more tedious, but Peg suggested I look at these too, dropped them on my desk, like roses that were … three thousand and twenty or so years old!'

'Romantic,' Rosie managed.

(It was romantic, though, that first night when they'd crammed onto a fire escape, drunk on tequila and ideas. Peg had listened to Dev's theories about the kind of reading that mathematical parentheses created, the information in the brackets to be read first, until Dev was proclaiming that parentheses explained the universe and demanded an eye that did not track things from left to right so linearly. *Exactly*, Peg had said, that first drunken night, when her thoughts were anything but exact; this was a kind of history she was interested in, she explained, one where linear progress might be disrupted and the marginalized privileged: a history where losing did not require silence. That first night, drunk on tequila and infatuation, sex sparkling in the air, there was no problem that they couldn't solve.)

'It definitely has an aura,' Rosie said, mercifully replacing the stone in the box before Peg snatched it; she'd bolt the doors when they left.

'Properly pagan,' Dev said, approvingly.

'I hope so,' Rosie said and they were off again, lost in some conversation about Celtic rituals and Hinduism, Peg tuning out until she heard Rosie pronounce: 'I mean, nobody in Ireland is *really* Catholic any more.'

Peg dealt with this sentence of Rosie's, stated as if it were a fact, though Peg knew that Rosie would not have any sociological data at her disposal.

'I mean, no young people,' Rosie continued, unabashed. 'I mean, not after everything the Church has done. I can't think of anybody who'd go to Mass voluntarily. I don't think it's even a consideration any more.'

The ease with which Rosie could shrug off Catholicism astonished Peg, as if the years between them meant they had sprung from different soil.

'Things have changed,' Rosie said, looking across at Peg, *since you left* dangling in the pause. 'Things that happened before wouldn't happen now.'

Rosie might have meant this as an olive branch but Peg only felt the poke of a stick.

This is my Master's thesis topic. Examining the educational practices of nineteenth-century religious institutions helps us understand the ways in which religion seeps into current secular pedagogical theory. Ideology has long tentacles. It seems premature to dismiss the effect of Catholicism on my – our? – generation. Catholicism is there, a pea at the bottom of a stack of mattresses, shaping our thoughts, even as we claim not to feel its presence.

These were the sentences that arranged themselves in Peg's brain as another sentence – *don't you see me?* – jagged across. The conversation had drifted on before she had any hope of assembling them into a coherent point and Rosie was on to the time that she had dared to put My Little Ponys into Granny Doyle's crib and Dev was wondering if unicorns had ever been worshipped and then he was checking a Wikipedia article he'd read on that very topic and Peg drifted off again until, getting ready to leave, Rosie looked around the dark corridors and asked, 'Don't you get lonely working here?'

They were too different. Rosie found the archive intimidating, while Peg loved the place. Rosie didn't think much of Manhattan while Peg loved its anonymity, its surprising pockets of quiet, its websites where you could order anything from sushi to sex, its hotel rooms, where you could lie naked on white sheets and say your name was Katie, Gloria, Gail, whatever, knowing that the stranger shutting the door behind him had not used his real name either and that the chances of him being friends with your cousin or cousins with your neighbour were next to nil.

'No,' Peg said, staying put by her desk. 'I don't.'

8

Rubik's Cube (2007)

'Howda ya rate my godfathering so far?'

Rosie laughed at Dev's terrible accent and joined him by the skylight window, an array of Sabharwals and neighbours below, in the New Jersey back garden of his childhood home.

'Well, you didn't drop the baby.'

There was Sara, happily gurgling away, as old ladies passed out food she couldn't eat.

'Phew.'

'And you did some excellent uncle-work.'

The children who could talk were already asking 'Where's Dev?', ready for another spirited dodgeball game.

'Helps that my mental age got stuck at seven.'

Rosie took a drag of her spliff.

'Though I'm not sure that sneaking up to your bedroom to find an old stash of weed is the *best* godfathering.'

'You're right,' Dev said. 'I should have invited Sara.'

Rosie laughed.

'I won't tell Gabriel if you don't.'

'Deal.'

At the mention of his name, the dreaded brother-in-law looked up; Dev ducked and pulled Rosie down with him.

'Smooth.'

'What can I say, I've had practice.'

Rosie settled into the floor and took in the room, bewilderingly stuck in time, with its games console and high

71

school textbooks and posters of *The Matrix* and a periodic table.

'I *was* cool,' Dev said, following Rosie's eyes.

'Your parents didn't want to use this room.'

'No, they kept it like this in case I moved back,' Dev said, with an eye-roll, every parental gesture of affection taken as an insult.

'Right.'

Rosie hadn't been inside 7 Dunluce Crescent since she ran away. She doubted that Granny Doyle had left the walls painted purple. Or carefully stored her crystals and dreamcatchers. For the best, no good getting bogged down with material things.

'So, wanna play Mario Kart?'

Dev used a tone that suggested a joke, though he seemed amenable to staying longer, picking up a Rubik's Cube and playing with it.

Rosie was in no hurry to return to the christening either. She'd agreed to come because she'd thought that Peg might appreciate an ally. But then Peg had felt sick after the ceremony and hadn't wanted any company on the train back, quite the contrary, and Dev had seemed so sad that Rosie agreed to stay, even though she felt an eejit, with her blue hair and Peg's dress too tight on her and the thin smile from Mrs Sabharwal, which assured her that she was used to disappointment from the Doyles.

Rosie needed a glass of water; she took another drag. It had been a mistake to come; she should never have left Clougheally. Apart from Peg, New York had nothing for her and suburban New Jersey was just as bad, if not worse. She had been a fool to think she could cross the Atlantic on a mission. She hadn't mentioned Pope John Paul III, let alone Aunty Mary's letter. It was as if Peg had some invisible force field which deflected any mention of the past and kept all talk small. She had nearly exhausted the generosity of the comrade whose couch she was crashing on; it was time to cut her losses.

'We should probably go back down,' Rosie said.

'Probably,' Dev agreed, rolling another joint.

Time stretched, the sun too.

When Rosie finished her joint, Dev was still playing with the Rubik's Cube.

'You're pretty quick.'

'Not bad,' he said, scrambling the puzzle again. 'My record was fifty-five point four seconds.'

Rosie let out an impressed sound.

'It's nothing: the record is twenty-two point nine five seconds. Or used to be, anyway.'

He didn't check Wikipedia, tossed the cube up and down instead.

'Dad entered me into a bunch of tournaments when I was younger. Like if I won, I could make it to the moon or Mensa.'

'You *were* a cool kid.'

'Oh yeah, I've got the medals to prove it.'

They were probably in the room somewhere, though Dev didn't search; he put on the voice he used to make fun of academia instead.

'Of course, it's really the unscrambling that's important. You know, there are approximately forty-three quintillion incorrect permutations but what if beauty lurks in truth? What if the Rubik's Cube is really a type of mandala, a portal to enlightenment, the gateway to nirvana!'

'Was that your pick-up line? No wonder you've got a poster of the periodic table.'

Dev pretended to be hurt.

'I'll have you know, your sister was very impressed by that speech. She made me a miniature paper Rubik's Cube for our first anniversary, little notes written on every surface!'

The smile on Dev's face faded.

73

'Well, our first month anniversary. For our wedding anniversary, she got me a brown paper bag …'

Peg was the problem that brought them together but neither of them knew how to talk about her. Rosie stood and joined him, no sign of the baby below.

'I should give it to Sara,' Dev said, looking out the window, where the dusk was clearing the garden.

'Yeah, she's bound to solve it in under twenty seconds,' Rosie said.

'Or, she has, what, forty-three million—'

'Quintillion.'

'She's got forty-three quintillion ways to fuck it up; I'm sure she'll find the one that works for her.'

Dev laughed but his eyes remained sad. Rosie followed his gaze down the length of the garden, where he looked at sundry nieces and nephews attempting to climb the cherry tree. She saw them, she imagined, the phantom offspring that Dev watched, the boy and girl who joked at their dad's jokes and their mam's food and smashed every record the Guinness Book had. Or perhaps his eyes tracked those alternative histories, the ones where he didn't give up on everything – Rubik's Cube tournaments, dissertations, marriage. Or perhaps he was looking at the young woman standing by the tree, some neighbour probably, Rosie hadn't been introduced, but perhaps if they'd shared the right sentences when they were teenagers, she could have been the person to make Dev happy.

'Perfection is overrated,' Rosie said, taking the cube from Dev. 'I think it looks better when all the colours are mixed up.'

Dev let out a laugh.

'Right! The completed Rubik's Cube is so big on colour divisions it's practically racist.'

Rosie laughed, relaxing into the conversation, as they ran off on absurdist tangents and composed imaginary letters to whoever Rubik was about the dearth of brown and black coloured squares.

Perhaps it had not been a mistake to come, after all, Rosie thought, finding the scrambling of the cube strangely soothing – possible, even, to imagine some universe where she and Peg might talk. Granny Doyle might have stuffed all of Peg's possessions into St Vincent de Paul bags, but they had history together; the Blessed Shells of Erris and Miraculous Fish Fingers could be summoned, still. Standing in Dev's childhood bedroom, high on weed and vicarious nostalgia, Rosie resolved that she wouldn't abandon her mission yet.

9

Blarney Stone (2007)

'Do you remember my christening?'

Rosie shifted in the bed, pulling the sheet towards her. Dev was away for spring break so Rosie was staying in their apartment for a bit, no questions asked about why Dev preferred his friends for camping company. The fan in the living room was broken, so here Rosie was, in the same double bed as her older sister, who hadn't lost her knack for pretending to be asleep.

Rosie focused on the stones arranged on Peg's windowsill, summoning their auras. She couldn't tell if they came from American beaches. It was certainly fanciful to imagine that Peg had carried one from Clougheally across the Atlantic (and yet, hadn't she loved to collect trinkets on the beach, their old bedroom filled with them until the St Vincent de Paul bags swept in?). Nonetheless, in the absence of Rubik's Cubes or carefully preserved rooms, the stones would have to do. Rosie focused on their aura, not minding about the detail – the feeling was important, not the fact! – and imagining magical properties contained therein. Why not? If stones could contain the oldest writing in the world or support the webbed feet of mythological swans, then couldn't they have the power to induce speech?

Rosie focused on one of the small stones; in the dark of Peg's room, it could have been the Blarney Stone, or at least a replica. It didn't matter that nobody in Ireland had ever kissed the thing. It was a coincidence that the Blarney Stone had been the site of one of John Paul's terrible Pope videos, where the Irish Pope puckered up alongside an elderly American tourist, who was induced to test his gift of the gab, shouting 'Póg mo thóin!' and beaming as he mispronounced everything, even the spaces between words. It didn't matter that the stone on Peg's windowsill might well have been purchased at Pottery Barn. Rosie had a mission to complete and so she plucked a stone from the mist of myth; it would have to do.

'Did we really get christened in coats?'

This broke Peg.

'No!'

'I remember being hot in that coat.'

'How could you remember? You weren't even one.'

'Babies have brains.'

'Not ones that can store long-term memories.'

'Well, not according to *Western* medicine—'

'You all had your own robes. There's no way you and Damien were christened in a coat.'

'That's what Dad told me.'

Peg sighed.

'They didn't have enough money for three christening robes, so John Paul got the nice one and Damien and I were shoved into some old white coat or a blanket, I can't remember—'

'*My* old robe, you wore *my* old robe—'

'And then Father Shaughnessy screamed when he saw the two of us in the same coat, like a two-headed demon. We were shocked so we started to cry—'

'All babies cry when they're christened.'

'And we were screaming and screaming until they took us away from the font and John Paul was christened and then we stopped like magic and the nuns started singing—'

'It wasn't *The Sound of Music*.'

'The nuns burst into song, all sorts of impossible harmonies, that's what I heard.'

Rosie followed scripture to the end.

'Some of them couldn't even sing. But they had beautiful voices that day, like angels.'

Peg stared at the ceiling, knowing what was coming.

'It was a miracle.'

Here they were, at the edge of Rosie's mission, the reason she had returned to New York, against her better judgement: the Unofficial Miracles of Pope John Paul III. Rosie stared at her imagined Blarney Stone; she could just make it out in the dark. Peg would take the bait, Rosie knew she would, letting the silence stretch, a task that years of sharing a bedroom had prepared her for.

'That's not what happened,' Peg said eventually.

Rosie waited a moment.

'What did happen, then?'

Peg sighed; it was too late to feign sleep. Part of her longed to, wishing she could kick Rosie and her sheet-hogging back into the living room. Another part of her liked this, though, the two of them in the same room, talking in the dark, they way they'd used to back in 7 Dunluce Crescent, Peg's snores never fooling Rosie, even then.

Peg shifted around. She could just make out Rosie's eyes in the dark. Here they were, at the edge of the Unofficial Miracles of John Paul Doyle. Peg had them all in her head.

Remember the Scarlet Communion Dress?

Remember the Blessed Shells of Erris?

Remember the Fish Fingers that Fed the Fifty?

Other historians might have picked a different miraculous origin (the bloody tea towel; the singing nuns at the christening) but Peg knew enough about alternative histories to select a miracle where she had a central role.

'Do you remember *The Chronicle of the Children of Lir*?'

Series III:
Communion

(1985–1991)

1

The Chronicle of the Children of Lir by Peg Doyle (1985)

Rosie chewed on her colouring pencil and looked out the window at Clougheally's blustery beach.

'I think when I grow up I want to be a swan.'

Peg gave the *Rosie!* sigh she'd been practising for several years. Even though she was almost five, it was clear that the boundaries of the world weren't certain for Rosie Doyle. Happily, Peg, nine years old and a fount of wisdom, was always there to clarify matters.

'Humans can't turn into swans in real life.'

'I'll be like the Children of Lir,' Rosie said, adding extra feathers to her doodle, as if this might help her point.

'That's just a *story*,' Peg explained.

'When I grow up I'm going to be a fireman!' John Paul shouted, not listening. 'Or … or Imma going to be a Transformer! And-and you can be a Transformer too, Dam'en, one of the bad ones, but-but then Imma save you and we'll fight Optimus Prime together, yeah yeah!'

Colouring on a rainy day was not John Paul's strong suit, so he was already hopping about the kitchen to demonstrate his firefighting and robotic abilities.

'And-and we'll have a BIG hose and we'll point it at the bad guys and then-then they'll be DOOMED!'

Damien nodded, content to play whatever role John Paul's narrative required, as long as he ended up a Good Boy when he grew up, his primary ambition.

'I think I'll be a swan. Like the Children of Lir,' Rosie said, as if Peg hadn't spoken.

'You want to be stuck here for hundreds of years?' Peg said, in a less understanding voice.

'Maybe,' Rosie said, finishing her picture. 'Then I won't have to be dead like Nanny and when I'm tired I'll just flap flap flap up to the sky.'

Peg shot Aunty Mary an *adults among adults* look: Nanny Nelligan's death was at the heart of Rosie's nonsense. Nanny Nelligan's wake had left quite an impression on them all, especially the sight of the withered old woman in the coffin. Nanny Nelligan had a great fear of being trapped underground, so she'd been cremated, a shock to the village, mutterings that you wouldn't want to be trapped inside a small urn either. The urn sat by the rattling window, the breeze coming in through the gap as if it was trying to upturn the lid and release a spirit. Peg felt a shiver down her spine, then remembered that she was practically a grown-up.

'You don't have to be scared of dying, Rosie.'

'I'm not. I just want to fly.'

'Fly' was the spell that roused John Paul: he'd been quiet for a full minute, possibly a record.

'Imma gonna FLY like a PILOT!' John Paul shouted, accelerating around the room and tugging at Damien's jumper. 'Dam'en, you be Chewie and I'll-I'll be HAN SOLO! I'm so fast you'll never catch me!'

'We haven't finished the story,' Peg said, as Damien threatened to stand up.

John Paul was so frustrated that he stopped moving.

'But-but I want to go OUTSIDE! C'mon DAM'EN! ROSIE!'

'*Ciúnas!*'

For the first time, Peg heard the schoolteacher in Aunty Mary's voice.

'Sit down and draw, would you? We have to stay inside while it's raining.'

'But-but it's ALWAYS raining HERE.'

John Paul had a point, Clougheally no threat to the Costa del Sol, but Peg shot Aunty Mary a pious *this is what I have to deal with* look. Granny Doyle and her dad were in Ballina for the day, so the balance had shifted. There was nobody there to praise John Paul's every step with the fervent belief that one day such legs might walk on the moon; Damien and Rosie were up for grabs. This was the dance that Peg and John Paul performed, daily. *I am a leader*, they said, devising games or schemes, waiting for their docile siblings to follow. Usually, John Paul won the battle, Damien and Rosie happy to follow him on some inane dash up and down Dunluce Crescent, leaving Peg with disappointment jigsawed in front of her. Today, Peg might have a chance.

'You can be Ardán,' Peg said to John Paul.

'I don't want to be a swan, I want to be a PILOT!'

'You can pretend to be a pilot tomorrow. Today, we're performing my book!'

'Book' was a grand title for the few pieces of paper that Peg had bound together but she couldn't have been prouder of her achievement. There had been lots of drizzly days while Granny Doyle and Aunty Mary had been busy with the stream of guests and the cleaning of the dusty old house, leaving Peg with plenty of time to work on her magnum opus. *The Chronicle of the Children of Lir by Peg Doyle* was its full title, *chronicle* a word that had leapt off the sides of one of the old books and danced inside Peg's head. After a few patchy years, when she missed large chunks of school, Peg was back on track. She'd been selected for the accelerated reading programme, so she could read about tractors that were *crimson* rather than plain red, allowing her to pick up the books from Nanny Nelligan's mahogany bookshelf with great authority. Most of them held little interest for her – a good deal were in Irish and

Peg had no *grá* for *Gaeilge* – but Peg loved the old bookshelf, with its mottled grain and friendly clumps of dust. There would be space for *The Chronicle of the Children of Lir by Peg Doyle* on it, pride of place if she had her way: stories were for babbies, but *chronicles* demanded respect.

'This is STUPID!' John Paul said, rejecting the squiggles that Peg had placed in front of him.

Peg gave him a look of infinite patience; she could have played a saint in a school play.

'Damien and Rosie can help you to read if you want. It's very simple.'

John Paul's cheeks flushed.

'I-I don't want to READ.'

John Paul hadn't the patience for Peg's generous tutoring sessions. A tornado of a boy, he couldn't sit still long enough for Peg's patient lectures, copybooks best transformed into paper aeroplanes. Damien and Rosie were more promising pupils. Rosie had the alarming attitude that the alphabet was arbitrary, but she at least sat still and listened. Damien actually showed signs of progress, concentrating hard on the puzzle of letters in front of him, ever eager to please. And both of them loved when Peg read to them, lapping up the voices she put on and her embellishments. Peg felt she had greatly improved upon the Children of Lir's story in her chronicle, adding several storms and adventures to the swan's three hundred years around Erris, with the eldest, Fionnuala, reliably capable of rescuing her siblings from whatever peril they found themselves in. Savvy about her audience, Peg added a section where one swan befriended a crab (for Rosie loved all animals) and another where one of the swans found a nice, warm cave (for Damien loved being cosy) and she even threw in a battle with pirates and Vikings, history's rigour compromised by the need to keep John Paul still. Even John Paul had gobbled up the tale the night before, the triplets squished into the one bed, eyes agog until Peg storied them towards sleep. However, listening to a bedtime tale was different from wasting valuable daylight hours reading, a position that John Paul continued to make clear.

'I don't wanna read, I don't wanna read!' John Paul recited, scrunching up his lines.

'Stop messing!' Peg shouted, her saint-like composure somewhat compromised as she tugged the paper from his hands.

'How about you lot have a look for some cardboard in the back bedroom? I need some children who might be brave enough to fight any monsters in the boxes ...'

Aunty Mary had John Paul at 'brave' and once he had signed on to the mission, it was only a matter of time before the other triplets bounded upstairs after him.

Initially furious, Peg was mollified when Aunty Mary returned and sat down at the table beside her. Alone time with Aunty Mary was precious for its rarity, like chocolate released from its tin after Lent.

'This is looking very professional.'

Peg beamed, the adjective better than any gold star.

'Aunty Mary?'

'Yes?'

'Did the Children of Lir make their Holy Communions before they turned into swans?'

Aunty Mary considered this.

'I'd say not. The world they grew up in was very different.'

'And then when they turned back into adults after nine hundred years, Saint Patrick gave them their Communion?'

'I suppose so.'

'But how were they allowed to take it if they hadn't made their Communions?'

The rules regarding First Holy Communions were at the forefront of Peg's brain as her own ceremony loomed. Peg's patchy attendance at school meant that she had missed her Communion, which meant that she had to take it at a mortifying age when she had clearly already acquired reason. The problem was that reason did not help Peg solve the puzzle of what Communion might taste like. Somewhere between her friends' helpful 'It's like dry paper, disgusting!' and Granny Doyle's 'Like the pure love of our divine Lord Jesus Christ, now would you get away from under my feet', lived various theological problems that Peg had no idea how to resolve. Peg seized her moment with Aunty Mary to push the matter further. What did baby Jesus' body taste like? How did he have so much body to eat that churches never ran out? If Jesus was made of bread how had he ever been killed? Peg presented these problems very seriously, so Aunty Mary, who always treated Peg as an intellectual equal, suppressed a smile and asked 'Do you know what a metaphor is?'

Peg turned her nod into a shake of the head, admitting ignorance as the price of knowledge.

'Sometimes the truth of stories isn't necessarily in the facts,' Aunty Mary said, searching for inspiration. 'We might think of the world starting with Adam and Eve eating an apple, because a story is easier to understand than science. Or we might say we are eating the body of Christ, but really it's a special loaf of bread that's been blessed. The metaphor helps us understand an important truth: that we should share with one another.'

Peg struggled with metaphor but nodded gamely nonetheless.

'So is the story not really true?'

Aunty Mary checked for the bustle of Granny Doyle's coat through the door.

'I wouldn't say that the story is not true,' she said slowly. 'But sometimes you have to be careful about what parts of stories you believe. You have to think about who is telling them and why they would want you to believe them.'

A door edged open in Peg's brain.

'Are the swans in this story a metaphor too?'

Aunty Mary smiled and tilted her head to the side, chewing on the thought.

'Hmmm … you could say they represented the transition between a pagan and a Christian era and also the shift between childhood and adulthood and yes, it's a good question …'

Peg focused on Aunty Mary's mutterings intently, keen to display that she was not some child who believed in fairy tales; no, Peg Doyle poked at stories until they revealed their secrets. In fact, she'd just had a brainwave regarding the ending of *The Chronicle of the Children of Lir by Peg Doyle*, an idea she kept folded up for herself, the better to be unveiled that evening.

*

The performance of *The Chronicle of the Children of Lir by Peg Doyle* was an exclusive event. Chairs were set up for Granny Doyle, Aunty Mary, and Danny Doyle. Nanny Nelligan remained in her urn by the window, an eerie wind keeping her company. The triplets sported cardboard wings. Peg held her little book proudly, one eye on the bookshelf, where she had already cleared a space. Aunty Mary even arranged some popcorn and mood lighting, ignoring Granny Doyle's cries of 'what is all this cod-acting about?'; this was to be a special occasion.

It started well enough. Peg's speaking voice shook the spiders from the ceiling. Aunty Mary smiled at Peg's liberal use of the house's dictionary, which helped hyperbolize the prologue, so that the children's stepmother was *vicious* and their time in exile was *horrendous*. Peg had the triplets standing on a line of chairs in an arrangement as adorable as any Von Trapp chorus. Damien read his sentence perfectly ('My Name is Fiachra') and whispered Rosie's sentence into her ear. The problem was, predictably, John Paul. All he had to do was say 'My name is Ardán' and flap his cardboard wings. He didn't even have to read the sentence: both Damien and Rosie were whispering it to him. His mouth stayed shut, his eyes fixed on the swirl of symbols in front of him. Panic opened a hole in his chest. Red rushed to his cheeks. The blobs of ink remained resolutely unhelpful, *YOU'RE STUPID* spelt out in their taunting squiggle.

'And one of the swans wasn't good at reading and he was called Ardán,' Peg said smoothly, eager to rush the story towards her exciting ending.

She flipped the page, ready to plunge into the narrative proper. She had learnt her lesson: *never work with children* was a maxim she was happy to adopt as an honorary adult. John Paul, however, had other plans.

'My name is HAN SOLO SWAN and I can FLY!'

He didn't look at Peg, only at his audience. Out went his wings, up went his feet and he was off, in his element, paper tossed to the ground as he whirled into the air in a death-defying leap. He was aiming for the windowsill, an impossible target to reach. Yet he did, his fingers at least, clinging to triumph, as the rest of his body clunked to the ground, his arms flailing and following, sweeping across the windowsill and crashing into—

Peg saw it happen: John Paul bashing into the urn on the windowsill, the urn tumbling over, the remains of Nanny Nelligan falling through the gap into the winds. Nothing she could do to stop it: her feet not fast enough, arms not long enough, brain not sharp enough. Disaster! Nanny Nelligan gone out the window, lost into the gulp of the wind.

Except that wasn't what happened. The urn, mid-wobble, decided to fall the other way, onto John Paul, who caught it before the lid came off, and held it in the air like a trophy.

It was Granny Doyle who broke the silence.

'A miracle!'

Gravity and stupidity were the forces at work, Peg knew, but Granny Doyle's gall stole the voice from her: how could John Paul be praised for averting a catastrophe he created? Lavishly, that was how.

'My little angel!'

Granny Doyle swooped over and picked up her beaming hero, who had just completed his First Unofficial Miracle: The Salvation of Nanny Nelligan's Ashes. Jesus might have brought the dead to life but John Paul Doyle made sure the dead stayed in place. Granny Doyle was clear where the blame lay.

'I don't know what you're thinking, keeping Mammy by the window.'

Aunty Mary didn't stop her sister as the urn was whisked off to a safer location.

'Thanks be to God John Paul has some wits about him,' Granny Doyle continued. 'Well, that's enough theatrics for one evening! I don't know what nonsense you've got them up to today but I've had a long one and it's bedtime!'

'Bedtime' was not a negotiable noun for Granny Doyle; Peg knew resistance was futile. John Paul bounded upstairs, not a bother on him. Rosie drifted over to show their dad her swan drawings. Damien stood smiling, relieved that he had said his sentence correctly: the house might have tumbled around them and he'd still have been content.

'Not to worry,' Aunty Mary said, proof that she was an ordinary adult after all, well able to disappoint when she wanted to.

Peg threw her book to the ground and stomped up the stairs. She hadn't even got close to her brilliant ending, where the swans decided not to turn back into sad withered humans and get Communion from St Patrick but stayed flapping about the bay, their wings light and lovely and probably metaphorical, Peg reckoned. Peg launched herself onto her bed. She hadn't made her Communion yet so filling a pillow with bitter tears wasn't a sin, an opportunity that Peg was ready to make the most of.

*

Some consolation came the next morning. Aunty Mary had given *The Chronicle of the Children of Lir by Peg Doyle* pride of place on the mahogany bookshelf. Peg couldn't help but gasp at how good it looked beside all the proper books. Then she remembered she was angry and tried to twist her face into a frown.

'We'll have to do another reading.'

This wasn't good enough.

'I had a look through last night: excellent work! I love what you did with the end. You're a real chronicler, aren't you?'

This was better.

'And I wanted to ask you something. Do you think you might have space in your room for the bookshelf? I haven't found a job or an apartment in Dublin yet, but I'm not sure if I'll have space for everything from this house and … well, it'd be a terrible shame to get rid of this bookshelf, wouldn't it?'

And this was enough for an ear-to-ear grin.

'You're moving to Dublin?'

Aunty Mary smiled, delighted that her move was the part that gave Peg the most pleasure.

'Well, I'm not sure yet, but I've been here with Mammy for a while and –' a sigh as she looked around the dusty old house: it had been a long year – 'well, there's not much for me here and instead of going back to Galway, well, I was thinking about moving back to Dublin. What do you think?'

'Move to Dublin!' Peg said immediately, the night's disappointments forgotten, because she was to have a bookshelf and her book displayed and, most importantly, an ally.

Aunty Mary smiled, the future appearing in front of her brick by brick.

'Well, maybe I will so!'

2

Blarney Stone (2007)

'Did Aunty Mary move to Dublin?' Rosie asked, shifting in the bed.

Peg stared at the ceiling: she was almost tired enough to drift into sleep.

'No.'

Rosie didn't need to ask 'why?' or 'what happened?'; now that the door to the past had been prised open, out stories could creep, the magical stone obliging. Besides, even if the details were blurry – in her defence, she had only been four – she had a sense of who was to blame. Aunty Mary was a dangerous topic – they hadn't mentioned her letter – but Rosie knew what she was doing.

'Did you know about Aunty Mary then?'

The truth lived somewhere between *yes* and *no*. Hard to believe that Aunty Mary had been so important to Peg's development – her fairy godmother! – yet at the time, Peg had never considered Aunty Mary's life outside of her own. Peg made a noncommittal sound, something she hoped bore a resemblance to a yawn, not that that would be any use: Rosie showed no signs of ever needing sleep. She could stay up for hours when they were younger, demanding more and more stories from Peg, who obliged usually, even when there were slim chances of happy endings.

3

Condom (1971–1985)

(1971)

Could something so small cause so much fuss?

Mary Nelligan looked down at the condoms in her handbag and suppressed a giggle; it was hard to imagine the men on the train slipping on something so like a balloon. Forty-one and she was as bad as the children in her class! Mary gathered her composure. This was a serious matter. All the meetings in Bewley's and the dinners in Mrs Gaj's restaurant on Baggot Street led to this direct action, a kind so direct that Mary wondered if she might explode with the tension. They – the Irish Women's Liberation Movement – had decided to protest against the ban on contraception by smuggling in condoms from Belfast, some of which sat innocently in Mary's bag as the train jostled along.

Were the other women as nervous? If they had any nerves they were hiding them well, chatting to each other or reading the newspaper. Mary looked out at the dreary towns passing by. She felt as if she had a bomb in her handbag. What if the customs guards arrested them on the train and carted them off to jail before they'd made their point? Mary's shoulders tensed in imagined resistance; she was prepared to fight beside these women, most of whom were younger than her, but had already figured out that the only real way to change the world was to grab it by the scruff of its neck. She might have died for them if it came to it. A foolish thought, absurd in its intensity, yet that was what Mary felt, the train hurtling towards Dublin, her heart hammering along with it, condoms jostling on her lap.

She'd imagine the guards with condoms on their head if they tried to stop them. A laugh burst out of Mary's chest, turned into a cough too late. Mary caught the eye of one of the other women: no judgement, a smile of solidarity. The train rushed past Drogheda: nearly there. Mary felt a rush of life, a blast so intense that she wondered it didn't bowl her over. She'd never experienced anything like it before. Maybe when she had been young, when she had fervently believed in God and found herself carried away by the music at Mass, transported to a space so big that she couldn't imagine a roof. This feeling was better, though: on that train, hurtling towards history, condoms on her lap, an army of women beside her, Mary Nelligan experienced the overwhelming potential that another world was possible, stops on the train she hadn't even imagined.

Connolly Station.

Mary stood up, her legs managing to hold her, the customs officers in sight. Out the condoms came, a theatrical flourish, up in the air, down to the feet of the guards, slippery snakes returning to the Republic's soil, refusing to be exiled again. Mary stood with her friends, the women she'd fight beside, and wondered how it was her feet stayed on the ground when she was so sure she was floating.

(1978)

'What are you doing with *this*?'

Searching for a corkscrew, Stella was surprised.

'Oh,' Mary said, with a delighted little laugh; she'd forgotten it was there. The Condom Train protest had been seven years ago and she never could keep drawers in order.

'*That*,' Mary said, already a little drunk without another bottle opened, 'that is a *story*.'

So Mary told the story, in the way that stories are often told when sex awaits, elaborations and embellishments expected, the details not as important as the eyes of the person listening. Mary didn't need to worry about Stella. Wasn't she here in her kitchen at 1 a.m. after all?

'I could make a pretty penny off it, perhaps,' Mary said, immediately regretting speaking, her accent too country, her words coming from an auld one – 'pretty penny', who said that? When had Mary, in fact, ever said that, and why should this be the time that she started, when the wine was still unopened, when that gorgeous mouth of Stella's still hadn't been kissed?

No matter; Stella was smiling, that lovely smile that had kept Mary at the conference. Mary had known that a Women and Lesbianism Conference held at Trinity College wasn't for her: the workshop on how to find your cervix; the cobblestones trying to trip you up with classiness; the assured way strangers talked to one another; the circles in the sun; the singing. But then there was Stella, a good fifteen years younger than Mary, with red hair cropped like some pixie and men's trousers fitting her perfectly and a smile that made everything okay: her accent, the way she was holding her wine glass, the fact that she was there at all.

'Maybe you should take it to Moore Street and see what you make.'

There it was again, that smile in action as Stella found the corkscrew like a superhero, held out a glass for Mary, everything easy and elegant.

'I should do,' Mary said, but she wished she hadn't said anything at all, because here they were, women for radical change, talking about condoms that they had no use for.

'I like your T-shirt,' Mary said, because she was getting chatty, which she never was, which was a blessing, because she was only ever saying the wrong thing.

'Thanks.'

Another smile: maybe, after all, the words didn't matter so much.

'It's sort of our armour,' Stella said. 'We are the "Lavender Menace" and all that.'

A different sort of smile, a twinkly one.

'We'll have to get one for you. If you're going to be part of the group.'

'Ah, I don't know if you'd have my size.'

Mary ducked from Stella's gaze: she was too clumsy for this life.

Another smile from Stella.

'I'd say we could find something that would fit.'

And then Stella had her hand, and the wine was left on the table, and the condom too, and they didn't find a T-shirt for her, the opposite, in fact, and it didn't matter that Mary didn't have the right words; what were words anyway when bodies could talk so beautifully?

(1985)

The porch of 7 Dunluce Crescent crackled with the news of the Health and Family Planning Amendment Act.

'An absolute disgrace it is,' Mrs McGinty said. 'We don't need Europeans poking their noses in. Charlie Haughey had it right before.'

'"An Irish Solution to an Irish Problem",' Granny Doyle quoted.

'This amendment says you won't need a prescription. All sorts will be at it.'

'Do you think they'll be selling them in Brennan's?' Mrs Nugent asked, a certain thrill in her tone.

'Not if she has any shred of Christian decency.'

'That one would sell the nails that hung Jesus if it would make her a scrap of silver,' Granny Doyle said. 'I won't be letting any of mine near the place, I can tell you that much.'

'All sorts of perverts shopping there now,' Mrs Nugent agreed. 'Sneaking contraceptives between the soap and the toothpaste.'

Mrs McGinty crossed herself.

'A disgrace it is, an absolute disgrace.'

*

Funny to think of it curled up quietly in a drawer. Could condoms curl? Mary Nelligan imagined so, thought of it jammed in alongside other knick-knacks, fancied that it twisted backwards to hug itself, a snake catching its tail in the mouth. Poor thing, it was probably lonely enough. Somehow it had survived the move from Dublin to Galway and here it was, a surprise as she finally packed up her things. Funny that she had kept it at all. A memento, she supposed, hard to throw away such a survivor.

It wasn't curled at all when Mary opened the drawer: it lay flat, as if defeated by its situation. *Well now, time for an adventure*, she thought, unaware of the miracle waiting to trip her up.

*

John Paul stood outside the Dáil holding a 'Children Against Condoms' sign. There were a fair few other children there, as well as a robust showing from the Legion of Mary and Opus Dei. A similarly large crew of counter-protesters stood in support of the amendment: the types of people who'd be wanting to buy condoms without a prescription – gays, sex workers, women's rights activists – the sorts that Granny Doyle was keen to shield John Paul from. She stood in a tight cluster with her neighbours, as if she could transport her porch's protection to Kildare Street.

She couldn't protect John Paul, though, not with a miracle to perform. Being stuck beside a boring building was a waste of outside time. The other children had been left at home, so nobody was there to suggest that taking a pram for a spin was a bad idea. One of Mrs Nugent's grandchildren was tucked inside, Mrs Nugent temporarily distracted by her other crying grandchild, so off John Paul went, his tiny hands reaching up, brakes released, wheels and feet in happy motion …

By the time Granny Doyle noticed, it was too late. She didn't even try to grab the air in front of her, her hands shot towards her mouth instead. The pram escaped from John Paul's grip, careening towards the road, a car zooming towards it. Then, just as Mrs Nugent's unfortunate grandchild was about to be annihilated, something – a gust of wind, the capricious flick of God's finger – changed the course of the pram. The beep of the car roused the crowd, including John Paul, who dashed onto the road and gave the pram a mighty push towards the pavement.

'Janey, he saved her!' Mrs Nugent cried, clear on who was at fault. 'Thanks be to Heavens for John Paul! Stop that crying, would you, your sister's after nearly dying because of you!'

Granny Doyle was distracted by John Paul's second miracle. Like his first, it relied on motion and gravity. This time, the results were more destructive: his Second Unoffical Miracle was the banishment of Aunty Mary. Aided by John Paul, the pram barrelled into one of the counter-protesters, an angry young man whose excessive stubble was proof enough of his moral lassitude. Over he tumbled, slipping on a condom (a detail to be savoured like lemon cake, delicious in its zesty ironies) down onto the ground with a break of his nose. Before the pram stopped, another two protesters skidded to the tarmac. Knees were grazed, egos wounded, flesh harmed. Granny Doyle was jubilant. She had got what she wanted: a battler on the front line against iniquity, a bruiser capable of breaking a nose when need be. She was wrestling the pram and John Paul away from some concerned counter-protesters when she recognized the shape of one of the faces.

Granny Doyle had always been suspicious of her sister's ideas but she was enough of a Charlie Haughey disciple not to press the matter, silence the best Irish solution to most problems. This was too far, though: the brazen stance of her, holding condoms like confetti. Not to mention the thing stood beside her: hair far too short for a woman, a quare one altogether. Granny Doyle couldn't have known the history of the condom that tripped the protester, but surely it was only getting its revenge for such neglect, leaping out of Mary's hands as soon as it got a chance, happy to expose her for all her cheek. Mary's face wasn't as defiant as it had been facing the customs officers; it blanched as Granny Doyle's hardened, quivered when faced with Granny Doyle's stare.

Granny Doyle's fierce gaze made her position clear. Aunty Mary had no business influencing her family. There would be no picking up Peg from school, no chats with fairies in the garden, no installation of any bookshelf. Mary felt winded, possibilities deflating in front of her; she might not move back to Dublin after all. Her strong voice, which rose above the chatter of schoolchildren and the drone of men and meetings, deserted her. She opened her mouth, in protest or plea, she wasn't sure, but Granny Doyle had already turned her splendid back. John Paul gripped her hand, not a hair on his head ruffled, no blame on his shoulders, the smile of the victorious stretching across his face.

4

Scarlet Communion Dress (1985)

It was not supposed to be the occasion of John Paul's Third Unofficial Miracle; the First Holy Communion of Peg Doyle should have been the moment when her family orbited around her for a change. John Paul would be sitting with the babies while she walked up to receive Holy Communion like a grown-up. She would develop a special connection to God that John Paul was years away from. And she would have a killer dress.

Shortly after her First Confession, Peg Doyle succumbed to the first sin that every Catholic girl commits once she reaches the age of reason: unbridled vanity in the face of one white Communion dress. Its powers were especially alluring to Peg, who had been denied both the fair-haired beauty of the Hennessys that Damien and Rosie had inherited and the rough dark-haired charm of the Doyles that John Paul had scraped together. Nine years old, with a shock of brown mousey hair, more pudge than she would want to be keeping, and a head that was more freckles than face, Peg was in desperate need of a Communion dress.

Surprisingly, the hand-me-down that Granny Doyle procured from Mrs Nugent did the trick, transforming her into a princess instantly. Peg paraded down the triplets' bedroom, a miniature Princess Di. Damien and Rosie watched appreciatively; John Paul's eyes flashed at the challenge.

'Let's go OUTSIDE and play!'

For a moment, Damien seemed genuinely torn. He did not need to be in constant motion like his brother and there was the gorgeous expanse of lace in front of him, fabric that begged to be admired.

'Come on! I'm-I'm going to be Optimus Prime and BLOW you up!'

There was no choice for Damien; John Paul would always win.

Rosie hovered by the door.

'Can I have a go of your bag, Peg?'

'No,' Peg snapped.

Rosie shrugged and trailed after her brothers. Peg was happy to see them all gone, the mirror a better audience than the triplets, her reflection as thrilled as she was to have something that the triplets couldn't ruin.

*

'It's all right love, we'll fix it.'

Danny Doyle opened his curtains and held the Communion dress up to the light. A zigzag pattern had been cut around the hem, whole chunks of the dress in scraps on the floor of the triplets' room.

'I'm going to kill him.'

'It'll be all right, love.'

'How?'

Danny Doyle sat down on his bed, already tired from it all.

'We'll take it to your gran. She'll know what to do.'

Peg should have known not to consult her dad; there was only one person who could help her.

'I want to see Aunty Mary.'

A rub of the brow, very tired eyes squinting back at her.

'You know you can't, love, you know you can't.'

'Why not?'

A look out the window, his daughter still there when his eyes returned.

'Because that's how it is. Your Aunty Mary's staying in the house in Clougheally.'

'I want to visit her.'

A sigh that stretched the length of the country.

'You can't, love, you know that, so stop asking me about it, okay? We'll take this to your gran and she'll have it right as rain.'

*

Granny Doyle's solution to the slashed Communion dress was the perfect fusion of thrift and fury.

'I want a new dress,' Peg sobbed.

'You'll be wearing this tomorrow.'

'No way! I'll wear my own clothes, I don't care.'

Granny Doyle gripped Peg's wrist.

'You listen to me, Missy. If I tell you you're wearing this dress, you're wearing this dress. You're a cute one. Thought you'd slash up this old thing and get your little brother into trouble? Well, you'd want to be getting up very early to pull one over on me: I know John Paul wouldn't do that. You'll get your lesson about staging a show, so you will.'

*

It wasn't long before the slagging started, the older girls in the choir setting the tone.

'Is that a new fashion?'

'Look, Peg Doyle's having her period!'

'Janey, I'd be scarleh if I was wearing that dress!'

'Move over, it's Scarleh Doyle.'

'It's Scarleh O'Huareh.'

The strips of fabric that Granny Doyle had sewn onto Peg's dress were bright red in colour, giving the alarming appearance of tongues of fire leaping upwards. It was not a fashion ever to be repeated in Killester Church.

Peg held her bag on her lap, wishing it were about ten times larger so it could have some hope of covering her dress. Nobody showed her a shred of sympathy. Her father stared ahead, all his energies expended in producing a smile. Granny Doyle stared at the altar piously, her shoulders radiating triumph. The triplets were no better. John Paul was busy poking everybody in the row in front of him, indifferent to the agony he had caused. Damien was practising praying like a Good Boy, face squeezed as if he was taking a giant shite. Rosie stared into mid-air, the way she often did, as if she could see into another world. Not for the first time, Peg longed for her mother, the kind woman whose face Peg could only just remember. She wouldn't have stood for this nonsense. She might have plucked Peg up in her arms and carried her out of the church, into a different life. Peg almost said a prayer to her, hoping that Catherine Doyle might prove to be the patron saint of dramatic interventions, looking down at the scene and sending some candle to the ground, Peg's dress forgotten in the blaze of the church. The words stayed in Peg's head; there was no more point in prayer than in believing that children could turn into swans, she knew that. Tears too were futile, the slagging would be much worse. Peg imagined that she was wearing a different dress – one made of armour! – and steeled herself for the fray.

Time to receive Communion. Peg stood up, feeling none of the thrill she had anticipated when she brushed past the triplets to become a proper adult in training. At least Rosie and Damien had the decency to look down. John Paul caught her eye as she walked past and gave her a grin that might have been sponsored by the devil. He had banished Aunty Mary and ruined her Communion; he was winning.

Father O'Shaughnessy swallowed his face in shock when he saw Peg's dress. He plopped the Communion wafer onto Peg's tongue like a bomb. It sat underneath Peg's tongue, hard as sin, unpalatable as ash. Peg returned to her seat, the rest of the pew indifferent to her mortification.

'Mortification' was the perfect word for what was happening to Peg, its medical definition particularly apt: *localized necrosis of tissue*. The spiritual cells of Peg Doyle, the ones that collectively organized to believe in a higher being, had become necrotic, digestion of Holy Communion thus impossible. Peg waited until nobody was watching, scooped the thin disc out of her mouth, and left it on the floor. The door that Aunty Mary had left ajar fell off its hinges.

Peg met John Paul's gaze without flinching. He might have banished Aunty Mary but she had gone one better: Peg Doyle had exiled God.

5

Blarney Stone (2007)

'Remember your Communion dress?'

Peg didn't answer; it didn't matter, Rosie would tell her anyway.

The fan whirred loudly through the heat of the New York spring; still, it was not loud enough.

'I did it.'

'What?'

Rosie gulped.

'I cut up your dress.'

Rosie had imagined this moment many times, a weight being lifted from her shoulders. Instead, she felt the air becoming heavier, as if the room had shifted to a different atmosphere, breaths becoming harder to take.

'Why?'

All Peg could manage. To admit that she had never considered this possibility was to admit that she had never considered Rosie capable of something so *solid*.

Peg's question reverberated in Rosie's ear: why? To get your attention? A thing she was incapable of, even now. Rosie swallowed. Any explanation was inadequate. She had thought that perhaps it was something they might have laughed about: Rosie had only been four, after all, *she* hadn't forced Peg to wear the scarlet dress, which Rosie didn't remember as quite so *scarlet*. Bits of fabric had been sewn on the bottom, yes, but hadn't they been cream with a red trim? In Rosie's mind, the incident had been on a spectrum of secret crimes she had committed during her anonymity at 7 Dunluce

Crescent, similar to the Barbie scalpings that Peg had blamed John Paul for. No malice had been involved, only jealousy, and, if anything, a strange sort of love, the kind that kept her in New York even when she knew it would be better for both of them if she left.

The silence expanded in space and time, a black hole swallowing words before they could leave Rosie's head. It would have been different with a lover. Rosie could have wrapped her arm around him, nuzzled his shoulders, forced his face to turn to hers. There was no moving Peg's back, though.

'I'm sorry.'

A very long silence; Peg was probably asleep.

6

Blessed Shells of Erris (1988)

Peg might have exiled God but she couldn't stop the Fourth Unofficial Miracle of John Paul Doyle: the appearance of the Virgin Mary in Erris three years later.

Peg had only herself to blame. She'd convinced Granny Doyle to return to Clougheally, waging a campaign that capitalized upon Granny Doyle's reliable concern for the happiness of John Paul Doyle. *Wouldn't it be great to search for pirates on a proper beach?* Peg suggested, and *can we go to Clougheally?* John Paul asked and *yes*, Granny Doyle said, for after three years without a holiday, she was ready to endure anything, even her sister.

Peg might have been glad to see Aunty Mary but Granny Doyle's reluctant truce didn't mean that she was comfortable being around her. Mary had made the house her own and knocked everything out of its place. Gone the St Brigid's cross and the old kettle and the leathery books in Irish that nobody read. Replaced with God knew what, all of Mary's trinkets and technology: electric kettles and figurines carved out of soapstone and a bookshelf bristling with ideas. Not to mention Aunty Mary, properly settled in Clougheally now that she'd bought Granny Doyle's share of the house (and didn't she need it, with Danny not showing any signs of getting regular work), putting some bright throw over the couch as if she owned the place, which, Granny Doyle supposed with a sigh, she did.

So, the Blessed Shells of Erris washed up at precisely the right time.

'Look, look, it's Our Lady, isn't it?'

Everybody squinted at the shell John Paul had found on the beach. It looked more like a meringue than a regular shell: white, round and very fragile.

'It's like the statue at the Grotto,' John Paul said, his fingers following the cylindrical groove in the centre of the shell. 'That's her body and that round bit at the top's her head.'

It could equally have been the outline of a cucumber.

'Would you credit that?' Granny Doyle said. 'Our Lady of Erris.'

'That's the outline of an old sea slug,' Aunty Mary scoffed. 'Those things are all over the beach!'

'I didn't see any slugs,' John Paul said, the truth, though he would have been well up for a lie.

'This is as bad as all that Ballinspittle nonsense a few years back,' Aunty Mary said. 'You remember that mania that swept the country: fools thinking a statue of Mary could move! There was chat here about the statue in Pullathomas moving then – little wonder, with it right beside the pub!'

Nothing could have convinced Granny Doyle more than the disapproval of her sister.

'No, this is Our Lady of Erris! A miracle, so it is! We'll have to collect them. And we'd better hurry before anyone else catches wind. There's a cute enough crowd around here and they'll be dying for a piece of this.'

'This is nonsense!' Aunty Mary said, to no avail. She might have settled into their old house, but she hadn't a hope of denting her sister's self-belief and there was nothing she could do to stop John Paul Doyle, already bounding out the door to fetch the other triplets, a lieutenant marshalling his troops.

*

All other leisure activities were suspended in service of collecting as many Blessed Shells as possible. The triplets worked as a team: John Paul scouting, Damien cleaning the shells, Rosie embellishing Our Lady's image with watercolours. Something for them all to enjoy: John Paul the adventurer, Damien the carer, Rosie the painter. Granny Doyle oversaw the operations, smiling as bucket upon bucket returned to the kitchen she grew up in. God was munificent (or the molluscs were promiscuous) and soon everything from the pots to the bathtub was full of the shells, Our Lady smiling serenely in blobs of blue and yellow paint. John Paul was inspired to search further afield, the other two running along beside him, leaping over rock pools, daring high tide together, the three of them as happy as froth in the sea, the elastic band tight between them in those days.

*

'Get your Blessed Shells of Erris, two for a pound! I'll do you a deal if you want, five for two quid, they'll look brilliant on the mantelpiece, they will.'

Even at eight, John Paul had sharp business sense. He kept Rosie and Damien behind the table outside the church, the two of them suitably angelic and trustworthy. John Paul worked the crowd, charming the old ladies and bringing a bit of Moore Street to Mayo.

'Today only: get your Blessed Shells of Erris, two for a pound! Special chipped range, only 20p each!'

Most of the parishioners assumed the money was going to charity, an assumption that John Paul did nothing to dispel. Granny Doyle's mantra echoed in his head: charity begins at home. John Paul paid his workers in Fat Frogs, green slurp dripping into the sea each afternoon as they combed the beach for fresh miracles. He kept a cut for himself, saved the rest of the money for Granny Doyle, the profits reaching double digits.

This was life, John Paul thought, loving the attention and the cut and thrust of commerce. He hadn't a head for school like Peg or

Damien; he was always in trouble or confused, or getting into trouble because he was confused, when it was hardly his fault that none of it made sense or that all the teachers were out to get him. Faced with such persecution, it was no wonder that he concentrated his energies on bringing the whole system down with admirable invention, the football pitch filled with forks and the inter-class milk-carton missile war already legendary. Here, though, was a scheme that John Paul could get behind, charming coins out of purses something he was born for; outside the church, John Paul didn't feel one bit stupid. Here, most likely, was the birth of Pope John Paul III, although it would take him years to grow into this identity, several stumbles from grace ahead.

He'd be doing even better without Damien and Rosie, not that he could fire them. Damien kept sneaking off and dropping money into the candle box in the church, even when John Paul promised to post some of the money to Ethiopia. Rosie was worse; she'd always been the only Doyle their father really cared about.

'Thanks, love, I'll drop it back to you later.'

John Paul flinched as his father swiped one of his hard-earned fivers from Rosie and tousled John Paul's hair with his other hand. Who knew where the fiver would go – smokes or a couple of pints – but John Paul was sure that Granny Doyle wouldn't see so much as a copper.

'That's my boy! Doing great business so you are, J.P! I'll see you at the house.'

John Paul folded his arms and glared at Damien and Rosie in a way that he couldn't at his father.

'You'll have to split a Fat Frog between the two of 'yis today.'

*

Damien dropped another fifty pence into the candle box and sat down on the empty wooden pew, his face shining as bright as the stained-glass windows. He didn't know the old lady who'd spoken

109

to him but he hugged her words to his heart: *you're a good boy, aren't you?*

He *was* a good boy, Damien felt, and it was nice to have somebody acknowledge this. Neither Granny Doyle nor his father had commented when he'd read more books than anybody else in his class in the Readathon for children with multiple sclerosis; they'd signed his form without remarking what a feat it had been for him to get through seventeen different stories. They hadn't noticed that John Paul had copied his sheet without opening a book, Granny Doyle thrilling that she always knew John Paul had the brains of a Nelligan.

It didn't matter. God and the Virgin Mary knew about the goodness of Damien Doyle, Damien reminded himself, looking up at the sparkling windows and swooning. God was like a radio channel that Damien could tune into and he loved hearing the soothing voice in the quiet of the church. God understood that even if Damien was picked last in football or had a head that was made to throw milk cartons at, he was a good boy who'd go far. *So you will*, the Virgin Mary seemed to say, smiling at him from stained glass.

The bobbing candle flames nodded in agreement, the one he'd lit for his mother particularly emphatic. Damien knew from the photo on her memorial card that Catherine Doyle would have been the kind of mammy to appreciate Damien; she would have noticed that Damien always picked up John Paul's dirty clothes from the floor and never complained when Granny Doyle dished him out the least crispy roast potatoes. The nice smiling lady in the photographs would have loved her quiet son with the same sandy hair as her and noticed every Twix he forsook so he could send more pennies to starving babies in Africa. *You are a good boy, aren't you?* Catherine Doyle would have said, or did say, for it was hard to say which channels crackled in the church and, for a moment, Damien heard his mother's voice inside his ears.

'Damo? What are you at?'

Damien turned around: typical John Paul to shout in a church.

'Come on, we've a shiteload more shells to shift,' John Paul said, swearing not beyond him either.

'I'm coming.'

'What are you like? Checking out the knockers on those angels, eh?'

John Paul was hanging out with some of their older second cousins in Clougheally, eager to prove that he had big talk in him, even as it strained in his mouth. Damien blushed; he wouldn't defy his brother, not then. John Paul gave him a playful punch and led him outside.

'Yer one there's not bad, if she wasn't stuck in that holy robe I'd say she'd have a decent pair of tits.'

*

Rosie smiled as she painted a big green line in the middle of one of the shells. One for Granny Doyle; one for her: a fair bargain. Rosie stretched out in the sun and added a pair of huge purple eyes: if the shells could contain the Virgin Mary, couldn't they also be the home for sea slugs? Rosie added a purple smile and some pink polka dots; she would not be bound by convention and besides, these alternative shells weren't for her, but decoration for the crabs and microscopic organisms that lived in Erris's rock pools. Pleased, Rosie plopped the shell into the rock pool beside her, smiling at the thought of the little creatures cosying up to their friendly new neighbour. (Later, Rosie cringed at the thought of all the chemicals she'd inadvertently released into the sea.) She picked up another white shell and prepared to paint another blandly smiling Virgin Mary.

'Here you go, love.'

It was Danny Doyle, jeans rolled up to the knee, returning from the sea with a few shells for her secret pile. He sat on the rocks and laughed at the sight of her sea-slug shell, already settling into his new rock-pool home.

'He's a friendly fella, isn't he!'

Rosie nodded. She knew the trick was to get her father outside and keep him busy. Some days he was up for a stroll along the coast, 99 ice creams shared between the two of them; smiles, too. Other days leaving the bed was too much to ask. Rosie knew the happiness of Danny Doyle was a tightrope, you had to be careful how to tread.

'Do you think the slugs mind their homes being turned into miracles?'

Another trick: keep him talking. Let him gaze out into the sea for too long and he could disappear into himself.

'I'd say they're not too fussed, love,' Danny Doyle said.

He could do better; she was the only one of his children with a bit of heart, he could keep her happy, at least.

'You know, actually, I'd say the slugs themselves are probably in on the whole business?'

'You think sea slugs believe in God?'

'Well, maybe not quite that. But if you think about what happens, how some slug at the bottom of the sea gets to make a home as beautiful as *this*, years and years it must take, and look at how detailed the yoke is … I'm no expert, mind, but you know, I suppose if you look at it one way, the fact that one slug can produce an incredible home, isn't that a kind of miracle in itself?'

He wasn't sure if he had the words right – he was never one for speeches – but from the smile spreading across his daughter's face he figured he hadn't cocked it up too badly.

'Yeah,' Rosie said, thrilled with the knowledge that miracles might have nothing to do with God, could just be another word for magic.

7

Millennium Milk Bottle (1988)

And what was Peg Doyle doing during this blessed summer? Staring at a milk bottle of inspiration. Not just any milk bottle, but a commemorative one, its bright red, yellow and blue crest announcing that this glass bottle had more important things to hold than milk. And hold more important things it did: perched atop scrunched-up newspaper, a variety of biros waited to compose Peg's latest opus, *A Children's History of Viking Dublin*. Peg hadn't been pleased with the Viking exhibition their class had visited. Dublinia didn't have one single story told by a child, Peg complained; in all the fuss with Dublin's own millennium (one thousand years since the Vikings had arrived in 988), wasn't there space for the histories of everyday children? *A very good point*, Aunty Mary said with a smile, letting Peg have the use of her desk (the one place in the house not covered with the infernal shells) to write her history. *Dublin's full of history*, Aunty Mary said, 'Dublin' catching in her throat, as if the word gave her pain. 'History' also sounded different in Aunty Mary's mouth, pain there too, though she smiled at Peg, telling her that she'd root out some books that might be useful.

Peg selected her favourite biro from the Millennium Milk Bottle, removing it with a flourish, as if the past were contained inside like ink. The pen itself contained four different inks, each one accessible by clicking a coloured rectangle at the pen's top, an action Peg loved. With such a professional tool, she was able to write the title (24 May 988) in red, continue the history proper in black, and reserve blue for dialogue (the green ink had no place in a serious project; it was Rosie's favourite). Peg hovered the black pen over her paper, ready for its satisfying scratch, as she plotted adventures for Ingrid, her heroine: a drudgy morning selling fish for her domineering grandmother and an exciting afternoon involving a smuggled manuscript awaited. Peg loved playing God, trawling through the books she'd got from Raheny Library to research the clothes she might have worn or the streets in Dublin whose names hadn't changed, the current of the past rushing through her pen, connecting her to a woman who might have lived a thousand years ago, while another woman hovered, bringing her books or cups of hot chocolate or simply standing by the doorway and watching Peg work.

8

Bermuda Shorts (1988)

Peg might have moved beyond the Children of Lir but the triplets hadn't; the Fifth Unofficial Miracle of John Paul Doyle took them up the swan's boulder in search of heroic flight.

John Paul looked back at Damien and Rosie.

'All right … you two count me in and then I'll jump!'

Damien looked down at the drop and felt dizzy.

'Are you sure you want to do this?'

'Of course,' John Paul said, trying to stop the shake in his legs. He hadn't jumped the other day, when some of the older second cousins he'd been palling around with had, leaving John Paul watching them like some poor sap in his bright Bermudas. Not today. John Paul had been double-dared and he had the triplets as witnesses.

'Go on, count for me, I'm getting cold.'

Damien was transfixed by the waves crashing against the rocks below so Rosie started.

'Three …'

John Paul steeled himself: it was only twenty feet or so, it was nothing.

'Two …'

But the drop looked like *something*, the water stern and uninviting.

'One …'

It was the moment to jump, John Paul knew it, but when he looked down he couldn't do it, he needed another second or so, but then before his legs were ready he saw a blur rush past him and leap into air.

'Rosie!'

Damien's voice was caught between fear and amazement. John Paul was frozen, another second before he caught on what had happened.

'It's great!' Rosie called up, head raised towards the sun like a seal. She'd bounded in, T-shirt and shorts and all. John Paul knew he should be furious but he couldn't help feeling relieved: typical Rosie, whoever knew what she'd do, but if *Rosie* could manage the leap, John Paul Doyle sure as certain could.

'All right, we have to do it *now*.'

Damien gulped.

'I'll mind the shells.'

'Come on, Damo. Think of how many we'll get down there. It'll be like we're scuba diving for shells.'

Damien had better sense than to believe John Paul but still he found himself taking off his T-shirt and shorts and folding them carefully beside the bucket of shells.

'Come on, we'll do it together.'

Damien nodded. He wasn't sure if the wind or God was responsible for his goose pimples, but he felt a fire inside him pushing him towards the edge; he could do this!

'Do you want me to count?' Rosie called up.

'No,' John Paul hollered, smiling, because he knew that Rosie and Damien would never rat him out to the cousins and it was a great thing, to shake off fear.

John Paul turned to Damien and *three two one* raced between their eyes and then they were into the air together, Rosie whooping with them as they crashed into the sea, bobbing immediately up with the cold, so that for one miraculous half-second, John Paul might have walked on water.

Peg was engrossed in a book about Viking Ireland when the triplets made their leap, so she didn't learn of this milestone in the triplets' lives until they dripped their triumph across the kitchen and shared suppressed grins as Granny Doyle rattled off her *you could have been killed!* and *would you look at that mess!* That she had not seen the triplets jump from the boulder was not a detail that curbed Peg's memory; she had a sharp sense of the moment, the three of them jumping into the water simultaneously in her imagination, never happier. Peg played with the memory in her head, allowing for an unlikely vantage point, where she was in the water, watching the triplets leap off the rock in unison. The sun was brighter in Peg's memory of the day, the water warmer, the triplets remaining miraculously suspended in mid-air for a moment: side by side, knees curled, huge smiles on their faces, fearless.

9

Lottery Ticket (1988)

While the triplets were collecting Blessed Shells and Peg was immersed in Viking Ireland, Danny Doyle found a passion of his own. It wasn't just the outside that was bringing a smile to his face; he'd discovered the new National Lottery, which acted like a defibrillator to his broken heart, restoring focus to his life. He had his lucky six numbers, almost memorized by yer man down the shop in Clougheally. The shops in Rossport had no luck in them, Belmullet equally unfortunate, so he tried out different machines across Mayo; when his windfall came it would be enormous.

4.

The number of their house on Baldoyle Grove. He remembered the first moment he had carried her inside, her shriek as he attempted the stairs too, no carpet yet to catch the two of them as they tumbled, although their laughs were like shields, no bruises possible on that day.

*

Soon scratchcards accompanied his regular numbers, the better to beat the odds. As the weeks progressed, more and more of the children's allowance siphoned into his Lotto fund, cheery pink slips crumpling onto the floor, as the numbers failed to come through.

12.

Her birthday. The first year, he'd got her a Stones record, and she'd arched her eyebrows – a signature move – and said there was no satisfaction to be got, though what more was there to be wanted, when her eyes were smiling all the same.

*

The itch got worse, more and more scratchcards keeping the pink slips company. Granny Doyle could sense them in the car on the way back to Dublin, competing with the Blessed Shells of Erris for space. She saw the scratchcards when she stuffed some shells in the glove compartment, knew that the reason they stopped for petrol six times was so the luck of different petrol stations could be tested. She massaged a Blessed Shell in her palms on the ride home, turning it over and over as a worry stone, the paint chipped by the time they reached Dunluce Crescent.

11.

This would be his number when he played for Shamrock Rovers, he assured her. *That's really your dream?* she asked with an arch of her eyebrows. *Aim big, you know?* he'd said, then, *and you?* She'd smiled before she spoke: *I've always wanted to cop off with a Liverpool player. You're a terrible one. I am.* She was.

*

The unveiling of the Blessed Shells of Erris to Dunluce Crescent was an event without precedent. Everything was scrubbed, even the dust. The dining room was opened up. The Blessed Shells were arrayed on the sitting-room table. Danny would pick up a nice bit of fish with the messages; it would be a spread like no other, the whole road invited. Mouths would drop open. Airs would be stripped off Mrs Donnelly next door. Granny Doyle would burst from the pride.

When Daniel Doyle returned from the post office, there wasn't a shopping bag in his hand. Granny Doyle's eyes flashed from the pink slips in his pockets to his face.

'Daniel Doyle, don't tell me you spent all the children's allowance on that Lotto again.'

He didn't tell her that; he didn't have to.

'Tell me there's some left.'

She had that Irish Mammy face on, the face that cannot believe that her beloved child could be capable of letting her down.

'We can have the do next week, Ma. Once this comes through I can get you a whole school of fish. Bound to be lucky, the Northside is due a big win. Buy a sailboat, eh, J.P., and we can get millions of those shells in your nets.'

John Paul looked away, hatred forming inside him, as clear as crystals.

19.

Their anniversary. She'd worn blue twice on their wedding day. Once in the austere necklace her mother had bequeathed; once, only for him, a secret to get the two of them through the day full of family, when there was the night waiting, all for them.

*

A surprise to Peg: Granny Doyle could look old. Peg was used to darting down the road to keep up with Granny Doyle's brisk pace; she'd never seen Granny Doyle walk like she did after she was refused credit from both the man at the post office and the young one at Nolans, more wobble than walk, it was. Another surprise: Granny Doyle taking out a box of cigarettes, pulling one out of the packet and lighting up, not a word about it. Peg felt too sorry for her to say anything – a final surprise, to be capable of this feeling. They sat on the bench by the bus stop on the Coast Road for a long while, several buses gliding past into town before they walked home.

31.

The bus to their house. He wanted to write a little A beside it when he placed his bets, because she always claimed that it was superior to the B; even when facts proved the opposite, she delighted in these little disagreements, only a fraction of the alphabet between them.

*

'Dad!'

Rosie rapped her knuckles against the door again.

'Come on, Dad, everybody is downstairs!'

Rosie tried to keep her voice calm. He was definitely awake: she could smell the cigarette smoke coming from underneath the door.

Another soft knock, one that said *it will all be okay!* but the door remained locked; he couldn't even face Rosie, that day.

29.

Her age, for ever. A cold number: harsh, indivisible, stuck, while he was up to 37, though he felt much older. He wished they could hit their prime together, but 29 wasn't budging, no, that's where she was now.

10

Box of Fish Fingers (1988)

The Sixth Unofficial Miracle of John Paul Doyle: a revision of the loaves and the fishes, a trick he would repeat in later life for a considerably wider audience.

The trial run in 7 Dunluce Crescent was no small success. When Granny Doyle returned home from her walk to find her house full of guests, she feared the worst. And then she saw the triplets at work. Damien handed sandwiches to the guests. Rosie drifted around the room with a teapot. John Paul stood by the Blessed Shells of Erris, in his Communion suit, as confident as Jesus chatting away in the temple to his elders. The meal that John Paul had conjured was beside the shells: a pyramid of slightly charred fish fingers beside two mounds of white sliced pans, jagged triangles of hard butter atop each slice. Danny Doyle was safely upstairs: door closed, curtains shut.

Most of Dunluce Crescent came to the event and who could blame them, what else was there to be doing on the sleepy little side street? All of Granny Doyle's porch friends were present. Mrs McGinty insisted that Damien bring in a hard-backed chair for her and eyed the Blessed Shells of Erris suspiciously, unsure if devotion or blasphemy were at work. Mrs Fay brought along her husband, who was as thin as she was large, though both were equally jovial, dispensing praise liberally, unaware of the impression Mrs Fay lodged in Rosie's mind when she complimented her *lovely* drawings on the shells or the warm somersault of Damien's tummy when Mr Fay told him he was a *brilliant* waiter. Mrs Nugent only had time for John Paul, who was well able to keep up with her, laughing along as she poked fun at her daughter's diet and whispered that they'd want to keep the spirits well hidden from Mr Geoghan. Most of the families on the road came too, for they all knew each other's business, had played handball and hopscotch on the road as children, but it was rare enough that anybody passed the threshold of Granny Doyle's porch. Only the Brennans didn't show, typical of a family who sold condoms in their pharmacy.

Granny Doyle surveyed the room and caught her breath.

'Sorry, I'm late,' she blustered, apologies not usually her thing. 'I was …'

'No matter,' Mrs Nugent said. 'John Paul has been entertaining us. Try one of these sandwiches, delicious they are, you'll have to come over and cook for me some time, won't you, John Paul?'

John Paul didn't smile yet, even though Mrs Nugent was tittering as though she'd made a joke; he wouldn't smile until Granny Doyle did.

'He's a better cook than me,' Mr Fay said, picking up another sandwich. 'Toast is about the extent of my expertise in the kitchen.'

'And you still burn it,' Mrs Fay said, a fond tone, the two of them still in love after forty years.

Mrs McGinty scraped some black breadcrumbs onto the side of her saucer but nobody minded about Mrs McGinty, the type of woman who would choose coffee creams first from a box of Roses. Equally, nobody minded about Mrs Brennan, who, this history must scrupulously report, knocked on the porch window the following day to report the theft of five sliced pans and four packets of fish fingers from her chest freezer.

Almost nobody minded about Mrs Brennan. Damien had a tough time with secrets, especially when sins were involved. Sins had a habit of multiplying: lying was added to theft, gluttony too, though Damien wasn't sure if enjoyment were necessary for that one.

'Relax,' John Paul said, finding his brother fretting in the kitchen.

'Maybe we should have left an IOU note,' Damien said.

John Paul didn't share his brother's scruples about honesty.

'I'll make sure to put one there tomorrow.'

Damien's forehead was still stuck on *worried* so John Paul found one of the half-drunk glasses of beer.

'Here, have a sip of this.'

'What is it?'

'It's like red lemonade.'

Damien took a huge gulp and then coughed violently, beer fizzing out of his nose, somehow, sending John Paul into fits of laughter, which Damien copied.

'See, you feel better now you're drunk, don't you, Damo?' John Paul said. 'Relax, it's all going to be fine!'

Things were going to be more than fine, John Paul thought, heading back into the sitting room with another pyramid full of fish finger sandwiches. He'd cut off the crusts to make them extra fancy, knowing that Granny Doyle wasn't in a state to complain that it was the crusts that gave you curly hair.

'Ah, there's the man of the house,' Mr Geoghan shouted, a bit plastered.

John Paul felt his shoulders rise in his Communion suit to fill out the description. He was the man of the house, wasn't he? More so than his Dad, that was certain. John Paul would have to get crafty. He'd forge his signature on the children's allowance. Pour water onto the poor sap's smokes. Punch some sense into him; in a few years, he might be up to that. He'd do anything to make sure he didn't have to see Granny Doyle's face in the shop when she realized there wasn't enough money for all the messages and, despite the careful list she'd written out, the rashers and the biscuits had to do a shameful parade backwards across the cash register. He'd show Danny Doyle and the rest of Dunluce Crescent, especially Mrs

124

Donnelly from next door, who, after one sherry too many, tugged at the side of his suit.

'Mind you, you clean up smart enough when you want to, don't you? This one is always dragging half of St Anne's Park across my kitchen floor, aren't you?'

John Paul made a mental note to stomp in mud before his next visit to Jason Donnelly's.

'Where did you get that suit? Dunnes, was it? Penneys? Mind you, they have some great bargains, don't they! We had to go and get Jason's in Louis Copeland, but isn't it mad when you think about it, all that fuss for a Communion?'

Nobody was listening to Mrs Donnelly, though that never stopped her.

'Mind you, *quality* is always worth the price tag, isn't it?'

Mrs Donnelly's face as she chewed on her charred fish finger made it clear that quality was not a noun one could associate with the Doyles. Behind her, Jason Donnelly rolled his eyes; it wasn't his fault that his mother was a snob or that he had a Nintendo and an official Manchester United shirt, so John Paul only hated him sometimes.

Peg stayed in the corner of the room, watching. It was a miracle of sorts, the way the triplets had brought the street together. They worked the room, John Paul spinning the story of the Blessed Shells while Damien and Rosie cleared plates. Mr Geoghan had brought over some cans and Mrs Nugent had unearthed a bottle of brandy from her kitchen and everybody was getting more relaxed, cigarette smoke hovering across the sitting room, chat and *craic* filling the air and soon Mr Geoghan was getting ready to sing some old union songs and Mrs Nugent was insisting that she saw an outline of Our Lady on the cushion she'd just sat up from and everybody was laughing, even Granny Doyle. Peg stared across the room at her grandmother, who was digging into a fish finger sandwich as if it were a Sunday dinner at Clontarf Castle. Granny Doyle beamed at her man of the house, a great lad, she agreed, love having achieved what the cigarettes hadn't: the regulation of her breathing, the relaxation of her shoulders, the sensation that everything, against all odds, might be just fine.

11

Blarney Stone (2007)

'Have you seen Pope John Paul III's loaves and fishes video?' Peg asked, one night.

Rosie should have smiled. They could bond over the villainy of John Paul Doyle; her mission was working. She had seen the video, some awful neocolonial thing where John Paul grinned as cheap special effects made loaves and fishes abound around him, all in aid of getting people to send money to Ethiopia, and, incidentally, support whichever company was organizing this bread sale.

'Yeah, it's awful,' Rosie said, although her heart wasn't in it.

I buy a scratchcard every year on Dad's anniversary, Rosie wanted to say, but the words stayed furled inside, because mentioning Danny Doyle would not be strategic for her mission. She did, though, scratching the card on his tombstone if she was in Dublin, promising to spend whatever winnings there were on fags and ice cream, stubbing her butt on the flowers that Granny Doyle left, because the bitch knew he hated chrysanthemums. Though at least Granny Doyle remembered the date. Rosie had bought a scratch-card the other day, some bright American thing, and had sat on Peg's fire escape, waiting for her sister to mention the anniversary.

'Did you see the video about the World Cup?' Peg asked now.

Rosie had seen it, from last year, when Ireland had reverted to hopeless form, knocked out of the World Cup before it began and Pope John Paul III had to controversially bless Italy as the team to root for, *Mamma Mia*-ing his way through the video.

'I did,' Rosie said quietly, realizing where the talk was headed.

12

Daniel Timofte Jersey (1990)

The mania began with the Holland match. The tension was unbearable: Holland a goal ahead, Ireland about to exit the World Cup in twenty minutes, despite all the pluck of them. Danny Doyle had already snapped the head off the Ciao keyring he was kneading in his hands, leaving a miniature soccer ball head stuck in the folds of his armchair. In desperation, he turned to his son.

'Say a prayer, J.P., what?'

It is true that John Paul responded. This history cannot verify the exact nature of that mumbled response, whether it was a 'Hail Mary' or a 'Fuck off, Da'. Relations between the pair had continued to sour: if John Paul had his way, fists would be involved soon. And yet, despite his feelings for his father, what happened next is undeniable. The ball sailed through the air, finding its way to Niall Quinn's head. Velocity took over as Quinn lunged his lanky body forwards, the ball whizzing past the outstretched hand of the Dutch goalie and bouncing satisfactorily into the back of the net. The Seventh Unofficial Miracle of John Paul Doyle: the Irish saved from elimination.

'You beauty!' Danny Doyle screamed, hugging John Paul ferociously.

In the absence of support from Granny Doyle, who did not approve of such secular miracles, Mrs Nugent became John Paul's chief evangelist. Her telly permanently 'on the blink', Mrs Nugent watched the game with the Doyles, recounted the prayer John Paul said, reported the goal that followed immediately afterwards, held out her arm to demonstrate the chills she had felt.

So, it was no surprise that Mrs Nugent turned up to watch the next Ireland match in an extra-large World Cup T-shirt.

'They're on special offer at Guineys at the minute, brilliant aren't they?'

Granny Doyle snorted.

'I think it's a shame to focus on a foreign sport when people could be playing GAA,' Mrs McGinty offered.

'Ah, it's only a bit of gas,' Mrs Nugent said. 'Anyways, I thought John Paul could sign it!'

Of course he could, John Paul was ever eager to please his fans. Granny Doyle didn't even try to stop him, distracted by the betting slips poking out of her son's jeans.

'Danny, what are you at?'

'Ah, Ma, everybody's doing it. It's only a bit of fun.'

'Fun' was something that Danny Doyle was learning to appreciate again. He hardly ever spent days in the box room and did the odd nixer for the neighbours; he strolled down the street with pride: the father of John Paul Doyle!

'What do you reckon, J.P. – Ireland 2, Romania nil?'

A shrug from John Paul, his shoulders stiffening immediately afterwards.

'What do you think, J.P., Houghton might get one this time?'

'Maybe.'

John Paul would have been happier spending the afternoon on Jason Donnelly's Nintendo. But there was no avoiding Ireland's showdown with Romania, especially as Mrs Nugent had rallied most of the street into 7 Dunluce Crescent, the better to witness another miracle. Even Mrs Donnelly had to have a look, thrilled by the prospect of disappointment, which seemed to beckon, as the match trudged along in a scoreless draw.

'Ah, they haven't a hope, do they?' Mrs Donnelly said, once the match dragged into extra time. 'Mind you, you wouldn't have thought they'd make it here in the first place, would you?'

'Peg, keep it down!'

Danny Doyle couldn't tell Mrs Donnelly to shut up, much as he would have liked to tell her and her lamentations of doom to fuck off home next door, where Mr Donnelly was having a quiet field day.

Peg shared an eye-roll with Denise Donnelly at the deficiencies of their parents. Best friends by proximity, Peg and Denise had finally found a shared interest: the legs of Italy's best striker, Salvatore Schillaci. It was clear that 'Nessun Dorma' played only for Schillachi. He was the player that encapsulated all that operatic drama: the skid to the grass in despair, the leap to the stars in jubilation when he scored, which he did, often, an intoxicating joy as he ran around the pitch in celebration. Unfortunately, Schillaci hadn't been drafted to the Irish squad yet, so Peg and Denise were left with disappointing specimens to admire, Peg responding to Denise's whispered question of 'which of those manky things would you ride?' with her usual answer (Paul McGrath; Tony Cascarino) while she waited for Denise to extol the virtues of Steve Staunton, 'if you had to, you know?'

Schillaci might have been a benefit to the Irish team for other reasons too; the minutes raced by and the ball trudged up and down but still no sign of a goal.

'Will they not bring on yokeymepuss to save the day?' Mrs Nugent said, pointing at the screen.

'Jack Charlton's the manager,' Danny Doyle said, a sigh abandoned, for now was the time for action; he made it off his armchair and rubbed John Paul's shoulders.

'Come on, J.P., say another prayer, what?'

The seconds of extra time ticked away.

'It's going to be one of those sudden death penalty shoot-outs,' Mrs Nugent shouted excitedly.

'Now'd be the time for a miracle,' Danny Doyle said.

'It will be a penalty shoot-out,' John Paul said, a pronouncement taken as prophecy.

When overtime ran into penalties there wasn't a sound in the room. Even Mrs Donnelly suppressed her queries about how penalty shoot-outs worked and her conviction that Kevin Sheedy looked a bit old in the tooth to be taking the first one. John Paul had a knack for ceremony. He said the 'Hail Mary' before each Irish penalty, the room with him. If Ireland won the game, they would make it into the top eight teams of the World Cup for the first time. If Ireland won, there would be no more rain, no more recession. Or, if they won, the rain and the recession and the tedium of *Live at 3* looping into the Angelus wouldn't matter because for one moment a whole nation had walked among gods. Number 7 Dunluce Crescent wasn't the only house to share some credit for Ireland's fate; sitting rooms and pubs across the country shouldered the same responsibility. If ever the collective prayers of a nation convinced a god to intervene in a sporting event, this was the day.

Sheedy scored. Houghton scored. Townsend scored. Cascarino scored. So did all the Romanians. It was 4–4, the last Romanian penalty. Daniel Timofte stepped up to take it. John Paul broke out an unprecedented 'Glory Be'. He had been silent for the previous Romanian penalties, but some instinct kicked in – cunning? luck? providence? – and he said a prayer.

'Glory be to the Father and to the Son and the Holy Ghost, let this damn Romanian choke!'

Timofte ran forward. Packie Bonner dived to the ground, hand reached out. The ball thudded across the grass, the back of the net unruffled.

'There you go, there you go! That's my boy!' Danny Doyle screamed in savage triumph.

Everybody else was looking at David O'Leary.

'Who's he now?' asked Mrs Donnelly, who would have been pushed to name more than two of the squad. 'Ah, God love him, he's going to bottle it!'

'No, he can do it, can't he, son?'

John Paul didn't respond, launched into the 'Hail Mary'. The whole room responded, even Granny Doyle. David O'Leary stepped forward.

The rest is documented history, legs in sitting rooms around Ireland leaping up in delight at the Eighth Unofficial Miracle of John Paul Doyle.

Peg Doyle stayed on the floor, transfixed by the pictures of Daniel Timofte, the poor Romanian bugger who had missed. He had lovely eyes, a face that was made to brood, only more beautiful in defeat. He swapped shirts with one of the Irish players, the regular ritual. Peg was struck by the oddness of the sweat-soaked shirt of the defeated being used as a talisman of success but everybody else *olé olé oléd* away, Danny Doyle replacing *olé* with 'J.P.' Peg continued to stare at Daniel Timofte, whose gorgeous face crumpled while Peg recognized the darker side of miracles: misery.

13

Italia '90 Shirt (1990)

No coroner would have blamed John Paul. The culprit in the death of Daniel Doyle was clearly one asphyxiation-inducing peanut (a final insult, that the object that ended his life was even more modest than his dreams. Of all the things people said would be the death of him – gambling, sadness, the children – peanuts were never mentioned; he wasn't even allergic). But Peg knew better. Perhaps no prosecutor would have convicted John Paul of murder, but the death of two parents was evidence enough: aggravated assault in the first instance, criminal neglect in the second.

The decline of Danny Doyle began five days after the Romanian match, on the morning of Ireland's fateful quarter-final showdown with Italy. The jersey he'd bought for John Paul, so clean it even smelled official, didn't quite have the result he'd hoped for upon its unveiling.

'Danny, where did you get the money for that?'

'It's grand, Ma. What do you think, J.P.? Thought you were due a new one.'

John Paul didn't let his eyes meet his father's.

'Should get you on the pitch more, too, you'd be a grand little midfielder. Maybe I could come coach, what? I didn't use to be half bad in my day, before I banjaxed this knee anyway, would have made the Rovers' reserves otherwise. Played in Lansdowne the one time, though, didn't I, Ma?'

'You did.'

Granny Doyle's mouth was tight, she could see sense the storm building. John Paul threw his new Ireland jersey on the back of the kitchen chair.

'Football's for losers. I'm going to play on Jason's Nintendo.'

Danny Doyle held on to the back of the chair for support as the door slammed.

'We'll play with you, Dad,' Rosie said.

'That's right, love, that's right, all on board! Just you wait until we win the World Cup, I'll get ones for you and Damo, I'll get new jerseys for us all.'

He didn't, of course. The rest of the day was spent brooding, cans shared with Mr Geoghan, as the match drew closer, and still John Paul stayed at the Donnellys', his fondness for video games involving Italian plumbers further proof of treachery. John Paul came home for the match, along with half the street, but he was in some mood, a gleam of triumph in his eyes when Schillaci scored, Danny Doyle could have sworn on it. John Paul sat calm as Buddha for the rest of the game, no expression on his face when the final whistle blew.

Danny Doyle went into the dining room, needing to escape from the shots of Schillaci racing around the field in triumph, the cries of 'Toto, Toto' in the stadium, Italy bound to win the World Cup. He felt the neighbours' judgement on the back of his neck, their eyes burning him: John Paul deficient, a fraud, a flop. Was it anger or sadness that got him in the end? Did his kicks and curses cause the peanut to go down the wrong way? Was it despair that kept him on the ground when he fell?

The sympathetic might have understood John Paul's actions: the beleaguered child was only right to shake off the mantle of responsibility. He hadn't asked to be the receptacle of his father's hopes; the pressure was too much for anybody. Peg rejected this reading, convinced that the little shit knew what he was doing.

(Schillaci, too, bore some of the blame, for Danny Doyle would have been too busy cheering to bother with peanuts had Schillaci's tears been ones of despair rather than joy. Later, Peg felt a squirm of guilt at her divided loyalties, aware that she had spent her father's final moments on earth admiring the legs of the enemy.)

It was Rosie who found her father's body, several minutes too late, his face a terrible colour.

'Dad!'

Nobody heard through the 'Nessun Dorma' and the cheers.

'Dad!'

The sighs of the commentators were equally indifferent to events in 7 Dunluce Crescent.

'Daddy! Daddy, wake up! Daddy!'

This summoned a crowd. Granny Doyle's hands rushed to her face. She'd seen enough dead bodies as a nurse to know. It was too late.

'Daddy! Help him!'

The men talked about doing CPR but Granny Doyle's arm stopped them: no point putting him through that, he hadn't a pulse.

'Daddy!'

Somebody called the ambulance (Mrs Fay?) Somebody put on the kettle (Mrs Nugent?) Somebody cleared the house (Mrs McGinty?) But even with the ambulance on its way and a fresh pot of tea made and the house nice and peaceful for once, Danny Doyle remained dead on the floor. He couldn't hear her any more; still, Rosie called.

'Dad!'

John Paul's face twisted. He should go over and hold his sister, that's what a man of the house would do. He felt his shoulders slump, his face twitch with guilt. He'd wished his father gone many a time – which of his friends hadn't wished the same? – but he hadn't wanted this, of course he hadn't. He stayed still as Rosie wailed and Granny Doyle leant against the wall with her hands up in her face, while he was stuck watching, not able to do a thing.

'Daddy!'

Damien needed to leave the house immediately. *Come on, now, let's leave space for the doctors to work.* That's what the voice was saying (Mrs Donnelly? Mrs Nugent? Some grown-up who knew what they were doing, at least) and Damien clung to this protocol. Chaos had entered the house; the best thing was to restore order. They needed to leave immediately, Rosie too, but she wouldn't stop crying.

'Daddy, wake up!'

Peg walked over to her sister and held her. She didn't always understand her sister but here was something she could appreciate: pain. Somebody had turned off the television – they must have – but Peg was sure that 'Nessun Dorma' was still playing, for nothing else could capture the depth of Rosie's grief. Peg saw its swell and storm on Rosie's red face, as the poor child seemed to move in tune with the song, sinking to the ground with racking sobs, raising her head for an anguished wail, finding the strength to yell one more 'Daddy!' though the word was hard to make out. It was too much for the grown-ups, but Peg gripped onto her sister. She didn't try to ssh her or say things would be okay. She couldn't even say that she knew what she was feeling, for what Peg felt was detachment, an awareness that she should have the same well of grief inside her, even as she failed to find it.

I'm here, Peg hoped her grip said, as she held Rosie on the dining-room floor, while John Paul and Damien were ushered away and sirens flashed through the net curtains. *I'm here*, Peg's hug said, as the stretcher arrived and Rosie's wails softened to sobs. *I'm here,*

Peg's arm said, as Rosie leant into it, the room empty now, the television definitely switched off, though Peg could still hear the traces of 'Nessun Dorma' in the air, the silence after the crescendo, heavy with the feelings that had gone before.

They stayed there like that for a time, an hour or an eternity, Peg wasn't sure, holding each other, like sisters.

14

Blarney Stone (2007)

Rosie was asleep. Peg could just make out her face in the dark; once, they had held each other like sisters. More than once, surely. Plenty of happy memories to choose from: the day of the Hula-Hoop Olympics in the garden in Clougheally or the night she'd finally added a dragon into one of her tales about the Children of Lir.

The day when she'd bought Rosie a hot chocolate with whipped cream in Bewley's, that was a happy memory, wasn't it? That day they'd met up with Aunty Mary and peeked into Áras an Uachtaráin, where they were sure they'd glimpsed Mary Robinson, no Granny Doyle or John Paul there to ruin things (though there was another figure in the shadows, tossing a book up and down, waiting for his cue to wreak havoc).

Peg turned back towards the ceiling. Who was she kidding? What was the point remembering? John Paul was always there, lurking, waiting for his last Unofficial Miracle: the disappearance of a sister.

15

Áras an Uachtaráin Candle (1991)

The days following Italia '90 were giddy with possibility, so perhaps it was no surprise that Mary Robinson grabbed the ball from the Irish squad and lobbed it through the walls of Áras an Uachtaráin, that grand home for presidents in Phoenix Park that had never housed a woman before. The first female President of Ireland! It didn't matter that the role was mostly symbolic; Mary Robinson had sensed the euphoria that came with the World Cup and channelled it in a different direction, one where a new Ireland could be called into being. After a month's work on a project about Mary Robinson for transition year, Peg had her favourite part of her inaugural speech off:

> *I was elected by men and women of all parties and none, by many with great moral courage who stepped out from the faded flag of the civil war and voted for a new Ireland, and above all by the women of Ireland, mná na hÉireann, who instead of rocking the cradle rocked the system, and who came out massively to make their mark on the ballot paper and on a new Ireland.*

Walking around the periphery of Áras an Uachtaráin, Peg gave Rosie a smile, one future system-rocker to another. They'd trekked to Phoenix Park for a sight of their new president and even though they hadn't spotted Mary Robinson, Peg could well imagine her, strolling down the grand corridors, clearing the cobwebs of history with her firm smile. They didn't see the famous candle she'd left by the window either, but it was clear in Peg's imagination, its beam flickering for all the exiled and the dispossessed, everybody welcome in her house of hope.

(Later, when Peg sat on a fire escape in New York, she wondered if the candle flickered for her. Probably not, she decided, resolving never to return; the problem with inspiring figures was that they traded in lies, showed you a place as it ought to be, not as it was.)

*

'Can I have whipped cream with my cake?'

In the queue of Bewley's Café, Rosie seemed to have forgotten the grandeur of Áras an Uachtaráin, where Peg suspected that Mary Robinson didn't even eat, ideas enough to sustain her.

'Of course,' Peg said, giving Rosie a smile to show that this generosity was a pleasure.

She'd insisted on buying the drinks herself, eager to demonstrate the financial independence that her part-time job afforded.

'Do you want to grab the spoons?' Peg asked.

All part of Peg's plan to sculpt her sister into something more solid: delegation of responsibilities. If she were lucky, one day Rosie might get an A for her project on feminist history or get her own part-time job at Nolans deli. Perhaps even more auspicious fates awaited: Celia Gallagher had a younger sister who declared with confidence that *she* would be the President of Ireland when she grew up! Rosie, unfortunately, had no such sense of purpose, drifting about and taking an eternity to pick up five spoons: Peg was sure that Mary Robinson had never *drifted* in her life. Worse, Rosie hadn't seemed all that fussed about Mary Robinson, asking all the wrong questions as they'd stood outside Áras an Uachtaráin. Were the deer happy in Phoenix Park? Rosie wanted to know. Were there still horses pulling carriages in Áras an Uachtaráin? And if so, who looked after them? It didn't matter who cleaned up the manure, Peg said, as long as it was a man, or an equal number of men and women being paid the same wage, as long as the women wanted the work. (Feminism was difficult to explain.) Perhaps Rosie could aspire to be a vet, Peg decided; she certainly hadn't any hope of becoming a decent waitress.

'Will we find the others upstairs?'

Rosie nodded, waiting for Peg to lead the way.

Peg strode up the stairs, eager for the second part of Rosie's feminist education. They might not have found the President, but another Mary waited upstairs. Working on her project, Peg had gasped in shock at one of the newspaper clippings she'd unearthed: Aunty Mary, smiling alongside radical feminists, on the infamous Condom Train. She'd arranged an interview, bringing Rosie along with her other project partners, Denise Donnelly and Celia Gallagher. Celia Gallagher was more of a rival than an ally – she was the only girl in the year with a better Junior Cert than Peg – but Peg had suffered working on a history project with her; they had a better chance of success if they pooled their brilliance, especially as Denise was only interested in certain aspects of Mary Robinson's story. Peg smiled at Aunty Mary as they sat down, Celia and Denise continuing their interrogation.

'So what was Mary Robinson like back then?' Celia Gallagher asked, pen hovering over a stack of index cards. 'Did you really used to have your meetings in this café?'

'Did she hold one of ...' Denise rolled her eyes at Rosie's presence '... you know?'

Celia glared at Denise.

'Did you have a sense that you were dealing with one of the country's finest legal minds?' Celia asked.

'Did she have better hair back then?'

Aunty Mary sighed.

'As I've explained, Mary Robinson wasn't on the train with us.'

'Yes, but she was part of the Irish Women's Liberation Movement, right?' Celia said, flipping through her notes. 'And she defended the group on *The Late Late Show*, right?'

'She did,' Aunty Mary said. 'But she kept her distance. She wasn't going to get involved in any of our antics, wanted to make sure there was a respectable face to the movement, I suppose.'

Peg hoped that Rosie might be alert to the interesting debate within feminism between radical and moderate tactics but Rosie seemed preoccupied with slowly spooning off the cream from her cake.

'What I want to know is if it's a precondition of being a politician that you have to have horrible hair,' Denise said. 'Maggie Thatcher: horrible louse hair. Máire Geoghehan what's her face: helmet hair. Barbara Bush: *Coronation Street* blue-rinse granny hair.'

'Barbara Bush isn't a politician,' Celia sniped.

Aunty Mary touched her own grey bob, which had become frizzier over the years.

'I suppose politicians have more important things to be doing than wondering about their hair,' she said with a laugh.

'Is yer one with the ginger hair a politician?' Denise asked.

Aunty Mary froze.

'Who?'

'The one you were talking to when we arrived,' Denise said. 'With the bright red hair: looks like she dyes it, I'd say, looked all right though.'

'She's not a politician,' Aunty Mary said. 'Just an old friend.'

Of course she'd run into Stella; Dublin could be as tiny as Clougheally. It was as lovely and heartbreaking as ever to see Stella, alternative lives opening up in front of them, as they talked small with their mouths and big with their eyes. It was Stella the girls should be meeting, Mary thought; she was still deep in the activist world. Lobbying Mary Robinson, in fact, the decriminalization of homosexuality essential if Ireland were to become a truly modern country. Mary Robinson had been one of the lawyers courageous enough to take on gay rights cases back in the Seventies. Stella would have told them all that, Rosie too, *because we can't hide who we are for ever!* Stella almost shouted, with every inch of her being. Meanwhile, Mary had run from the fight, back into the house in Clougheally, which might as well have been shaped like a closet, no space in its drawers for revolutionary condoms or lube or whips. Ah, but she was too old for it all, wasn't she? She'd stepped into herself late, small wonder the skin hadn't quite fitted. Past sixty now, she was best off leaving the revolutions to the young.

'I brought you these,' Aunty Mary said, placing a bag of books on the table for Peg.

'Thanks,' Peg said, examining the contents.

'Are there any ones with pictures of the train in there?' Denise asked, eager for a better glimpse at some condoms.

'I'm afraid it's mostly Greek texts,' Aunty Mary said. 'You're still into that, aren't you?'

'Yes,' Peg said, though that had been last summer's obsession. She pulled out a few of the dusty paperbacks and checked her disappointment that the Greeks hadn't any more explicitly feminist works. Rosie was more interested in a bright paperback at the bottom of the pile.

'Oh,' Aunty Mary said. 'That was more of a joke.'

Peg rolled her eyes. It was some fairy tale about the Children of Lir, which Rosie still liked, even though it wasn't a very appropriate story: if Fionnuala had been a proper feminist she would have left her squawking brothers to clean up their own swan-shite and flown off somewhere more revolutionary, Cuba perhaps.

'You keep that,' Aunty Mary said, smiling at Rosie.

'Thanks,' Rosie said, thrilled to have a book of her own.

'Rosie, do you want to ask Aunty Mary any questions about the President?' Peg said, keen that Rosie not waste any of their time free from Granny Doyle's shadow. 'They used to sit here and meet and talk about important issues, you know?'

Rosie looked thoughtful.

'Do you know who looks after the deer in Phoenix Park?'

Peg decided that she needed another coffee.

*

Peg had used the last of her change buying a second coffee when she saw Celia Gallagher charge down the stairs, flustered. Peg was sure that Rosie had caused some catastrophe but then she saw the source of Celia's interest: the gang of teenage schoolboys sauntering through the door. The Gonzaga French Debating team, their main rivals in the tournament at Alliance Française. Celia was captain of the team and was certain that the sudden appearance of the Gonzaga team while she researched feminism (an upcoming debate topic) meant that they were spying on them. Celia stared at them too long, causing the Gonzaga captain to stroll over. So, what happened next was Celia's fault; any historian would have concluded as much.

How to describe Ruadhan Kennedy-Carthy? A Grecian god for the twentieth century? One of the tricksier ones, Hermes or Dionysus. No, something more prosaic: Captain Wickham in a school uniform. History had seen his type plenty before, he'd cadded up to many a *cailín*, but Peg Doyle hadn't a clue.

'You're on the Holy Faith debating team, aren't you?' Ruadhan asked, for he'd sussed out the competition too.

'Yes,' Peg said as Celia said, 'Why are you asking?'

Ruadhan acted as if Celia Gallagher didn't exist, reason enough for Peg to fall for him.

'You're studying Plato?' he asked, eyeing the book on Peg's tray.

'Yeah,' Peg lied.

'No way!'

He swivelled his bag around and removed an identical paperback copy of *The Symposium*. Seconds later, he'd snatched Peg's and had the two Platos flying up in the air, then in separate hands behind his back.

'Know which is yours?'

'Give her back her book,' Celia Gallagher said.

Peg, however, was transfixed, pointing to his right arm, sure that static electricity clung to his school jumper.

'Wrong choice,' Ruadhan said, as Peg opened the book to find Ruadhan's many notes inside. 'You'll have to play again …'

Ruadhan flipped to the cover of Peg's book but no name greeted him.

'Peg. Doyle.'

'You should write your name on your possessions, Doyle. Otherwise you don't know who might take them.'

'And you should head back to your mates and leave us alone,' Celia said. 'You can keep your copy, I'm sure Peg will survive without your dazzling observations.'

Ruadhan put on a wounded look, followed by a grin as he leant closer to Peg.

'Want to get a drink somewhere else, Doyle? This kip is a bit crowded.'

Mary Robinson would not have followed Ruadhan Kennedy-Carthy out the door. Mary Robinson would not have asked Celia Gallagher to bring Rosie home and to furnish some emergency excuse for the others. Mary Robinson certainly wouldn't have left Rosie upstairs, like some forgotten umbrella. But not everybody could be a president, could they?

'You ready, Doyle?'

Peg chugged her second cup of coffee as if it were a shot.

'I am.'

Series IV:
Confirmation

(1992)

1

Fallons French Regular and Irregular Verb Book (1992)

The courtship of Peg Doyle and Ruadhan Kennedy-Carthy was inextricable from the French Debates at the Alliance Française that threw them together and was best charted through the irregular verbs that Ruadhan spent so much time practising.

savoir (to know)

Peg kept an index of facts about Ruadhan Kennedy-Carthy in her head, as if he were a card she was collecting.

Height: 5 ft 11
Age: 17
Eyes: glacier Blue
Hair: blond
School: Gonzaga
Address: 'Glendale', 13 Eglinton Grove, Donnybrook, Dublin
    4, Ireland.
Interests: Rugby, debating, travel, Peg Doyle (?!)

connaître (to know)

Ruadhan helped Peg understand the need for two verbs for 'to know'. Peg knew facts; Ruadhan knew how to live. Ruadhan knew the varieties of cheese beyond 'shredded' and the types of wine beyond 'red' or 'white'; 'Bordeaux' and 'Gorgonzola' as familiar as friends. Ruadhan had parents who dined with the Attorney General and a sister who had gone on a date with The Edge. He had been to almost every country in Europe, even the new ones that kept cropping up; Slovenia was news to Peg, 'the most amazing kayaking' to Ruadhan.

gésir (to lie helplessly or dead)

Competing for attention with Ruadhan's eight Leaving Certificate subjects, Peg dangled the strange facts she had accumulated before him, titbits that might give him the edge in essays. Ruadhan was determined to beat his older brother's score of 580 points, a car in it for him if he reached 600. So, defective verbs, irregular verbs that could only be conjugated in certain tenses, impossible due to the strict policing of the Académie Française to use *pleuvoir* in the first person singular or *gésir* in the conditional or future tense.

'Why would you want to, Doyle? Why would anybody want to use that verb *ever*? How could you be "lying helplessly *or* dead"? Christ, you'd think they could find another verb: don't know if this bugger is *gisant* helplessly or *gisant* dead, guess we'd better bung him in the coffin!'

Not the point: it was the bizarre precision of the grammar that attracted Peg, the urge that it compelled in her to break the rules, because why couldn't multiple skies rain or why couldn't one lie helplessly or dead in some conditional future? Ruadhan, at least, was intrigued enough to keep listening.

sortir (to go out; go out with)

There was some linguistic uncertainty to the arrangement, a lack of clarity as to what their explorations of mouths and minds constituted, exactly. Peg felt that she was balanced on a tightrope, perilously close to happiness or despair, desperate to secure

Ruadhan's attentions, aware that defective verbs alone were not sufficient.

lire (to read)

A book about love had brought them together, but Peg wasn't sure if Plato was the best person for advice. *The Symposium* was about transcending the material, Ruadhan said, the sensory world merely a rung towards the appreciation of abstract forms.

'So the ideal kind of love is platonic?'

Ruadhan's blue eyes flashed (surely no form could be more perfect?)

'I wouldn't exactly say that, Doyle.'

prédire (to foretell)

'It won't end well,' Celia Gallagher warned. 'I've always found that the cockiness of the male involved is in inverse proportion to his addendum. I think you should break up. Unless he's sharing any debate strategy with you? Peg, come back, I haven't given you your index cards yet ...'

médire (to slander)

Celia Gallagher was not impressed with Ruadhan's debating style.

'All style and no substance, no index cards, and what a terrible opening: there's no way a team that opens a serious debate with "*J'accuse!*" can be rewarded.'

vaincre (to vanquish)

The judges disagreed.

boire (to drink)

Ruadhan poured drinks in his brother's empty flat for them after the debate, Shiraz and Merlots mixing in with the flagon of vodka that Peg had used for courage.

devoir (to have to)

Peg thought of the other women who had knelt in this position. Did Helen of Troy regret her fate when Menelaus gripped her by the hair and shoved her to her knees? Was crouching in front of Paris any better? Did Maud Gonne do it for W.B.? Princess Di? Marilyn Monroe? She was taking her place in a time-honoured tradition, securing her spot in history with each reflex of the lips.

pouvoir (to be able to)

The combination of a variety of fluids and a foreign appendage poking about required collective action from the body of Peg Doyle. At first, she feared murder by botched blow job, Ruadhan screaming in pain as teeth clamped too hard. Then, it was worse, something else stirred up inside her, a shade of vomit that comes only from an excess of red wine, defying gravity, reaching the white shirt, blue eyes and astonished face of Ruadhan Kennedy-Carthy.

aller (to go)

The bus home had never felt lonelier.

rire (to laugh)

'It's not funny.'
    'No, you're right, it's very serious.'

Denise Donnelly let out another peal of laughter.

gésir (to lie helplessly or dead)

'It's terrible. He won't return my calls. Our relationship is a defective verb: there's no future tense, we're doomed!'

'Jaysus, relax, you've spent too much time with those French Debate cunts. You know what I do in these situations?'

'What?'

'I ask myself, "What would Madonna do"?'

vouloir (to want)

Ruadhan answered the phone. Peg spoke the one French sentence everybody knew.

2

Chrism Ointment (1992)

Damien Patrick *Francis* Doyle floated back to his pew. His teacher had been unclear about the mechanics of Confirmation, vague about how tongues of fire or maturity would descend upon his soul once Father Shaughnessy dabbed a bit of chrism on his forehead. Damien fretted that he might mess the procedure up (especially without Peg, who was supposed to be his sponsor, until she fell ill and left his soul in the care of Mrs McGinty) but he needn't have worried. The Holy Spirit had found him; he felt a lovely warm fire tickle his insides, while his legs floated down the aisle, wings likely to follow.

Damien knelt down and closed his eyes, no need for a glance at Jason Donnelly's leather jacket. If St Francis of Assisi was happy to empty his pockets for the poor, then Damien Patrick Francis Doyle certainly wouldn't covet a coat, no matter how nice and new it smelled. Damien felt warmed by the Holy Spirit and the possibilities of his new Confirmation name, only a few years before he floated off to cure the sick in Assisi (or some far-flung island, his teacher also vague about Assisi's current leper population) and grew into the person God meant him to be. *I'm ready, God!* Damien said, the radio in his head pulsating with the Holy Spirit's new frequency; in no time at all he'd be giving his clothes to beggars.

First, prayers for those in immediate need. One for John Paul, whose current symphonic farts suggested that the Holy Spirit had yet to discover his soul. One for Mrs McGinty, who had stepped in to be his sponsor at the last minute, and done a fine job, even if she'd only given him a prayer book as a present (he would not be covetous!) A prayer for Peg, too, he couldn't forget that. Perhaps this was the most important one, the test of his future healing abilities. Poor Peg was sick at home, she'd have sponsored his soul otherwise, guided him gently down the aisle and calmed the thump of his heart, like she had when he'd made his Communion and she'd promised him that he wouldn't choke.

Protect Peg, Damien asked the Holy Spirit, feeling the fire blaze brighter inside him. He could make her a hot water bottle and a cup of tea when they got home. Perhaps he could even try cooling her forehead with his fingers, which tingled at the prospect of goodness and glory.

3

Fallons French Regular and Irregular Verb Book (1992)

confirmer (to confirm)

'What's your Confirmation name, Doyle? Mary? Bridget? No, something more political would be your game, Doyle. Maud? Rosa? What's Lady Gregory's first name … Lady?'

Peg focused on the boiling kettle: a normal thing to be doing, making tea for a friend.

'My Confirmation name is Hildegard,' she lied.

She turned to Ruadhan.

'What's yours? Aloysius? Ignatius?'

'You've got me all wrong, Doyle. I'm a humble Jedi: Luke.'

Peg allowed herself a glance.

'Patron saint of boys with lightsabers?'

Peg turned back to the kettle, careful not to look for too long.

Ruadhan put his arms around her dressing gown.

'Well, Doyle, I hope your young brother isn't adrift without your expert sponsorship to steer him down the aisle.'

'I could probably make the ceremony if I tried.'

'No. *Confirmer. Con*, together. *Firmare*, strengthen.'

Peg felt Ruadhan's hands glide downwards.

'I'm sure we could find some alternative way of strengthening things together.'

The essence of Ruadhan Kennedy-Carthy: a seventeen-year-old whose idea of foreplay was a lecture on Latin.

Even so, Peg switched off the kettle and turned around.

4

Lynx Deodorant (1992)

'Mind you, you're better off not splashing out, aren't you? I mean, between Jason's jacket and the cost of a table at Clontarf Castle, it adds up, doesn't it? Mind you, only once in a lifetime they get confirmed, isn't it? Where is it *you're* eating? Not at the Castle anyway, Jason told me, aren't you the wise ones!'

John Paul scanned Granny Doyle's face nervously. Usually, Granny Doyle could dismiss Mrs Donnelly with a snort. Something was up. John Paul turned to Jason, who mouthed 'Two hundred and eighty-five,' the lucky git. Boyler had two hundred. Keifo had one hundred and eighty, apparently, though the gobshite could barely count. Not to worry. John Paul had managed one hundred and thirty pounds fifty (cheap Mrs McGinty with the fifty pence): a tidy sum for a piggybank. He might manage new runners and deodorant that would make Clodagh Reynolds notice him. Who cared about the Donnellys?

'Anyway, we'd better dash! Parking will be only mad at the Castle! I hope you have a great meal; I'm sure the Yacht is much improved.'

Granny Doyle cared, that was what had her agitated. John Paul saw the problem immediately. Peg would have been grand to share a children's meal with one of them, but Granny Doyle couldn't ask the same of Mrs McGinty. Mrs Nugent had been his sponsor and Mrs Fay had sponsored Rosie and now Granny Doyle didn't have the money in her purse to treat the lot of them. He could donate the money from his cards, John Paul decided, anything to stop the blush on Granny Doyle's cheek and the fret of her fingers. He was on the verge of offering as much (the deodorant that might make Clodagh Reynolds stop and sniff him evaporated) when another idea struck him.

'I'd murder a takeaway!' Mrs Nugent agreed, ever an ally. 'There's not a food that isn't improved with a bit of batter!'

Mrs McGinty lamented that far too much fuss was made of Confirmations, these days, and the Fays thought a takeaway would be *lovely* and Granny Doyle demurred just enough, until they all agreed, and then John Paul saw he'd done it, brought a smile back to her face, saved the day; his insides glowed with relief.

'Maybe we can check in on Peg and see if she wants some,' Damien suggested, inspired by altruism.

'A lovely idea,' the Fays thought.

Mrs Nugent wasn't so sure.

'A spicy burger might be the last thing she wants if she's feeling queasy, in and out faster than Bishop Casey into an American floozy, that's what I'd worry about! Ah, Maureen, what are you staring at me for? I'm only joking and aren't they old enough now! Sure, this one will be doing a line with a young one soon, won't you?'

I will, John Paul thought, enjoying the walk and the notes in his pocket that meant he wouldn't have to choose between Lynx's Nevada or Oriental range; he could buy the whole shelf, all the sets, the world in his grasp.

5

Fallons French Regular and Irregular Verb Book (1992)

permettre (to allow)

'You're sure this is what you want?'

He looked lovely, standing naked in the middle of the bedroom, his face lit up by the scrap of light poking through the curtains and the red of the statue, a vulnerability to his smile, the rare moment when it felt as though they were equals.

'Yes.'

admettre (to admit)

'I broke it when I was practising,' he said, that rare moment when he looked younger.

Neither of them were old enough to buy condoms in Brennan's, even if they'd had the nerve.

She gripped his hair.

'It doesn't matter.'

mettre (to put)

'We can try again, if you want.'

'No, that was fine.'

remettre (to postpone)

Lying in his arms *was* fine, more than fine, time stretchy and wonderful, possible to stay there for ever.

admettre (to admit)

'My favourite part of *The Symposium* is the part where the four-legged creatures are split in two and then they hop about the world trying to find their other … half.'

Soulmate remained stuck in her throat.

'Aristophanes' speech? You do know that bit is satirical?'

remettre (to put back in; to postpone)

Even so, they fitted better, the second time.

promettre (to promise)

The words were easier to say in French: *Je t'aime.*

That he responsed in the formal tense ('that's what they'll use in the oral exam!') diminished the moment, but only slightly.

6

Walkman (1992)

Peg was lucky to be sick, Rosie thought, as Dunluce Crescent loomed into view and soggy chips and chat about *Coronation Street* beckoned. Maybe she could babysit Peg; Granny Doyle probably wouldn't even notice her absence. She hadn't even commented on her Confirmation name. *I haven't heard of Saint Danielle* Mr Fay had admitted and *it's a lovely name* Mrs Fay had offered but Granny Doyle hadn't even bothered to snort.

Danny Doyle would have been her sponsor, if he hadn't gone and died. Rosie hadn't realized how nice it had been, to have her father depend upon her. She had done it for him, she thought, the cheery chat about her day and the *let's go for a walk before it gets dark* and the *maybe you'll win big on the next one*. She hadn't realized how much these chats had kept her going too, especially with all the girls in her class ignoring her, because she'd never mastered the rituals of fancy paper swapping or Take That worship. Other older sisters might have provided some counsel but Peg was no help; nobody else managed to make 'Rosie!' sound like such an insult.

'Rosie! Are you coming in or out?'

Though Granny Doyle could give Peg a run for her money, when she remembered. They had reached the porch of 7 Dunluce Crescent and Rosie was dawdling and daydreaming as usual, no harm, for who really wanted to pay attention to Mrs Nugent's account of the ill-advised time she'd tackled a battered sausage on top of a tummy bug.

In, Rosie decided, her legs pushing into the hall as Granny Doyle and the others fussed in the porch. She could make sure Peg hadn't died. And, as long as she was still sick but not dead, Rosie might be able to borrow her Walkman. With *Nevermind* in her ears, Rosie might be able to get through the dinner. Rosie had *almost* tried to smuggle it into the church; Nirvana could have cleansed her ears from the hymns. She might have chanced Kurt as a Confirmation name – or at least Courtney – if her Dad hadn't gone and died. Danny Doyle would have been a cool sponsor, seeing the funny side. He might have loved the tape too – his room had been full of records – and here was another thing to make a heart heavy and send feet trudging up stairs, her ears in search of the only voices that knew just how broken the world was.

'Rosie, hurry up!'

Some affection in John Paul's tone, at least, though his legs charged past, his piggybank calling. Damien was right behind, eager to be the first to check on Peg, which annoyed Rosie, so she picked up her pace until *three two one* they bundled up the stairs, lightly pushing and shoving each other, the way they used to, still friends then, motivations tangled, until somehow it was John Paul who opened the door to Rosie's bedroom.

7

Fallons French Regular and Irregular Verb Book (1992)

voir (to see)

For once, John Paul Doyle was speechless.

The girl in the bed looked like his sister, but she didn't bear any resemblance to the bookwormish wagon who could sour a room with her face. The cow who was always making sure that John Paul knew how much smarter she was couldn't be scooping a sheet up around her, with the curtains drawn and the red light glowing, as if she were in some tawdry porno that even Keifo'd be embarrassed to watch. Yet there she was, Peg. Who the fuck knew who the lad was, some gobshite whooshing out of the bed and scrambling for his clothes.

John Paul's brain whirred into overdrive as Peg caught his eye, desperate. Granny Doyle and the other biddies were still in the porch. He could call her, heroically. Or he could push the blond gobshite down the stairs and boot him onto the street, man-of-the-house style. Peg would deserve it and all, the cheeky cow; he'd never disrespect Granny Doyle like that, not under her own roof.

Or …

He could fix this. Peg knew as much, her eyes flashing in desperation. The man of the house could help everybody. Shield a sister. Spare Granny Doyle a broken heart.

And …

John Paul could help himself too, he realized, his brain whirring ahead, aware that every opened door had to reveal an opportunity.

8

Nike Runners (1992)

John Paul stretched out his legs, the better for Clodagh Reynolds to notice his new runners. Bright enough to blind, the runners couldn't be missed, yet somehow Clodagh Reynolds' eyes continued to display no interest. John Paul gripped his fag and exhaled in a way he hoped was cool. His heart was doing its thump-bump, its rhythm attuned to the bounce of Clodagh Reynolds' tits, though it wasn't just that: a glimpse into the blue of her eyes was enough to send John Paul's heart a-plummet, a wonder it was possible to breathe afterwards.

Clodagh Reynolds leant against the wall and waited for her friend to buy cigarettes from John Paul. She was thirteen like the other Holy Faith first-years, but she'd easily get into a 15 film, 18 if she had her make-up on. She lived in a posh house off the Coast Road and ironed her auburn hair so straight it could slice envelopes, and was a secondary school principal's daughter and was perfect in every way, except that she never noticed John Paul, even when his shoes were fluorescent.

'Thanks, J.P.,' Clodagh's friend said, some gobshite, like all his other customers, skittery things who giggled and played with their ponytails and acted like the purchase of a few Marley Lights made them Sharon Stone in *Basic Instinct*.

Most of the first-years had a crush on John Paul, because even though he was only in sixth class and nowhere near as tall as Jason Donnelly, he had the chat and the smile; it was a pleasure doing business with the cheeky little ride.

'Cool runners,' Clodagh Reynolds' friend said, the stupid tit, because this only made it worse, the glance of Clodagh's as she walked away, nothing she saw enough to cause a crinkle across her perfect face. John Paul gawped at her as she stalked off, the chat stolen clean out of him in her presence, his heart dragged along on a leash after her razor-sharp hair and the peep of leg between tartan skirt and grey socks.

'All right, mate?'

Jason Donnelly's words dragged John Paul back to his senses.

He brought the gang with him because Jason Donnelly was cute enough to pull over some customers and Boyler and Keifo were thick enough to help out without getting any commission. Without doubt the leader of the group, John Paul was sure he came off all *Goodfellas*, except when Jason, too clever for his own good, took the mick. John Paul could see a smile forming across Jason's smug face so he struck first.

'I'd be cool, man, if I didn't have to stare at that Saturn of a spot of yours. Is that a new one? Jesus, you've got the whole solar system on your chin!'

Boyler and Keifo laughed because they knew what was good for them and John Paul kept it all under control, *blackhead? more like a black fucking hole!*, the mention of acne enough to stop Jason's smile. *I'll tell you what black hole I'd like*, John Paul's heart returning to normal, *fuck off, you dirty geebag, that wasn't what I meant!*, no chance of Jason daring to mention Clodagh Reynolds' name out loud, *be phoning your ma, so I will*, order restored, *don't I have her number after last night, hey!*

'You saying something about my ma?'

It was Denise Donnelly, Peg beside her.

John Paul put on his innocent face.

'Wouldn't dream of it.'

Denise rolled her eyes. John Paul would never tell Jason about the time he'd crept into Denise's empty room just to cop a lungful of her perfume, because Clodagh used Dior too. There was certainly no danger of Jason falling for Peg; she looked worse than ever, a right puss on her as she slapped a few cartons of cigarettes into John Paul's hand.

'Pleasure doing business with you too,' John Paul said.

'Fuck off.'

It was the coldness of these two words that had John Paul bounding after Peg, leaving the gang behind for a moment, Denise busy giving Jason an earful about what their mother would say if she caught him smoking.

John Paul caught Peg before she crossed the road.

'Wait, we can do a deal, you know I've said—'

'All I want is for you to leave me alone. I've told you to do this shit somewhere else.'

John Paul put on his cheekiest smile.

'Don't you like hanging out with your little bro?'

'No.'

It was the truth of this that had John Paul saying what he did next.

'Can do you another deal if you want. Write off some of your debt. Poor Boyler over there has never copped off with a soul, but he'd be well keen. He's not blond, of course – not your type – but I could ask Jason, he's almost thirteen, and he'd be glad of a BJ, I don't know how many packets that'd be worth but we can do a deal ...'

Peg's face was finally enough to drain John Paul's courage. She could have slapped him. She'd certainly wanted to; slapping John Paul had been a frequent wish since the day of the triplets' Confirmation. She should have slapped him when he'd made her buy the cigarettes to keep his business going. She should have slapped him when he'd forced her to spend all her wages on his new runners. She should definitely have slapped him that afternoon. Peg wasn't sure she had the strength for a slap, though, it was enough to keep the tears back, so her arms remained fixed by her side and all she managed was a 'just fuck off, okay.'

Peg was the one fucking off down the road though, leaving John Paul frozen for the second time that afternoon, his insides performing another complicated loop-de-loop. He couldn't deny the satisfaction he felt at finally having the better of his stuck-up older sister. There was guilt too, a sense that he'd gone too far; Peg wasn't to be spoken to like Boyler or Jason Donnelly. *I was only messing*, he might have said, with his best smile on, though Peg had always been immune to his dimples. *This is only business*, he might have said – the truth, or part of it, for he couldn't deny the satisfaction he had in finally seeing Peg squirm. *I'll give you a cut*, he might have said – also the truth, because between his Confirmation money and his profits he was loaded, and it was only business sense to keep the supplier happy.

I'm sorry, he might have said, if he'd bounded after her, which he had the instinct to, though his feet remained stuck – a shame, when he was wearing the fastest runners in Killester.

9

Fallons French Regular and Irregular Verb Book (1992)

revoir (to see again)

Damien stood transfixed by the scene in front of him: Peg swooping a bed-sheet around her, a teenage boy leaping out of the bed, squeezing a white bottom into a pair of dark blue Levis, the curtains drawn in the afternoon, the statue still on, filling the room with an odd red light. Did he know then that this would be an image fixed upon his retina, sharp as any photograph?

There was more. The boy shuffled into a T-shirt and turned around. *Help!* the boy's face said, though Damien's legs couldn't budge. He stayed there, as the boy gulped and ran his fingers though his wavy blond hair and barely looked at Peg. Damien stood still while John Paul headed downstairs and chatted to the ladies out the front door and Rosie kept lookout and summoned the boy down the stairs. Peg was as stuck as Damien, not a breath out of her until Rosie returned.

Then, Damien moved, walking over to the window beside Rosie, watching the boy stride through their garden, his cool returned, his ascent of the back wall smooth and swift, escape accomplished in seconds, though not before Damien, with a horrid lurch of his heart, could clock another glimpse of that Levi-clad bottom, easing its way over the back wall, taunting, somehow.

10

Trócaire Box (1992)

Damien dropped another twenty pence into his Trócaire charity box. John Paul took a break from admiring his runners to let out a sigh.

'Jesus, Damo, Trócaire'll be feeding half of Africa by the time Lent's over. Why do you keep chucking in change?'

Damien blushed; impossible to tell John Paul the truth. John Paul was shrewd enough to glean some of it.

'Paying for your impure thoughts, are you? Fuck, man, you're better than me: I'd be broke if I had to give money to charity every time I thought of Clo.'

'You'd be broke if you had to put in money every time you *talked* about her.'

'Fuck off,' John Paul said, laughing and throwing the nearest thing he could find – a rolled-up sock – across at Damien.

Damien groaned and tossed it back, lobbing a 'so did you see her today?' across too as insurance against escalation. Damien's calculation was correct; John Paul flopped down and launched into an account of the latest sighting of Clodagh Reynolds. Damien was the only person John Paul could trust with such secret information, so Damien was treated to daily updates. Not that Damien minded, any distraction welcome at the moment, an evening listening to *and the way she wears her jumper round her waist, fuck, man, I thought I'd die* preferable to dealing with the thoughts jagging about in his head.

March had been a difficult month. Whenever Damien closed his eyes, Ruadhan Kennedy-Carthy's buttocks appeared like magic, crowding out the poor Holy Spirit. When Damien thought of Jesus on the cross, he had Ruadhan's chest, those beautiful biceps that Damien had seen shuffling into a T-shirt. When Damien imagined Daniel valiantly running towards the lion, it was Ruadhan's rear that bounced across the Colosseum. When Damien thought of his island, of all the pure poor he would help, Ruadhan was beside him, no need for many clothes in the heat of the island sun. God was no help. Damien had lost the trick of finding the channel and no matter how many coins he shoved into his Trócaire box, a certain pair of buttocks always reappeared, squeezing into jeans or easing over a wall or—

'Jesus, not again! Don't tell me *you've* been thinking about Clo?'

Damien flushed; he hadn't even realized that he'd dropped in another twenty pence.

'What's to say I'm not looking after your soul?'

John Paul laughed.

'You're too generous. Maybe I'll get Peg to buy you a pair of these to pay you back.'

John Paul's runners were kicked up towards the ceiling, the better for Damien to re-admire them.

'I'm all right.'

Damien knew well enough why Peg suddenly cared about the state of John Paul's footwear; he had enough sins to worry about without adding blackmail.

'You can't be wearing runners from Dunnes next year, everyone will slag you to bits.'

'I'll be okay.'

They both knew that Damien would be slagged to bits in September, new runners or not. It was the way of the world: Damien got the piss ripped out of him, John Paul beat up the piss-rippers, secondary school sure to be no different.

'Your loss,' John Paul said with a shrug, finally taking off his beloved Nikes and shuffling into bed properly.

This was the part of the day that Damien dreaded most. John Paul could only talk about Clodagh Reynolds for so long; soon his snores would fill the room and Damien would be left with Ruadhan Kennedy-Carthy's buttocks. He'd have to add more money in the morning; Damien had a terrible feeling he was getting further and further in debt to God and wasn't at all sure he'd be able to buy his way out. Sleep wasn't even safe; who could tell what his mind would get up to in the dark. He needed something to stop the horrible parade of arses dancing across his brain; a lobotomy was the only answer, but Damien didn't have enough money for that either.

11

Fallons French Regular and Irregular Verb Book (1992)

deçevoir (to deceive; to disappoint)

As soon as Rosie saw Ruadhan Kennedy-Carthy, she understood what she had to do. Sibling solidarity kicked in and Rosie shifted into crisis mode. Gone was all the daydreamy fuzz; in a crisis, Rosie could be counted on.

It was remarkable how calm she could be, really. She waited until John Paul had charmed and chatted the ladies out of the porch, some urgent photo opportunity at Mrs Nugent's enough to buy enough time for Rosie to lead Ruadhan downstairs and out the back door. Damien she led too, into his room, where John Paul made their strategy of silence clear, not that Rosie needed to be told. The elastic band was in place, the three of them united by the crisis, getting through the takeaway dinner together, John Paul supplying the chat for the old ladies, while Rosie made sure Damien ate. There was talk about Deirdre Barlow's antics in *Coronation Street* and Bishop Casey's antics in real life and the whole afternoon seemed normal until Rosie went back upstairs.

Peg was in bed, looking genuinely sick.

'Don't worry, Peg. It'll be a secret.'

It would; Rosie felt a tingle at the thought that the secret might bind them together.

Peg didn't turn. She had her earphones in, well enough to listen to her Walkman, not that Rosie needed it any more.

12

Cosmopolitan Magazine (1992)

Rosie frowned. She was sure Peg had heard her; she was too perfectly
still to be asleep. She chanced the repeat.

'What was it like?'

Rosie sighed into the silence. Other older sisters would have sat
on Rosie's bed and told her all about the dances at the Grove and
who was the biggest ride at St Paul's. Other older sisters would have
told Rosie about what *it* was like. All Rosie had were the smuggled
copies of *Cosmopolitan* she had stolen from Peg's dresser, the quizzes
already filled out by Denise Donnelly, riddles that Rosie didn't
know how to start deciphering.

> *Which toy does your man fantasize about:*
> *a) body cream b) a strap-on dildo c) handcuffs d) all of the above?*

'Peg …'

> *Who do you fantasize about:*
> *a) Kevin Costner b) Patrick Swayze c) Tom Cruise d) all of the*
> *above?*

Rosie had already clocked five minutes of furtive fumbling by the
bike sheds with Stephen Daly. When Rosie wanted something, she
leapt in, whether it was diving from a boulder into the Atlantic or
sending a hand down Stephen Daly's trousers. The five minutes
behind the bike sheds had not evoked any particular feelings in

Rosie, boredom swiftly replacing curiosity, but Stephen Daly had told the yard, so nobody in Rosie's class was talking to her. Rosie had always been a bit too odd for the other girls but now they looked at her as if she were contaminated – a *slut* as well as a *weirdo* – even though she'd only done what they all whispered about. John Paul had given Stephen Daly an unasked-for thumping, but he couldn't attack a class of girls, not that Rosie wanted him to, because she was fine in her own dream world, happy enough to spend the day doodling, self-sufficiency one of the first things she'd learnt in a house where she was invisible.

How regularly do you perform oral sex for your man:
a) once a month b) once a week c) daily d) all of the above?

I'm here, Rosie wanted to call across, wondering why Peg felt a million miles away, when their hands could have touched in the space between their beds if they'd tried.
'Peg …'
She tried the name a bit louder.
'Peg, what was it like?'
Nothing.

Is your older sister:
a) a bitch b) a selfish bitch c) an oblivious bitch d) all of the
*   above?*

Peg turned and faced her in the dark.
'Rosie, go to sleep. I don't know what you're talking about.'

13

Fallons French Regular and Irregular Verb Book (1992)

se taire (to keep quiet)

Peg's phone calls to Ruadhan received a variety of responses, all equally heartbreaking.

The brisk severity of his father: 'He's not home.'

The acid curtness of his mother: 'I'm afraid Ruadhan is busy studying.'

The awful kindness of his younger sister: 'I'm sure he'll call you back.'

être; suivre (to be; to follow)

No accident that they had the same conjugation in the first person singular: how could she exist without him to follow?

seoir (to fit; to suit)

'Forget about those D4 bollixes: Stevo's sound. And he's more in your league, you know? And anyways, you're still probably a virgin after being with Speedy Gonzago: sounds like he was in and out faster than Flo-Jo. You're better off without the prick. Ah, what's wrong? Peg ... what is it?'

confirmer (to confirm)

Denise Donnelly looked at the pregnancy test and sighed.
  'Most of those yokes are rip-offs. We'll try another one.'

avoir (to have)

History sighed, stubbed out a cigarette. She'd seen it all before. The name changed, Tamar into Clarissa into Tess, lots of them, sitting in each other like Babushkas, their unwanted offspring swelling in their bellies, shame and zygotes bulging out the folds of the flesh. Even the shock of the tale – the awful awareness that while Peg's heart was shrivelling, something else was twisting and growing – even that sting of the pregnancy was nothing new for history. Girls had sex from time to time and out the babies came.

ouïr (to listen; obsolete)

'Ruadhan, hello … did you hear what I said? … Ruadhan?'

14

Piggybank (1992)

The Ninth Unofficial Miracle of John Paul Doyle was swift and brutal. Peg didn't know why John Paul ratted her out. Maybe he'd leached her of enough runners and fags. Maybe he felt sorry for Granny Doyle. Or perhaps he was just eager to finally put an older sister in her place. Peg didn't care what motivated him; as soon as she saw the fury on Granny Doyle's back, she knew that her secret had been unveiled.

Granny Doyle was quick to show Peg the door. Out she was, the house finally rid of her, possessions stuffed into a schoolbag, John Paul's piggybank smashed and raided on the way out, the least the little git owed her. Damien sat sobbing in the bathroom, but Peg hadn't the time to reassure him. In any case, what was there to say?

She used up all her words once she was outside, cold and lonely in the rain, Granny Doyle at the kitchen window, her back inflexible. She pushed more words through the letterbox of 5 Dunluce Crescent, but Denise Donnelly wouldn't open the door. Then she turned to look at her home and saw John Paul sitting in the porch with the door locked. One last sentence, she owed him that, one to knock all the twitching curtains of Dunluce Crescent off their rails.

'You fucking bastard!'

John Paul sat there unrepentant; he'd won.

Then Peg was around the corner, disappeared in seconds.

15

St Vincent de Paul Bag (1992)

Granny Doyle stripped Peg's bed, duvets and sheets stuffed into St Vincent de Paul bags. Fresh sheets for a fresh start. She pressed the new sheets down on the bed, checking the corners, the way she'd been trained to as a nurse. It had always struck her as remarkable what a fresh set of sheets could do: marvellous how the rows of freshly made beds in the hospital looked, so neat without the complications of human limbs. Yet this bed looked sad. Not a moment's pity for that one; this was the mantra that got Granny Doyle through the day. Hadn't she brought somebody home – into *her* house, in the middle of the day – and worse, letting the triplets see what was going on, the secret tearing away at them over the weeks, though only one of them had the decency to tell her. No, not a moment's pity for that one. People made their beds; they lay in them.

Granny Doyle sat down on the bed, ruining the sheet's crisp calm. She was too tired for this world! She'd murder a cigarette, but she hadn't the energy to go down the stairs and fish one out from the dining-room cabinet. She caught the eye of the statue of the Sacred Heart; what was it to him if she had a smoke? He'd kept quiet too, hadn't he, the lot of them in conspiracy against her, when all she was doing was trying to keep the place going and everybody healthy and she was too old for this, too tired, and Danny had a lot to answer for, leaving her with this mess. Though she'd got what she prayed for, hadn't she? That was the joke of the world, giving you what you wished for in a way you didn't want. She'd sat in this very

178

bedroom and prayed for more babies: it was shameful to have only the one, especially with so many buggies bustling across Dunluce Crescent, as if something was wrong with her. Well. There was Danny and the two miscarriages, scars in her heart each of them, and that was it. So, she should have been happy with all the rooms in the house finally full, shouldn't she?

Granny Doyle gripped the side of the bed, her knuckles whitening. It was a wicked world, there was nothing she could do to protect them, and that one always had her eye cocked for trouble. Not a moment's pity for that one: this would get her through the day. Peg didn't want to keep the baby; that was when Granny Doyle knew the door was the only direction Peg could head. She might have been able to work out some old-school solution – Peg sent off to Mayo for the while – but she wasn't having anything to do with the other business. It was bad enough with the papers full of this X girl – poor child, *she* hadn't asked to get pregnant at fourteen – who was denied passage to England and so there was all this uproar about the rights of women to access information when you'd hardly be giving out pamphlets in school about how to knife somebody, would you? The whole thing was a disgrace, especially considering how much women went through to get pregnant – the prayers she'd said in this room, the nights she'd lain there while Mick heaved and told her to 'just stay still' – and then that one said she didn't want it, as if it were a toy to be thrown away. It was too much, this world.

Granny Doyle sighed. She needed a smoke or a lie-down; or an axe, perhaps. Well. She'd have to take the bags to the St Vincent de Paul before they closed. The clothes too. Not a bit of pity for that one. That was the mantra that would see her through. People made their beds; they lay in them, or they should if there was any justice in this wicked world.

16

Fallons French Regular and Irregular Verb Book (1992)

dire (to say)

'.. I had an abortion.'

Peg later learnt to recognize it, the catch before somebody sounded the words they rarely, if ever, shared. Though it was unusual that the words to follow were so stark; even in New York, 'I had an abortion' was a sentence that needed working up to. So it was too on the ferry to England, when she heard that pause before the unsayable sounded the first time, as Kay Gallagher looked down at her cold coffee and said,

avoir (to have)

'You should know it's something you'll carry. I still carry it. Not every day, not all the time. But it's a decision that sticks with you, just as deciding to have a baby is not something you can forget. I don't regret it – don't regret it at all – but it's not something that is easy.'

voir (to see)

Mrs Gallagher kept her eyes fixed on the rim of her coffee cup: this was what she looked at, but Peg had the sense that they were seeing each other, bare.

vouloir (to want)

'… It was a long time ago. I was older than you, older enough to know better. Back when I was in Trinity: Hilary term of my Senior Sophister year. I don't doubt that I made the right decision. He wasn't the right boy; it wasn't the right time. I could never have had the two daughters I love now, I couldn't have given them the lives they deserve if I'd gone through with that pregnancy …'

rire (to laugh)

Mrs Gallagher drank some cold coffee and spat it out.
   'God, this is enough to send you to the drink.'
   The laugh caught on the Irish Sea.

se taire (to keep quiet)

Mrs Gallagher turned to Peg, her eyes watered with the wind or something else; who could say.
   'I've never spoken about it. Not to Cathal, not to my parents, not to anybody.'

savoir (to know)

Peg only knew a handful of facts about Celia Gallagher's mother: she was a successful barrister; she had forced Celia to join the French Debating team; she had a closet full of shoes; she had once grounded Celia for getting a B; she successfully petitioned the Corporation for the removal of the street sign from her outside wall; her house boasted a dishwasher and modern art rather than framed pictures of the Beatitudes.

ouvrir (to open)

But Mrs Gallagher had done what Granny Doyle and Denise Donnelly had not.

dire (to say)

Aunty Mary, too, had been a disappointment, the sentence sharp down the phone after she'd heard the story: 'Peg, you stupid, stupid girl.'

connaître (to know)

And if Peg hadn't understood why Mrs Gallagher had insisted on accompanying a girl who was only barely an acquaintance of her daughter's, she thought she did now.

se taire (to keep quiet)

'I won't say anything.'

Mrs Gallagher smiled and this time there was no doubting what was causing the water in her eyes.

'Thank you.'

17

Megaphone (1992)

Aunty Mary joined the crowd of women outside Leinster House. Cardboard signs were held by arms quivering with fury: 'No Eighth Amendment' and 'My Body, My Choice' and 'Get Your Rosaries off my Ovaries'. She might have been too old to have ovaries that the state wanted to interfere with, but Mary Nelligan wasn't too old for this after all. She could make the train to Dublin and she could raise her voice to a shout, a necessity for the times.

Stella had the megaphone, a voice to break through iron.

'It is an outrage that this government is denying a fourteen-year-old girl who was raped her right to travel to England to have an abortion.'

The crowd raged in assent, Mary's voice among them.

'It is an outrage that Miss X – or any woman – has to go to England to get an abortion in the first place.'

Stella caught her eye but she couldn't be distracted now.

'It is an outrage that this country exports its unwanted problems across the Irish Sea. It is an outrage that this country has the rights of foetuses enshrined in its constitution but denies us the right to make choices about our own bodies, denies us the right to talk about abortion, denies us even the right to get on a ferry!'

The crowd cheered.

'It is an outrage that our constitution has an amendment that protects the rights of foetuses more than the rights of women: we cannot let the Eighth Amendment stand!'

The chants started, Stella leading the crowd confidently, her new partner beside her, no shame to the pair of them. Mary bellowed out her responses; if shouts could drown out past sentences, this might be her chance. She was the stupid one, of course, immediately regretting what she'd said to Peg. She'd called back, though the payphone kept ringing. Granny Doyle had been no help. It had been a bad day – bad year? Life? – and Mary hadn't expected this, not from Peg, who had so many opportunities in front of her, who could go ahead and live the life that Aunty Mary hadn't had the chance to, at least at the right age. And then, it was all so prosaic, so familiar; she couldn't help the bitterness of her reaction, much as she regretted it. She hadn't expected Peg to hang up the phone.

Well, she had. And Mary Nelligan had woken up; she wasn't too old for this yet, she'd decided, catching Stella's eye and finding strength there, and all around her, lots of women angry at the injustice of the world. She picked up a placard from one of the volunteers and held it towards the clouds. They would shout at government buildings until the stones cracked in solidarity and the country changed; it had to.

18

Fallons French Regular and Irregular Verb Book (1992–1993)

dire (to say)

Peg heard the same catch in the hospital when the girls told their stories, afterwards.

voir (to see)

They were all looking away – at the clock, the magazines, their feet – but they all saw each other, Peg knew that.

lire (to read)

To glimpse at any newspaper was to know they were not alone.

pouvoir (to be able to)

Somehow the closing of the ferry barriers to Miss X also opened up a space, conversations cracking open, possible to talk about the injustice of laws in the light of day.

gésir (to lie helplessly or dead)

Not that this was much help to Peg, knees curled to chest on a bed in Birmingham.

parvenir (to reach; to achieve)

Or that such perturbations did anything to stall the ascent of Ruadhan Kennedy-Carthy, the A1 secured in Higher Level French suggesting a paper unscratched by guilt.

se souvenir (to remember)

'What's the matter, Doyle?'

'Stay still: I want to remember this for ever.'

Ruadhan obliged, posing heroically, until he dropped the pose, and there he was, naked in red light, a vulnerability to him, that rare moment when they were equals.

revenir (to return)

Some actions were impossible to imagine.

se souvenir (to remember)

'It makes sense in French. *Se souvenir.*'

'You're not going to get all clever on me, Doyle, are you?'

'I just like it. The idea that things can come back to you.'

Peg imagined memories coming through a crack in a window, the lost restored.

Ruadhan had the fortune not to have lost anything he wished to be returned, so he said:

'Speaking of *coming* ...'

défaire (to undo)

But who was Ruadhan Kennedy-Carthy? History had seen his type; who was Ruadhan but Captain Wickham in a school uniform? He was nothing, a thing to be forgotten

aller (to go)

and there were many directions that didn't involve 'back'.

19

Green Card (1994)

Peg sucked in her stomach as the plane hopscotched over Ireland, terrified that the land might rear up and drag the plane down. Only clouds out the window, but Peg knew that the fields were down below, grass stretching hungrily upwards, the land itching to trap more souls in its soil. There were other Irish people on the British Airways flight from Birmingham to JFK – tricolours throbbing with World Cup fever – but they seemed to suffer no allergic reaction as the plane cruised over the homeland, no dip of the stomach, no tightening of muscles.

Peg looked at the rectangle that had liberated her from Birmingham and the friend's pub that Mrs Gallagher had set her up in. It wasn't even green: Peg's first exposure to the gap between the talk and the thing in America. It was a beige blank slate, the rectangle that allowed her to reinvent herself, the photograph of Peg Doyle one that contained no traces of the past. When the customs officer asked her if she had anything to declare, it was easy for this Peg to say 'nothing'.

*

Then, the statue wasn't even green either. Or, it was green, but it was a green leached of colour, nothing like the headbands on sale in the shops, no trace of chlorophyll. It wasn't even that big. Shadowed by the skyscrapers behind it, the statue seemed squat, could only be a disappointment.

Triona didn't do disappointed. The other new barmaid at Mulligan's, she was determined that her J1 visa would deliver the best summer of her life. She refused to be disappointed in Peg as a friend, even though Peg was sure that she was too shy, too bookish, too uninterested in Baileys diving into pints of Guinness. At least Peg was handy with a disposable camera, somebody required to document Triona's variety of poses: pure glee, fingers pointing at her headband, hands holding an imaginary torch. Triona insisted on taking the Staten Island ferry in a loop as the boats to the island were a rip-off and Triona had no interest in visiting Ellis Island, the opportunities for posing limited in a museum. Besides, the view was better on the ferry and you couldn't drink cans on the tourist boats.

A couple of years earlier, Peg might have objected or gone off on her own to Ellis Island, meandering in its halls for hours, absorbed in the history of immigrant America, the things people carried with them, the ballast they refused to drop. This Peg tried to ignore the familiar bobbing of the ferry, the feelings churned up by the motion of the boat across water and focused instead on the image she was capturing: Triona facing sideways with her mouth agape, the statue so small in the distance that it looked like she was gobbling it whole.

*

It was too green, a horrible colour for a pint, but *that's how St Paddy's Day rolls here*, the owner of Mulligan's said, a shake of the head to say *we know better*. The green beer looked out of place in Woodside, a location that was technically part of New York City, although it was hard to imagine that a place where Barry's tea could be bought in bulk and you could find a priest to give you a proper Confession could inhabit the city where skyscrapers could tickle clouds. Peg kept the green pints flowing as she looked around the bar with its picture of Mary Robinson on the wall and Tayto crisps in vending machines and lads who had GAA jerseys, cheese and onion breath, and smiles which turned to grins after a few more pints had been drained.

Peg held her head in her hands in the bathroom of Mulligan's and stared at the stripe on the pregnancy test.

Triona struggled to find the right face. The owner told her that Mulligan's wasn't that kind of pub. Peg heard Granny Doyle's voice: *I always knew you were a dirty little hoor. I'm warning you, Peg Doyle, Hell is a cold place and you can't be relying on me for a coat.* She had fallen again, one of the many women falling out of history; it was too late for her.

20

Fallons French Regular and Irregular Verb Book (1994)

valoir (to be worth)

Except, *fuck that*, Peg thought, riding the subway across the Manhattan Bridge for the first time after she escaped Mulligan's, skin prickling at the possibility that *no!* it wasn't too late at all, there was no need to get trapped in a cycle of Guinness and Ireland playing Italy and *whereabouts are you from?*

voir (to see)

because this was a city with its problems placed in full view, steam rising off trash on the sidewalk, all sorts sitting on the subway, no need to hide anything. It wasn't too late for Peg, eighteen and New York City unfurled in front of her,

pouvoir (to be able)

she would find support, because women were rising, not falling, rising out of history, out of the margins, into the air, *parvenir (to reach)*

like the train pushing forwards, her first sight of the Brooklyn Bridge from a subway car an incredible thing, something that demanded the pressing of noses against glass, sun catching on water, steel suspended across air, a thing to stir the soul, a bridge that showed the smallness of each of the stories that shuttled past.

dire (to say)

This was a city where 'I had two abortions' was a sentence that could be sounded

cueillir (to gather)

as Peg imagined herself in the centre of a library, stories coming towards her, slotting into boxes, until a line of boxes streched along the length of a desk, paper bulging against lids

coudre (to sew)

or perhaps the stories could be stitched together, hung in a large room with a vaulted roof and big open windows, calling out: *you are not alone*

écrire (to write)

because *fuck it*, Peg thought, riding the subway across the Manhattan Bridge for the very first time, all sorts of histories could be written, subjunctive moods might be explored, the conditional tense could be reclaimed, anything – everything! – was possible.

21

Confession Box (1994)

'… I had an abortion. And then I ripped up a picture of the Pope into pieces on national television.'

'Child,' the priest would say.

Peg would ignore him.

'Fight the real enemy, I said. Fight the real enemy, I say.'

'I don't know what you're—' the priest would try to say.

'My name is Sinéad and I have not sinned.'

'This isn't how—' the priest would start but Peg would interrupt him.

'I'm not sorry, Father, because I can't remember how long it is since my last Confession. I had sex and tried to have my baby by the Grotto of the Virgin Mary, because nobody would talk to me about being pregnant, but the Virgin Mary didn't do anything when I died. My name is Ann and I have not sinned.'

The priest would shuffle in the box, the priest would think about leaving.

'Don't move! You have to stay where you are, that's the ceremony,' Peg would say.

'Child,' the priest would say.

'I've got fire and knives in my knickers,' Peg would say. 'Don't you dare fucking move!'

The priest would stay still.

'I tried to leave the country after I was raped but I wasn't allowed and I had to wait for all the pain of a miscarriage. My name is X and I have not sinned.'

'Child, you must have some sickness,' the priest would say.

'I had an abortion. My name is Mary and I have not sinned.'

The priest would shift in the box but he would not leave.

'I had an abortion. My name is Nuala and I have not sinned.'

Peg's voice would open the door and step into the aisle.

'I had an abortion. My name is Fidelma and I have not sinned.'

Peg would have flaming torches enough to burn the box down.

'I had an abortion. My name is Amanda and I have not sinned.'

But her voice would be enough to do that.

'My name is Melanie and I have not sinned.'

Her voice would be enough to shatter stained glass.

'My name is Molly and I have not sinned my name is Annie and I have not sinned my name is Grainne and I have not sinned my name is Clare and I have not sinned my name is Ciara and I have not sinned my name is Clodagh and I have not sinned my name is Grace and I have not sinned my name is Peg and I have not sinned ...'

She would have fire and knives in her knickers and the statues in the church would gasp at the blasphemy but she would not care, for she would leave it all in her wake, everything in splinters and cinders, while she would walk out towards the sky, smiling.

22

Blarney Stone (2007)

'............ I had an abortion,' Peg said, on the night that she and Rosie talked.

Peg focused on the whirr of the fan and the dark of the ceiling. Rosie didn't say anything, but the turn of her head was a *go on*.

So Peg told her the story of the two abortions and Rosie held her and cried. Rosie was unusually quiet, so Peg wasn't sure if she had understood, but then Rosie put her arm around Peg and that was enough.

Later, before Peg went to sleep, Rosie said, 'I had an abortion.'

There was no catch before the words; she might have said, 'I had an avocado, for lunch.'

Peg looked across. Rosie was staring at the ceiling.

'When I was in Paris. There was a second, before I told him, when I thought *maybe* ... but it definitely wasn't the right time. There was no way he was leaving his wife. And he was such a dick about it. Asking me if I'd take a half-day to work his poetry reading. I guess he was a dick about everything, but that was the first time I let myself notice.'

Rosie chanced a glance; Peg was looking at her.

'It was easy. I mean, comparatively. It hurt a lot that night, like a really bad period, but I didn't have too much bleeding. And he was with her, so I was alone, which wasn't brilliant, but I was okay, I really was, and I thought how mad it was, how glad I was to have it happen in a strange country where I could barely speak the language because …'

Here was the catch. Rosie thought she must have an extra chamber in her lungs, to house the pauses before she talked to Peg about the past.

'… And I thought of what it would have been like, if I'd been back home and had to figure out a way to get to England, what it would have been like if I'd been younger …'

Rosie looked across; Peg's eyes were still there.

'Peg …'

Peg couldn't look away now; she could just make out Rosie's tears in the dark.

'It's okay …'

Peg started to cry too.

'I'm sorry about everything that happened …'

'You don't have anything to be sorry about.'

Peg allowed her hand to touch Rosie's shoulder, the smallest of gestures, but it was enough to pull Rosie over, sobbing into her skin, so that one arm of Peg's had to wrap around Rosie's shoulder, and the other wiped tears from their eyes, as Rosie lay on Peg's chest, so that they would sleep in each other's arms that night, like sisters.

Later, when Rosie wasn't sure if Peg was asleep, she said:

'It makes me so angry.'

Peg stared at the ceiling and then she said:

'Me too. I get angry too.'

They looked at the ceiling together.

Later, when Peg wasn't sure if Rosie was asleep, she said:

'You know what Catherine is the patron saint of?'

'No.'

'I didn't know when I picked it for my Confirmation name, I did that because …'

'Yeah.'

'But then I came across it a few years ago. It turned out that there's a Catherine who is the patron saint of librarians, which seemed apt, but then it turns out that there are lots of St Catherines …'

'Yeah …'

'And there's one Catherine of Sweden who's the patron saint of protection against abortion.'

They thought about this until one of them laughed and then the other did too.

'Not very fucking good, is she?' Rosie said and when Peg laughed she did too, the sheet rising and falling in time with the howls.

Later, when Peg wasn't sure if Rosie was asleep, she said:

'You know, I love you Rosie, you know that.'

Later, when Rosie was sure Peg was asleep, she twisted her head to look at Peg, so she'd remember.

Series V:

The Revolutions of Rosie Doyle

(1992–2007)

1

Tattoo Gun (2007)

'If you're going to buy the juice with the pulp, at least be sure to rinse the glass properly.'

Could such a sentence be possible? Not after they had cried and held each other. An alternative alphabet had been found, that night; it was impossible that Peg could waste words on something so trivial.

There Peg was, though, holding up a glass to the morning light, the kitchen too small for the three of them now that Dev was back.

Dev took the fall.

'My bad! I'll lick every piece of pulp next time.'

The vigour of Peg's drying indicated that this was not a laughing matter.

'Actually, I think that was me,' Rosie hazarded. 'Sorry.'

'It's fine,' Peg said swiftly.

But ...

'I think it's good to rinse things after you wash; the coffee I had the other morning was very sudsy.'

'Of course,' Rosie said.

'The American way,' Dev said with a smile. 'Use as much water as possible!'

'Just a small thing,' Peg said, attempting a smile.

'Sure.'

Oh, but nothing was small with Peg! Every action reverberated with feelings, the opening of the cupboard or the careful examination of a bowl alive with deeper meaning. And where to put the feelings of Peg Doyle? Rosie wished bodies had a more sophisticated emotional infrastructure. Food and fluids came in, got processed, and out they went again. Air too, there was some order to that: oxygen in; carbon dioxide out. But what sort of internal plumbing was there for feelings? What use were the oesophagus or the kidneys when it came to digesting emotions? Rosie absorbed people's stories and emotions, but then there was no method to expel them and she ended up bloated with the problems of others. She needed some sort of chimney on her head to let feelings out but she only had her hair, which, Peg had reminded her, she should remember to remove from the shower-drain.

Was Rosie any better, though? They had talked, yes, but she'd only completed the first part of her mission: confront the past. This had been done, more or less, a little too successfully (Rosie squirmed at what hadn't been said) and now the second step loomed: address the present; talk about Aunty Mary's letter. How, though? They had only just begun to accept who they were as children; how could they see each other as adults?

'Did you manage to make the Obama equation for your students?'

It was easier to talk to Dev, who revealed all his feelings on his face; he didn't ask anybody else to store them.

'It's not really an equation, more exploring probability and statistics in relation to the election.'

'Right.'

Ordinarily, maths bored Rosie to tears but Dev got so excited talking about it that it was hard not to be charmed.

'I should get them to take the latest funding figures into account,' Dev said, remembering the *New York Times* article he'd just glanced at. 'Obama's catching up! And so I guess I'll get them to take the current amount of funding into account, and the number of months left before the primaries, and maybe the number of counties they've visited in Iowa – that's always key – and then ...'

Rosie didn't follow the maths and she didn't exactly see its relevance to probability theory, but she nodded; Dev was so passionate, it was difficult not to. Obama was sure to win the nomination and his students were certain to ace statistics and everything was possible, including, perhaps, plotting the outcome of the Irish election.

This aroused Peg's interest.

'Don't bother,' she said. 'The odds of change happening are nil.'

'It is a more complex system,' Dev said, Wikipedia already open. 'I wouldn't say Fianna Fáil – is that the name? – have it in the bag. They're like the Irish Republican party, right?'

Rosie said 'more or less' as Peg said 'no'.

'It's complicated,' Rosie said. 'Fianna Fáil and Fine Gael are the two major parties and they're both centre-right, more or less, and basically indistinguishable, except for their opinions about the civil war.'

Rosie saw Peg flinch at her *more or less*, the type of imprecise talk that Peg loathed, but this only gave Rosie more courage; she was the one living in Ireland, wasn't she?

'But yeah, Fianna Fáil have been in power for ten years and they're pretty evil, but this is our chance to kick them out.'

'Yes, Ireland can!' Dev said.

'Exactly!' Rosie said, forgetting her reservations about Obama and the whole process of electoral politics, and clinging instead to the electricity of agreement, the possibility that they were on revolution's cusp and the world really might be changing for the better.

'It doesn't matter,' Peg said, with a clang of the cupboard. 'They're all the same.'

Rosie wondered if Peg was following the Irish news. Another anonymous girl had made the headlines, Miss D, a seventeen-year-old in state care who'd been stopped by the health services when she wanted to travel to England for an abortion. The High Court had let her go, eventually, but not before the case had been dragged through the papers, every detail examined. Fifteen years and nothing had changed, not really, an alphabet of women (Misses A, B, C, X) waiting for the men in power to figure out how to spell 'justice'. Peg had to have heard the news, but in the light of day, Rosie wasn't sure how they could talk about it.

'The Greens have a chance of getting into a coalition,' Rosie said. 'That would be something different.'

A cop-out of a sentence, but one that steered her closer to Aunty Mary's letter.

Peg shrugged, absorbed in the turmeric stains on a spatula.

'They have six seats and an outside chance of ten,' Dev said, finding a blog to consult. 'Five to one odds of getting into a coalition. Says they might stop warplanes fuelling up in Ireland. I'd love to see Bush's face if that happened!'

'No Irish government will turn away warplanes,' Peg said, certain. 'There's an equation for neutrality and American dollars are always greater than principles. And there wouldn't be any point in turning planes away from Shannon; they'd only find somewhere else to fuel.'

Another cupboard was shut with finality: case closed.

Oh, but if only Rosie could open the doors in Peg's mind, because another world was possible – it had to be! – and Rosie had friends who had locked on to runways in Shannon to stop the planes and Rosie and Dev had both marched in different cities holding cardboard signs against the war, along with millions of others, while Peg fiddled with folders in a library. It was especially frustrating, because Peg had once taken Rosie to see Mary Robinson and brought her to quiz Aunty Mary about Women's Lib and this was the sister Rosie longed to find, a comrade against a cruel world.

'What does that say?'

Dev leant forward to examine Rosie's tattoo. It was too hot for anything other than a tank top so the words were exposed.

Rosie tensed. This was something, a key that Peg might use to unlock Rosie Doyle, the adult waiting behind the door.

'Fight the real enemy,' Rosie said slowly, waiting for a reaction from Peg, whose back remained immobile, no sense that the words meant anything at all.

'Huh!' Dev said. 'When did you get that?'

'Goth phase.'

'No way! Did you have the Elvira hair and everything?'

'You got it. Henna all over the bathtub.'

Nothing from Peg, not a twitch of curiosity; if she turned, she'd have the key.

'You didn't want a Chinese character?'

Rosie stared at Peg's back.

'No. I didn't.'

2

Picture of the Pope, Ripped (1992)

Years before she got the words tattooed on her arm, Rosie clutched them to her heart.

Sinéad O'Connor seemed to speak directly to Rosie Doyle, staring through the camera as she ripped up a picture of Pope John Paul II on *Saturday Night Live*. Catching a glimpse of it on the news before Granny Doyle shooed her out of the room, Rosie knew the words were for her, one rebel to another.

Fight the real enemy, Rosie wrote in Tipp-Ex across her schoolbooks, the nuns oblivious.

Fight the real enemy, Rosie wrote in marker on the faded yellow walls of the box room, her new home at 7 Dunluce Crescent.

Fight the real enemy, Rosie doodled in pen at the bottom of the petition; it was doubtful that the government would listen to the message, or the petition, but she had to try.

'Here we go,' Aunty Mary said, placing two cups of coffee onto the table.

'Thanks,' Rosie said, although she had asked for tea.

'You're welcome,' Aunty Mary said, ignoring the extra chair at the table, where only a year ago Peg had sat and quizzed her about Mary Robinson.

'Is that your petition?' she asked, peering at the page that Rosie was doodling across.

'Yep.'

Schoolchildren didn't have a vote in the upcoming abortion

referendum but that didn't mean they couldn't have a voice.

'You might want to clean it up a little,' Aunty Mary said, something of the schoolteacher in her voice.

She smiled.

'You'll learn that it's vital to present as respectable a case as possible. You don't want to give the government any ammunition to dismiss your point.'

Rosie wasn't sure she agreed, but she took out the Tipp-Ex from her bag.

'It's very impressive though,' Aunty Mary said, rallying.

'Thanks.'

It was amazing the difference that starting secondary school made. Some girls still called Rosie *weirdo*, of course. *Slut* too, that hung in the air, because word of why Peg had gone to England had spread across the yard and Rosie was as bad, so the whispers went. Rosie didn't give a shit. She had found an older crew of Nirvana fans, allies who would mosh in pits and sign indignant petitions, the organization of which might be enough to get Rosie expelled, not that she gave a shit about that either.

Who could care about school when the world was opening up? Rosie couldn't feel any remorse, not when the times demanded action, not when the protest had been so … *fun* was the word that entered Rosie's head, although it seemed inappropriate. The energy on O'Connell Street, though, Rosie had never felt anything like it! Women were furious at the government, but there was something exhilarating about the afternoon, the sense that Rosie had found kindred spirits, adults who admitted that the world was broken from multiple angles.

'Are protests always this … big?' Rosie asked, fun something she shouldn't be thinking about while the chair beside her remained empty.

'I wish!' Aunty Mary said. 'Plenty I've been to where there were almost as many guards. But, on we go.'

Aunty Mary fished in her handbag.

'I found these pamphlets from the IWLM when I was rooting through stuff at home, I thought you might be interested in them, for a project or something …'

'Thanks,' Rosie said, taking the faded leaflets, though they seemed more of a gift for Peg, who would have pored over any materials from the early days of the Irish Women's Liberation Movement.

Rosie noticed Aunty Mary's eyes on her and felt a familiar pressure to fill the shoes of the departed. She was named after a dead woman who she was the spit of, apparently, so she recognized the gaze and felt her cheeks burn with the knowledge that she could never have just the right questions to ask about feminist history or fill the chair that Aunty Mary wanted her to.

When Aunty Mary spoke, it wasn't to admonish her, though, but to ask 'And how are things at home?'

What to say? Granny Doyle acted as if nothing had happened, a spell cast at her cauldron, probably, for the walls of 7 Dunluce Crescent would crumble before anybody dared to say 'Peg'. Not that Rosie was talking to anybody in the house. As far as she was concerned, her brothers were equally to blame for Peg's disappearance; the elastic band had snapped, leaving her all alone in a sad box room where nobody even noticed her graffiti.

'Okay,' Rosie said.

Aunty Mary stared at her coffee, though it wouldn't speak for her.

'No news?' she asked, eventually.

Rosie stared at the coffee she wished were tea.

'No.'

Aunty Mary inhaled sharply, ageing with the word.

(It passed, like a wind across the room, the chance to talk about Peg, the opportunity to say 'do you think she's okay?' and 'how can we find her?' and 'I miss her.')

'And how's school?'

The kind of sentence Aunty Mary never would have asked Peg.

'Fine,' Rosie said.

'Good.'

Peg might have known a way to fill the silence but Rosie hadn't the words. She focused on her petition instead, carefully Tipp-Exing across her doodles, thinking privately that she might add another *Fight the real enemy* before she posted it, even if it was written in invisible ink.

3

Ordnance Survey Map (1993)

New possibilities continued to push against Rosie's brain. She hadn't found anything of use in Peg's books in the shed (old Greek things without a single picture) but revelation came, surprisingly, in geography class.

'Sister, why does the Church have a special symbol?'

Sister Margaret adopted her briskest tone.

'Churches have great cultural and social significance and are often placed at the heart of a settlement. Now, perhaps we can move on to questions that are likely to appear on your Junior Certificate …'

Rosie continued to examine her geography book, crosses puncturing the contours of the ordnance map. She could feel her brain stretching towards a new thought: maps were lies. If she asked a rabbit or a seagull to draw a map, they wouldn't put a special symbol for a church. And when she thought about it, half of the words on the map were about humans owning space, like dogs pissing their territorial boundaries with an alphabet instead of urine. *Cill Easra*, St Esra's Church. *Rath Eanaigh*, Enda's fort. Half of the names on the map in front of her began with *cill* or *rath*, churches or forts. Or they did for the moment, Rosie's bottle of Tipp-Ex out, a small smile crossing her face.

4

Moonstone (1994)

Other names bristled with pagan mischief, holding histories before forts and churches (Erris would not be *Cilled* by Catholicism!) including Clougheally's name itself, the Stone of the Swans.

The Children of Lir's boulder became Rosie's favourite space in Clougheally. Aunty Mary had something of Peg's whirr about her – her brain was always moving towards the next task to tackle or book to read – so Rosie liked to slip away and climb up the cliff. Despite Aunty Mary's protestations, she did *do* things there occasionally, from sketches to song-writing to spliffs. Mostly, though, the boulder was a place to *be* away from the clutter of the world, Rosie's birthstone placed on top of the rock, as the stones shared energies. The birthstone she'd bought in Temple Bar was a 'sodium potassium compound, not *actually* from the moon', Damien helpfully informed her, but Rosie didn't care; the moon understood.

Rosie loved climbing up the boulder at full moon, its friendly light a guide for feet and minds, for alone on the rock in the moonlight, Rosie felt the world's tingle, the pulse in the air that connected her to the other creatures of the night, bats swooping and beetles testing the night air with antennae and blades of grass gently growing and so many stars and oh the rush of life! The interconnectedness of living things! Rosie didn't need anything or anyone on that rock in the moonlight; there, she felt full.

5

'Free the Ogoni Nine' Amnesty International Urgent Action (1995)

Rosie felt the currents of the world connect her to Ken Saro-Wiwa and the Ogoni Nine, who only wanted their rivers to be clean. They hadn't asked for oil to clog up their streams and creeks. *Environmental activist* was an alien term to Rosie, but when she saw the photographs of dead fish and oil spills and gas flares spewing smoke towards the sky, she knew in her gut that nobody should be jailed for trying to protect their homes.

And if Shell continued to cooperate with a Nigerian government who planned to execute the Ogoni Nine, well, she would show them how she felt. Rosie had already responded to the Urgent Action letter that Amnesty had sent; it was time for escalation. Dunluce Crescent was, unfortunately, not the best place to launch a boycott of Shell. Mr Fay agreed that the situation was terrible, but was puzzled because people had to fill their cars somewhere, didn't they? Mrs Nugent was happy to add her autograph to Rosie's petition, but didn't seem to fully grasp the boycott concept, waving at Rosie as she emerged from the Shell garage with a packet of Monster Munch, 'Ah, it was only an emergency; I'd be dead from the hunger, otherwise!' John Paul's signature was equally meaningless, for he wondered immediately if Rosie might start a petition against *his* persecution by vindictive teachers.

Not that it mattered. The Ogoni Nine were executed despite the efforts of Rosie Doyle. A new petition was circulated, calling for 'Justice for the Ogoni Nine', *justice* the saddest word Rosie knew, only voiced in its absence. Petitions and boycotts weren't enough and Rosie felt her tininess in the world, all her imagined actions absurd, for she suspected that the last thing the Ogoni protesters needed was a fifteen-year-old white girl from Dublin rocking up with some half-baked plan to smash Shell's equipment.

Rosie lit nine sticks of incense for the men instead, this action equally absurd in the face of injustice, though it seemed important to Rosie.

6

Spice Girls Calendar (1996)

No, Rosie told Mrs McGinty, they weren't really her thing.

Yes, Rosie told Mrs Fay, it was brilliant that her Grace knew all the words to the rap.

Ha!, Rosie told Mrs Nugent, no, she didn't want to be Goth Spice and *ha!*, yes, Mrs Nugent was a shoo-in if they ever needed an Irish Baby Spice, and *help!* Rosie thought, as nothings continued to bounce around the porch, 7 Dunluce Crescent possibly the furthest point in the world from anything relevant; Rosie's mind had long fled, it was only a matter of time before her body caught up.

7

Wooden Dreamcatcher (1997)

Rosie turned over on their tree-house floor and held out the drawing of her next tattoo for Conor to admire.

'What do you think?'

It was the oak tree they were lying in, the finest in Wicklow.

'Sweet. Though there's somebody important missing.'

'Fidelma's there, she's scampering across one of the branches,' Rosie said, with a smile to torment him.

Conor shook his head.

'You know your squirrel-friend is a he?'

'You've asked Fidelma, have you?'

'Hard to argue with a pair of nuts!'

'You're jealous.'

'And you're not a Disney princess entertaining your animal kingdom; you know you shouldn't waste food on … Fidelma.'

He wasn't really mad; he wrapped his arms around her. There was the slight patter of rain on leaves, a lovely sound.

'Anyway, the thing you forgot is the person who built the tree house.'

'I thought it was a collaborative effort.'

'Of course it is – you'll have to add a pink-haired girl next to those bits of twig that … what does it do again?'

'Catches your dreams!'

'Oh that's where they've been going! Anyway, you'd want to be adding in the guy who made the best tree house in the camp.'

'You want to hang out on my arse for ever?'

215

'I thought the tree was going on your back?'

'The tree is, yeah, but not the arrogant eejit I pushed out for making fun of my friends.'

'You wouldn't!'

A gentle push, a kiss to pull him back in, giggles, as they lay in each other's arms, the rain soft outside.

It *was* the best tree house in the camp: Conor knew what he was doing and it would hold up through the winter, the two of them snuggled in sleeping bags like cuddling caterpillars. It was the best room she'd ever had, even if rain dripped through the roof. Her first proper home! She'd been glad to escape 7 Dunluce Crescent, where every effort she made to push against the sadness of the box room, from purple walls to wind chimes, was defeated by the house; it wasn't a structure where joy was possible. She hadn't hesitated when Conor had told her he was heading to the Glen of the Downs Camp. She'd packed a satchel that night and left a note on the kitchen table for the battleaxe, who might not have noticed otherwise.

She hadn't looked back. They weren't just protecting the Glen of the Downs woods from a road expansion, they were creating an alternative world; Rosie couldn't have found a better place to escape to. It was incredible, to lie in an oak as generations of leaves greened and reddened and wrinkled. To get away from the cars was to hear the hush of ancient woods, to stand barefoot in a clear spring over stones that had felt the rush of water for thousands of years. She'd barely thought about the Doyles once.

Until that morning.

'Is that somebody knocking?'

Rosie was in no mood to get up.

'It's Fidelma; she's pissed off with you for calling her a fella, that's all.'

Conor stirred.

'That's definitely someone.'

They could have snuggled for the morning but Conor found his clothes, the traitor.

'Sorry about that ... hiya!'

'Is Rosie there?'

No, Rosie thought, recognizing the voice but failing to become invisible in time.

*

'Thanks,' Damien said, peering at the dandelion tea as if it might be poisoned.

'No bother,' Conor said, handing a tin mug full of tea to Rosie too.

It was strange to see them side by side in the camp's makeshift kitchen. Damien, out of place in his corduroys and tucked-in shirt (he might as well have brought a Legion of Mary handbook!), taking in Conor's tattoo and piercings.

'I'll leave you to it,' Conor said, taking off before she could stop him.

Rosie clocked Damien taking in Conor's arse too, and thought about all the things she might say to him, incredible that they were technically the same age, when Rosie had grown into herself and found a world beyond Dunluce Crescent.

'I'm not coming back,' was what she said, though.

'Sure,' Damien said, startled by her directness.

'Did she send you here?'

'No!'

Damien looked up from his tea.

'It's ...'

He had to work up to what he'd come to say.

'It's amazing here.'

'Yeah.'

'Really! It's so organized.'

Trust Damien to find the most boring part of the camp to admire. It was a feat though, the logistics required to have thirty people live in trees for months, the meetings that stretched on into the night, which Rosie didn't mind, because she loved the care that went into every collective decision, from where they should compost to what time the fiddle players should stop.

'I like this installation.'

Damien pointed to the jars of spices, arranged by colour – Rosie's doing, so she allowed him a smile.

'Seems like you're well stocked.'

'We've had a bunch of donations.'

'That's good that local people are supporting you.'

'Of course they are!'

Some of them, at least. Some were keen for the dual carriageway to be finished, an ancient oak forest no competition to convenience. That was all Fianna Fáil cared about, building roads and houses and shopping centres; it was enough to make her cry.

'You're not missing the Cookeen too much, then?'

This warranted another smile; they always had the shared enemy of Granny Doyle, at least.

'Not exactly.'

Damien smiled and even took an experimental sip of dandelion tea.

'She's okay, is she?' Rosie found herself asking, against her best instincts.

'Yeah.'

It's …

But Damien had a great interest in examining his mug.

The conversation trundled on in fits and starts for a while, Damien expressing amazement at every facet of the camp, while his tea grew cold and his resolve faltered. Finally, he found the words.

I'm not coming back, she thought, *whatever it is*.

'It's John Paul.'

And ...

'He's ... not great.'

Rosie couldn't be annoyed at Damien's prevarications because she sensed the crisis coming, felt some triplet-twist of her insides, knew a tear was forming in her eye in sympathy with Damien's.

'Rosie, you have to come home ...'

8

Box of John Player Blue Cigarettes (1997)

Rosie fumbled for change in the hospital gift shop. After months of living in the woods, she was disarmed by the gaudy parade of commerce, the multiple options of fags available, when her pouch of tobacco was fine. The picky git wanted his John Players, though, so Rosie obliged, secretly glad of the mission, because she wasn't sure how much longer she could have stayed by the hospital bed, while John Paul stared into space and Damien reached for small talk.

At least his pickiness showed some signs of life. Otherwise, Rosie might have been hard placed to connect the boy in the bed to her brother. Things had been tense before she left – John Paul and Damien had been fighting about something or other – but she couldn't believe that John Paul was capable of such silence.

She hadn't a clue what to say. Not when she saw the bandages, which were covering the scars, which were where he'd slashed a razor blade into his wrists. Impossible that such an action could occur in the bathtub she'd once stained with henna. It had though, not that John Paul or Damien talked about it. Or that she had anything to say either, in fairness, directness disappearing when she copped sight of John Paul. She needed a smoke herself. One on her own before they shared one together; they'd talk, then.

She wasn't alone in the depressing smoking area, however. Some poor cancer patient puffed defiantly away and a couple of nurses shared fags and gossip and, leaning against the brick wall, there she was.

'I didn't think you'd be here,' Rosie blurted out.

Damien had promised.

'Where else would I be?' Granny Doyle said.

Rosie had never seen Granny Doyle smoke before, though she knew she had a secret stash. She'd aged too, in the few short months Rosie had been away. Though she hadn't lost her capacity for indignation, taking in Rosie and managing a snort. Rosie steeled herself, rolling her own fag for support, eager to be on equal ground, an adult, now.

'Have you been to see John Paul?'

Something softer in Granny Doyle's voice as she approached her favourite noun; of course they weren't going to talk about what Rosie had been up to.

'Yeah.'

'He's okay, is he?'

Rosie gave a shrug: how could she begin to communicate how far from okay he was?

'They're not feeding him right,' Granny Doyle said, glad of a pair of ears. 'Of course he won't eat with that muck they serve here! I've told them, he needs a good cut of meat and fresh spuds, not some slop they call soup, but they won't let me into the kitchen!'

Her eyes caught sight of the box in Rosie's hand.

'They're not for him, are they? You're not helping, he's to stop all that, not healthy for him at all,' she said, incredibly, as she let out a puff of smoke. 'Fresh air is what he needs. Up out of the bed and back into school, or some job; out of the bed, that's what I tell them – if they'll only let him home, we'll have him back on his feet, but I might as well be speaking in tongues.'

Rosie squirmed at the 'we', wondering if it included her; panic seized her body and this fag wasn't strong enough to calm her. She had to leave.

Perhaps Granny Doyle sensed this resistance; she squinted at her and sighed.

'What are you after doing to your hair?'

She had to leave, now.

'The nuns will never take you back, looking like some flamingo-floozy. There's a reason God didn't gift us with pink hair and as soon as you meet a mirror again you'll be discovering it!'

'I can do what I want,' Rosie said, hating how suddenly seventeen she sounded.

Granny Doyle snorted.

'So you've made clear.'

Granny Doyle stubbed out her cigarette.

They were going to talk about what Rosie had done, after all.

'John Paul was worried sick about you.'

'Right.'

'You've no right to be gallivanting around in trees while your poor brother is sick—'

'I'm not gallivanting—'

'A load of codswallop, so it is, chaining yourself to trees when there are good men only glad of the work, having to twiddle their thumbs while you eejits drum and dance about—'

'It's a protest, not a party—'

'What would your father say about this? He would have been glad of that work – he spent his life building things, roads too, do you not remember when he had that Corporation job? He'd turn in his grave, so he would.'

Rage boiled inside Rosie – how dare she mention Danny Doyle! – but she waited until it cooled before she spoke.

'I don't think he'd be too happy with what you've done to John Paul, either.'

Granny Doyle looked like she needed another cigarette, but she leant against the wall instead, catching her breath, not dignifying Rosie with a response. Rosie wouldn't regret the words. Granny Doyle had ruined the lot of them; love or neglect, the effect was the same. ('Peg' hung in the air, unsaid.) She deserved to hear the truth; Rosie wouldn't regret the words, even as her hands shook.

Granny Doyle composed herself, snatching for control of the conversation.

'Your bed is still there for you. And the room's had a good clean. The number of candles and smelly sticks you had in there, it was a wonder you didn't burn the house down! And I had to throw out some of that tofu stuff from the fridge – you're not to be at any of that nonsense this Christmas, you'll be glad of the turkey, I won't be having you under my feet and taking up all the pots and pans with your beans—'

'I'm not coming back.'

'Don't be daft! You're not spending Christmas in a tree. I've enough on my plate without worrying about you.'

'Then don't.'

She had to leave. Immediately.

'Give these to John Paul. I won't ask anything else of you again. I've my own family now.'

Rosie walked away before Granny Doyle could guilt her into staying. She should say goodbye to John Paul and Damien, of course, but her legs headed towards the bus stop, beyond it, she'd walk to the next one; it was too much to ask of her, she couldn't look after the lot of them.

Rosie managed to light a cigarette and find her rhythm, her heart returning to normal, the closer she got to Wicklow. It was a question of priorities. John Paul could sort himself out. Her being back wouldn't help. And somebody needed to protect the Glen of the Downs from the pickaxes and the guards and the chainsaws. It wasn't just the glen Rosie was protecting, it was a whole way of life, the right to say *slow down, stop!* She *had* found a new family, a group of people who felt the same pull of the world that Rosie felt, the sense that there was no need to sit in front of a television and fill cupboards with clothes and get a good job and buy a big house and switch the channel if it looked like the world was falling apart; in a world of the dead, Rosie had found other forms of life.

Rosie picked up her pace. She had to get back to Conor and Fidelma the squirrel and the spindly branches she could climb, as guards and chainsaws waited below, futilely, for Rosie Doyle would not come down. The Glen of the Downs was where she belonged, where she could hear the hum of the trees and the swish of squirrels' tails and the drums played by campfires; she would stay there, for ever.

9

Tattoo Gun (2007)

'They kicked you out of the trees eventually, right?'

There was no malice in Peg's question, merely a desire for accurate history.

'Yes,' Rosie said.

There was no denying it: the camp had been demolished; the trees felled; the road widened (oh, but the Glen of the Downs campaign had seeded something, a moment, a movement, the idea that *stop!* might be possible to sound.)

A shame, Peg's sigh said.

Then, *to be expected, though, wasn't it?*, communicated through a shrug of her shoulders and a dip of her head back to her book, the Glen of the Downs already history to her.

'It's a beautiful tree,' Dev said, admiring her tattoo; she could have hugged him for it.

It was. She had wept when they chopped it down and Conor carved its dates in the sad bare stump left on the ground.

'Thanks.'

Dev peered at her back.

'You drew this?'

'I did.'

'I love this little squirrel!'

Fidelma! She didn't know where any of her friends had retreated to once the road widened; even now, it hurt her heart too much to return to Wicklow.

'Thanks!'

Rosie lowered her T-shirt: Dev's turn.

Peg continued to read her book. If she minded Rosie's and Dev's Tattoo Show-Off Session she didn't let on; Rosie suspected she was glad to have the pair of them distract each other. All of Dev's tattoos were mathematical in nature ('Nerd phase' – an eye-roll from Peg at 'phase') and he showed Rosie the *pi* symbol on his back ('I know; I was sixteen!') and the dot that represented zero on his ankle ('You know an Indian astronomer invented the concept, Brahmagupta; I edited his Wikipedia entry!') and the Fibonacci sequence that stretched along his elbow ('Isn't it beautiful?') Peg's eyes remained fixed on her book, no matter how hard Dev stared at her, her face inscrutable, for she was not fool enough to carve her self on her skin.

'Anyway, don't be mocking me: you have numbers too!' Dev said, once it became clear that Peg might never look up.

Rosie blushed as he looked at the numbers on her shoulder.

'I don't recognize that sequence.'

4, 11, 12, 19, 29, 31.

'Just some lucky numbers,' Rosie said.

(Some things they might never talk about, Rosie realized, the words on the small of her back also remaining unexplained, for she'd already told Peg about her time with the poet in Paris, exaggerating the details – how awful his revolutionary poetry! How greasy his silver ponytail! How crushed her heart had been! – so that the episode had the comfort of a cartoon, when the truth was she still felt the scars. Still, rejection could be the making of you, Rosie reflected, a revelation that gained an edge as Peg's eyes remained fixed on her book, though she must have finished the page.)

It was time to confront the second part of her mission.

'This is my most recent,' Rosie said, rolling up her skirt to reveal the tattoo of a triumphant bird on her ankle.

'Is that one of those swans you were talking about?' Dev asked, bending down for a closer look, while Peg didn't budge.

'Yes. The Children of Lir.'

It was time to talk about Aunty Mary's letter and what had brought her back to Ireland.

'What's that in its beak?'

'A pipe,' Rosie answered, a long story coiled in those words, though she wasn't sure that Peg would listen.

10

Pipe (2005)

'Is that a *swan*?'

Damien peered at Rosie's doodle.

'It's the Children of Lir.'

'I see,' Damien said, in a tone that suggested he didn't.

'The Children of Lir would hate the pipe,' Rosie said, grimacing at the view from Aunty Mary's porch in Clougheally. Cranes and construction fences gutted the horizon. Ugly trucks juggernauted down narrow roads. The Children of Lir's boulder surveyed the changed beach, a pebble to progress.

'It's not fair to fossils to turn them into fuels,' Rosie continued. 'This beach used to be full of amazing creatures …'

Rosie could picture them if she closed her eyes, long-necked creatures that roamed through towering-fern forests while – why not? – swans swooped around them.

'They could have squashed humans with their feet, if we'd been about, and now we're squishing them into canisters to power blenders. It's not right.'

'Uh-huh,' Damien said, although what he really said was 'Rosie!' because while the shade of her hair dye changed – black to pink to blue – the core of Rosie Doyle was preserved in amber; she remained the teenager who insisted that crystals had the power to repel mobile phone radiation.

The pipe *wasn't* right, though, on so many levels that Rosie didn't need to summon the Children of Lir. It was in the wrong place, for starters; An Bord Pleanála's initial report said as much. It wouldn't benefit the community; the money wouldn't even be staying in Ireland, let alone Mayo. Not to mention the Rossport Five. For the first time in history, the government had signed a compulsory purchase order in favour of a corporation, and the five farmers who refused Shell access to their land were now in jail in Dublin, sending half the country – so it seemed – frenzying towards Erris. Including Damien Doyle, newly employed by the Green Party and not afraid to share this fact.

'I think it's important to have broad messaging,' Damien said, as if this were news. 'Focus on the nationalization of resources. Shell can talk about job creation but it's outrageous that all the profits from the pipe go to a corporation instead of citizens. If you look at the Norwegian model …'

Damien! Rosie thought, the voice in her head suddenly seventeen, because Damien remained the teenager who wore sensible cords and kept fastidious minutes of the Legion of Mary with colour-coded pens.

Rosie tuned out of Damien's lecture and peeped in the letterbox. No sign of Aunty Mary. They were on time – Damien had made sure of that – and Rosie felt a twinge of irritation at being pulled away from the Solidarity Camp when there was the road to blockade and banners to be painted and the Rossport Five stuck in jail. Still, they might recruit Aunty Mary to the cause. The pipe wasn't going to pass directly through Clougheally, but it was close enough, and the campaign could benefit from experienced local energy.

'Hello?'

No response from the letterbox. Damien paused from excoriating Fianna Fáil's tax policy and looked around nervously.

'This place gives me the creeps.'

'The *creeps*! Are you five or what?'

'You were the one who said the house had a strange aura.'

This she couldn't deny.

'As if Nanny Nelligan were still roaming about upstairs, wasn't that what you used to say?'

That was John Paul or Peg. Rosie couldn't remember. It didn't matter; neither sibling was to be mentioned.

'The only person roaming anywhere is Aunty Mary. She's probably out for a walk or pottering around the back. I'll go have a look.'

'I'm coming too – there was a reason Hansel and Gretel stuck together.'

'I hope you're not suggesting that Aunty Mary's a witch—'

'I very much hope so too,' Aunty Mary said, emerging from the back garden and startling Damien, whose shriek confirmed Rosie's suspicion that Gretel would have got on grand without Hansel slowing her down.

Aunty Mary looked unperturbed.

'I'm doing some gardening; come on, ye can give me a hand.'

*

There was only the one spade, so they took it in turns, digging new beds while Aunty Mary did some weeding. In the ramshackle garden, with its cheery cabbages and triumphant lettuces, Rosie felt a bubble of affection for her great-aunt, the spry thing in an over-sized shirt who seemed glad of her new white hair. She *would* make a great witch, Rosie decided: a wise woman who lived at the edge of the world and would be glad to share subversive teachings and sage blessings with the Solidarity Camp …

'Let me have the spade if you're not going to use it!'

Rosie! Aunty Mary's gaze said, for here Rosie was daydreaming when there was work to be done.

'Sorry,' Rosie said, back into it.

'Ah, it's grand,' Aunty Mary said, turning her attention to another weed. 'I'd say this plot has had the most it'll get this season, these new things are only experiments to keep an idle mind busy.'

There's plenty at the Solidarity Camp to keep you busy, Rosie almost blurted out, excitement bubbling at the prospect that the pipe might be the thing to unite the Doyles, finally.

'Is this kale?' Damien asked.

'It is.'

'*Cool*. Oh, I didn't think we'd be having lunch, so I didn't mention this, but I'm a vegetarian now.'

'No bother.'

'Rosie's vegan,' Damien added, with the sense that she was always taking things a step too far.

'Right so.'

'Anyway, if you need a hand I know a great salad where you just massage the kale and ...'

(As if they'd invented vegetarianism, Mary thought, a secret smile at the confidence of the young. Hadn't she spent days in Stella's cooperative house in Dublin, with its soaking chickpeas and crisped kale and weed growing in the shed? That would have been before either of them was born, not that they'd ask. Not that she'd say.)

'Did Nanny Nelligan farm here?' Rosie asked, once Damien had finished sharing his recipe.

'A bit,' Aunty Mary said.

'It must be a terrible thing for the soil to be disturbed too much,' Rosie said, suddenly respectful with her shovel.

'Isn't that what gardening is about?' Damien asked.

Rosie shot him a look.

'This kind of farming is grand. I'm talking about those diggers, coming in and ripping everything up, so they can lay down that monstrosity. It's not fair to the ground.'

Aunty Mary didn't seem too perturbed about the sentience of soil.

'Aren't there pipes running under every house in the country?'

'Not with unrefined gas running at 345 bar,' Damien said, all the numbers in his head. 'If there were an explosion at that pressure, it could extend for seventy metres, so ...'

231

The facts wouldn't convince Aunty Mary; Rosie saw it in her face. Nor would fancies about the memories of soil or flying swans.

'It's a human rights issue, really,' Rosie said. 'Shell has a horrific record in Nigeria; they continued to work there even after the government killed the Ogoni Nine!'

Aunty Mary had signed Rosie's petition, back when she'd asked, but all she said now was 'the world can be a terrible place.'

(As if she didn't know about the injustices of the world, Mary thought; hadn't her voice gone hoarse from shouting? She'd seen plenty of causes of the day cycle through, enough to think that progress wasn't shaped like a line; some zigzaggy thing it was, one that didn't mind what folk at the arse-edge of Ireland did about trouble in other countries. Nobody in Clougheally had been bothered about the revolution until it knocked at their door. Perhaps it was spite that kept her from the Solidarity Camp or perhaps it was tiredness or perhaps it was sense, but she wouldn't have her twilight days stolen by a squabble over a bit of gas.)

Aunty Mary collected a final flourish of lettuce.

'We'd best eat this salad,' she said, the pipe pushed underground, for the moment.

*

'Delicious,' Damien said.

'Glad you liked it,' Aunty Mary said.

'Thanks for having us,' Rosie said, detesting the sound of her voice. The food might change, but dinners with the Doyles were the same, symphonies of knife-scrapings and 'pass the salt' drowning out the chance of any meaningful interaction.

Rosie shifted in her seat, eager to escape the creaky house and its sad aura. It was horrible to be indoors when she could have been at the Solidarity Camp, where a rectangle of light seemed to illuminate the stretch of road, exposing only the good in the world. Mary Moran Horan's canteen poured out tea and community. The

Bitchin' Kitchin radical collective provided vegan meals. Kids played tin-can football tournaments. Farmers chatted to punks. Songs were belted out, in all keys and languages. Ciarán Delaney wandered around, recording interviews for a radio documentary by day, keeping Rosie warm in her tent at night. Here was the future, laid out in all its non-hierarchical glory, if only Aunty Mary would bother to look.

Rosie stood and walked over to the overflowing bookshelf in the corner, in search of a sideways path towards the pipe.

'This is a great collection.'

'Too much clutter!' Aunty Mary said. 'I should box up the lot.'

'There's some interesting stuff,' Rosie said, although there *was* a lot of clutter, old history books and faded Penguins but no pamphlets from the Irish Women's Liberation Movement, even as her eyes searched the shelves. Dust stared back at her, atop some ancient Irish things that might have belonged to Nanny Nelligan and some leather-bound *chronicles* and …

Here was something else not to be talked about; Rosie felt its presence, as her hands passed over the gap. Her eyes met Aunty Mary's. Knowledge and longing flickered between them, Rosie could have sworn it, 'Peg' unsayable.

(*The Chronicle of the Children of Lir by Peg Doyle*, Mary thought, heart soaring and plunging at the memory. She'd mislaid the opus. Thrown it out, probably. They might have laughed about it, had Peg been in the room, her fingers delighting at the spines of books, the way they'd used to. A genius! A dote. A fool, that too. Weren't they all? Rosie certainly was; she hadn't even the stamina to finish reading a pamphlet before she'd drawn some nonsense creature on it. And to swan back to Clougheally, all over some pipe, what a waste of a life! Mary had a baton to pass on; all she needed was the hand of an eager grand-niece who would listen to tales of Women's Lib and the Gay Rights Movement. To drop the baton in the ditch, distracted by gas bubbles, it was too much.)

Aunty Mary stood and gripped the sides of the table.

'There's scones if you want. Though you might not be able to eat them.'

No! Rosie thought, not caring about the dairy, only wanting to block the flow of food that seemed designed to stopper all conversation, as Damien said, 'Yes please!'

*

'Delicious,' Damien said.

'Thanks,' Aunty Mary said, standing. 'Well. Thanks for the help with the garden.'

'No bother,' Damien said, as Rosie's head threatened to explode.

'There's a spare bed upstairs if you ever need it.'

'Thanks,' Damien said. 'I'm just in for the weekend; I've a room at a B&B with a friend.'

(A *friend*? Mary thought, wondering if she was reading her grand-nephew right; did *friends* exist in 2005? Stella had relished *lovers*. Mary didn't have a word for Mags; they had the warmth of their bodies. Long walks with Mags's dogs. Crosswords pieced together over coffee. Space in their own houses when they wanted it, a healthy number of miles between them; they were too old to be disrupting routines, even as Mary felt a twinkle at the thought of her semi-secret, *what-business-was-it-of-anybody's* lover. Or *friend*, she supposed, filling the word with mischief, as she remembered Peter and her actual friends in Dublin, who she might have introduced to Damien, except poor Peter was long dead – half of the queens she knew had been snatched by the plague, that bastard – and even if he had been around, he'd never have trekked out to Clougheally, and Mary didn't have the words to say any of this to Damien, who might, after all, have a perfectly innocent friend whose only interest in room-sharing was frugality.)

'Well. If you ever need a place.'

'Thanks.'

234

Aunty Mary turned to Rosie.

'And you're welcome to tea, any time. So long as you don't mind it black.'

'Thanks.'

Rosie found her courage.

'You should come by the Solidarity Camp some day.'

'Maybe.'

'You've seen it?'

'Hard to miss.'

'We'd be glad of you.'

'Ah.'

(She might make it to the camp, Mary thought, wondering how many revolutions a life could hold before all the spokes fell off. She'd been worn out and rejuvenated so many times, what was another? Whatever she thought about the pipe, she wouldn't disagree that Fianna Fáil couldn't be trusted; across a long life, here was one constant. And Rosie and Damien might be fools, but they meant well; even if they lacked Peg's sharpness, they had good hearts. She might make it to the camp, yet.)

Aunty Mary opened the door.

'Thanks for coming.'

'No bother,' Damien said.

'I'll come back,' Rosie said.

'Do,' Aunty Mary said, shutting the door.

11

Spade (2007)

Rosie clutched a glass of red wine and a fag – appropriate props for a funeral – and gazed at the spade in the drizzle. Did metal have memories? Could it remember all the generations of soil it had communicated with? Did its wooden handle remember the hands that had gripped it, through downpours and gusts and flashes of sun, something heroic about the growing of cabbages by the edge of the Atlantic?

Rosie! sounded in her head; it was typical of her to daydream through a funeral. She should pick some lettuces to serve, that would be a useful activity, but there was already more than enough food inside and not enough people to eat it. (*What would happen to the garden?* crossed Rosie's brain, before it was swiftly banished, for this was a sentence that led to thinking about Aunty Mary's surprise letter and the new owner of the sad old house by the sea.) She should go inside and talk to the neighbours, Rosie knew, as she stayed staring at a spade, which, at least, didn't judge her. She should have called back. Only a stone's throw down the road and she hadn't made the journey. *The pipe!* loomed in her head, an easy excuse, for she hadn't time for anything else. Though she hadn't wanted to visit Aunty Mary either, Rosie admitted, squirming at the truth that she didn't feel guilty enough about this neglect, her brain daydreaming off about spades or, worse, thinking about the pipe.

'Rosie!'

Ciarán filled out the word with love, a sound to glide a cloud to earth.

He wrapped his arm around Rosie's waist and gave her the gentlest of touches. *It'll be okay*, his fingers said, for he wasn't alone; he'd brought the one person who could be relied upon for insults at a funeral.

'Have you not given up those?' Granny Doyle said by way of hello, before turning to Ciarán and tutting: 'Disgraceful it was, really, she crammed her mouth full to the brim with blackberries, no mind what I said!'

Neither Damien nor John Paul had been able to make the funeral (Green Party business and something diabolical, no doubt) so Granny Doyle had latched onto Ciarán, a local lad who knew the right sounds and nods to make and could steady her arm, evidence of his fine character, though Rosie wasn't entirely disposed to see things in this light.

'She was a divil for the blackberries,' Granny Doyle continued, as if this instead of a stroke had been the cause of Aunty Mary's death.

'Aren't we all?' Ciarán said, as his fingers massaged *I love you* into the small of Rosie's back.

'I told her she'd be sick,' Granny Doyle said, obviously not for the first time. 'But she wouldn't listen, didn't even mind the hiding she got from Mammy, she'd eat them again, she said. God, but she had a mind on her!'

Rosie felt disarmed by this accidental intimacy, unable to tell if any affection hovered underneath the words. There were ten years between Granny Doyle and Aunty Mary – a chasm between children – though somehow Rosie had never really thought about them being young in the same house.

'The blackberries were *glorious*, according to her,' Granny Doyle said, the incredulity fresh. 'Did you ever hear the like! *Glorious*, she says to Mammy, and it's lucky she didn't earn a second slapping, oh, she had a head full of words …'

Granny Doyle gave out a long sigh at such a danger (for a second, Rosie wondered if 'Peg' lurked in that silence) before she recovered with 'she always did have a good appetite,' as close to a compliment as she could get.

I'll make you a blackberry tart, Aunty Mary had said, the last time she'd seen her. Or had she? Was it vegan scones she was promising to bake? Or some gluten-free *braic*? Rosie cycled through the possibilities and tried to remember if she'd ever seen Aunty Mary eating blackberries, but the picture was fuzzy and she wasn't even sure if she could place Aunty Mary's face accurately, and suddenly Rosie felt floored by finality, grief sledgehammering towards her at the thought that she'd never get to eat whatever Aunty Mary might have promised. Guilt added another blow to her chest, for it was too late now to make Aunty Mary something in return; there would be no time for tea or questions about the time she'd smuggled condoms onto a train. Shame delivered a final jab, for Rosie had been a fool not to call when she'd had the chance.

Grief was getting to Granny Doyle too – or the red wine was – for instead of getting at Rosie for lighting another cigarette she stared at the spade and said: 'That teacher was the one who filled her head with ideas, you might have heard of him, ah, the one who discovered the Céide Fields …'

Ciarán had the name.

'Patrick Caulfield.'

'Himself,' Granny Doyle said, her eyes scanning the spade now. 'Oh, sure he was full of stories about finding the oldest Neolithic settlement in Ireland and him only a history teacher with a spade in his hand and an idea in his head. And sure Mary lapped it all up, all the way there on a bicycle, and only to tap at the ground with a spade in search of stones!'

'I'd say the Neolithic farmers would be shocked to see a pipe cutting Erris apart,' Rosie said, hoping that *pipe* might reveal a battleaxe she recognized. The word could usually be relied upon to slap sense into a conversation. Two years after she'd moved to Erris, the pipe continued to divide the community. The Rossport Five were out of jail and most of the media had left but the pipe remained, lurking underneath birthdays and christenings and funerals, ready to slice any gathering apart. Rosie waited for Granny Doyle to endorse the pipe; hadn't the Bishop of Kilcommon blessed the rig with holy water in a special ceremony and weren't Shell sponsoring the local GAA team and – most importantly, whatever had gone on between them – hadn't Pope John Paul III himself come out in favour of the pipe?

Incredibly, though, Granny Doyle looked out at the sea and said, 'A fierce shame, that thing.'

She turned to Ciarán.

'I told you about my father and the crab pots?'

'You did.'

Ciarán was making a radio documentary about the pipe and he had a gentle way with people, easy for him to get information for interviews. Still, it was incredible that in a few hours with Granny Doyle, he'd found more stories than Rosie had in a lifetime.

'Haven't folk been fishing in that bay for years?'

Granny Doyle looked out at the sea, which was soon to be off limits for small fishing boats.

'There'll be graves upturned with the shifting under at what's going on here,' Granny Doyle said. 'And all for gas that won't make its way to any taps here; the country's gone to the dogs.'

'It has,' Ciarán agreed, while Rosie stared.

'Families driven apart because of that monstrosity,' Granny Doyle continued. 'There'll be generations here in the future not talking to each other and they won't know why ...'

(*And aren't families good enough about making their own fights already?* Rosie heard, or thought she heard, in the pause.)

'My father wouldn't have stood for it; he'd have been out in his currach blocking that thing.'

Ciarán attempted a smile.

'Sure, maybe we'll get a wetsuit in your size; I'll make space for you on my surfboard.'

So he'd told her about their plans to surf in the path of the ship when it came, attempting to block the laying of the pipe; like *daft things* Granny Doyle was sure to say, though instead she laughed and said:

'Keep at it; you'll stop that pipe yet.'

'We will,' Rosie said, annoyingly hopeful that when Granny Doyle's eyes turned towards her a trace of the admiration she directed towards Ciarán might remain. But no, the battleaxe might as well have been dressed in leopard-coat, no chance that she'd change her spots, inevitable that she'd squint and declare: 'What have you done to your head now? Lord save us, I'd say you had to skin a dozen Smurfs to get that shade! Would you not show some respect and find a hat?'

Rosie gulped at her glass, making the decision there and then, as Granny Doyle railed against the state of the world and Ciarán nodded when necessary. Later, she couldn't prise apart all the different factors that led to her trip. One motivation was escape; she could get away from Granny Doyle and the sad house and the pipe campaign, with its meetings and tussles in ditches and lock-ons and late nights. A fresh mission held its appeal too, as Rosie saw a plan crystallize in front of her. She wouldn't let the house be sold. Granny Doyle didn't seem to want it, glad of her life in Dublin. So, Rosie would just have to convince its surprising new owner. In her wildest dreams, she imagined the creaky old house as a community centre, a winter-proof place to continue the revolution; imagine what could be done if it could house protesters and meetings and communal dinners and training! Peg would understand; she'd have to.

Or, Peg would see her. That motivation couldn't be denied, an excuse to recover a long-lost sister. As Granny Doyle returned to the story of when Aunty Mary had made herself sick with blackberries, Rosie felt a familiar twinge of longing in her chest, a response that finally she might act upon. Perhaps, if she were honest, her mission had nothing to do with the pipe and when she looked out at the Atlantic she didn't see the gas rig or the construction cranes but the long-lost sister on the other edge of the ocean, waiting.

12

Blarney Stone (2007)

'Peg?'

She was feigning sleep; Rosie was sure of it. Dev would be back from his weekend in New Jersey in the morning and who knew if another chance would present itself? Certainly, such a conversation would not be possible in the daylight.

'Peg!'

She chanced the repeat, sharper. The imaginary Blarney Stone sat on the windowsill, encouraging her.

'What is it, Rosie?'

Peg didn't bother to turn. It was late, the fan loud, the room hot. It was time for Rosie to leave: her bedroom, New York, her life. They had talked and cried and held each other like sisters: couldn't that be enough?

Rosie stared at the Blarney Stone. She'd convinced herself that her mission would be easy: prove the perfidy of John Paul Doyle and Peg would be quick to do anything to spite him, keeping the house included. But, lying in the bed beside a long-lost sister, Rosie knew she couldn't leave without telling her the truth, even if it jeopardized her mission. She understood that what she was doing was dangerous, a match held up towards accepted history. Still, she spoke.

'It wasn't John Paul who told Granny Doyle.'

Peg stared into the dark. It would be better to craft histories out of more durable material, she resolved. Words and memories were too fragile: one breath and away they went. The silence stretched, though Peg knew that Rosie hadn't drifted into sleep. It was best to leave things be, Peg decided. It didn't matter now. Still, she spoke.

'Who was it, then?'

Series VI:
The Pride of Damien Doyle

(1992–2007)

1

Pride Flag (1983–2007)

(2007)

Damien closed the stall door and unzipped Mark's fly. Hands dived in, lips lunged towards lips, stubble scratched stubble. The toilet was a bit awkward, Mark's long legs bashing into it, but there was something strangely erotic about it all: the door that might open; the tang of piss that pushed them towards each other; the savage shuffle of jeans to ankles; the clang of belts against the tiles. Damien led it all, manoeuvring Mark against the wall, taking time off canvassing, even with the election looming: it was alarming how turned on he was by guilt. Mark whispered in his ear, laughter bubbling under the words.

'Are you sure this is your first time in a toilet?'

'I'm a natural.'

Too many feelings for Damien to cope with – freedom, excitement, guilt, fear. He buried his head in Mark's hair, every force in the world pushing them towards each other.

(1983)

Mary Nelligan quickened her pace once she spotted Liberty Hall, a whirl of feelings – anger, fear, sadness – propelling her legs. She needed to get to the safety of the crowd; she needed to be beside Stella. More people than she had imagined were there: hundreds, maybe even a thousand. Some faces she knew from meetings, many she didn't; there was a strong show of solidarity from the unions, a group called Mothers of Gay Men, speakers from the Rape Crisis Centre. Mary caught her breath at Declan Flynn's photo on some of the placards. He'd been beaten to death in Fairview Park by a gang of five lads, who boasted that they were out to bash a queer, something that 'could never be called murder', according to the judge, who released them on suspended sentences, for what was one dead fairy when the lives of five young men were at stake? 'This could never be called justice,' another placard read, words to galvanize.

Finally, Mary spotted Stella, talking to Peter, one of their friends from the Dublin Gay Collective, the group organizing the protest. Stella squeezed her arm when she walked over, something that she wouldn't do in other public spaces. Mary looked into Peter's lined face and thought she saw some reflection of her own: the tears gone, a desperate force inside, the kind that pushed bodies into streets.

'You know what the little bastards sang when they got off?' Stella said. 'We Are the Champions.'

'Maybe somebody should tell them about Freddie Mercury. They might not want Queen as their anthem then.'

No smile from Peter, his face as grim as Stella's; he had known Declan a little.

'Not here *now*, are they, the little shits,' Stella said. 'If they show, I'll rip them apart.'

'This isn't about revenge,' Peter said. 'We can't condone violence of any kind and we're not asking that the gang go to prison – we can't support incarceration as a radical group.'

'I know,' Stella said, her face illuminating the difference between knowing and feeling.

'We're not engaging with the gang at all,' Peter said, slipping into his organizer mode. 'We have a series of demands: decriminalize homosexuality; give gays equal legal protection; stop job discrimination on the basis of sexuality. We have to focus on the gay community, not the people who hate us.'

'That won't be much good if they come to beat you up,' Stella said.

Mary spoke before the two of them could get involved in a dispute about tactics; she had been in Dublin for the week and had attended enough meetings for a lifetime.

'They won't come; they haven't the courage. And if they do, we'll ignore them, won't mind what they say or shout at us, because we are in the right and we won't be beaten, we won't be scared, we won't be hidden. We're stronger than them because when we walk, we move out of love rather than fear.'

It was the kind of speech she might have made through a megaphone, in a different life.

Stella clenched Mary's hand in hers, a grip almost tight enough to crush her.

(2007)

Damien felt a surge of electricity as his arm brushed against Mark's. Damien was glad it was getting darker; he was sure his face was crimson. The car park of Westview Gym was full of people off to work out, *normal* people, Damien almost thought, before he corrected himself (Damien wouldn't put it past Mark to be capable of telekinesis). Still, the pair of them, having sex in toilets in a gym; it was a bit much. *Hot*, too, Damien thought, letting his fingers loop around those of Mark, who was walking to his own beat, something bothering him.

'It's so hard to believe that anything happened here: not a plaque, not a memorial, but a giant fucking gym. In a country so great at putting up statues of men with guns, you think we'd be able to do something for Declan Flynn.'

'We could talk to the Greens on the local council; Trevor might be able to organize a plaque and it could tie in nicely with our Equal Rights campaigning—'

'No.'

Mark's voice was surprisingly sharp; Damien felt it like a cut to the face.

'I don't want some bullshit plaque! They should have a sign in the toilet, painted up in rainbow colours: have a good ole screw here in honour of Declan Flynn. That's what he was doing when they gay-bashed him, out cruising. And we shouldn't be ashamed of that history, shouldn't force ourselves into the straight fucking establishment.'

'You want us to have more sex in toilets? I mean it was good, but there's a few logistical problems.'

No smile from Mark: he wasn't in a mood for banter and had started to walk ahead.

(1983)

'What do we want? Gay rights! When do we want it? Now!'

'Give us our rights by day and night!'

'Bigotry is your pollution! Liberation is our solution!'

Mary walked in the middle of the street, aiming her voice towards the sky. It was easier for her. People couldn't see the lavender T-shirt, hadn't a notion that there was something 'quare' about her. It was harder for her. She felt invisible, parts hidden, no language to talk about her relationship with Stella with her colleagues. And, simultaneously, she felt too visible: a 'single' older woman who dared to walk places on her own. Now, here she was, walking down the middle of Amiens Street, Stella beside her, hundreds behind them, suddenly visible in a different way, propelled by a swathe of bodies and a swirl of emotions: anger, sadness, fear, pride.

(2007)

'I guess I don't really feel *proud* to be gay.'

Walking back to Mark's flat, feelings stuck to Damien like glitter, hard to shake unless he was forceful about it.

'I mean, being gay is like having blue eyes or being Irish. It's just a fact, not something I achieved: I don't know what there is to be proud about.'

'It's because Gay Pride has been divorced from its political context,' Mark said, hands sweeping through the air, while his eyes lasered in on Damien's. 'It's a dance party sponsored by the fucking banks. But we can't forget our history: the first Irish Pride march was the year after the Declan Flynn murder, only twenty or so fags behind a rainbow flag in 1983. Saying you were *proud* to be gay meant something when people wanted to beat the shit out of you.'

Damien clenched. It was hard to talk to Mark when he was off on one of his riffs, Mark perpetually disappointed that Damien didn't know the things he did; Damien struggling to piece his thoughts together.

'But the *language* of pride, it seems excessive. Can't we be content to be gay without being proud?'

'No!'

This 'no' threatened to shatter the stained glass of St Patrick's Cathedral across the road.

'That's part of internal homophobia. And there are lots of places in the world that aren't safe spaces yet *and* it's not like Dublin is the safest place in the world; most fucking places aren't safe for fags! Why are you flinching when I talk loudly? See, this is part of your internal homophobia. You don't have a problem fucking in a public toilet but you can't talk about gay rights in case somebody hears.'

Damien stared ahead, ears blushing; there was no talking to Mark when he got like this.

'I love you.'

Mark's voice was always softer after they fought. Damien nuzzled into Mark's chest, still glittery from last night's party.

'I love you too, you miserable bastard.'

A punch from Mark, as soft as his voice.

'I just hate this fucking season, you know?'

'The summer?'

'All this shite coming up: Pride; the Twelfth; televised sports!'

'Ah well, once your dissertation proves that religion and nationalism are pointless you won't have to worry about the last two.'

'Are you making fun of me, you wee shite?'

'Wouldn't dream of it.'

Mark shifted Damien off his chest, then moved onto his elbows, the better to glare at him.

A thing to love about Mark: he was trying to be serious, even with glitter all over his face.

'What's so funny?'

'I think glitter suits you.'

'Don't get me started. I can't think of a better symbol of modern Pride than indestructible plastic crap being scattered everywhere. Maybe the Greens can release a pamphlet.'

For once, Damien did not want to talk about the Green Party. Lying beside Mark, he felt a dizzying sensation, like the first time they'd tried poppers together, eye to eye, Mark squeezing each nostril shut as Damien inhaled, pores opening wide as pupils dilated and cocks pumped and mouth met mouth; only this was better, because the chemicals were natural.

'I prefer direct action: maybe somebody should lick it off.'

A thing to love about Mark: his belly button the perfect shape for a tongue.

'You're a dirty fucker.'

'And you're a miserable bastard.'

What else was a tongue for if not to touch?

*

To talk, unfortunately.

As soon as he got home from work, Damien knew that Mark was pissed.

'The question is: how do you queer history?'

Mark poured another glass of wine and pondered the drawing in front of him. 'The problem with history is that it's just a catalogue of reproduction.' Mark held up the family tree he'd scrawled. 'See, it's all Mary meets John and out they pop seven little leaves. Family trees are another hetero-normative tool to lay claim to "the natural".'

Damien went to the sink and poured two pint glasses of water; it was hard enough to follow Mark's train of thought when he was sober.

'And history's the same shite, back from the epics onwards – sons singing the great deeds of their fathers, the only way to ensure a legacy is to have a fuck-load of children so some of them will survive the arrows. The problem with history is that it's all about mitosis.'

Damien took a long gulp of water.

'*Mitosis* is basically some shite romantic comedy where pollen is played by Matthew McConaughey and he's off on a quest to find Kate Hudson, who plays the stamen or whatever and they're dividing cells like goodo, leaves popping up everywhere, except for the dud ones, the Johns who don't find their Marys, or the Kates who have no time for their Matthews. The rest of the story speeds along, but these poor leaves are left stranded, the odd uncles and the spinster aunts, and who the fuck knows who our queer ancestors were or how many rainbow leaves are hidden in our trees? Even Ma gets all quiet when I ask her, oh Uncle Tom was only a wee bit strange, she'll say, and there's no way of knowing, and that's the problem.'

Mark reached for his wine glass in triumph as Damien put the water beside him. The problem, Damien realized, was with the whole concept of family trees, which bore little resemblance to either the science of tree reproduction or the tangle of real families. He would not say this yet; Mark had stumbled upon another thought.

'But meiosis – *meiosis* is different. Meiosis is also *natural*.'

Damien edged the water closer to Mark's hand.

'You want us to reproduce asexually?'

Mark shooed away the brambles of confusion with his hands.

'No, no! It's about alternative ways of reproducing. Ideas. Or legacies. Or, I don't know, memories. People to tend to the weeds on graves. See, queers don't need to adopt children –' (Damien saw her in a flash, the little girl who would straddle Mark's shoulders and smile when Damien read her stories to sleep, there and gone in a blink) – 'we need to look after our own. Like, there's all these empty stools in gay bars, where arses that wiggled away to Madonna should be sitting, because there's a whole missing generation that AIDS snatched away and we need to … remember them.'

'Here, drink this.'

Mark gulped the pint in one go.

'And that's why Pride is important to me. It's about acknowledging – celebrating – our queer family. Which, fuck knows, can be as annoying as any biological family. But Pride is a way of remembering. Or it should be. Could be. Would be. Family's important, you know?'

Damien knew what was coming. He went to clear up the dishes. He didn't care that he would be the one to wipe Mark's sausage-grease, he'd do anything to avoid this conversation. But Mark was drunk and holding a picture of a family tree; there was no escape.

'I think you should tell her.'

Damien let the frying pan puddle onto the countertop and picked up one of Mark's many mugs to wash. He reminded himself that he couldn't be mad at Mark's messiness at that very moment; he couldn't avoid a conversation by picking a fight.

'She won't want to know.'

'It'll be a weight off you.'

'I feel fine.'

Damien knew that if he turned around he would see Mark's face screwed up in incredulity, or worse, pity; Mark, of course, had come out to his mother at sixteen, when there was just the two of them in the house, which she'd nearly kicked him out of, but she hadn't, ultimately, because who could win an argument with Mark? Now the two of them were as tight as thieves, talked to each other in a way that Damien could never fathom, Mark egging on his mother to try online dating, the two of them laughing raucously at the results. Mark had talked to his mother about teenage loves, while Damien had been pining over Rory O'Donoghue, so far in the closet he was practically in Narnia.

'I can come. Or you can go on your own. Or phone her. Or write a letter. Or do nothing at all; it's your choice. I'm only trying to help, because I hate seeing you carry this. It's armour, but it's also a weight: lugging a giant wardrobe everywhere you go.'

Damien might have snapped, if Mark hadn't been standing beside him then, his voice lovely and tender and pissed.

'I'm out to everybody who matters to me,' Damien said. 'She's different; you don't understand.'

Mark's hand against Damien's cheek: *let me*.

'She said I was moving to a "den of iniquity" when I told her I was moving to the Southside.'

A small smile from Mark: *well …*

Damien sighed. He saw the porch of 7 Dunluce Crescent looming across his day, some ghost of Rory O'Donoghue sauntering down the cul-de-sac.

'I couldn't care less what she thinks at this stage. Honestly.'

A look from Mark, his eyes as fiercely focused as ever: *well then* …

Damien sighed. There was the future in front of him – the Greens with a chance of getting into government, ten seats within reach if only they knocked on enough doors and wrote enough blogs – but here was Mark, dragging him back to the past.

You'll go back, Mark's eyes said.

'Fine,' Damien said, though he felt far from it.

2

Nail Polish (2007)

Mrs Fay fumbled with the keys at the porch door.

'Oh, dear, it must be one of these! George was always the one who kept track of these things – he could tell just by looking at the shape of it, imagine! – but, oh dear, they're all the same to me.'

'You're grand, no rush,' Damien said.

'It'd make you long for the day when you could keep the door unlocked, but when you read the papers now, oh, it's terrible, isn't it?'

'It is indeed,' Damien managed.

'She'll be having a nap, that's how she can't hear us. I'm the same, away to the world once I close my eyes – oh dear, not this one either – and this weather would wear you out, wouldn't it? Not that I'm complaining, isn't it lovely to have the bit of sun?'

Damien was preparing a press release about the relationship between global warming and Ireland's record heat wave and while remaining cautious about the difference between weather and climate, he was sure that some of the impacts of global temperature rise would be far from lovely, further proof that it was time to have the Greens in government.

'It is indeed,' he said.

'Oh dear, I can't remember which is which, don't tell Helen! She's always after me – *you'll forget your own name*, she says and *how could I forget Audrey Hepburn?* I say but she doesn't laugh like George did ...'

'Do you want me to try?' Damien asked, gently taking the keys.

'Oh yes, dear! George always spoke very highly of *you*, you made a great impression that time you brought the statue to our house with the Legion. *Isn't it brilliant to see young people doing a bit of good in the world?* George said – did I tell you we met in the Legion? – and isn't it a shame that you wouldn't read about *that* in the papers … oh, look at that, you've got it, I knew you'd be able to do it!'

Damien slid open the porch door, not stepping in, yet. He left his hand by the door, hoping that Mrs Fay might say something about his nail polish. Words might not be necessary, then. Perhaps he should have chosen a shade other than peach. Perhaps he should have placed an earring in his left ear. Perhaps he should have draped himself in a Pride flag, for, as Mark was fond of telling him, gender and sexuality were different things, not that Mrs Fay had anything to say about either of them.

'Go on in, that one must be for the front door. She'll be asleep upstairs, so she will. It wears you out, the heat. And the chat. Don't be worried about waking her; I'm sure she'll be thrilled to see you, feels like years since you've been here! Go on in, dear, go on in …'

Damien hovered by the door, wary of historical precedent and the last time he'd told the truth to Granny Doyle.

3

Trócaire Box (1992)

Damien stepped inside the porch and met Granny Doyle's gaze.

'That fella not got a home to be going to?'

She was staring at Rory O'Donoghue, who was still standing by the gate, his eyes on Damien.

'Why's he loitering outside?'

'He's in the Legion of Mary too,' Damien should have said, a perfectly innocent explanation available – they'd just said the rosary with the Fays – but he couldn't find the words, his heart racing at the thought that Granny Doyle could read minds.

Granny Doyle released a snort when Rory finally started to walk home, his step too close to a skip for her liking, the kind of boy who'd hold funerals for butterflies.

'You wouldn't want to be getting too pally with him.'

Damien felt all the red in his body rush to his cheeks. Was he too pally with Rory O'Donoghue? Before his Confirmation, he'd been glad to have a friend in the Legion of Mary. *We're the Incredible Legionnaires*, Rory joked, as they delivered the statue of the Virgin Mary to a different house each week, like superheroes with rosary beads. Rory had an arch way about him so Damien was never sure when he was being serious – he couldn't tell if Rory had genuinely complimented Mrs Fay on her potpourri earlier – but he was a friend, Damien's only friend, and before his Confirmation, Damien had looked forward to their weekly chats.

But then the rear end of Ruadhan Kennedy-Carthy had disrupted Damien's universe. Even as he tried to focus on the Second Glorious

Mystery (The Ascension! This physical world and all its temptations transcended!), he was aware of Rory's buttocks pushing against his jeans as he knelt over in prayer. Rory's gentle smile was worse, puncturing the calm of the Fifth Glorious Mystery (The Coronation of Our Lady! *You're a good boy, Damien Doyle*, she'd say, from her castle in the clouds) and opening a well in Damien's chest, one whose depth he could not sound, where bright creatures twittered towards the sunlight.

'What are you doing standing there, are you going in or out?'

Damien managed an 'Actually …'

Granny Doyle swivelled to look at him properly and Damien balked under her X-ray vision. She probably knew already; wasn't it best to get the words into the open? He couldn't afford to keep loading his Trócaire box up with twenty pences, and thinking about Rory O'Donoghue's smile must be worth at least fifty pence and he'd never be ascending anywhere with all the secrets inside him and—

'Well, what is it?'

Damien swallowed.

'There's something I have to tell you.'

But then he couldn't do it! Not to Peg, who had taught him to read and always answered his questions carefully. *You're very good at reading*, Peg had told Damien, once, and he'd clung to the praise and powered through a record number of books for the Readathon. He couldn't do it!

Yet something had to be done. Granny Doyle's eyes bore into his soul. He wouldn't be surprised if she could see his thoughts; she'd be reaching for the bleach in a moment, if there were any mercy in the world.

'What is it?'

The words caught in Damien's throat: he couldn't do it to Peg!

'For the love of God, would you ever spit it out!'

But there was Ruadhan Kennedy-Carthy shuffling into Levis, robbing Damien of all the change from his pockets. The breadth of Damien's blush sent fear into Granny Doyle's heart.

'Is it John Paul?'

'No! It's …'

Damien couldn't say it, not standing in the porch with who-knew-who watching, the Geoghan kids coming back from school and Mrs Brennan pulling out of her driveway and the words stuck inside him, jabbing.

'Is it that sister of yours?'

'No, it's not Rosie …'

That was where Damien told Granny Doyle, in the pause after 'Rosie'. The pause gained weight at an exponential rate, gathering gravity until it seemed to bulge against the windows of the porch. 'Or Peg' became an impossible utterance. Granny Doyle parsed the pause; she knew. Damien felt as if he might be flattened by the silence.

'I saw something I shouldn't have.'

This was better: Damien was the one who should be confessing. The weight Damien needed to get off his chest was all about what he saw. What he couldn't stop seeing. If he could tell somebody about Ruadhan Kennedy-Carthy, perhaps oxygen would return.

Granny Doyle, though, had no interest in Damien, her voice sharp and solid.

'When?'

She disarmed him with direct questions. 'On the morning of my Confirmation' slipped out easily and then 'where?' was answered with 'upstairs' until 'who?' could only have one answer; Granny Doyle understood the rest, or most of it.

'Was John Paul with you?'

This was what she cared about most: the corruption of John Paul Doyle. Damien hadn't a lie in him.

'Yes.'

(And Rosie too, though she didn't count.)

Granny Doyle gripped the sides of her folding chair. She couldn't credit it. Not for a minute had she suspected it. A bookish thing with dangerous ideas, Peg Doyle had always been that, yet Granny Doyle had never imagined she'd do something as brazen. The cheek of the little hussy! In what used to be her bedroom! In front of the Sacred Heart of Jesus! In front of the triplets! Exclamation marks abounded in Granny Doyle's head, slicing away at her. Here was one cut: John Paul had known! And not a peep out of himself, full of chat that very morning, while all these weeks and months he'd known. The whole house had, the walls even, a conspiracy against her, all started by that one, who'd been a great help over the years, she couldn't deny it, and now – after everything she'd done! – this. Granny Doyle scanned the street. What if somebody else had seen the chancer escape? Her friends would have told her but you couldn't count on the Donnellys and the Brennans, there'd be plenty who'd be glorying at this piece of gossip. They might have known all these months, whispering away at her, while she shuffled off to the shops and picked up John Paul's favourite biscuits, like some fool. Rage tore at her. There in front of her was Damien, the only one who'd told her, yet the sight of the trembling thing filled her with disgust.

'Go on up to your room now.'

Damien stood still. She hadn't said *thanks*. She hadn't said *you're a good boy, Damien Doyle*. No word to say that he had done the right thing. Outside, there was no sense that life had changed. Mr Kehoe hacked at his hedge. Some young lad washed Mrs O'Shea's windows. Jason Donnelly arrived home next door, dribbling a football. He nodded at Damien, only because he was John Paul's friend, but Damien felt something swell in his chest and then the football drifted away and Jason had to bend down to pick it up and Damien's eyes zoomed to his shorts, like a horribly precise missile, and

262

Damien knew he was cursed. It didn't matter that he had told the truth; it was too late.

'Go on upstairs now.'

Damien caught the fury in Granny Doyle's eyes. He had to warn Peg. He'd dash out the door and run to Nolans supermarket or Peg's school or wherever she was and make amends. He could be brave. Once, he'd jumped off the rock in Clougheally and not looked down. Damien knew he had to leave the porch but the door he reached for led inside; there was nothing he could do for Peg now.

He waited for Granny Doyle to come upstairs.

She didn't.

He concentrated on disappearing.

He didn't.

The afternoon passed. Drizzle came, then a downpour. Peg came home. Words followed. Shouts threatened to split the house in two. Damien hid in the bathroom. He heard Peg's stomp up the stairs, though he daren't open the door. He heard the banging and breaking of things, though nobody knocked to see if he was okay. He wasn't.

And then Peg was gone and she didn't even knock for her toothbrush.

A bomb might have exploded in the top floor of the house; that was how it felt to Damien, pressed up against the bathroom door. Granny Doyle stayed downstairs, pots clanged, the radio on. They might have been on different planets. Damien heard John Paul come home, more shouts. He stayed in the bathroom, the stairs impossible. He wondered, perhaps, if he might live here for ever; the sink was certainly convenient for tears, which had finally come, in an awful racking rush.

John Paul made it up the stairs, eventually. Damien ventured into their bedroom. John Paul was on the floor by his smashed piggybank. Peg had raided Damien's Trócaire box too, not that it mattered, for Damien deserved it. John Paul looked up and knew from Damien's face what had happened.

'I'm sorry.'

He was.

John Paul walked over to his bed.

'John Paul ...'

'Fuck off, you little faggot.'

The word was an iron to Damien's face.

'What ...'

'You heard me: I said, fuck off, you little faggot.'

John Paul got into bed, though it hadn't even gone nine. Damien didn't dare move. Even the thought of running into the bathroom and curling up in the bathtub for ever was impossible; to breathe was to do something wrong. He stayed still so, while John Paul pretended to sleep and Granny Doyle clattered about downstairs and Rosie came home. Rosie saw her room and rushed into his and looked at Damien in the dark; then, she knew. Rosie wouldn't look at him again, not really, not in the same way; this, he understood.

Damien sat on his bed, alone. None of the triplets would get any sleep that night, but there was no elastic band pulling them onto the one bed. Damien searched for God's channel, but all he heard was static, as if God were a pirate radio station and Damien had missed the latest secret frequency. Instead, Damien listened to the sound of Rosie through the walls, crying into her pillow, and the shift of John Paul's sheets in the bed across the room, not even a snore to be sent in Damien's direction now.

4

Soundings (1993)

Happily, God was waiting for Damien in the pages of Peg's poetry book, rescued from a St Vincent de Paul bag by a scared boy in search of an older sister. He hadn't found Peg in the pages, even though he squinted at all her markings and marginalia, but there was God, waiting in the poems of Gerard Manley Hopkins, not caring if Damien couldn't understand most of the words, the feeling was what mattered, and God swooped off the pages of 'The Windhover' and fluttered towards Damien, whose *heart in hiding/ stirred.*

'The language is quite … excited … for a poem about God,' Rory said, peering at the book.

Years until they'd be studying for their Leaving, but Damien offered *Soundings* as treasure to Rory, proof that school might get more interesting than 'Colonel Fazackerley Butterworth-Toast', the poem they were supposed to be studying (Peg too had started *Soundings* too early, a precedent that Damien was unsure about).

'I guess the idea is that the bird represents God,' Rory said.

'Uh-huh,' Damien said.

Rory's mind continued to speed ahead, a bicycle zipping through cars and running red lights, while Damien's chugged along behind, stuck in traffic.

'But there's something *terrible* about the bird,' Rory said, peering at 'The Windhover' for hidden clues. '*Brute beauty … pride* and *plume* … but then God is even more terrible – and beautiful! – and he describes God like a fire, more *dangerous* but also *lovelier.*'

Absorbed in the book, Rory probably didn't notice that his knee had got too close to Damien's.

'It's weirdly like a romantic relationship, I guess.'

Damien felt a tilt of his heart.

'Uh-huh,' Damien managed.

5

The Symposium (1994)

The Symposium! Peg had written beside one of the poems in *Soundings*, followed by *true love!?* It was from a Yeats poem, 'Among School Children', where he went on about his long-lost love for Maud Gonne, remembering the pair of them as schoolchildren, two souls finding each other, *into the yolk and white of the one shell.*

Damien was curious enough to search through Peg's old books in the shed for *The Symposium*. It was quite the surprise to find a story from thousands of years ago where, among the two-legged creatures in search of their other half to make them whole, were men in search of men and women in search of women, no way for their bodies or souls to slot in easily with anybody of the opposite sex.

Oh, the Greeks! Rory said, when Damien told him, the noun loaded with knowledge, though as far as Damien knew, Rory hadn't been to Athlone, let alone Athens.

6

The Colour of My Love
Compact Disc (1995)

Damien couldn't contradict Rory's assertion that Celine Dion was a *poet*. Rory's tone might have been arch and his enthusiastic crooning ironic; even so, Damien felt a swoon of his soul as Rory O'Donoghue, with twinkling eyes and soprano voice, declaimed his full-hearted readiness to learn 'The Power of Love'.

7

Legion of Mary Handbook (1996)

I've been writing a poem, Rory said, when the two of them were sharing a hotel room in Knock for a Legion of Mary trip. They'd drunk a bottle of wine between them, pledge and Mrs McGinty be damned: dangerous territory. Damien had thought they would top and tail in the one bed, but then Rory clambered in beside him in his tartan boxers.

You'll approve; it's about God.

Damien did not search for Rory's eyes. Rule one of his alternative handbook: do not look into Rory's eyes under the influence of alcohol, even in the dark. Especially in the dark.

Well, Jesus.

Rule two: stay silent. Do not provide any encouraging words or sounds.

And his disciples.

Rule three: ignore the movement of the body.

Did you ever think it was weird that they were just men?

Rule four: especially ignore the bristle of hairs as Rory's ankle touched against his or the fact that his pyjamas were too short to stop skin meeting skin.

I thought it would be cool to imagine their relationship.

Rule five: regulate breath.

You know?

Rule six: ignore the slight movement of Rory's leg.

Jesus, travelling with those young fishermen ...

Rule seven: clench eyes; sleep will come faster.

But there it was, as vivid as ever across Damien's retina: the glowing buttocks of Ruadhan Kennedy-Carthy, white globes squeezing into blue jeans.

Rule eight: tune into God. Tune into Mary's frequency. Any of the saints, anything.

Damien, are you awake?

Rule nine: sleep, sleep, you are asleep!

Damien?

Rule ten: In the morning light, it is acceptable to look at the sleeping face of Rory O'Donoghue. If legs have draped over legs while sleeping, if a wrist has dozed across a chest, best not to disturb, best to admire, for doesn't every beauty lead us to the beauty of Our Lord?

8

Purple Marker (1997)

The graffiti artists in the school bathroom seemed to favour prose over poetry: 'Cocksuckers' was followed by 'Rory O'Donoghue' and 'Damien Doyle', with telephone numbers helpfully supplied.

John Paul was furious, making it clear who was to blame with a good thump directed towards Rory O'Donoghue's face. He couldn't hit Damien, so he shoved the school desk in front of him instead.

'You haven't an ounce of fucking cop-on, do you?' John Paul said, still mad, for it was his phone number too and Granny Doyle might answer some messer's call and Damien hadn't even thanked him.

Damien gripped his desk, shaking.

'You …'

'I told the fucker to leave my brother alone, that's all. And if you know what's good for you, you'll stay left alone. Only trying to help you, I am, fuck knows why, not as if you ever say thanks.'

No 'thanks' forthcoming, John Paul swiped Damien's English homework and started to copy it, while Damien shook, searching for words to make things right: *I didn't ask you to* or *how could you?*

Words remained stuck inside him, however, even as Rory entered the classroom, the wrong walk about him, defiant instead of defeated. Rory was terrible at being invisible, that vital skill for getting through secondary school; Rory talked too much in class and dropped his crisp packet into the bin too daintily and seemed to prance rather than walk, all details that he might have reined in, if he had any consideration for Damien. Damien might tell him, one day. For the moment, he focused on Jason Donnelly's arse as

Jason leant forward to chat to somebody, the inviting stretch of grey flannel a treat for Damien's eyes. Easier for Damien to stare at Jason Donnelly's arse than to turn towards Rory, who was looking in his direction, an ugly bruise under his eye and a tender smile that was waiting for a reflection, *Damien!* and *talk to me* at the ready.

John Paul was looking at Damien too – it felt as if the whole room was – and Damien knew that he was passing a test, staring fixedly ahead even as Rory whispered his name. The teacher entered, mercifully, and Rory at least had the sense to say 'nothing' when quizzed about what had happened to his eye. This, Damien interpreted as a move towards the right attitude but then Rory had to ruin this progress by bringing a purple marker to school the next day, 'So what?' written in bold beside 'Cocksuckers'.

From this point, it became impossible to acknowledge Rory O'Donoghue; surely he understood that? Damien avoided Rory's gaze but he followed the battles that took place across toilet doors. Rory hadn't a clue how to respond. Instead of ignoring the cartoon-cock beside his name, Rory added 'Bit bigger next time please' in purple marker. 'Faggot' was crossed out, replaced in purple with 'Fabulous'. 'Like I'd touch any of you mingers' was added beside his phone number; no wonder he earned himself a proper beating, purple pen flushed down the toilet, the bruises on his face traitorously turning an unflattering shade of turmeric.

Incredibly, Rory refused to learn this lesson, unveiling part of some Walt Whitman poem in purple the next week, for he'd moved beyond the confines of *Soundings*, didn't attempt to catch Damien's gaze any more, fuck-it-all fearlessness powering him through the yard, 'All this I swallow' and 'It tastes good' and 'I like it well' proud and loud on the toilet door.

Damien was left sitting on the bog and puzzling at the strange words, which, even behind a swarm of cartoon penises and scrawls of 'faggot', seemed somehow to shine.

9

Soundings (1998)

Damien stared at Peg's old book. The poems made more sense, now that he was studying them, the teacher plodding the class through each metaphor and reference. Yet, Damien had lost the joy of them; back when he was thirteen and thrilled at Gerard Manley Hopkins, God had skittered off the page like a bird, *O my chevalier!* Now, Damien read the same words – even understood that *chevalier* was a reference to Christ – but his heart felt no ping of solidarity. Instead, he was stuck with *Comforter, where, where is your comforting?* and *Mary, mother of us, where is your relief?*, from the later poems of Gerard Manley Hopkins, when he had lost the certainty of his faith, his voice reaching across centuries to sound Damien's despair with precision.

(There was no consolation in poetry, generally; when Damien flipped to the Yeats poem which had led him towards *The Symposium*, he saw that Peg had written *satirical?* in the margins, underneath *true love!?*, coming back later with a different pen to underline the question, twice.)

'I think he's making himself sick,' Rory said, talking about some Gerard Manley Hopkins poem that Damien didn't want to think about.

Rory still hadn't learnt not to talk too much in class, though now that they had reached sixth year nobody seemed to mind as much; Jason Donnelly even took notes, sometimes. Rory went out in town now, so Damien heard, with a gang of friends from Loreto, 'bitch' and 'babe' the salt and pepper of his sentences. John Paul wasn't there to beat him up; he'd been expelled after the controversy about the tablets, which, perhaps, was Damien's fault. Damien wasn't sure if he should feel guilty about what had happened to John Paul; he would normally have asked God or Rory, but neither was talking to him.

Instead, Rory was talking to the class, as if he'd already made it into Trinity's English department.

'He's trying to experience God through Communion, I guess, but he only tastes himself – *my taste was me* – but he can't reach God, just some sour *selfyeast*.'

Damien stared at the book that Peg had never got to use for her Leaving; she'd worked out the Communion imagery too, markings that Damien had glossed over all those years ago. Rory sat straight in his chair, on the precipice of a new thought.

'I think he's figured something out, sir. It's as if he's realized that God is just a projection; he's trying to reach God again, but he's stuck with himself, because that's all God ever was, a voice in his mind.'

Damien could never be sure if Rory's head turned slightly or not.

'I feel sorry for him, sir.'

10

Nail Polish (2007)

Damien stepped inside. The holy water font was inside the door, mocking him. There wasn't even the sound of the television. Granny Doyle was asleep upstairs. He should leave, Damien felt that immediately, though some instinct led him to the kettle in the kitchen. He'd leave her a note, he decided, no shock that the spare biros were still in the same drawer. The only thing that had changed was the dirt; Granny Doyle wouldn't have stood for grime on her tiles, back in the day. Damien resisted the urge to pick up the forlorn J-cloth from the sink; the stains would need more than water and he was sure that the cleaning products would not be environmentally friendly. He'd focus on the tea. A quick cup, and he'd be off. The mugs were brown on the inside, more stain than mug, but he left them be. Once you started, the day would be gone: there were mouse droppings in the drawer with the biros and the oven was crying out for a scrub and somebody should cut the grass before they got too deep into the summer. *Somebody*. Damien Doyle had an election to win. Besides, with what he had to say, chances were he wouldn't be back.

One cuppa; he owed her that. Damien got out a saucer for biscuits, sighing as he opened the tin to find a packet of Bourbon Creams. Next time – if there was a next time – he'd stop by Marks & Spencer in town and get some expensive biscuits, chocolate and orange ginger nuts or some things with designs latticed across in white chocolate. Mark was right: he could do better. Perhaps they could visit together. Mark had the knack of chat, he was a brilliant canvasser, talking the ear off anybody, always finding a way to get them to agree that yes, the country needed a change, they'd give the Greens a think after all. Damien smiled at the thought of Mark knocking his way down Dunluce Crescent, agreeing with Mrs Fay that her flowers were *lovely* and shooting the shit with Mr Geoghan and charming Granny Doyle – Mark could manage that, surely. Damien poured the tea, losing himself in a fantasy where Mark cut the grass while Damien found a delightful apron and baked scones and Granny Doyle glowed with gratitude—

'What are you at?'

Damien nearly spilled the milk with the fright.

'Why are you the one leaping up? Aren't you the one who's let yourself into my kitchen?'

The real Granny Doyle was far from glowing. More wrinkles than he remembered. Red eyes, from tears or tiredness, he couldn't tell.

'Sorry, I rang the bell …'

'That thing's buzzing all day, as if I didn't have anything better to be doing than talking about the election.'

Damien bit his lip quite hard.

'Sorry, I should have called.'

'Well, I might have had something in the oven for you then.'

'It's grand, I ate before I came.'

'Oh!'

'I didn't want to trouble you.'

But Granny Doyle was determined to find trouble.

'I'd never turn my nose up at a meal – that was how I was reared, but oh, well, isn't everything takeway nowadays? And is that *tea* you're attempting to make there? Lord preserve us, I've seen less milk come out of a cow's udder! Would you ever throw that sickly concoction away and make a proper pot?'

She was tired after her nap, Damien reasoned, pressing the teabag against the mug quite vigorously.

'*Winning Streak* will be on in a minute.'

How could he forget?

'Right. I'll bring in a pot.'

'Grand, so.'

And with that she was shuffling off into the sitting room. Damien clicked on the kettle and found some steel teapot that had generations of tea clinging to its spout. The jingle of ads sounded from the next room. Nothing that she couldn't have skipped, if she'd wanted to spend a couple of minutes chatting with him. She had not noticed the peach nail polish. He shouldn't have come; Mark was mad.

'There's biscuits in the tin if you want,' Granny Doyle called from the sitting room.

'Thanks,' Damien called in.

He'd deposit the tea and the biscuits and leg it out the door before *Winning Streak* started. Or, he'd get it over and done with. Like ripping a plaster.

The thing is, Gran, I'm gay!

No, he needed some smooth conversational transition, difficult when the chat was as dry as Bourbon Creams. Maybe *Coronation Street* would be on afterwards?

The thing is, Gran, I'm like Sarah-Louise's boyfriend. The one who went out with a nurse. Yes, the male nurse.

That might do the trick, at a pinch.

The thing is, Gran, I used to watch Coronation Street!

Not to mention that he borrowed Rosie's *Smash Hits* to keep the Take That covers or used to plait the hair of Peg's Barbies; when he assembled the evidence, it seemed to Damien that he should never have needed to come out to anybody, least of all himself.

'You're missing the start!' Granny Doyle called.

That was how visits went: Granny Doyle refused to budge from her routine and imagined that nobody else would dream of missing a minute of her scheduled thrills.

'Coming!' Damien called.

He found a tray for the pot and the biscuits. Some steel jug so the battleaxe could pour her own milk. He hesitated at the door, wondering if there were any hope of whiskey in the house.

'Are you coming in or out?'

She had bat ears as well as X-ray vision: it was the only explanation.

Damien entered and placed the tray by Granny Doyle's armchair, *Winning Streak* providing enough distraction to avoid opprobrium.

'Thank you,' Granny Doyle managed. 'Nice to see you.'

I have something to tell you hung in the air, giving Granny Doyle space for:

'Though you really should ring before the next time. Give me the chance to get some dinner into you; I've a bit of lamb needs using up.'

'I'm grand,' Damien said, so Granny Doyle tutted and turned back to the television and Damien sighed for he saw the way the evening would go, all *grands* and *would you not have a bit to eat?* and *did I tell you a Polish crowd moved into number 9, poor Mr Kehoe would turn in his grave* and the chance of saying anything important would vanish, *the thing is, Gran, I'm gay* retreating back inside Damien, until he exploded.

'Are you all right?'

Granny Doyle squinted across at him in the ad-break.

'I wanted to …'

He needed to turn on a light; he couldn't do it like this, with ads for fizzy drinks flashing across Granny Doyle's face.

'Do you need the toilet?'

'No. No.'

The thing is …

'Er, is *Coronation Street* on?'

278

Granny Doyle snorted.

'I don't watch that any more. It got awful quare.'

Damien tensed: in what sense was Granny Doyle using 'queer'? Country-speak for something strange? Mark's way of identifying himself, where the word contained both alternative politics and sexual identity? Or the derogatory term for a soap opera that had been contaminated by the appearance of flaming gay nurses? It was too late for Damien to ask: Granny Doyle had started a rant about the decline of television, dating back to Miley's fumblings with Fidelma in the hay. *Glenroe* was no use to Damien: the gayest thing about it was Teasey's hair, but he wasn't sure that 'the thing is, loads of drag queens I know emulate that hairstyle' would be the best of openings.

'Are you sure you're all right?'

Winning Streak was back on but Damien felt the glare of Granny Doyle's eyes.

'I'm grand.'

'Stop fidgeting so, would you!'

Why did this house stammer him? Wasn't he a proficient adult, capable of dealing with an array of irate Green Party members or prospective voters with impeccable patience? Hadn't he, once, jumped off the side of the Children of Lir's rock without looking down?

'Actually ... there's something I wanted to talk to you about.'

Granny Doyle's shoulders tensed.

'Right.'

She kept her eyes on the television, suddenly immersed in whatever cash prize somebody was about to win.

It can wait until the ads, Granny Doyle's shoulders said.

It can wait until never, Granny Doyle's back said.

Damien pretended to be enthralled by *Winning Streak*, a blur of bright colours in front of him. He'd forgotten why he needed to tell her. What if she knew? What if he was going to mess it all up by putting brash words around the already understood.

The thing is, Gran, I'm queer as folk, gay as glitter, the fairy on top of Dunluce Crescent. What if he killed her? Murder by truth, another casualty of the closet's swinging doors; he couldn't even remember how to do CPR.

The thing is, Gran, I'm in love with a man.

He should have brought Mark, after all; Mark would find the words.

The thing is, Gran, I'm in love with a man called Mark and I'd love for you to meet him.

Mark had gone with him to the graveyard; a stupid idea, Damien had thought, but then he'd cried when he'd told them, the words whispered to tombstones, and Mark had been brilliant, holding and hugging him and not even minding when he wanted to say a decade of the rosary.

The thing is, Gran, you reared me and even if we've had some rocky years and even if we've never got on, the thing is you mean something to me and so does Mark – the world, actually – and the thing is, I want to bring him here so we can all sit and watch whatever you want and eat stale biscuits and chat about nothing and the thing is that would mean so much to me that I might weep.

'Well.'

Damien blinked: the credits of *Winning Streak* flashed in front of his eyes.

'Thanks for the visit.'

It was too dark for her to see the water in his eyes, he hoped.

'Right. I just wanted to …'

She didn't turn off the telly; she wasn't ready for silence, yet.

'I just wanted to tell you something.'

'Right.'

She turned to face him, ads flickering across her face.

'The thing is …'

' …'

'The thing is, Gran …'

'…'

'…'

'What is it?'

She stared at him in the dark. She couldn't make out his eyes, he hoped. He was an independent adult. He didn't need her blessing or her support. He hardly saw her any more. But then the thoughts of what she might say reared in front of him and Damien froze, terrified.

'The thing is …'

'Yes?'

'The thing is, Gran … I'm a vegetarian.'

11

Love Hearts (2007)

'The thing is, if you're going to be vegetarian, you might as well be vegan, right?' Mark said, as he dug into a sausage bap. 'Though that might have killed her, eh?'

Damien blushed.

'Ah, I'm only teasing.'

Mark moved in for a kiss but Damien didn't want a taste of beer and sausage.

'You did great.'

Mark put his arm around Damien, though this somehow made things worse too; Damien had been searching for pride and he'd found pity.

Damien picked up his phone from the coffee table, ignoring the mug of mouldy tea that Mark had left there since the morning. This movement was enough to shrug away Mark's arm, which swooped down to pick up his laptop. Damien clenched; he could tell Mark was about to play something on YouTube and he wanted to lose himself in his work. The election was only a few days away and Fianna Fáil were polling well. The Greens still had the chance to squeak into a coalition government but the window for change was closing and they needed to cling on; every blog post mattered. So of course Mark chose this moment to put on one of John Paul's bloody videos.

'You seen this one?'

Mark was drunk, otherwise he wouldn't have played the Pope video or teased Damien about his grand plant-based coming-out.

Sober, he would have seen how tender and on edge Damien felt, the future precarious, because if the Greens didn't get into government it would be five more years of shouting from the sidelines and writing press releases that nobody read and Damien might never emerge into his most promising self.

'It's not bad,' Mark said, pressing play.

Damien watched.

The colours were too garish: the fake green grass too shiny; the blue-sky backdrop too bright; the rainbow straight out of a primary school classroom. Pope John Paul III didn't notice, flashed a smile as blinding as the fake sun bobbing above his hat.

'Everybody knows that rainbows can bring miracles,' Pope John Paul III said. 'And we've got something better than a pot of gold to give you.'

The contents of a bright pot emptied into his hand: lots of brightly coloured heart-shaped sweets.

'Love,' the Irish Pope explained, because his videos left nothing to chance. 'Fiannix supports equal rights for everybody. So they're offering unlimited texts this month for all sweethearts: straight, L.G.T.B.Q, any other letter you can think of!'

Damien looked away, certain his face was cycling through several shades of indignation. He didn't want to look at his brother, so his eye strayed to the comments, where a stink was being kicked up, words thrown about that Damien didn't want to read. Controversy was good for clicks, so Pope John Paul III didn't mind; he was happy to put hand on hip and wink at the camera.

'So pick up your phone and go get 'em, girl! Or guy! Or whatever!'

Tiny terms and conditions whirled across the bottom of the screen, much smaller than the love hearts thrown upwards by an enthusiastic Pope.

'Fair play!'

'What?'

'Well, it's more than the current fucker in the Vatican would say, isn't it? Good on him. And at least he's not afraid to get people talking—'

'That's all he wants to do, as long as they're paying Fiannix every month for the pleasure.'

Mark would hate Fiannix, Damien was sure. It was one of many new phone-providers, unleashed since the telecommunications industry had been deregulated. Fiannix promised to be more than just a place to get cheap calls, however. Its name evoked old Ireland, and its logo – a cheeky bird chirping out of flames – appealed to young people. Pope John Paul III was only too happy to promote Fiannix; this was the new Ireland he believed in.

'You know Fiannix is his girlfriend's shitty phone start-up company?'

'*Fiancée's.*'

How could Damien forget the gold-dusted wedding invitation? (Mark, unfortunately, hadn't.)

'Which makes it even more dodgy that he's playing Rent-a-Cause for something that he has a stake in.'

'Maybe so, but fair play to him for getting into something controversial: Fiannix support gay marriage too.'

Damien wanted to scream; sometimes he felt Mark made up his politics on the spot.

But, Damien thought, he's only doing it because it's fashionable.

But, Damien thought, this is the very corporatization of queer culture that you're always complaining about.

But, Damien thought, he called me *faggot* and punched Rory O'Donoghue.

But, Damien thought, it's John Paul …

This was what it came to: Damien could not support any endeavour of his brother. Nor could he ever tell Mark about why John Paul got at him so he tried to move the topic to safer ground.

'I thought you didn't believe in gay marriage.'

Mark shrugged.

'I don't! It's a normalizing trap to straighten out queer culture and force us into fucking boxes and buy shite we don't need. But it's like the vegan thing, isn't it – *if* you care about it you might as well go the whole fucking hog.'

There was definitely an edge to this: the Greens were pushing for same-sex civil partnership in their manifesto after many debates and strategy sessions. Achievable, incremental aims could lead to greater change; this Damien believed with a quiet passion that would never make its way onto a YouTube video, but kept him going nonetheless. So it was galling to see Mark give John Paul credit for mincing about in a video, praise that seemed to say *if your brother can do this in front of your granny* (as if she knew how to get onto a computer) *why can't you?*

Damien tried a different tack.

'I can try and get his number for you, if you want. He might be able to get you a ticket to the Galway Races.'

Damien could count on Mark's hatred of Fianna Fáil, at least, and the video that John Paul had made at the races was the epitome of everything that Mark's dissertation was trying to attack. Mark had been on YouTube a lot for his 'research', which Damien felt increasingly prickly about; he wasn't even watching the Green Party's channel.

'Ah, come here, you jealous wee thing.'

Mark yanked Damien's tie in for a kiss, sausage and beer breath be damned.

'I'm not jealous, just embarrassed by your taste.'

'Says the man with the Ronan Keating calendar in his office.'

'That was left behind by the last occupant!'

This was nice teasing, though, and had Mark put his arm out on the back of the couch, Damien would have leant into it. The last few weeks of the campaign had been difficult, with Damien canvassing every day after work, while Mark sat at home watching videos, despair steaming off his clothes, papers and mugs scattered around him, never dinner to come home to, only recriminations at his choice of takeaway, Damien responsible for the gentrification of the Liberties. So this tone was a welcome change; Damien would have leant into Mark's arm if he'd extended it.

Instead, the treacherous limb reached for the blasted wedding invitation.

'Maybe Ronan Keating will be at this?'

Damien rolled his eyes.

'It's going to be in *VIP* magazine, so I heard!' Mark said.

'I thought you hated weddings?'

Mark screwed up his face.

'There are worse things.'

'I thought weddings were a "hetero-normative nightmare that have to be boycotted at every opportunity"?'

Mark sighed.

'This one might be interesting. The First Pope of Ireland tying the knot! Anthropological research. And I bet they'll have some free Love Hearts; I'd murder a pack now.'

Mark was pissed, otherwise he wouldn't be going on about John Paul or craving sweets that he should probably be boycotting for some reason.

'It might be a chance to talk to your brother.'

Damien clenched: here they were pulling up to a familiar argument.

'I'm not *not* talking to him. We just don't see each other.'

'This would be a chance, so. He invited you. *Us*, actually. And Rosie's probably going.'

Mark had met Rosie in the Rossport Solidarity Camp, because Ireland was actually the size of a stamp and whichever deity or geological force was responsible for its tininess clearly had a malicious intent to ruin Damien Doyle's life. Mark and Rosie got on great, so Mark couldn't understand why Damien and Rosie hardly ever talked. Damien definitely didn't want to talk about Rosie because that would mean confronting Aunty Mary's letter, a document he had postponed dealing with until after the election, when with any luck it might have disappeared.

The bloody wedding invitation hadn't disappeared, so Damien felt the need to banish it.

'The whole wedding will be on YouTube. We can watch it there, save some money.'

Mark dropped the invitation onto the table immediately, the mention of money an easy way to quiet him. He'd lost the funding for his PhD – which was fine, Mark said, because academia was a con, he was tired of acting like he was lucky to get some shite teaching gig that didn't even give him benefits; he'd finish his dissertation, he'd pick something else up, so he said, although the only thing he was picking up was more cans.

Mark stood up.

'I'm going to hit the sack. Want me to kill the light and save us some cents?'

Damien didn't rise to this.

'I'll turn it off; I've a bit more work to get done.'

'Right.'

'Night.'

Damien stared at his phone. He had a heap of work to get through – checking in with the canvassers and tweaking a press release about housing for tomorrow and finishing the bloody blog about the Greens' plan for early education – but his eyes wouldn't focus and his hands wouldn't stop shaking. After the election: he'd deal with everything then. Once the Greens had ousted Fianna Fáil and set up a new Rainbow Coalition with bright green stripes, then Mark would appreciate the work he'd been doing and they could find a shady spot in Phoenix Park and lie in each other's arms and not talk about families or politics or anything really; just the whites of each other's eyes, that would be enough for the day.

12

Ballot Box (2007)

Could Damien feel proud about the election result? The Greens had only won six seats. There wasn't going to be an alternative coalition government. The only hope they had of getting into any government was to join Fianna Fáil's coalition, something their leader had deemed as improbable as flying pigs, creatures which were likely flapping over the Mansion House, as the whole of the Green Party had an emergency meeting to determine whether they should join Fianna Fáil in government.

Damien avoided the protesters as he brisked through the rain. He'd answered the phone in the Green Party headquarters enough times to know the objections: the Greens couldn't enter government with a party that allowed US warplanes to refuel in Shannon; the Greens couldn't enter government with a party that was going to build a motorway through Tara; the Greens couldn't enter government with a party that cared about builders more than badgers. The Greens couldn't enter government with Fianna Fáil, so the protesters shouted, as the Party prepared to stomach this prospect.

There was one protester Damien couldn't avoid.

'Hey.'

'Hey.'

'It's not too late to stop this.'

Damien sighed; they'd travelled over the tracks of this argument several times.

They're offering two ministries, Energy and Environment, Damien would say.

Fianna Fáil won't let you get anything done, Mark would say.

Going into government gives us a chance to change as well as complain.

Minority parties are always screwed by coalition governments.

Think of the policies we can pass: climate change, planning laws, civil partnership!

'You're going to vote yes.'

Damien shrugged his shoulders.

'I have to see where the room is.'

Mark knew he was lying.

'I have to go,' Damien said, a convenient truth.

'I don't want to keep you from the corridors of power.'

'That's not fair. This is about the chance to act upon the promises we've been making …'

It wasn't Mark staring at him, but the Iraqi girl on his placard, Mark already walking back to the protest.

*

Damien knew that Mark was in the minority, he was confident they'd get the seal of approval from two thirds of the membership. There were dissenting voices: Patricia McKenna making a passionate speech against joining government; Mark, equally impassioned, using his vote even though he was already severing himself from the party. Then it was time to vote. The intimacy of the ballot booth surprised Damien, the paper in his hand so flimsy, given its significance. Damien did what 86 per cent of the assembled Green Party members did – weighed up his choices, assessed the risks and rewards, voted a resounding 'yes'.

*

Outside, Mark could barely look Damien in the eye.

'We're going to Café en Seine for a drink, if you want,' Damien attempted, knowing that Mark would decline.

'No thanks.'

It was Mark's face that prompted Damien's response.

'You know what your problem is?'

'I'd say you can't wait to tell me.'

'You can't bear to compromise. You know where that gets you. If you'd been nicer to your adviser, you'd probably still have funding.'

The colour drained from Mark's face.

'I should take lessons from you. Your tongue's so far up Bertie's arse you could lick his shites.'

So, here it was, the end. Colour returned to Mark's cheeks before he stormed off. Damien stayed standing on Dawson Street like an eejit, surprised by the sense of loss as much as release: he wouldn't feel Mark's stubble scratch against his face again; he wouldn't rest his head against his chest; he wouldn't be there to hold Mark when he got sad; nobody would be there to make fun of Damien in the morning when he blow-dried his hair.

He should go home, he knew. Start to pack. Apologize? Leave. This he couldn't face, though, not yet, so when 'are you coming for one?' was shouted in his direction, his legs headed for Café en Seine, Damien revelling in the fact that the establishment was one of the villains of Mark's dissertation. He'd show his face; have the one. Or two. Eamon or John might buy him a beer and there was a lot to talk about, policies to be perfected and new beginnings to be toasted, no need for Mark to drag him down.

But then there was somebody else in Damien's path before he could find Eamon Ryan or John Gormley. Damien froze, taking it all in: the ridiculous hat; the half-second of panic before a grin was found.

'Damo!'

Here was the figure who had punched Rory O'Donoghue. Here was the boy who had called him *faggot*. Here was the embodiment of everything that was wrong with modern Ireland, stretching a grin to breaking point and gesturing towards the bar.

'Can I get you a drink?'

Series VII:

The Tricks of
John Paul Doyle

(1992–2007)

1

iPhone (2007)

The trick was to keep moving.

Pope John Paul III worked the crowds in Café en Seine, shaking hands and slapping backs and holding up the exclusive prototype he'd managed to snag. *Brilliant, isn't it?* he asked, unclear if *it* was the phone, the picture, or the Greens' decision to go into government with Fianna Fáil. Why not all three? John Paul couldn't be happier – the trick was to keep smiling – and it was brilliant to record every moment of the night. Some of the shite ones he'd delete, where the flash was too bright or the bar too dark or his cheeks strained at the edges. Maybe there was some technology that could airbrush in the perfect smile if you'd messed up in a photo; if this didn't already exist, he'd have to invent it, he'd write it down on his phone. In the meantime, more drinks – the trick was to keep buzzed; the trick was to pay on credit – and a photo with his brother.

The appearance of Damien Doyle threatened to awaken the black hole inside him, but John Paul had it under control; keep the liver busy and the black hole got confused. Damien had a better suit than he did and a mad grin on his face, hammered out of his tree he was, he could never hold his drink, though perhaps that had changed. Years since they'd had a pint. Had they, in fact, ever had a pint? Cups of tea and strained chat and cans at Christmas, the odd times they overlapped at 7 Dunluce Crescent. Sharing a pint, so, was an historic occasion and even though John Paul had an agenda, there was a part of him that was glad to sit in a bar with his brother (he wished that they could flee the chandeliers and the dark wood and the coffee cocktails and find some old man's pub where they could chat into the dawn) despite everything Damien had done.

'Here we go!' John Paul said, depositing more drinks with a smile.

'Let me,' Damien said, fumbling for his wallet and almost falling off the stool with the effort.

'Don't even!' Clodagh said. 'It's a small price to pay for your advice.'

Another sin to add to Damien Doyle's ledger: he was siding with Clodagh.

'*Damien* thinks that gold cufflinks are a terrible idea,' Clodagh announced, as Damien stared at his pint. 'And he is *not* a fan of novelty boxers for the groomsmen either.'

A point in his favour: Damien had agreed to be a groomsman, ensuring that Clodagh's desire for symmetry would be satisfied.

'I see you've been catching up!' John Paul said, his best gormless grin on.

'And you can't be spray-painting peacocks for the lawn,' Clodagh continued. 'Bad for the environment, isn't it, Damien?'

John Paul tried his catchphrase: 'Ah now, I wouldn't know anything about that!'

They needed some stunning images if they were to make it into a decent magazine – Clodagh was the one who'd suggested finding golden butterflies and releasing them as confetti, hardly approved by the Green Party, John Paul imagined – but John Paul knew what Clodagh was at, coddling Damien into solidarity, the things *we* have to put up with!

'And Rosie can't have blue hair if she wants to be a bridesmaid,' Clodagh said, waving her finger through the air. 'Personally, I *love* that she's got her own sense of style but from a colour scheme perspective, I just think it might clash, you know what I mean?'

Damien did, or he pretended to, sitting with his pint like some nodding dog. John Paul relaxed; Damien didn't want to talk about Rosie, which was fine as far as he was concerned. He didn't even know if she'd come to the wedding and he hadn't thought he cared until he felt some powerful stretch in his chest at the idea of the three of them together again; he had to sit down.

'I'm just glad the Green Party isn't that *extreme*,' Clodagh said. 'I mean, you have to compromise, don't you?'

He had to credit her, she was a great veerer of conversations, leading Damien smoothly from how prickly Rosie could be to what a good thing it was that the Greens weren't going to be kicking up too much fuss.

'I just think we're lucky to be free of all these regulations,' Clodagh said, swooping her hands through the air like she was performing a dance move. 'I mean, that's what was holding us back from developing, wasn't it? Like, haven't we had enough of people telling us what to do in this country! I mean, I am all for choice: everybody should be able to love who they want.'

Clodagh gripped Damien's hand; it was magnificent, the way she could keep focus, even when she was pissed.

'And it's the same everywhere, isn't it? All we want is freedom! Nobody should be telling us what to do, do you know what I mean?'

John Paul saw the struggle on Damien's face – perhaps there were circumstances when a government should tell citizens and corporations what to do and *perhaps* economic and personal freedoms were different fights – but Damien had had enough arguing that day, all he could manage was a nod. On Clodagh moved, to the blissful deregulation of the telecommunications industry and her success in setting up Fiannix, a nimble operation that would only be possible in a light-touch environment ('and isn't that what we all want, a light touch!' Clodagh said, gripping Damien's hand and laughing, the best of mates), and by the way, did Damien have any inside information on who might be the Communications Minister, between friends, and the Greens didn't have any plans to interfere with corporate taxation, did they, not now they were in with Fianna Fáil? She was magnificent, the perfect partner for John Paul; they could conquer continents together.

John Paul remembered to smile. Some gobshite wanted a photo, which meant the pope's hat went back on; uncomfortable, with the heat of the place. He longed to run away to a less crowded bar or even to slip outside for a fag, but he wasn't sure that he should leave Damien with Clodagh. Damien was turning the wrong shade of green – he still couldn't handle his drink – and Damien puking in Clo's Dolce & Gabbana bag might put a wrinkle in their best-of-friends business. But why did he need to protect his brother? Couldn't Damien cop on himself and know when to head to the jacks? Damien, certainly, hadn't protected John Paul, had he? *All in the past*, John Paul wanted to say, through a hearty back-slap, but his hands had turned into fists. Something was stirring inside John Paul's chest too and he wasn't sure if it was the black hole or the oyster tacos or the too many shots or the past, poking away at him, when all he wanted to do was forget.

The trick was to keep moving.

'J.P., you all right?'

'Hey, it's the Irish Pope!'

'Pope J.P. is in the house!'

He felt completely scuttered, all of a sudden, a miracle that his legs could wobble around the crowds. Jason Donnelly *heyyyyed* him from across the bar. The chandelier danced down from the ceiling and swirled in front of his eyes. A patterned rug launched from the floor. Fat-faced gobshites chuckled.

'J.P., are you all right?' Clo called.

The trick was to say *yes*, but he hadn't the words.

The trick was to find a smile, but he couldn't find the shape.

The trick was to keep moving: out of this bar, away from the past and – most especially – steer clear of the Doyles, because when he thought about it Damien had a lot to answer for.

2

Piggybank (1992)

John Paul read the room immediately. He was fairly buzzed after a couple of cans of Bulmers but the sight of Granny Doyle sobered him instantly. She was still as stone, hands planted on the sink, eyes fixed on the wall, as Peg shouted in through the kitchen window, a wet and wild thing. If any of Peg's words made any impression, Granny Doyle's body didn't show it; she could have been a statue, there by the sink, the tap trickling into an overflowing saucepan. Peg continued to shout and sob outside; John Paul remained frozen, his eyes fixed on Granny Doyle's unflinching back.

So Damien had told. An entirely predictable course of events when he thought about it, yet John Paul had never considered the possibility. He felt the shift in the room, the carpet ripped from under his feet, all the furniture of his life struggling to figure out a new arrangement.

'Get out!'

John Paul started at the sound of Granny Doyle's roar. She had turned, finally, but it wasn't Peg she was looking at, but him. She'd never shouted at him before, not with any weight behind the words, and John Paul shook, startled by the rage in her voice. Her face trembled but the rest of her body remained calm and John Paul wanted to go over to her and hug her or tell her he was sorry or turn off the trickling tap but before he could move she let out another shout.

'I've told you now: get out!'

She was exerting all her energy to stay still, he could see that. The cider had made his legs wobbly, so he wasn't sure if he'd be able to walk over to her and quiet her. A thousand actions seemed possible in the fuzz of his brain, opening the window and letting Peg in from the rain included, but when his legs decided to move, they did what Granny Doyle suggested; John Paul got out.

He leant against the stairs, the cider catching up with him. Minutes passed, the quiet of the house threatening to kill him. The walls seemed ready to come for him too, so he opened the door, not expecting Peg to be out there, but there she was, through the glass of the porch, banging the door of 5 Dunluce Crescent. The Donnellys were definitely home but their door remained closed. Peg battered her knuckles against the wood, *Denise!* pushed through the letterbox, but the only thing to move were the curtains. Other curtains twitched on Dunluce Crescent. John Paul had the sense that the whole road was watching, peering out at the desperate figure in the wind and the rain, while Granny Doyle stayed rooted in the kitchen, hands either side of the sink while the water continued to run.

Peg turned and saw him. It would have been the easiest thing to open the porch door. A simple slide of the latch and she'd be in. John Paul didn't open the door. Instead, he stared at his older sister, watching the cogs turn in her brain. *You ratted me out, you bastard,* her face said and even though he might have cleared things up, John Paul's head did not shake from side to side nor did his hand reach for the latch. 'You fucking bastard', Peg shouted. John Paul waited for a *fuck off* but Peg was beyond that now, a purer form of hatred sent towards him, an energy that he returned, because how dare she look at him like that?

Then she was gone, disappeared around the corner.

*

John Paul's legs swayed and he found himself on one of the porch's folding chairs, staring out at the rain. She'd be back later. Granny Doyle's temper would cool. She'd forgive John Paul for not telling her too; she'd have to. Curtains shifted next door and John Paul knew that Mrs Donnelly was only too eager for the news of what was happening, though she didn't show her face. The road was completely quiet, the lash of the wind and the rain against the glass the only sound. Peg hadn't her coat on, something that Granny Doyle might scold her about, eventually, when everything shifted back to normal and John Paul's knees stopped knocking into each other.

John Paul walked upstairs, a mistake: the rain would have shaken off his feelings. Rosie was still out, up to who knew what with who knew who; John Paul had an urge to go and thump him – one sister at least he could protect – but the man of the house found his legs leading him to his own room, where a smashed piggybank greeted him.

Peg had cleaned it out. She'd taken all of his Confirmation money and his profits from the cigarette business, something that Peg wouldn't be facilitating any more. It hit John Paul then that she'd turned a corner she might not come back from; he crouched on the floor and picked up the pieces of his piggybank for the sake of something to do.

Damien appeared at the doorway and wrung out words through tears.

'I'm sorry.'

John Paul glared at his brother, fists ready to push him down the stairs if it came to it. John Paul couldn't shout at Peg or Granny Doyle so here was somebody to blame, the poor sap who John Paul had always stood up for; he'd never imagined Damien could do something like this.

So he told the little faggot to fuck off, making every word count, the last he'd speak to Damien, so he resolved, as he flopped down

302

onto the bed and wriggled under the covers, tears threatening him too, but he'd keep them in, steel coursing through his veins, fists balled for a fight, sleep a long way off.

3

Triple X Mints (1993)

The trick was to stay away from 7 Dunluce Crescent as long as possible.

Some days he went back to Jason Donnelly's to play Nintendo, but even 5 Dunluce Crescent was compromised: the ghost of Peg hung around Denise's room, beside the cloud of perfume and cigarette smoke.

'You're lucky, I wish *she'd* disappear,' Jason said, one day when Denise was wrecking his head with her Enya phase, but once he saw the face on John Paul he never mentioned Peg again.

Most days they went deep into the woods of St Anne's Park. Some days, they experimented: glue, the vodka that Jason stole off Denise, the weed that Keifo's cousin got them. Some days they brought spray cans and swirled out their immortality in squiggly capitals or wrote glorious revenges against the teachers who tormented them. Some days they sat in some empty ruin that stank of piss and chatted shite about the birds they'd bang and the teachers they'd batter and the glorious goals they'd score that would make even Eamon Dunphy cum in his kacks.

The trick was to always come prepared: a couple of Triple X Mints strong enough to blast away the trace of most things, cider or vodka or weed soon replaced with minty freshness.

The trick was to keep a good distance. Granny Doyle always pottered about in the kitchen until he came home, but if he hovered by the doorway they could get through the chat without her seeing anything.

Or without her *saying* anything. Granny Doyle's nose was sharp enough and some nights he was sure she could smell the weed on him. Whatever her olfactory powers, the tongue of Granny Doyle could be silent when it wanted and most days they could make it through the ritual with a nod and a 'night' before John Paul stumbled upstairs to copy Damien's homework.

4

Riverdance Video (1994)

The trick was to keep her happy.

Granny Doyle squinted at the video in front of her.

'Ah, you didn't need to be bothering with this nonsense! Where did you get this?'

'I picked it up at HMV in town,' John Paul said, which was technically true, though he hadn't taken it to the till: the trick was to deal in half-truths.

'We had a half-day,' Jason Donnelly added, which was also technically true, although their teachers might not have seen it that way.

'Would you look at the cut of them!' Granny Doyle said, examining the box. 'Yer man Flatley prancing about in leather pants and *that one* beside him, flailing her arms about like she's drowning! It's a great gladness that Mammy didn't have to see this like!'

Granny Doyle was chuffed to bits, though, in her element when she was giving out about something and could dangle some controversy in front of the rest of the porch.

'I think it's lovely to see all the young people getting involved in Irish dancing again,' Mrs Fay said.

'I wish Anuna got more credit,' Mrs McGinty sniffed. 'The singers were the real stars of the show, not that infernal tapping: I had a headache by the end of it.'

'Michael Flatley is welcome to give me a headache any day!' Mrs Nugent said, grabbing the box from Granny Doyle. 'Look at those leather pants!'

Mrs McGinty attempted to shatter glass with her tut.

'Ah, don't be at me – I'd say half the girls in that choir of yours have their eyes on him as well; sure, all the "nourishing" and "cherishing" they'd be singing about, there's only one man they could be talking about – they'll have to get in line, though!'

'Lord preserve us! This whole country has gone too American altogether.'

'Well, I think it's absolutely brilliant to see the country showing a bit of confidence,' Mrs Fay said. 'Three Eurovision wins in a row, could you credit it? We'll be winning the World Cup, yet, George says.'

'You'll sort us out, won't you, lads?' Mrs Nugent said. 'Though maybe you'll take up the dancing too?'

'He will not!' Granny Doyle said.

'They're crying out for boys, so Clare says,' Mrs Nugent added. 'And you've a nice long pair of legs: I'd say *you'd* be very popular!'

Christ! Jason Donnelly said with his eyes, backing as far against the porch window as he could. *That lot are even mentaller than my ma*, Jason said whenever he had to spend a couple of minutes in the porch, incredulous that John Paul ever lingered there. Ah, but Jason didn't understand. John Paul loved the *craic* and the chat of the porch: the jokes with Mrs Nugent and the challenge of making Mrs McGinty smile and the treat of seeing Granny Doyle happy. On her own in the kitchen, she'd be sighing and shuffling, the ghosts of the dead and the disappeared at the windows. The porch brought insulation, chat that could swaddle her, while she sat quiet enough in the middle, content to pass the day discussing the gall of Fiona Brennan (parading about in poms, as if she invented Irish dancing!) and the cheek of a divorce referendum (it couldn't pass!) and the general goodness of John Paul (a great lad, isn't he?)

John Paul was a great lad, at least in the porch, where he liked to see himself reflected in the eyes of the old ladies, a boy bringing presents to his grandmother, the kind of figure who might one day summon the future through smiles and dry ice, the breaths of audiences stolen clean from their bodies at the sight of such brilliance: a hero.

5

CK One Bottle (1995)

The trick was to keep distracted.

They found each other at a free gaff in Clontarf, some posh prat's party that John Paul was only at because Jason had an in with one of the girls. John Paul hadn't exactly forgotten about Clodagh Reynolds, but he hadn't spent the years pining for her either. He'd gone far enough into St Anne's Park with Emer Clancy to shake off the burden of virginity and there'd been bits of fun in various bushes by the coast but the feeling in his chest at the sight of Clodagh Reynolds was something entirely different. She'd graduated from Dior to CK One and John Paul longed to nick a bottle for himself; it was a brilliant thing, a scent that could be worn by a guy and a girl, a sleek glass bottle that could make two people one. By the end of the night he was sure he was wrapped up in some of it: Jason was up in a spare bedroom with some chick from Loreto while John Paul stayed outside freezing his balls off, a small price to pay, because Clodagh Reynolds had shared a smoke, then a whole packet, with him.

'All right, how about heads you give us a kiss and tails I give you a kiss?'

'Chancer. How about heads you take a long walk off a short pier and tails you take a bungee jump without a rope?'

John Paul's turn to laugh.

'You know it's the season of goodwill and all that.'

'What, think you're some charity case? It's the second of December, not exactly Christmas.'

'You'll have plenty of time to pick me a good present so.'

She was still standing there, a nod to her friends through the French doors: *it's okay*.

'If I throw three heads in a row, you give us a kiss. Whatever you want, just a Christmas peck, no pressure. Tails, I'll leave you alone, let you go back to the conversation inside: you know, they were talking about breaking out the Scrabble and I don't want to ruin your night.'

'All right, hurry up though, I'm freezing to death here, seriously.'

'*Seriously?*'

'Fuck off!'

Heads. Heads. A smile between them, a spark.

Heads.

John Paul put on his best irresistible face, confident and vulnerable at once.

Clodagh examined the coin. She was sharp, a year above him in school, six As in her Junior Cert. Out of his league, but still she stood in front of him.

'This one's messed up: it's heavier on one side where the crest is. It will always land on heads.'

A different face, one John Paul had never made to a girl before: *yeah, you've caught me, you've got me*.

'You fucking bastard,' she said, giving him a thump on the arm.

'Fucking' said softly, the thump a way of bringing them closer. He held her arm there, the two of them looking at each other in the dark. Kissing was different with Clodagh Reynolds, an activity unrelated to 'snogging'. She controlled John Paul's excitable tongue, slowed him down to her rhythm, the meeting of mouths somehow new, proof of the brilliance of the whole world, somehow related to the stars in the sky above.

6

Wonderwall (1996)

They didn't know what it was; they did know that, for the other, they were it.

7

Tablets (1997)

The trick was to seize opportunities.

John Paul hadn't been thrilled when Granny Doyle forced him into the Legion of Mary after a school report that even she couldn't ignore, but he'd found something about the organization that wasn't a complete fucking waste of time. John Paul skipped the meetings and the rosaries but he loved volunteering at the nursing home on Sundays. He'd turn up, chugging a bottle of Lucozade for his hangover and greeting Mrs Nugent, who was also a volunteer, not that she ever did any work. Damien worked in the kitchen, scrubbing pots with some sour face on him, but John Paul loved serving the lunch to the guests, a familiar joke for each table.

'What's on the menu today?' Mrs Lacey would say, and John Paul would say 'caviar', and she'd say 'in that case, fill me up', and then they'd laugh as he put a plate of grey meat and boiled potatoes in front of her. John Paul would flirt with Miss Hardy at the next table and Mr Davis would pretend to be jealous: 'Pistols at dawn,' he'd say, 'we'll have to settle this with pistols at dawn.' Mr Lally would say something incomprehensible in a thick Cork accent and John Paul would smile and nod, all that was required. Mrs Garvey would say how well he was looking, ask if he was 'doing a line' with a young one, John Paul would say he was saving himself for Sister Angela. The nuns were great *craic* too, teasing him about his wedding plans with Sister Angela and giving him time for a smoke break with Mrs Nugent. He had an idea, actually, that he might get a job there instead of wasting time with school (which was a conspiracy: every teacher out to get him). They could use someone strong to help move some of the auld ones, heavy as heifers some of them were. He could help out in the main kitchen downstairs: it would be a handy bit of money and he'd be able to get a place of his own soon (Clo would love that), especially with the tablet income.

The tablets were a great trick: textbook example of seizing your opportunities. It had started with Mrs Flannigan. The daft old duck kept getting lost so John Paul escorted her to her room and there she told him about all the extras she had. A favour to her; that was how it started. John Paul didn't even keep any of the money himself, just wanted to help her because of how bare the room was and how happy she was with the frames for the photos of the grandkids. A small cut the next time, commission. It was easy enough – lots of tablets lying around, expired, no longer needed. John Paul made sure none of them were dangerous. Many of them were basically fancy paracetamol and it was a joke selling them off at schools. It was even easier at clubs; young ones would give you fifty quid for a Tic Tac if they thought it was E. Taking the tablets from the dead residents didn't sit entirely right with John Paul. But better him than the grasping relatives, those creatures that popped up when one of the rooms emptied, when they would have been hard pressed to find the nursing home on a map before. John Paul was doing people a favour, no harm to anybody, a little extra cash for himself, his own apartment on the cards soon, a place Clo would love; he'd get her a welcome mat in zebra print.

*

But then some fucker called Plato intervened.

Clodagh had started at Trinity; it was inevitable that she'd have a different crowd, no matter the promises to wait for John Paul as he finished sixth year. But then she'd devoured Plato's *Symposium*

313

under a tree one afternoon, going over it with her highlighter, tracking the rungs of Plato's ladder of love. Or, Diotima's ladder of love, Clodagh supposed: Diotima, the woman who gave the best speech about love in the book, who had no need for a lover, who would definitely be played by Meryl Streep in the movie. Love, according to Diotima, was about transcending the physical, moving from sex to an appreciation of beautiful bodies, to an appreciation of beautiful customs, on and on, up and up, rung by rung, until you were on top of a ladder looking across a wide forest, gazing up at the beauty of beauty itself. It was related to the theory of forms, that was what the lecturer had said: there were abstract forms that were invariably superior to their cheap manifestations in the material world – no chair could be as perfect as the idea of a chair, no beautiful boy as worthy of admiration as beauty itself. Clodagh felt something stir inside her, beyond her body or mind: who needed a boyfriend when there was philosophy?

So, Plato was the cad responsible for the first sundering of Clodagh and John Paul. Or, perhaps, more prosaically, it was Niamh Rooney, the floozy from the Gaeltacht who John Paul claimed meant 'nothing at all, Clo, I promise'.

It didn't matter to Clodagh that she was breaking up the gang. The nights they'd spent together – Clo and J.P. and Jason and Dee, even their names in synch – were nothing to Clodagh, she probably didn't remember the night at the Plex when they'd raced down the bowling lanes until they were kicked out or the time they did mushrooms in the Wicklow mountains until Jason swore he saw a bear, something he still hadn't heard the last of. Or the afternoons in Clodagh's bedroom when they lay on the bare floorboards and looked into each other's souls. No, Clodagh didn't care: she had her own Trinity friends, didn't mind that John Paul could hardly hang around after Jason and Dee like some third tit.

So Clodagh was the domino that set it all in motion. John Paul might not have punched Rory O'Donoghue otherwise. The reasons

314

were 80 per cent frustration and 20 per cent altruism; Damien would always be a stupid sap who never thanked his brother for what he did. Things might still have worked out okay – the trick was to keep moving – and the mood might have shifted, John Paul continuing on at the nursing home, looking to pick up work there.

And then Damien, fucking Damien, told the nuns about the tablets and ruined everything.

*

The trick was to disappear.

If John Paul got deep enough inside the duvet he might just manage it and his head would be free of any thoughts about the expulsion or Clodagh changing her phone number or whatever the police might do.

'John Paul!'

Granny Doyle couldn't leave him be.

'Open the door, I'm carrying a tray!'

'I'm not hungry!' John Paul called from the depths of the duvet.

'I'm after making rashers.'

Go fuck your rashers off a cliff, John Paul almost shouted, because all he wanted was a spliff and to disappear. If he pretended to be asleep she might just deposit the tray and shuffle back downstairs. No such luck. She was determined to get in the door and that was when it happened: the tray dropped, rashers and tea tumbling to the floor and landing atop a pyramid of clothes. John Paul clenched his eyes: if he pretended he couldn't hear she might just fuck off.

'Get up out of bed, would you!'

Up the duvet came, wrenched with surprising force.

Granny Doyle dropped it on top of the ruined breakfast and the clothes: what did it matter?

John Paul curled into a ball, shocked at this sudden exposure. How dare she! Barging in, while he was in boxers and T-shirt, a creature not fit for her eyes, definitely not ready for daylight.

315

'Some light and fresh air, that's all you need,' Granny Doyle said, wrenching open the curtains. 'Come on, now, up out of bed before I drag you!'

The tablets had broken her. Mrs Brennan's stolen loaves and Mr Kehoe's smashed windows could all be brushed away with *boys will be boys*, but here was something that she couldn't deny. The whole street knew: Mrs Brennan fat with the gloating; Mrs McGinty shadowed with the thought that the Legion of Mary had been compromised; Mrs Donnelly keeping Jason safely inside, for *her* children made it through their Leaving Certs. Granny Doyle looked at the pathetic creature curled in front of her and saw him for what he was: another bitter disappointment the Lord had sent to test her.

'Come on now, get—'

'Don't touch me!'

John Paul surprised himself with the rage in his voice; it was her fault though, for pulling off the duvet, him practically naked. He managed to stand.

'Just chill, all right, there's no hurry, is there?'

'Plenty of things for you to be getting on with: you can start by cleaning up this mess!'

'I will!'

'A waste of good bacon, that is.'

'I didn't ask you to make it, did I?'

This hurt her more than anything: what use was she if she couldn't feed him? John Paul wanted the words back as soon as he saw her face – he would have knelt down on the ground and gulped the tea from the carpet – but then the guilt got at him and the only thing he wanted to do was rescue the duvet and hide inside it.

'This room is a holy disgrace!'

John Paul shrugged. Damien had moved into Rosie's room – what was the point of keeping things tidy?

'Once you've got this done we can get you sorted in another school.'

'There's no point: it's all a load of bollix.'

Granny Doyle found the thunder in her voice.

'What did you say?'

There was no use pretending any more.

'I said it's a whole heap of bollix and I don't want anything to do with it.'

Granny Doyle had her hand raised before she stopped herself. He almost wished she would slap him.

'You'll watch your language when you're under this roof.'

'Or what?'

This deserved a slap, he was asking for one, standing right in front of her, taunting; if she was going to fuck around with his morning, she could learn her lesson.

'Just mind your language.'

Granny Doyle was backing down but all John Paul could see in every direction was red flags; the fight was coming whether she wanted it or not.

'Or what? You'll kick me out? Two down, two to go, you'll have the house to yourself in no time!'

These were words he definitely wanted to take back, as soon as he said them; he didn't even need to see the collapse in Granny Doyle's face to know that he'd gone too far. They never talked about Peg or Rosie. Usually, John Paul did the opposite, bringing home a stream of chat to keep things light. Until he'd gone ahead and shoved her face in it: she should slap him to the ground, maybe he'd disappear then.

Granny Doyle walked to the window very slowly.

'I don't know what's gotten into you.'

This is me! John Paul longed to yell, but he was out of words now.

Granny Doyle yanked at the edges of the curtains. She'd already opened them, but clearly they could go further, off the poles if necessary.

'Fresh air and a decent amount of light, that's what you need! It's indecent to be keeping the sun out at this hour. You'll clean up that mess and then we'll sort you out.'

She turned and saw him still gawping at her.

'And get dressed, would you! And a bath! You stink.'

She couldn't hide the disgust in her voice.

'You're as bad as your father, do you know that?'

This was the slap she was capable of. John Paul thought he might topple over. Rage he could take but the sadness of that sentence was too much: he needed the curtains shut, the duvet around him, all sound to disappear. That was the trick he hadn't mastered – the ability to disappear – though he had an idea how; he'd do it in the bath the next day. The trick was to stay ahead of the game, to get out before you got done.

8

Nokia 3110 Phone (1998)

'Ah no, don't worry, love: sure we'll say a prayer to Saint Ultán!'

Mrs Nugent tittered and went to light up another cigarette. John Paul helped her with the flame, difficult with the winter wind on Clougheally's beach. He had another fag too; this was a rule, no limit on the amount he could light up to get through the day.

Mrs Nugent continued to extol Saint Ultán's virtues.

'Don't I always say, you're better off praying to one of the more obscure ones! Can you imagine what Saint Anthony's phone lines are like and poor Saint Jude, I'd say the man needs a saint of his own. No, no, pick some fella that nobody's ever heard of, says I, and I'll tell you what, Saint Ultán has never once not found me keys! I'd say he's glad of the work, wouldn't you? Don't worry, love, he'll find your phone!'

Whatever, John Paul's shrug said. This was another rule: not caring. To care too much was dangerous; caring could lead to razor blades pressed against skin.

John Paul pulled down the sleeves of his hoodie; if he couldn't wear a duvet, he'd hide here instead. Another rule: always cover his wrists. *You'll have sick scars*, Jason said, when he came to the hospital, aiming for the old jokes, faltering when he saw that wouldn't work. Dee was worse, floods of tears and shite streaming out of her, Clodagh to blame, definitely, she'd turned right snobby since she'd gone to college, but Dee would be there for him – for ever! – which only made John Paul long to tell her that he'd never really liked her and that her highlights looked shit. The deep of him was dark, that was the problem. He could cover the scars with his sleeves, but there was a black hole inside him; it would swallow him, eventually.

'I tell you, we'll comb this beach later,' Mrs Nugent said. 'We'll find it!'

Whatever, John Paul's exhalation of smoke spelt, though underneath his *fuck this world* face, his heart gave a tiny twist, a pea bothering a princess; he did want to find his missing phone because it had all of Clodagh's old texts saved. It didn't matter that she had a new phone with a zebra-case and the capacity to store picture messages from whatever Trinity twerp she was seeing; in his saved messages on the Nokia 3110 Clodagh Reynolds professed her love for John Paul Doyle in ALL CAPS.

'Janey, maybe I should get Saint Ultán to sort out this weather,' Mrs Nugent said as the drizzle started. 'Doesn't he know I came to Clougheally to get my tan?'

Whatever, John Paul's shrug wanted to say, though he coughed a laugh out too. Mrs Nugent had the trick of it, she had the words to pierce through the armour and tickle that blackened heart of his. She was the only one who knew what to do, playing penny poker with him and going for strolls and knowing when to keep the chat in the air and when to let silence settle and – crucially – always having a packet of fags at the ready. He couldn't bear the gaze of the Doyles, looking at him like he was saviour of the family or the scourge of it, depending upon whose eyes were involved. Mrs Nugent saw him, the worst of him, and still thought he was worth looking at, a task that should have been Clodagh's but she hadn't returned his gaze when he'd thrown pebbles then rocks at her window and her eyes hadn't known where to look when she'd come to visit him in the hospital, for all of five minutes; it would have been better if she'd worn sunglasses.

'Should we head back?' Mrs Nugent asked, looking up at the clouds.

John Paul didn't answer, but his legs led them to a bit of the cliff they could shelter under. He couldn't face the house; the Doyles would be waiting there and one of the major rules was to avoid their gaze. Aunty Mary clearly blamed him for the presence of the lot of them in her house, disturbing the curated quiet of her Christmas and New Year's. Damien didn't know where to look, spent all his time in his room, wanking to the Virgin Mary or listening to the Corrs, who the fuck cared. Granny Doyle was the worst. She was in early in the morning, yanking the curtains open. *Go on and mow the lawn, would you? I've a list of messages for you to get. Mary needs the gutters cleaned, come on now, up out of bed, we've no time for this.* She'd already decided that what John Paul had done in the bath was taboo, 'a little accident' the preferred vocabulary for the events of late 1997.

John Paul fumbled for another cigarette, every second without it a terror and a torture, the wind out to get him, until Mrs Nugent cupped her hands and then – *relief!* – the pins and needles in his head stopped.

Mrs Nugent leant in for a light and let out a titter.

'I hope you haven't dragged me over here to seduce me: what will Sister Angela say?'

John Paul managed a laugh.

Oh, there'll be murder, he might have said once, but the sentence was stuck.

'Sure, we won't tell her,' Mrs Nugent said.

They were all asking for him at the nursing home, Mrs Nugent had said. Even the nuns. Who'd petitioned to the guards on his behalf: he'd have some community service to do, though that was what got him in trouble in the first place. Sister Angela had sat with him in the hospital and she hadn't a word of judgement. *They could say a prayer*, she'd said, and they had, 'Our Fathers' and 'Hail Marys' stones that he didn't need to think about, the familiar words helpful in quieting his mind.

'God, maybe we should ask Saint Ultán for some feathers,' Mrs Nugent said, blinking as the rain found a way to move sideways. 'I'd say they'd come in handy here, though poor craters, wouldn't you be wanting more than feathers to get through three hundred years in this place?'

She looked out at the boulder where the Children of Lir were said to have huddled as swans, the same rock that the triplets had dived off into the sea together, back when they were eight and oblivious, incredible that a leap from such a piddly little thing could have seemed so terrifying.

'Though who knows what Clougheally was like back then,' Mrs Nugent continued. 'Maybe it was hopping: jammers with tourists and theme parks and discos to rival Dublin.'

John Paul coughed out a laugh.

'Tanning salons,' he said, surprised at the words coming out loud.

Fuck it, though, wasn't he only seventeen and the world ahead of him? He'd climbed up onto that rock once, back when it had scared the shite out of him; he could get out of this hole. He didn't need a Leaving Cert or Clodagh Reynolds. Wasn't there nothing that John Paul Doyle couldn't do?

'Hookah bars,' John Paul said, earning a laugh from Mrs Nugent.

Talking about shite would be a rope to climb up. This would be another rule. Keep things light and breezy. Avoid the dark.

'One of them inflatable slides down to the sea,' Mrs Nugent said.

He wouldn't rummage around for some missing phone; he'd get a new one with his own fancy fucking cover.

'Bouncy castles on the beach,' John Paul said.

He'd pick himself up. Keep going. The trick was to keep moving.

'Them toadstools with the waterfalls that they have at Mosney,' Mrs Nugent said.

The rule was not to look any of the Doyles in the eye.

'A big casino at the edge of the cliff,' John Paul said.

He'd keep things light. The trick was to avoid Clodagh Reynolds and Granny Doyle. The rule was not to care too much.

'Ah, they would have had great *craic* altogether,' Mrs Nugent said, laughing. 'I'd say they asked to stay here another three hundred years.'

9

Furby (1999)

The trick was to keep things light.

'Isn't this the most ridiculous contraption you've ever seen?' Granny Doyle asked the porch, thrilled.

'It's all the rage,' John Paul said, holding up the bright purple and yellow toy for display.

'Go on, say hello, they have their own language – Furbish!'

'A load of nonsense it is,' Granny Doyle said, chuffed. 'He's even trying to teach it my name, aren't you?'

'Oh lovely,' Mrs Fay said.

'Lord preserve us! The better to call out your name when it murders you at night,' Mrs McGinty said. 'Those eyes have the devil inside, I'd swear on it!'

'Furby reeeeesha,' the Furby said.

(Mrs Nugent didn't say anything, because she'd died earlier in the year, Saint Ultán fuck all use in the face of cancer. A shame – Mrs Nugent would have loved the Furby, a successor of sorts to the Tamagotchi that she'd borrowed from one of her grandchildren, back when she was still alive, leaning forward on her chair and trying to get a rise out of Mrs McGinty by mentioning electronic poo.)

'Mind you, you'd want to be careful what you say in front of them,' Mrs Donnelly said, sitting in Mrs Nugent's chair. 'You wouldn't know what they'd repeat. Denise is processing very *sensitive* information at the bank: did I tell you she got a promotion?'

'So you mentioned,' Mrs McGinty said.

'She's run off her feet, so she is,' Mrs Donnelly continued. 'And did I tell you Jason has a summer internship at the Central Bank?'

'You did.'

'Off to Amsterdam for the weekend, he is, isn't that brilliant! Mind you, that kind of schedule wouldn't be for everyone, it's very *demanding*. I'd say you're happy in the building site, aren't you, John Paul?'

The trick was not to let the likes of Mrs Donnelly get to him.

'I am.'

'Well for you, like father like son!'

The trick was to punch something, as soon as he could.

'I always say, once you have your health, aren't you doing grand? Mind you, I wouldn't say no to a weekend in Amsterdam either, ha!'

Mrs McGinty stiffened in her chair.

'Goodness gracious, if you don't take a breath this poor contraption will never get a word in.'

John Paul grinned at the width of Granny Doyle's smile. The Furby had done the trick; it would keep her happy for days. Damien had moved out and John Paul did some night shifts as a kitchen porter, so the Furby might make her less lonely in the dark. *He could get a different job*, Granny Doyle said, but that wasn't what he wanted: the trick was to keep his distance. The trick was to keep her content with bits of plastic, because the things she asked for (love; time) were too much for him to trade with now.

The trick was to keep things light.

'Furby meeesho dooopla,' said the Furby.

'There you go,' John Paul said. 'Isn't it already trying to say Doyle?'

10

Smiley Face Stress Ball (2000)

The trick was to keep smiling.

People can hear your smile over the phone, his team leader said, like a wanker. He left John Paul alone, though; his stats couldn't be argued with so he could bounce as many stress balls off the ceiling as he wanted. John Paul didn't need to finish school to sell shit to people. Selling phone plans turned out to be mostly about the chat and John Paul could switch between banter like a pianist, *sound as a pound* for the students, flirty *hiyas* for the mammies at home, *God blesses* for the auld ones, all business when he needed to be, the weekend rates to Warsaw at the tip of his tongue.

Smiling was useful for the part-time promotions work he picked up, too. Most of the staff were girls with blonde hair and a thick layer of fake tan and self-belief, but John Paul did well too, grinning at festival-goers as he handed out free ice cream samples or cajoled them into filling out a quick survey or asked them if they wanted to enter a draw to win a car. He was a natural, his manager said, before she slept with him.

Smiling was helpful too for when he slept with some of the promotions girls; it did well to look happy as they Maniaced away on the dance floor or Woo-hooed up and down in some field that was meant to be a festival. A smile can stretch as big as a black hole, that was what he liked to think, dancing fiercer and faster if he felt any dark feelings bristling inside. Pills were great at keeping his mouth fixed in its *Time of My Life!* position, *I love you, I do* easier to say with some tabs inside.

And smiling got him up and down Dunluce Crescent. Bat away Mrs McGinty's tut with a grin. Smile like he couldn't be happier when Mrs Donnelly asked if he knew Jason was off to Slovenia. Grin like his teeth might crack when he saw Jason's 00 licence plate. And smile and nod at whatever Granny Doyle said.

Would he not make it to Mass with her in the morning?

Would he not stay for a bit of dinner?

Would he not get a job with more regular hours?

No, John Paul said, as he nodded his head and grinned, he'd catch the evening Mass or pick something up in town or look for something else soon, all unfortunate events, but the great thing about a smile was that it made everything you said seem positive, even a refusal. Refusing Granny Doyle was absolutely necessary; the trick was to keep everyone at a distance, he couldn't forget that.

11

High Heel (2001)

Rules, though, were made to be broken, especially when life could be like a fairy tale, Clodagh Reynolds at the Trinity Ball, auburn hair tied up, gorgeous as ever, one gold heel trapped in the cobblestones. It had to be Fate, because John Paul was only escorting one of Jason Donnelly's mates, her name already forgotten, because their love wasn't fated; *they* weren't like Ross and Rachel from *Friends*.

'Clo,' John Paul shouted, her heel in his hand. Then she turned and he smiled and all the lights in Front Square flashed fluorescent at once; it was a wonder there wasn't a power cut.

Clodagh couldn't help returning his smile, because there was John Paul in a tux, her heel in his hand, an excellent occurrence as she was a bit pissed and she'd left her bag with the spare shoes somewhere, and the cobblestones had always been out to get her, had probably been laid in the 15whatevers with the express purpose of thwarting Clodagh Reynolds, except that, actually, they were her friends, the equivalents of fairy-tale mice, bringing John Paul back to her, her heel in his hand, her name on his lips, bright lights transforming all the stones. Clodagh knew then that it was tough titties for Marcus and whoever John Paul was escorting; she was going to shag John Paul, preferably in the Provost's garden, and that was that.

12

Euro-holder (2002)

The trick was to bring her offerings, bits of plastic to keep her distracted. Then, instead of 'I don't know what you're at with Clodagh Reynolds again, do you not remember (… *the little accident* hung in the air, unsayable)' Granny Doyle would hold up the purple coin-holder and say: 'Ah, what is this nonsense!'

John Paul could write the script.

'Goodness, don't they think of everything!' Mrs Fay would say.

'No proper punt would fit in those tiny holes,' Mrs McGinty would say. 'The only thing you can trust the European Union to make is a mess!'

'Mind you, won't the euros be very handy for the travelling?' Mrs Donnelly would say, as if any of them ever went beyond the Howth Road. 'Did I tell you that Jason's off to Thailand?'

Thank you, Granny Doyle would have to say, instead of *will you be home tonight?* or *are you sure you can trust that one?* or *did I tell you Grace Fay broke up with her boyfriend, a lovely young one she is, she was always very fond of you.* John Paul would be down the drive before she got any of that out, headphones in the ears before he reached the gate, leaving Granny Doyle with the sad circle of plastic to hold coins she didn't want – not that it mattered, because the trick was to keep moving forwards.

13

The *Irish Times* Property Supplement (2003)

'What about that one?'

Clodagh rolled her eyes: *I've told you.*

'I know, I know,' John Paul said. 'Even-numbered postcode. But Croke Park is crying out for regeneration. It might be funeral homes and flats now, but give it a decade and you'll get vertigo from the skyscrapers.'

They were in the Gravity Bar of the Guinness Storehouse, the city laid in front of them. John Paul moved around the curved glass window and pointed towards O'Connell Street.

'That one?'

Clodagh folded her arms; she wasn't going to be moved by John Paul's dimples. Finding the right apartment was a serious business – she had a colour-coded spreadsheet and the property section of the *Irish Times* marked up – and she didn't have time for John Paul's messing.

'We'd have a great view,' John Paul said.

'I'd chuck you off the fucking top.'

'Very well situated for amenities.'

'Every shade of fast-food vomit on our doorstep!'

'And it would only cost what, a couple of mill?'

Clodagh rolled her eyes but she couldn't resist a tiny smile; she was powerless against the dimples of John Paul Doyle. She turned to beckon to Jason Donnelly, who sleeked over with his latest girlfriend.

'Tell J.P. we're not moving into the Spire!'

Jason Donnelly laughed and raised up his pint of Guinness in salute. Jason already had a couple of 'properties' alongside some consultancy job in the Irish Financial Services Centre that John Paul didn't understand; ah, but he was sound, even if he went by 'Jay' now.

'Niche,' Jason said. 'You could probably carve out some space in the middle.'

'Prime real estate!' John Paul said. 'And it's not like they're using it for anything: stupid cunts built a giant telegraph pole and you can't even walk up to see the view. That's what we can do, Clo, we'll charge people to …'

Clodagh was already deep in conversation with Jason's girlfriend.

The smile froze on John Paul's face as he gazed at the Spire. It would be great to live inside, he thought, madly; it could be a cocoon for the two of them, where nobody could find them, all sleek and steel and perfect. Better at least than the task of actually finding an apartment, the numbers involved terrifying, even with Clo's parents helping; it was enough to stir the black hole inside him.

John Paul remembered to smile.

'My round,' he said, even though Jason could probably have bought the bar if he wanted.

'Or I could swipe us a couple of fresh ones,' he added, eyeing the many nearly full complimentary pints that tourists, content with a sip and a photo, had abandoned.

'Ha,' Jason Donnelly said (he was sound, even if he said 'ha' instead of laughing), so John Paul laughed and headed to the bar, ignoring the criminal waste of good Guinness and the chance to pull a fast one. They weren't thirteen and knocking about St Anne's Park any more; the trick was to grow up.

Or, the trick was to grow up in the right direction, towards a Southside postcode and another property to rent out in Marino and a Friday night where they could stand above their shining city and watch the sun gleam against the glass as they thought about where next they might descend, like gods.

The trick was to have aspirations.

The trick was to pay by credit card.

The trick was, whatever the situation, to always say *Cheers!*

14

Couch (2004)

'Cheers!' John Paul shouted, clinking his flute against Clodagh's.

Careful of the couch! stuck in Clodagh's mouth; she would not turn into her mother.

'Cheers!' Clodagh said, sitting down into the couch and looking at the magnolia walls in front of them.

Not for the first time, John Paul threw the keycard up and down in the air. It was sleek and aerodynamic and nothing like the chubby keys that opened 7 Dunluce Crescent. Clodagh sipped her Prosecco; she wouldn't tell him to stop. Not for the first time, John Paul admired the couch.

'Amazing, isn't it!'

Cream and classy, the type of couch that would recoil before a patterned carpet.

'It's great!'

'Admit it: you were worried when I said I'd ordered something.'

'I wish you'd asked me—'

'Because you thought I'd deck out the place like a Batmobile or something—'

'I did fear the presence of a ping-pong table.'

'There's still space!'

Clodagh took another gulp.

'But this is perfect, isn't it? The Platonic ideal of a couch!'

The trick was to have aspirations. John Paul had googled the little book that had sundered them, the first time, and he thought he had the measure of Plato.

'I don't know if that's exactly what Plato had in mind when he said there was an ideal form of everything.'

'Plato didn't have the internet! No way Plato could plonk his arse on this baby and say that some *idea* of a couch is better.'

'Plato didn't have an arse.'

'Of course he did! Aren't they all falling over each other trying to sit beside Plato?'

'That was Socrates,' Clodagh said, although she wasn't sure; she'd transferred into business and economics after first year, for the best, as she wasn't sure that philosophy would be much use in setting up a telecommunications empire.

'Whoever,' John Paul said, pouring more Prosecco into their glasses and giving Clodagh's arse a playful pinch. 'The moral is that there *is* an ideal couch on earth: you just have to find the right arse to share it with.'

Clodagh stood up.

'Keep the seat warm, will you, I'm going to go and see if I can find this Plato fella; I hear he's a ride.'

John Paul grinned, a proper smile that came from somewhere deep inside. The trick was to find smiles like these and capture them; if he could sell something to produce genuine smiles he'd be a millionaire, could buy a warehouse of couches and spend the afternoon fucking Clodagh Reynolds across each and every one.

15

Mitre (2005)

The trick was to seize every opportunity.

'I've had a brilliant idea,' John Paul said, diving down beside Clodagh on the couch in Lillie's Bordello.

'Go on.'

'Well, okay, this is a bit mad.'

'Shocking.'

He ignored this, the idea too brilliant to be contained.

'What if I became a pope?'

Maybe it was the coke or maybe it was the espresso martini from earlier but John Paul was certain this idea was a keeper; it was destiny, in fact. Pope John Paul II had died the other day and John Paul saw the empty space, as clear as a wall crying out for a billboard. He heard the fuss in Granny Doyle's porch, Mrs McGinty indignant that the shops wouldn't be closing for a national day of mourning. He saw the shock of the young Poles in the call centre, where he was now a centre manager; whatever their feelings about the Church, they had affection for the first Polish Pope, may he rest in peace, and here was the gap that John Paul was born to fill. Ireland was due a pope but not one who bothered about Mass or sins or all the shackles they'd shaken off; no, it was time for a new pope for a new millennium and John Paul had an idea for a video in his head – getting baptized in his boxers with a bucket of ice chucked over him – and this he knew he could sell. Selling nothing was his speciality and here was something, an ideal form for the ages. The idea was clear in his head – brilliant! – but he wasn't sure how it came out, because Clodagh had her forehead wrinkled from trying to understand.

'You're serious?'

'I am,' John Paul said immediately.

'Pope John Paul III?'

John Paul beamed; the trick was to have aspirations.

'Exactly.'

16

Camcorder (2006)

The trick was to seize every opportunity.

There was Pope John Paul III blessing the opening of the Dundrum Shopping Centre and there he was in Waterford steering a tall ship into port and there his mitre was in Down, bobbing outside Hillsborough Castle as Mary McAleese met the Queen and there he was in Tralee, anointing the edgier Roses in the Sacrament of Hotness, until they stripped him starkers, only a well-placed bouquet to keep his modesty.

The Official Miracles of John Paul Doyle courted controversy. Pope John Paul III walked on water buoyed by natural gas or 'healed' Jason Donnelly of his Man U support or performed exorcisms on people with poor phone plans. *Ah, now, I wouldn't know anything about that!* the catchphrase for whenever he got into hot water, but that was seldom; he was good at judging the temperature of the zeitgeist, as adept as any Beyoncé or Steve Jobs (or, why not, any Michael Flatley or Mary Robinson). Pope John Paul III was achieving his goal – ubiquity! – and he was chasing history's heels, like Forrest Gump with a better business plan.

So, inevitably, there was Pope John Paul III at Fianna Fáil's tent at the Galway Races, ignoring the hippies protesting against a gas pipe outside, elbows edging instead against the Very Important, as he promised to bless a new complex of condos and professed that he wouldn't know anything about running for office and turned to the camera with a huge grin to say: 'Now where do I collect the award for Best Hat?'

17

iPhone (2007)

The trick was to throw up when necessary.

John Paul found his reflection in the bathroom mirror: much better. The floor stayed put under his feet. He'd be grand; of course he would. Damien, on the other hand, was making a right production out of getting sick in one of the other stalls. John Paul longed to bang on the door and tell him to stop retching and groaning and get it over with – he'd feel much better! – but it wasn't his job to look after his family.

No, his job was to smile, which he did, a gracious grin for the prat in the suit who didn't get that the bathroom wasn't the place for pictures. The price of fame: he was happy to pay. John Paul smiled at his reflection; against all odds, he'd made it.

'Pope J.P.'s in the house! Wasssupp!'

It was Jason Donnelly, barrelling into the bathroom as if he owned the place. (There was a chance he did.)

Ah, but he was sound, even when he put on an American accent.

'How's the form?' John Paul asked.

'Cracking. You sure you don't want me to set you up with Gosia's mate – you seen the legs on her?'

Jason had half of Eastern Europe rotating through his bedroom and he was sure to let you know it; ah, but he was sound.

'I'm grand,' John Paul said, holding up his engagement ring. 'And anyways, I've got an appointment with your ma later!'

'Ha!'

Damien emerged from the stall; John Paul had forgotten what a magnet Jason Donnelly was for him.

'Damo Doyle! What's the buzz?'

Damien nodded, concentrating on keeping in the vomit as Jason slapped his back.

'Congrats, congrats! Have to say, I never thought I'd see the Greens getting into bed with Fianna Fáil!'

'I guess it's worth keeping your options open.'

'Ha! A man after my philosophy! I think it'll be good for the country, though, all this sustainability stuff is very on brand.'

Damien looked like he might vomit over Jason Donnelly's one-thousand-euro suit; a dark part of John Paul wanted him to.

'You'll have to get Damo's deets for the stag do,' John Paul said, before Jason got going about sustainable investment funds and the need to keep the red tape snipped.

'Sure thing,' Jason said. 'Have to get you some carbon credits too, ha!'

'Right,' Damien said.

It took a moment for it to sink in.

'Wait, where are we going?'

John Paul caught Damien's eye before Jason answered. He had to play this carefully. His best innocent expression. *Ah, now, I wouldn't know anything about that!* The truth, or part of it, for John Paul did want Damien to come – he was surprised by the force of this feeling – and despite the dangers of the black hole and all the rules (don't dwell; stay away from the Doyles; the trick was to keep moving) there was a part of John Paul Doyle that wanted nothing more than for the lot of them to be together again, happy.

Jason answered Damien's question, his accent ready.

'Get ready, baby, cause we're going to New York city!'

Series VIII:
Boom

(2007)

1

Clock (2007)

Peg looked at the clock on the library wall. Twenty to six; she'd definitely be late by the time she got downtown. She picked up another folder and sifted through the documents. The stacks were blissfully quiet on the weekend. Peg had the pleasure of a magazine's records to work through: she greatly preferred archiving the impersonal files of institutions to the mess of working on somebody's personal papers. Here, she was happy. Staples removed. Alphabet adhered to. Order imposed.

A quarter to, somehow. She ignored the buzz of her phone. Another folder: she could get through that. *She* didn't have months to drift about the world or slouch on somebody else's couch. *She* had a real job: she didn't pretend to be a pope or spend her days holding up cardboard signs that cars sped past. Peg Doyle had come to New York with nothing but a green card and a rucksack and now she had an education and a job she loved; *she* deserved this life.

Including the house in Clougheally? Peg had no idea what had motivated Aunty Mary. Guilt, she supposed. *You stupid, stupid girl,* Aunty Mary had said and Peg had dedicated a life to proving her wrong. Why had Aunty Mary left her the house? She didn't want it, not a brick. Why had Rosie told her the truth about Damien telling Granny Doyle about Ruadhan? She didn't want to know it, not a sentence. All she wanted was to be left in peace, *A Manual of Archive Administration* the only company she required.

Five to! Peg tensed. They were all waiting for her in the bar downtown: John Paul had arranged it all, like some magician, the trickster. If she wanted to get downtown in time, she needed to leave immediately.

Peg picked up a fresh folder and wrote out its title in impeccable handwriting. Plenty of other documents to deal with first.

2

Three Pint Glasses (2007)

John Paul came back from the bar with their pints like a returning hero.

'Check that out!' he said, for the pints had shamrocks carved into their foam.

'Cool,' Damien said, nervous.

Rosie didn't say anything.

John Paul would not be deterred. He had found the Blarney Stone, like a pioneering explorer; Fate, surely, that such a bar would be near their downtown hotel.

Ten past. He hadn't bought one for Peg; he'd get her one as soon as she walked in the door. He hoped she wasn't somebody who wanted wine; the bar had more varieties of sport on telly than bottles, he'd bet on it. They could go somewhere else, if she wanted; she could provide a local's perspective beyond the blur of bars and burgers and billboards.

'Sláinte!' John Paul said.

'Sláinte!' Damien repeated, his hand shaking.

He was nervous, the poor thing. They all were. Ten past, still, of course. She'd be here soon.

'Would you say that at home?' Rosie said, the judgemental cow.

John Paul could take a slagging.

'Begorrah, I would, to be sure, to be sure!'

Rosie rolled her eyes but there was the hint of a smile too; he could still manage that.

'We can do some last-minute wedding planning,' John Paul said, *while we're waiting* hanging in the air.

'Lucky us,' Damien said, which for Damien was a joke, so John Paul laughed.

Rosie said, 'Cheers.'

Drinks were clinked, supped, returned to the table. They hadn't been talking while he was at the bar, John Paul noticed, adjusting to this new dynamic.

A quarter past. Fashionably late; she was a New Yorker now, sure.

'So, take your pick for your table partners: Mrs McGinty or Mrs Donnelly?'

They didn't have parents to complain to each other about, so they would slag off their ancient nemeses from Dunluce Crescent; this was safe territory, confirmed by a laugh from Damien, an eye-roll from Rosie.

'You're really selling this event,' Damien said, and John Paul laughed again, wanting the three of them to have a relationship where laughter was easy.

'Have you invited the whole street?' Rosie asked.

'Of course,' John Paul said. 'I wanted to have the afters there, but Clo wouldn't have it.'

'You can sit beside Mrs McGinty, Damien. You can reminisce about the Legion of Mary.'

A slight edge to Rosie's voice, something else that John Paul didn't remember.

'No thanks.'

Something that had not changed: Damien still turned beetroot at the slenderest of slaggings.

'We'll be at the family table, though, won't we?' Damien said, his voice suddenly serious.

'Ah yeah, absolutely,' John Paul said, realizing how happy it was going to make him to have them there; it didn't do to start a new family without an old one to wish you well. 'I just thought you might appreciate a little quality time with some of your favourites.'

'Do you have a separate chair for the Furby?'

This was another surprise, to hear Rosie be so cutting about Granny Doyle, but John Paul laughed, hating himself, slightly, as he did so.

'Yeah, we ordered it a special menu.'

'Make sure there's no salt.'

This was a joke of Damien's that elicited genuine laughter from John Paul and then they were off, describing the menu as designed by Granny Doyle, globs of Cookeen and corned beef sandwiches, things that she hardly ate any more, but that didn't matter, they were safer in the past, especially one whose architecture was principally crafted by imagination.

'Remember that time you brought home tofu?'

Damien's question to Rosie was slightly more dangerous territory – the time when they were teenagers – but Rosie smiled, game for the story.

'I carried that thing halfway across Dublin.'

'You wouldn't be getting that at SuperValu, thanks be to God,' John Paul said, making the other two laugh with his impression of Granny Doyle, the way he used to, when they had been united against the world.

'God, that thing must have cost half of my wages in those days,' Rosie said.

Damien, already laughing, started to snort.

'And then you didn't know how to cook it!'

'I *did*!'

'You spent half an hour watching it in the frying pan, wondering why it wouldn't change colour—'

'And then you turned the frying pan on!' John Paul said, because he couldn't resist a punchline, however bad, however far removed from the truth.

'And then you put brown sauce on it!' Damien said, loving this detail.

'And ketchup!' John Paul added.

'It *was* delicious,' Rosie said, irritation bubbling up underneath her laugh.

'It looked like somebody had murdered it!'

'*You* looked like you might die eating it.'

'It's not my fault that soy sauce hadn't found its way to Nolans.'

Rosie seemed annoyed, so John Paul tried to make peace.

'There's a great vegetarian spread at the wedding. Mushroom risotto, I think. We can even get you a bottle of brown sauce if you want!'

'Piss off!'

This was a bit softer, so John Paul thought that the crisis was averted, especially when they got on to slagging him about whether or not Grainne Keogh or Emer Clancy or other characters from his past would be there, and that led to a discussion of which Mayo cousins would try to shift which of Clodagh's friends and it seemed to be going well. So John Paul was surprised when, out of nowhere, Rosie asked if he'd invited Peg.

'To the wedding?'

'Yes.'

John Paul turned his head. No sign of Peg. Forty-five past: she had turned very fashionable.

'Eh … well …'

'I thought not.'

Rosie challenging him was definitely new and he wondered if inviting her had been a mistake, alongside coming to New York and getting in touch with Peg and getting born.

'I thought I'd …'

See how it went? There could be no inviting Peg; Granny Doyle wouldn't stand it and John Paul couldn't break her heart another time. Rosie was out to pick a fight, which was ungrateful, as he was trying to bring them all together. Ten to: she'd be here soon and they'd sort it out. John Paul drank his pint for something to do, thinking that he would get another in a moment, but then Damien, who was sporting a blush that looked more like a rash, announced that it was his round, standing up before either of them could stop him.

3

Mayo Stone (2007)

Peg stared out at the water. There was the Statue of Liberty and there was Ellis Island and there, just over the horizon, was Ireland. *I can feel its aura here*, Rosie might say, her hand hovering towards the horizon and attempting to reach Clougheally. (The real Rosie was waiting for her, blocks away, though movement was impossible.) Rosie had declared that the Irish Hunger Memorial downtown had an aura and Peg, who had never bothered to go, could see her point. A large mound of bright green grass and stones assembled into walls, it was remarkable; if she turned her back to the skyscrapers and looked out at the water it was as if New York disappeared.

Peg checked her watch. Five to seven: she might as well wait and be an even hour late. She didn't dare consult her phone; its buzzes over the last hour suggested several messages and missed calls. It was time to go, beyond time to go.

Tourists ambled past and snapped pictures of the stones. Peg hid behind her sunglasses. On a different day, she would have consulted every stone carefully, cataloguing each of the different counties that people had fled from. She would have read the informational panels and the poems. *Aura* would not be a word that crossed her consciousness.

Cracking location for a video, John Paul might have said, whipping out the pope hat and recording a special message for the Irish diaspora. The Irish had suffered through their Famine. It had made them a generous people. So donate now to fight world hunger and keep the Pope's saviouring in business—

All this romanticism about the Famine is misplaced, Peg might have interrupted. Everybody acts as if they're descended from the victims, a historical impossibility. The survivors did desperate things to get through. Stole clothes from the dead. Stepped over the bodies of babies. Ate seaweed, worms, worse. *You don't know what people did to survive*, Peg said, in her conversation with an imaginary John Paul, while the real one waited in a bar not ten blocks away. (She'd go in a minute, once her legs permitted.)

Peg felt the buzz of her phone and resisted the urge to fling it into the Atlantic. Or, rather, the Hudson: she had explained this distinction to Rosie, many times, but Rosie remained impervious to facts, Ireland visible in every direction once she reached a bit of water. Peg was as bad, though, wasn't she, standing on some bit of transplanted grass and weeping like a fool (she was glad of the sunglasses) and staring out across the water and picking imaginary fights with her brother because she had to blame him for something.

I'm sorry, Damien might have said and *it's okay* got stuck in Peg's brain. In a different life, she might have marched ten blocks and had it out with him in a blazing bar-fight, the little shit, for she'd taught him to read and watched him cycle with his stabilizers and he had repaid her by ratting her out. In a different life, Peg would have screamed and shouted and hugged and forgiven and held the three of them in her arms in some drunken embrace, while sports played on different screens and a bartender from Queens carved out foam shamrocks.

Peg stood, watching the water. A clock chimed, somewhere: an hour late. The sun slanted across the stone in front of her, another timepiece to torment her. The three of them were waiting in a bar for her. She could see them, didn't she long for that? She could call Dev and he would come and smooth things over, delighted, and they could eat buffalo wings and talk about baseball.

Peg felt the tick of a clock in her chest and started to walk.

351

4

Three Pint Glasses (2007)

Damien took his time at the bar, checking his phone for a good minute or two before he attempted to get the barman's attention, which took another few minutes, because he was 'polite to a fault' as Mark used to say, in an endeared tone, at least initially. He resisted the urge to text Mark. Mark had tried to get him to email Peg, as part of his grand project, Damien Doyle Confronts His Past! Look at me now, Damien longed to text: see how I have grown, ready to have a drink with my long-lost sister. Who was an hour late, Damien noted, sneaking a sip of his pint before he returned to the table.

He didn't need to feel guilty, he reminded himself. He had only been twelve. 'Not your fault,' Mark had said, when he'd coaxed the story out of Damien, when he was being tender ('you suck on guilt like a fucking lollipop,' a later, less consoling, assessment). Damien took another sip, a bigger one. He could leave, he realized. Dash out the door. Head to the hotel. Hail a cab to JFK. Damien didn't leave. He couldn't shirk his duty, even if it meant delivering pints to two people he'd rather not talk to.

John Paul and Rosie were both on their phones, probably texting Peg, a thought that made him nervous, so he grasped at wedding chat.

'So are any of the Mayo lot coming? What about Colm?'

'I hope so; he's great *craic*,' John Paul said immediately, treating the comment like a life-jacket. 'Remember when he got wasted on *poitín* at his sixtieth?'

Rosie didn't say whether or not she remembered, said instead: 'I don't know if he'll be able to make it. He's worried about what's happening in Clougheally.'

When John Paul didn't ask either, Rosie continued.

'You heard there was trouble down on the Pullathomas pier in June?'

Damien looked at the time on his phone. Five past. Peg was more than an hour late; perhaps she might not come. Damien gulped, unsure if this was the outcome he wanted. He took another sip, forgetting his resolutions about pacing himself as Rosie went on about the installation of a Shell portaloo on a farmer's land without his permission as if it were the greatest crisis since the assassination of Franz Ferdinand. Another sup, longer. To be a Good Boy: that was his desired outcome, always. He could convince Rosie of this, surely.

'Eamon is working on an announcement soon,' Damien said, once she broke for air; perhaps Rosie had not heard the rumours.

'Look at you, on first-name terms with the Minister for Energy,' John Paul said, raising his pint as if in salute. 'You'll be running the country next.'

'He's my boss,' Damien said, suppressing a small smile.

'It's a cop-out.'

Rosie's voice was hard; so, she had heard.

'It's a big deal. An additional resource tax on the oil and gas sector for all new licences.'

'Good old Greens and their taxes,' John Paul said.

Damien focused on Rosie.

'It's making sure that what happened with Corrib Gas won't happen again; from next January, Irish resources will benefit Irish people.'

He sounded like a press release, he realized, an occupational hazard: half the job of being in government was convincing people that you were doing the right thing.

Rosie leant forward; she'd been waiting for this moment.

'The resource tax is a PR move so he can wriggle out of launching a new independent review.'

Damien sighed.

'There's already been a review of the pipe.'

'By a company that works for Shell!'

'Maybe we should change the topic? Did I mention I'm getting married?'

Damien and Rosie glared at John Paul; in that instant, at least, they were united.

Damien leant forward, ready to explain the principle; they couldn't protect the forest if they got stuck worrying about the fate of every tree. He would articulate the Green Party's programme for government slowly and clearly and Rosie would understand the compromises that were necessary to achieve legislative success, although he would have to wait until she came back because, once he got a couple of sentences out, Rosie chugged her pint and declared it was her round.

5

Blinds (2007)

Peg sat on the mattress on the floor of Matt's downtown apartment and let out the wrong kind of sigh. Matt had gone to the bathroom to check out his chest or overdose or wait for her to leave; she could still make it to the Blarney Stone, if she really tried.

What do you want to do? Matt had asked and Alyssa had said *whatever*, happy to try any pills from Matt's goody bag. (Younger men might not be able to afford hotels, but at least they had access to better drugs.)

Then, *what do you want me to do?* Matt had asked, and *I want you to know!* Peg had sighed as Alyssa said *whatever*.

Peg picked up her phone, wondering if it was too late to find an older man in a hotel. Sex was like take-out: sometimes it was great and sometimes it was unsatisfying and she had nothing to feel guilty about.

Where are you? a variety of messages asked, in different words, from John Paul and Rosie and Dev. None from Damien, though Peg knew he was asking the question too, waiting to say 'sorry' while she searched for 'it's okay'. She couldn't face any of them. She'd stay on this mattress on the floor, for ever, behind her new best friends, Matt's light-cancelling blinds, which obligingly erased all traces of the outside world, the flicker of digits on Matt's games console the only indication that time was moving at all.

6

Three Pint Glasses (2007)

Rosie sloshed three pints onto the table, with a barb of satisfaction as Damien removed his phone with a yelp. She was pissed and pissed off, not a brilliant combination. The problem was that Rosie got drunk very easily – a pint was enough to make her tipsy – and she was annoyed at her brothers for putting her in this situation. She was annoyed at herself, because she was drinking through far too many rounds, partaking in a competition where there could only be a loser, whose name would always be Rosie. She should have ordered herbal tea for this round – the sixth! – but she hadn't even considered the possibility at the bar.

Nine o'clock. Peg had got the better of John Paul, again. Rosie might have felt a twinge of sympathy for her brothers, if they hadn't been shiteing on about Fiannix when she returned, something she couldn't listen to.

'I thought you'd given up!' John Paul said as Rosie snatched his fags.

'When in Manhattan …'

'I knew you hadn't,' John Paul said, seeming thrilled by this fact, momentarily abandoning his pitch to Damien; it seemed unlikely, anyway, that the Green Party would want a Fiannix account, although who knew what they might get up to next – a skyscraper on the Hill of Tara that shot missiles to Iraq would not be out of the question, in Rosie's current opinion.

They didn't even ask if Damien wanted to join them outside; he was grand with his phone.

John Paul lit up in solidarity.

'You used to *always* steal mine, when you'd run out of that filthy pouch of yours.'

'Two words: Marley Lights.'

'Okay, I borrowed Clo's stash sometimes—'

'Just like James Bond.'

John Paul coughed and smiled; the opposite of Damien, he accepted slags like gifts, grew fuller with the knowledge that people were talking about him. Rosie couldn't help smiling back and for a moment it was nice, the two of them puffing together outside while Damien checked out how to bomb Iraq on his phone, probably. But why did it need to be like this? Why was it always two of them united against the other? Even when they had been a tight trio – the days when they had collected the Blessed Shells of Erris on the beach or the time they had toddlered through the Big Snow and made their own epic Snowbear – there had always been some sort of conspiracy between them, a desire to keep others out: Peg; their father; Granny Doyle.

'Does *she* know you're smoking again?'

It took a moment for his face to recover from the shock; the same face as when she'd mentioned Peg, like she'd punched him. Good.

'She probably wouldn't believe it, anyway,' Rosie said, answering the question. 'Or, she'd say it was medicinal.'

'Ah, yeah,' John Paul said, recovering. 'What she doesn't know …'

His motto all through childhood, bolstered by Granny Doyle's excellent capacity for not knowing things when she wished.

'Does she know you contacted Peg?'

Again, John Paul looked shocked at her ability to be direct and for a moment she hated the lot of them, because she was an adult, and still none of them could see her.

John Paul searched for his catchphrase but he couldn't manage it.

'I really need to give up,' he said, stubbing out the cigarette and heading back to Damien.

Rosie clung to her fag. She should go home. Not to Peg's apartment: she'd been ignored enough for one trip. She should pick up her rucksack and toss everything in and hail the swiftest flight she could to Shannon: *I'll hitch a warplane*, she thought about joking to Damien, except it wasn't funny.

When she got inside, John Paul was still shiteing on about Fiannix.

'The clusters on Fiannix might be good for your group, too, Rosie – you can send blasts of text messages at no extra cost if you register the group. What is the group called again? Shell to Sea? Or is there another one?'

'There are four distinct protest groups,' Damien said.

Damien's voice was wry; so, he was following what was going on in Erris.

'It's not as if the Green Party is a united front,' Rosie said. 'Patricia McKenna will probably stand as an independent in the next European elections.'

Damien grimaced.

'Patricia has always been very *difficult*.'

Rosie's turn for a grimace.

'That's just a word that men use about women who have an opinion.'

'No, what men say when women have an opinion is "time of the month".'

Rosie glared at John Paul.

'You're not on camera; there's no need to share your shit jokes.'

A crack in John Paul's composure; she had managed that.

Damien, meanwhile, had only just recovered the ability to talk.

'No! *No!* I say that about men! Men are difficult all the time.'

'Who? Mark?' Rosie said.

This was something she regretted later; it wasn't nice to see Damien's face empty of all life, no matter how smug it had been.

Mark was not the point, though; she wasn't going to get distracted, spoke over the awkwardness, aware that she was being *difficult*, embracing it.

'Difficult is what the guards say – "don't be difficult" – when they're the ones with the batons pushing us into ditches. I think more people – more *women* – should be difficult because we're living in a world that *is* difficult, where companies can walk all over little people and their land, or guards can joke that they want to rape you if you look at them the wrong way, or they'll look at you like you deserve it, because you're a tease, going out to shout about justice when you should be lying in bed waiting for—'

'Hey, Rosie, why don't you calm—'

'I don't want to be fucking calm!'

'How about I buy us all a shot? Or some chips, maybe, some food to line the booze?'

'I don't want you to buy me anything,' Rosie snapped, secure in the knowledge that had John Paul sat in Solomon's chair and eyed the two women fighting over the one baby, he would simply have bought another baby, one for everybody in the audience.

'I should go.'

'Ah, Rosie, wait—' John Paul started.

'For what? She's not coming.'

Damien looked up. She couldn't tell if he was relieved or disappointed.

'Stay,' John Paul said. 'She's just …'

'Three hours late! She's not coming. And –'

Rosie was drunk enough to say it.

'And she's not selling the house either.'

John Paul sighed: here was the conversation he wanted to duck. She wouldn't let him.

'I know what you're at and it's not going to work: she'll never do it.'

'She already has.'

Rosie stared at John Paul.

'What?'

He looked right at her, he gave her that.

'She's already sold the house.'

She couldn't have.

'What?'

The words remained the same, meaningless, impossible. Rosie shook her head but John Paul continued to look at her, like he was very sorry about it, while Damien pondered his beer mat, his face reddening, until she realized he knew, which meant it wasn't bullshit, after all.

'Who to?'

Shell, he was going to say 'Shell' and she needed her things in a rucksack, immediately.

John Paul gave a smile before he provided a carefully moderated answer, not too triumphant, though he couldn't hide it: he was pleased.

'Me. Peg sold the house in Clougheally to me.'

7

Swimming Goggles (2007)

Sometimes, Peg felt that she was only truly herself immersed in water. Lapping the pool in the 92nd Street Y, life was reduced to the essential: the sideways gulp of air, the quick kick of limbs, the space just in front of her the only thing to reach for.

Peg liked to imagine that there were many histories one could carve through a life; surely there was another story she could swim through, with no sex or siblings or popes, where she was a woman whose only exceptional quality was an above-average breaststroke.

8

Cuneiform Stone (2007)

A Manual of Archive Administration, while clear about the necessity of cleaning hands after eating food, remained silent about what to do after giving an undergrad a hand-job in the stacks. It hadn't been worth the ethical compromises or wasted processing time. The student had let nerves get the better of him, leaving Peg with an unsatisfied mind and sticky hands.

Peg imagined that immediately starting to process correspondence would not be the best course of action, so she'd made her way to the bathroom, where she stared at her reflection in the small mirror, the water continuing to run, even after her hands were clean. She might have splashed some water on her face – that seemed like an appropriate *wake up, Peg Doyle!* action – but she knew from experience that such an action would leave her wet but unrepentant.

She knew she should go home, but she couldn't face her empty apartment. Rosie had crammed her stuff into a rucksack and headed out the door in minutes. Dev had followed; Peg had told him about the house in Clougheally and Gina and Gloria and Alyssa and now she was left with a quiet apartment which she couldn't bear to clean. The thoughts of collecting Rosie's scarves or shelving Dev's dog-eared books made her long to disappear under a duvet; she couldn't even close the browser on her laptop, because Dev had left open a Wikipedia tab about the numbering of *Star Wars* episodes.

She couldn't face work either, so Peg walked to the section where they kept the library's oldest treasures, the material they pulled out to woo undergrads. Here was the cuneiform stone that Dev loved, the oldest form of writing, though all it contained was a statement of accounts. A small grey thing that could fit inside a palm, its inscriptions etched out the purest form of history: records of the transfer of assets.

In certain records, the history might be simple; Peg Doyle had acquired property she did not need, so she had sold that property to a willing buyer. The financial transactions of Peg Doyle were a private matter, certainly not affairs she needed to disclose to her sister. If said sister were upset at the party to whom the property had been transferred to, well, this was an unfortunate occurrence but business should not be clouded by emotion; Peg Doyle needed capital more than property and John Paul Doyle's proposal made perfect financial sense. In this account, timing would be incidental, demonstrating either the admirable capacity of Peg Doyle to conduct business dealings without emotion or the adroit manner in which Peg Doyle could respond to new information and rectify misperceptions with reparative decisions.

Peg gripped the stone in her hands; she had the sense that if she crushed it she might feel better. Nothing. Evidently, she needed to work out, a thought that produced a dry laugh in the quiet of the library, though nobody was there to hear. *Pull yourself together, Peg Doyle!* sounded in her head, the stone dropped back into its protective box, though this action too afforded no relief.

She hadn't asked Aunty Mary for the house, she reminded herself. She was American now, walking proof of the nation's trademarked dream – hadn't she crossed an ocean with little more than a schoolbag (all that ballast shed) and carved a life for herself? She didn't need some anchor to Ireland. So she'd said 'yes' to John Paul's first email, eager to be clean of the haunted house, sure that Granny Doyle wouldn't be happy with whatever a fake pope did to her home. That would be the end of it, no Doyles knocking at her door, she'd hoped, but then Rosie had arrived, oblivious as always, and they'd talked and cried and held each other, like sisters, while that other history rumbled along.

I shouldn't have told you the truth, Rosie had said, through tears, the night she'd stuffed her things into one rucksack, thinking that Peg's actions had some relation to her news about who had told Granny Doyle about Ruadhan. Rosie had almost looked disappointed when Peg explained that this decision had nothing to do with that, *you don't actually care about any of us, do you?* a question that probably should have been met with a response.

The words hung in the air, following her to the archive, Rosie's and Dev's voices layering over each other, alternately hurt and angry, *don't turn your back on me!* and *I don't care about the money!* and *all this time, and you didn't say a thing!* and the crescendo: *you're fucked up, Peg, you know that?*

Oh yes, Peg thought, closing the cuneiform's protective box with a sigh, she knew all about that.

9

Duty-Free Bag (2007)

John Paul gulped the last of his Guinness in the airport pub; they'd be calling them for boarding soon and he still had more duty-free to stock up on. He'd got the booze and the fags but, when he reflected upon it, he wasn't sure that he had enough items that combined chocolate and peanut butter. Or Oreos. He'd bought Clo a couple of packets, but he could probably stuff more in the duty-free suitcase. Perfume, too; he could never bring enough of that back for her. He had a lot to do, certainly not time for another pint, but then Damien was up with an 'I'll get these' and John Paul hadn't the heart to say no.

Fuck it, they'd skull them and then they'd do a blitz of the duty-free, dashing around like they were on some game show where they had to fill up a basket with as much swag as they could before the time ran out (a metaphor for life? He'd write it down, see if it could be material for a stocking filler). A quick message to Clo. Let her know that he had the perfume and Oreos. Anything else she needed? Jason had already shared some of the photos from the stag do, the bastard. Clo had been game: *Ah, now, I don't want to know anything about that!* He hadn't told her about the meeting with Peg. The house, yes, of course they'd consulted about that, but he'd skirted around the personal parts. That was the trick of things between them; if they kept things light, they could conquer continents together.

Perhaps it was for the best that Peg hadn't shown. He felt a strain in his chest: the shots or the pizza or the stretch of a black hole, he couldn't tell. He'd have to stock up on peanut butter and chocolate, every colour of candy; if he filled his insides, there'd be no space for anything else. He'd get some as soon as Damien got back. He picked up his phone. Nothing from Clo, not even an 'xx' or a 'mwah!' A quick call to Granny Doyle? Tell her he was about to board and he'd said a prayer to Saint Joseph of Cupertino (patron saint of air travel); she'd love that.

He'd say the prayer first. One to Saint Ultán too. Perhaps Mrs Nugent was there beside him, talking the ear off the poor man. Perhaps this could be good material for a video? Saints like air traffic controllers, something about Fiannix's excellent reception – he'd write down the idea. He'd text Clo; she'd love it. The trick was to keep focus. Was there a patron saint for that? He'd look it up. Or family? Was there some magician in Heaven who'd sort that out for him? He'd ask Granny Doyle, when he gave her a buzz, in a minute.

They'd be grand. Rosie would calm down. Maybe he'd let her keep her hair blue for the wedding. (He'd buy Clo a suitcase full of perfume.) She'd love what they did with the house, eventually. It wasn't as if Peg had ever been planning to live there. It was for the best that she hadn't shown up (something expanded in his chest). Best to keep things focused: texts and emails and crisp phone calls. They could all have pints one day, once the development was finished: they could sit on the balcony and toast the safe, invisible movement of gas underneath their feet and laugh at the day that anything had ever divided the lot of them.

'I'll be back in a sec.'

It was Damien, the pints deposited with unusual haste. He was up and away before John Paul could stop him. Typical, Damien buried in his phone with some government shite when John Paul needed him to help carry some of the giant Toblerones.

It wasn't government business, though, John Paul could tell from the worry creased on his face. He clocked what Damien was up to and he had an urge to stop him. Ah, now, you wouldn't want to know anything about that! Damien did, though, that was always his problem, and John Paul drank his pint instead of stopping him, the black hole inside his chest stirring; he'd need another round, after all.

10

Boarding Card (2007)

'Hello?'

'…'

'Hello?'

'Peg?'

'…'

'It's Damien.'

'…'

'…'

'Hi.'

'Hi.'

'I'm at JFK.'

'Right.'

'…'

'It sounds busy.'

'It is.'

'…'

'…'

'Damien, I'm … the other night … I'm …'

'It's okay.'

'…'

'…'

'I'm at work at the moment.'

'The library?'

'Yes. It's …'

'Probably quieter than here!'

'Yes. I …'

'It's not a good time. No problem! I have to go too. Work. The flight. Duty-free! I just …'

'…'

'The thing is …'

'I don't know what Rosie …'

'Nothing. I just …'

'…'

'…'

'Maybe we can find a better time for us both. When I'm not at work. It'd be a bit easier. Things have been a bit difficult, the last few days, to tell the truth …'

'Yes. Of course.'

'…'

'…'

'Peg—'

'Damien—'

'I'm sorry.'

'…'

'…'

'I shouldn't have said anything.'

'It's …'

'…'

'…'

'It's all a long time ago, now.'

'Peg—'

'I'm sorry, Damien, but this isn't a great time. I have a meeting and—'

'Sure. They're calling our flight now, anyway. I hate being late.'

'Right.'

'…'

'…'

'Thanks for—'

'No problem. I'll let you go, so.'

'Right.'

'...'

'...'

'Damien ...'

'That's our flight there! I'd better go! Maybe we can talk again, a better time?'

'Sure. Have a good flight!'

'Bye!'

'Bye!'

11

Surfboard (2007)

To Ciarán's great credit, he didn't say anything. He didn't get at Rosie for how long she'd been away or for how difficult the campaign had been. He didn't ask about New York; he listened to as much as she wanted to say and held her when she cried and didn't say a word about whatever monstrosity John Paul wanted to erect in the big garden where once they'd laid out the Blessed Shells of Erris to dry.

Nor did he say a thing when Rosie walked into the sea in her gold bridesmaid's dress. She should have returned it – or at least searched for the fecking receipt – but Rosie felt a savage satisfaction at ruining the dress; she might slash it to strips, later. She looked a right sight, she knew, but wrecking a dress was nothing in comparison to the damage humans could wreak (in front of her was the gas rig; behind, the house that John Paul would gut into apartments for Shell workers). Rosie longed to scream but she was crying instead, tears sliding into a sea full enough with its own sorrows.

Rosie … Ciarán's arm said, gentle around her back as the waves crashed towards them. *We'll get you on a kayak or a surfboard*, his grip said, *get you good enough to stop any ship*. They wouldn't look behind. They'd surf out to meet whatever digger Shell sent into the bay. They'd ride the crests of waves, fearless.

Come on home, the tug of Ciarán's arm said, a movement Rosie was keen to follow, the dress dripping along the beach, Ciarán having the sense not to say anything except to ask if he'd get to wear the gold dress now, which he would, without a bat of one of his extremely kissable eyelashes, reason enough for Rosie to put her arm around his waist, a lifetime of blissful, radical, unmarriedness ahead of them if they wanted it.

12

VIP Magazine (2007)

'Mind you, I didn't think much of the dress. Not for the cost of it.'

Denise Donnelly gritted her teeth and waved to John Paul, who was making a complex series of hand gestures that conveyed, she imagined, the location of the castle in relation to the church. She didn't need them with her satnav, or with her mother, who would surely give her unsolicited suggestions for the majority of the drive. She was only jealous, Denise reminded herself; she was disappointed that Denise and Keith showed no sign of formalizing things while Jason treated his girlfriends like toothbrushes, too hard if you kept them for too long. Denise felt unaccountably irritable, when usually she loved weddings, when this one promised a free bar and minor celebrities, and the chance that her outfit might feature in the background of *VIP* magazine; it must be because Keith wasn't there, off at his son's soccer match while she was stuck with her parents, her dad no help, having tuned out her mother's frequency long ago.

'Mind you, I think wedding registries can be a bit tacky. Though maybe they need every gift they can get! Weren't you saying you saw John Paul in at your branch looking for a loan?'

Denise swerved a little too aggressively.

'No, I wasn't, and if I was I shouldn't have been disclosing confidential information.'

'Sure, *I* wouldn't breathe a word! I'm only making conversation. And I'd say little enough has been well spent if that service is anything to go by. Why in the world you'd need gold confetti is beyond me, some people have no appreciation for subtlety.'

'Mam, would you shut up for a minute, you're wrecking my head, and I need to find this bloody castle.'

The rest of the drive was spent in silence: Mrs Donnelly's mind occupied with a flurry of thoughts about filial ingratitude, the superiority of Jason's driving over Denise's, and the selfishness of holding a wedding in a location with so many potholes; Mr Donnelly lost in deep contemplation as to whether he might choose smoked salmon or lamb kebabs for his starter.

*

Mr Donnelly dropped his menu in disgust, unclear when it had become fashionable to eat seaweed.

*

There hadn't been that carry-on at her wedding, Granny Doyle was sure of it. That lad from next door telling all sorts of stories about John Paul; Granny Doyle was glad she was going deaf, though, the voice on Jason Donnelly, Helen Keller couldn't have missed what he was saying. And then *she* couldn't resist speaking either, calling John Paul 'J.P.,' or worse, 'babe'. But then John Paul had spoken, said he'd been reared by the best woman in Ireland, raised his glass to her and smiled, a proper smile, no danger of his eyes winking, and she knew that nothing else would matter that night; she was happy.

*

'Let's move before he comes back. Did you know him?'

A small shrug of Rory O'Donoghue's shoulders: what was there to be said about Damien Doyle?

'He's probably downloading more petitions to bore us with,' Olly said, forking up a last morsel of cake. 'The way he was going on, as if being in government made him a celebrity. *Hello*, there's nothing cool about a club that includes an Ahern: they don't even know which boy band to be marrying into.'

Olly shook off his irritation as soon as he stood up, happiness his natural condition, especially when there was a floor to be danced on, Rory to be danced with, fetching in his bow-tied professor get-up. Olly felt a twinge of guilt at dragging Rory along; it wasn't as if he had kept in touch with Clodagh Reynolds since Trinity, but he knew he had to go, because now she was marrying the cutest ever Pope, who just now had tipped his glass to Olly – as if there were a real connection between them – and Olly felt that he was thus only one step away from dating a pope. Not that Olly had any complaints – how could anybody be unhappy with a man so adept at the moonwalk that the floor had already cleared for him?

*

Damien stared at his phone, happier to be reading the news than listening to Mrs Fay, who was remembering her own lovely wedding. He wished that he were dating Mark, so that he would have a shield at such events, somebody to be in a grumpier mood than he was. Somebody to introduce to Rory O'Donoghue or to stand opposite the smiling dope of a boyfriend that Rory was dating. *He* was the person Damien had ended up talking to, not Rory, who listened as Damien gabbed on about the Greens, mentioning the civil partnership bill, hoping that Rory would understand that he, Damien, was out now, had been happily gaying it up for years since he'd left the Legion of Mary, but instead Rory had started talking to one of Clodagh's friends and Damien was stuck in a conversation with his idiotic boyfriend, the kind that would dress up to go to the STD clinic.

Damien wanted Mark to walk over, an earlier version of Mark, perhaps an imaginary one, who would stride through the door, whisper something dirty in his ear, and pull him off to the castle dungeons. When somebody did come over to the table, though, it was only John Paul.

'Hey big bro.'

'I'm only a few minutes older than you: you don't get to call me that.'

'But so much wiser.'

'Ha, doesn't that mean Rosie's supposed to be wise too?'

'Well …'

They drank.

'Have you heard from her?'

'No.'

Damien pulled out his phone, but there were no messages from actual humans, just more list-servs and petitions. Mrs Fay had left them to it.

'Thanks for coming.'

'Sure. It's great.'

'Good to have some family here.'

'Yeah.'

'You okay for a drink?'

'I'm grand.'

John Paul plonked another beer in front of Damien, listening never his strong suit. He scanned the room, nodding to a few people.

'Any form? I can put in a word for you if you want. Give you my blessing!'

He had to credit John Paul: he was trying.

'I don't think I need a pope for a wingman.'

'Ah, come on, it's what weddings are for! Let's see. Aha!'

'The waiter?'

'Yeah, the Spanish one, he's been throwing eyes at you. And you'd make Gran's day.'

Damien nearly choked on his beer.

'Are you joking?'

John Paul raised both of his eyebrows: *would I do such a thing?*

'You know the way they'd have all sorts of different names in Spain? Guess what yer man's called.'

'What?'

John Paul grinned, the face he had on before he was about to deliver a quip on a video. 'Jesús.'

*

There was magic in the air, there had to be. What else would have Mrs McGinty pulling out her handkerchief again, an item which, prior to that day, had most likely not been unfolded since the Second World War? She had accepted a medicinal Scotch from John Paul, and then another, and then, there she was, blowing into her handkerchief at the sight of John Paul and Clodagh Doyle slow-dancing together, telling Granny Doyle that Mr McGinty had been a fine dancer in his day, surprising Mrs Donnelly, who sat beside her hoping for some judgement but instead found herself listening to 'ah well, isn't it nice to see young people in love?'

*

Something had to be in the air, because what else would have Mrs Donnelly leaning on her daughter's arm and pronouncing John Paul Doyle a charmer, a man whose word carried weight when the phrase 'best hat I've ever seen' was uttered.

*

Magic was in the air. Fairy lights twinkled in the marquee. Everything flowed freely – drinks across the bar, jackets across chairs, limbs across dance floors. Rory O'Donoghue loved weddings because everybody was a little bit gay, the aunties and young lads YMCAing with the best of them, obstacles to dancing to cheesy songs removed, because you could pretend you were being ironic, because who cared?

And then – magic – 'It's Raining Men' coming on, the dance floor filling up, Clodagh and her pals clustering around Olly, who delivered each 'hallelujah' with the fervour of a Baptist minister. Rory had a following too – he could lip sync the song in his sleep, was every straight girl's best friend, the guy they could grind to without consequence. *Everybody* was on the dance floor: Jason Donnelly pulled over by the girl he had been kissing; John Paul sashaying over to the group; lads from school that Rory could never have imagined dancing to this song with, layers of clothes left at tables, drinks in hand for elaborate gestures, nobody minding the sticky floor, or caring if beer sloshed towards them as somebody pointed to the sky; magic was in the air, or drunkenness, or, perhaps it was that John Paul and Clodagh were genies, or geniuses, enchanting every foot to tap, every torso to shake, every mouth to cry 'amen!'

Damien was there too: drunk, shuffling his shoulders awkwardly, doing a sort of bemused dad dance, his face hovering between mild bliss and slight terror. Rory caught his eye and then they were dancing with each other, on either side of the tent, and words were not necessary: Rory knew how Damien felt about a sky of raining men; Damien knew that Rory held no bitterness, was only glad to see him dancing with a weight off his shoulders. Then, they were *really* dancing together, Rory a great person to dance with, gifted, generous, somebody to mimic who could also take your lead, which he did, as Damien unleashed a force of imaginary rain from the roof of the marquee, pushed back his head, in parody or ecstasy, the lines had all blurred, imagined what it was to be *absolutely soaking wet*, eyes twinkling at Rory, because this was Rory's speciality, innuendo, and it was a pleasure to share, especially with John Paul walking over, leading the Spanish waiter towards Damien, not missing a beat of the song in the process. Rory shot Damien a different kind of smile, and Damien blushed, before turning to the waiter, who had a smile more like Damien's – bemused, unsure, excited – and

Rory felt a complicated twinge, mostly sweet, the small measure of bitter. The song was still going, Olly bounding over, lovably dishevelled, pulling Rory into the circle, pointing at him, to suggest he had just fallen from the sky; Rory knew the exact coy face to make, shook his limbs in the light of Olly's smile, gasped with the rest of the crowd when rain started, real rain, thundering against the tent, further evidence of the magic of the night, which was only getting more wonderful, because when the chorus of 'It's Raining Men' was about to start, instead

*

it was Rihanna, Clodagh's favourite song at that minute, everybody's favourite song at that moment, perhaps; certainly, its intro was instantly recognized, elicited a whoop of joy, a gasp at a DJ so inspired, a smile from Clodagh, who caught John Paul's eye, the way they had all night, as they satellited around the groups, keeping glasses full and people happy, nudging strangers towards each other, steering prickly relatives towards other rooms, a wonder of choreography that, between them, they had it all under control, as splendid as their movement now, limbs dancing in tandem despite all the bodies between them, both songs playing together, as everything merged, John Paul miming an umbrella as Clodagh pointed to the sky, where the roof of the tent ballooned up, as if it were talking to the rain, which was shooting sideways into the marquee now, not that anybody minded, because everybody was making the same sounds in their mouths, pushing their hands in the air to the beat of each 'ella', mouths wide as John Paul opened the champagne, which rocketed towards the sky and fizzed down like miraculous rain, towards the open mouths of dancing bodies, everything special and in slow motion, as if they were in a music video, wine raining from the sky, Clodagh not needing any alcohol, so full of life that she felt the movement of her limbs was absolutely necessary, as everybody danced, to Rihanna and the

379

Weather Girls, the songs converging happily, like Clodagh and John Paul, who were getting closer, coming here to each other, shining together with the sun, everybody dancing around them, imaginary umbrellas all shaking out their spokes in delight.

Series IX:
Bust

(2008–2009)

1

Anglo-Irish Bank Sign (2008)

And then it all fell down.

2

Brick (2008)

They were supposed to be solid, a safe place to shovel money, but they might as well have been made of clouds.

3

Keys (2008)

It must be especially hard for them, it was said: what use a key without a door to open? Some, it was said, had gone wild, roamed through what was left of the hills and forest. Some lurked around the half-finished estates, scratched at abandoned holes, lamented that there was only one door to fit their grooves. Some stayed put, remained with owners who had no use for them, existed to provide the meaning of cold comfort.

4

Medical Card (2008)

It was all mixed up. Things that seemed solid – with letters and numbers and indentations – could nonetheless be taken away, a government's responsibility for the health care of the vulnerable apparently not fixed.

5

The Ryan Report, or The Commission to Inquire into Child Abuse Report (2009)

It was all mixed up. Priests and nuns who were supposed to be above the physical had fingers and hands that were all too solid; men in power had ears that were all too blocked (it was not a good time for popes).

6

Envelopes, Multiple (2009)

Some objects would not be stopped, insinuating their way through letterboxes and demanding what could not be paid (it was not a good time for companies).

7

Incandescent Bulb (2009)

And what were the Greens in government doing during all this? Outlining their strategy to ensure that illumination within Leinster House complied with EU standards. Fiddling with bulbs while a city burned, the media said. An unfair assessment, perhaps, but the media could not always be relied upon for fairness; this was not the moment for a government to focus on objects whose benefit would outlast an election cycle (it was not a good time for governments).

8

Fibre-optic Christmas Tree
(2008–2010)

It was state of the art, it was said, worth the 300,000 euros.

Its baubles lit up O'Connell Street, cycling through bright, hopeful colours.

The toughest budget in years was passed.

Its baubles flashed red, blue, green.

Banks were propped up.

Shutters came down.

The tree flashed green, blue, red, white.

Another budget came.

Floods.

A Snowpocalypse.

The IMF.

And the tree flashed red, blue, green, hope!, until it was shuttled off to Smithfield, the gap between its confidence and the street it lit up too stark for any eye.

9

'For Sale' Sign (2009)

9 Dunluce Crescent

It was sad, Maria Hernandez thought, to see a garden like that. The old lady had always loved her garden. She sat out in her porch admiring it all of last summer, was there every morning when Maria went out to work and every evening when she returned. She had reminded Maria of her grandmother, who had a lovely garden back in Valencia, one that overflowed with things you wouldn't find here, tomatoes like happy little hearts. The thought of her grandmother sitting alone in her big garden added another layer to the sadness of Maria Hernandez, because she wouldn't be going back to Spain, not yet, not while she was clinging to her job here, while, by all reports, the situation was even worse at home. She would tend to the garden when she got home from work, Maria resolved, looking back as she turned the corner, feeling a bubble of affection for the old lady she had only ever nodded to, thinking that she might have to borrow shears for the weeds, that the hedge could use a trim, that she would phone her own grandmother that evening.

2 Dunluce Crescent

Would it have been different, Maureen McGinty wondered, if she had offered the spare bedroom? She had turned the idea over and over in her mind, gone as far as to clear out the wardrobe of the copies of *Irish Catholics* and old coats that she stored there. It was, after all, a thing that they had used to joke about – it had been Mrs Nugent's idea: they would all, eventually, move into the same house, like the Golden Girls, Mrs Nugent had said, adding that she would need her own entrance for all her fellas. Mrs McGinty couldn't have borne Mrs Nugent's cackle, but she could, she had thought, have handled Mrs Doyle; she would have driven her to Mass in the mornings, maybe even have brought her to the Legion of Mary meetings, to bring her out of herself, take her mind off her grand-children (it was a blessing, Mrs McGinty thought, that *she* hadn't a family to disappoint her). Bridget would have had something to say about the developments on the street: a Nigerian family renting out the Nugents' (at least they were Catholics, the boys good members of the Legion), some gang of foreign young things renting out old Mr Kehoe's place (*they* were not religious), poor Mrs Fay. It would have been nice to have the bit of company in the evening, nice to go to sleep with the knowledge that if somebody broke in in the middle of the night she wouldn't be murdered alone.

7 Dunluce Crescent

Cool, Chike Okorocho thought, watching Amara hop over the wall too, instead of waiting for him to open the back gate. *No big deal*, his face said, as Amara looked at him wanting something – praise? flirtation? – before her face also shifted into a 'no big deal' stance.

She looked around the back garden, face stuck on 'unimpressed'. Chike shifted on his feet, because he *did* want her to be impressed, because she was the coolest girl in second year, and he couldn't help it if he looked five rather than fifteen at that moment; he wanted her to be excited.

'So who lives here?'

'Some old witch used to,' Chike said, shrugging his shoulders.

'No such thing as witches. What rubbish is your mam teaching you?'

392

'Bet you think there's no such thing as ghosts too?'

Amara raised her eyebrows: *are you kidding me?*

'Don't scream too loudly,' Chike said, glad that his hands didn't shake as he picked the lock, happy to see that Amara brushed against his arm as he opened the door, almost holding on to him, a movement he replicated moments later as they walked in, Amara first, making a big deal of being fearless, not caring what ghosts the house held, thinking only of what would happen there that night, a different kind of tingle animating her arms.

4 Dunluce Crescent

She could do the hoovering in her knickers now, Irene Hunter thought, pouring the third glass of wine, saluting out her window to the empty porch, finally free of the binoculared battleaxes. Barry could park in the driveway and nobody would be taking down his registration number, remarking that his second name wasn't Hunter, that he hadn't fathered either of her two girls. His car was parked outside all the time now; he was 'in between' things, it made sense to share the rent, especially with Irene's business in trouble. More opportunity for them to do as they wished, for them to play strip poker in the sitting room, for the blinds to remain drawn all through Sunday morning. Except, Irene thought, filling up Barry's third glass, there wasn't much to be spied upon these days: the two of them sitting on the couch, draining cheap bottles of wine while watching *Fair City*, corks and cable television suddenly luxuries.

At least the contents of her recycling bin would no longer be subject to scrutiny, she thought, placing the Lidl bottle beside its empty predecessor. Another thought, less pleasing: she would cut down on the wine. Once she'd made some other cuts. Toilet paper for sanitary towels. Fewer hot showers for the girls. Sliced pans, no more things with seeds. She was wise to her pennies, because the thought of the amounts that she owed, or the size of the figures associated with the cards in her wallet, summoned vomit to her throat, a substance that could only be stopped with another glass of wine, something that would be cut, at a later date, another number that she couldn't face just yet.

5 Dunluce Crescent

'I could have sued the little prick, if he had more than fuck all in his account!'

'Didn't I always say he'd come to a bad end, Jason?'

Jason Donnelly rubbed his temple. It didn't matter whether or not he responded; neither his mother nor sister had any need of communication from him. Denise was in the middle of her story describing how John Paul Doyle had ripped up a pen from the bank counter – weight and all! – and flung it at the cashiers. Each time the story passed across the table it gained more details; soon, Jason was sure of it, Denise would be due a medal, the first bank manager to survive near death by projectile pen.

'And the cheek of people clapping,' Denise said. 'Different faces they had on when they were begging for loans and now they're acting like it's all the banks' fault.'

'I've always said: you reap what you sow,' Mrs Donnelly added, a statement Jason could not disagree with, its wisdom proffered on many an occasion. He, too, had reaped what he had sown, shares and property offloaded at the right moment, hardly his fault if others weren't so lucky. And yet, thinking about John Paul made Jason's insides twist in a way he was sure wasn't good for his abs. Jason made his excuses and sleeked into his car, confident that he too had made sacrifices (one of his properties had barely made a profit), contributed to charity (he had participated in two separate fun runs) and could not be responsible for the myopia of others. Denise said she wouldn't stay for her dinner either, leaving Mrs

Donnelly with all the satisfaction of sharing the accuracy of her prophecies with an empty kitchen.

6 Dunluce Crescent

She would google the price of the house across the road, Nnenna Okorocho decided, once Onyema got off the computer, which might be never; he was at that game again. No good, to have one son out all the time (and where was Chike, with homework to be done?) and the other attached to the computer, the chair grooved to his bottom at this stage. She would lift up those huge head-phones and bellow in his ear to *move!*; she had to Skype her sister in Lagos and first, she would have to check the price of the house, so she would know how many trips in a taxi Igwebwe would have to make before they could buy their own place. Not a place like *that*, Mrs Okorocho would not be having such a house, fat with sadness, a porch that collected rain. She would get a house that could be boasted about. Could it be so much more than the rent? It was going up again, a rip-off, as they said, as she had learnt to say, holding up sandals in a department store, fruit at a stall (or, what they called fruit in Ireland; if her sister could see the pale things they called bananas, she would not be jealous). They might have been better off following her other sister to America; Chiamaka claimed her house was a mansion (a lie, Onyema had said: at least he was able to use Google Maps). But then what would happen to Chike in America? Mrs Okorocho did not like to think of it, because men would shoot at him and they were better here, even if black boys weren't safe in Ireland either (she would clutch Chike to her heart and not let go, as soon as he came home). No, they would not go to America; Igwebwe would drive enough drunk people home, they would buy their own little house, would call it a mansion, and she would ask Onyema if there was any way to lie about the dimensions of a structure on Google Earth.

'We'll have to tell Emma,' George Geoghan said, fiddling with the volume on their computer's speakers (his wife kept it too low; impossible to hear their daughters).'She was in the same school as one of the Doyles, wasn't she?'

'Maybe,' Mrs Geoghan said, absorbed in *Coronation Street* (she would refuse to Skype with Emma until it was over), uninterested in any news that did not involve Tracy Barlow. And why would she be? She hadn't grown up on the road like her husband, hadn't played handball with Danny Doyle, couldn't remember what 7 Dunluce Crescent had looked like before its porch. Emma would be interested, or at least she'd pretend to be (she was a brilliant daughter, a shame that she was stuck over in England); she always listened to the news on the street, was game to hear any of her dad's rants, rolled her eyes when he'd talk about the good old days of the unions or the punt, pronounced 'Dad' in the tone he loved, enough affection to ease the irritation (terrible that she was stuck in England; emigration was supposed to be a thing of the past). Emma would be interested, would want to know the story (and yet, the truth of it was she seemed to be loving her life over there).

'Rosie,' Mr Geoghan said, remembering the name of the Doyle that Emma had gone to school with; the blondie one, 'a bit of a quare one,' Mr Geoghan had said, eliciting a 'Dad!' from Emma, who was always telling him what he shouldn't be saying any more.

'No, that one's Sophie,' Mrs Geoghan said, her eyes on the telly, her voice taking on the tight tone she used whenever anybody talked during *Coronation Street*.

8 Dunluce Crescent

'I wonder how much it will go for?' Sarah Brennan asked, news as ineffective a condiment at her table as salt: nothing could revive the conversation or dried meat.

Carl shrugged, all he did since he'd moved home, impossible to get a word out of him, even after she'd cooked chicken curry, his favourite, for dinner.

'I'd say they'd be lucky with whatever they get.'

Carl turned the pages of the *RTÉ Guide*, a publication that had never held much appeal for him before, but was currently indispensable.

'Although, who knows if they'll be getting anything.'

Mrs Brennan hadn't forgotten any of it: the time John Paul had raided her freezer, the night he'd smashed her windows, the cheek of his grandmother, not setting foot in their pharmacy when it had been open, acting as if the Doyles were better than the Brennans. They'd got their just deserts, Mrs Brennan thought, wishing that Carl would provide some echo of her thoughts, even a nod would have sufficed, but instead he stood up and walked into the sitting room, leaving Mrs Brennan with her thoughts and the table to clear. An awful thing, how a house could be too big and too small at the same time.

1 Dunluce Crescent

'What happened?' Kathleen Fay asked, her eyes roving over the hedge to the empty porch of 7 Dunluce Crescent.

Helen Fay caught her breath and clung to her mother's arm, the tables turning for a second as she was the one needing support. It startled Helen, these flashes of lucidity in her mother, when the fog cleared across her forehead, when her eyes attempted to focus again, when there was a chance that she would remember who she was.

But no, the moment passed like clouds, and Mrs Fay smiled serenely and tottered down the street, no more perturbed by the sign than she was when Helen had told her again, that lunchtime, that she was moving to a new home, that Daddy wouldn't be coming with her, because he was dead, they'd visited the grave only that weekend. Helen brushed a tear away; her mother was asking her again about when they were going to the strand, mistaking her for Kitty, her aunt, who was also dead, like almost everybody her mother knew, so it was no wonder she didn't want to know what happened to the Doyles. Easier for herself too, Helen acknowledged, supporting her mother as they walked down Dunluce Crescent for what might be the last time, unless she drove her out from the home, but what would be the point, when it was already vanishing for Mrs Fay, bricks and memories losing their solidity, the shape of the street changing for Helen too, no longer possible to play hopscotch in the road the way she had with Clare Nugent, no big hedge in number 9 to hide behind any more, nothing left in 1 Dunluce Crescent, only bits in boxes; to forget was to survive.

10

Drawing of Snowbear (2009)

Rosie rushed over the threshold into the glass porch, no time for ceremony with the amount of snow outside. *A snowpocalypse*, Mrs Nugent might have pronounced with glee, waiting for the disdain of Mrs McGinty, who would be sure to point out that snow had always fallen in the country without so much fuss, in a different time, when the folding chairs of 7 Dunluce Crescent's porch bounced with the arrival of fresh gossip and no weeds tapped against the glass. Rosie fumbled for the keys; it was too cold for ghosts. She opened the front door slowly, worried that the past might jack-in-the-box towards her. The hallway of 7 Dunluce Crescent was empty, of course, the grubbiness of the wallpaper unfairly exposed with no other objects to shield it. It would be stripped, the triplets' childhood scribblings painted over. The garden would be paved, one of the few in Dunluce Crescent not to allow for a car. The porch would be knocked down.

Rosie heaved inside two bin-bags full of cardboard, mostly shoeboxes, all she had until reinforcements arrived. Pathetic. In his heyday John Paul would have hired somebody to clear the house – he probably would have founded a company to tackle such tasks – but he wasn't likely to do so now. Damien would have made a schedule and a spreadsheet – he was a great disciple of Excel – and approached the emptying of the house with the attitude he adopted to cleaning a fridge, top to bottom the only way that made sense. Peg would have been the ideal candidate for the task, archival boxes brought to store items adequately, faded photographs placed in protective sleeves, figures identified on the back in pencil.

Rosie sat on the stairs and rolled a cigarette. She might not be the ideal Doyle for the job, but she was the one who was here. What did it matter if she got distracted and started to peel back wallpaper, years of measurements and her thoughts about Bananarama waiting to be rediscovered on bare wall? Nobody was left to shout at her. Rosie exhaled and felt a rush of pleasure at this transgression. The house seemed smaller, suddenly. The details of the hallway remained the same – holy water font, coat hooks that nobody used, beige-and-blue-flower carpeting up the stairs – but she felt the dizzying gap between memory and perception, as if she were an adult returning to her primary school, shocked at the paltry size of a yard that had seemed as huge as a universe.

She would come up with a plan, once she'd searched her bag for a biro that worked. Or perhaps there were still some spares in the second drawer in the kitchen; perhaps everything would be as she had left it. No, she would not become sentimental. This was a house she had longed to leave. Rosie would not hesitate in the donation of radios to charities. She would not pause before consigning an armchair to a hard rubbish collection. Such was the cycle of life: most lives were sized so that their essential contents could ultimately squeeze into a shoebox. The more ruthless she was, the better. She would not succumb to nostalgia. She would take a trip upstairs if necessary: there would be the statue of the Sacred Heart, there the room Granny Doyle had stripped.

Though she had come to know a different side of Granny Doyle, Rosie had to acknowledge that, even if she struggled to do the arithmetic: could two years really outweigh a lifetime of neglect? Granny Doyle had come to Clougheally a few times, staying with Rosie and Ciarán, not that she had a choice; the flats that John Paul had planned remained stuck in mid-construction, a monument to a different time. She couldn't credit the sight of Shell's giant *Solitaire* ship in Erris, stopping tiny fishing boats from catching crabs, all so that they could lay down a pipe that would pump money to a foreign country. So she banged pots on the beach, shouting at the navy who were escorting the Shell ship as they removed small fishermen from the sea. Rage, she had that in her, plenty of it, a lifetime's worth. Kindness too, this was the surprise to Rosie; she scrubbed Ciarán's surfboard, a ridiculous action, but if he was going to be out getting in the path of the construction diggers in the water, then she wanted to make sure his surfboard was presentable, especially with the news watching. (Rosie's kayak she didn't bother with.) She could be flexible, telling Ciarán that she *would* have the drop of honey in her tea (though she still greeted Rosie's soy milk with suspicion, 'an insult to cows, so it is'). She remained a difficult woman and Rosie had no illusions about her politics (Shell got in her way so they earned her rage; other issues were not to be discussed) but finally, despite herself, Rosie could regard her with something close to affection.

So, to work. Rosie went upstairs, ignoring the box room, still painted purple. She'd start in Granny Doyle's room, where dust was already gathering, even though she'd only been in hospital for a couple of weeks. Rosie stared at the neatly made bed, the corners tucked in the way Granny Doyle insisted upon. John Paul should be doing this. He was responsible for the stroke, as clear a cause as any. Fiannix had collapsed, alongside his marriage, the property development in Clougheally, and even the Irish Pope, not popular in such times. The bank was after 7 Dunluce Crescent, too; that was what had broken her. Granny Doyle had taken out a second mortgage for him years ago (he'd kept that quiet) and so that was in trouble too, but he'd sort it out, John Paul had promised, he'd fix everything: no bank would throw an old lady out on the streets in the snow! But then she'd had a stroke and they were selling the house and she'd never sleep in this bed again, let alone make it carefully.

Rosie tackled the wardrobe. What to do with the coats and the carefully dry-cleaned skirts and the stack of summer clothes that she'd probably never need? She'd be in her hospital gown for the next while, the stroke severe enough that the nurses didn't think she'd be leaving. Hospital had shrunk her: one side already paralysed by the stroke, she had thinned as well, veins pushing against skin. Her hair had lost its curls, hung limply by her side, the same off-white shade as the pillow it rested upon. It was difficult for her to talk; strange sounds came out instead. All this made her eyes appear more alive than ever, pushing out against the carapace of a body they were trapped inside, boring into whoever hovered over them. She might last a few months, the nurses said, but she wouldn't be getting on a surfboard, the way she'd joked with Ciarán, and she wouldn't be banging another pot on the side of the road, and she wouldn't ever be telling Rosie what it was like to have grown up on Clougheally strand and it was too much: just when they'd started to talk, the words had been stolen out of her.

Rosie focused on the boxes of random documents and old photos, not the most efficient choice, but she was the one here, she could do it as she pleased. There had to be a photo of the Big Snow, she was sure somebody would have snapped them: the lot of them in their winter coats, the largest snow-creature ever assembled triumphant in the garden. She wanted to hold it up against the window and compare the levels, sure that the news had it wrong; the snow in 1982 had definitely been higher.

The only evidence preserved was Rosie's drawing of the Snowbear, an early masterpiece.

'You can't use white crayon on white paper,' Peg had said.

'I can't see anything,' Damien had said.

'Ah, you'll be an abstract genius, won't you love? A budding Picasso!' Danny Doyle had said.

'Where am I?' John Paul had said.

'Don't be wasting paper; I've the messages to write out,' Granny Doyle had said.

Yet, she had kept it, Granny Doyle. Here it was, pressed between John Paul's school reports; she had kept it over the years. A mystery. She should throw it out, Rosie thought, extinguishing her fag on one of John Paul's reports (his 'well-developed sense of self' hadn't worked out so well for them all, had it?). There was far too much stuff to be dealing with, no space for it in her rented house in Erris. A lot of junk: dead-eyed Furbys and tea-stained mugs and rusted pans and pieces of Lego that had once made a Millennium Falcon. Rosie had the wrong attitude, thinking that she could salvage things, shoebox by shoebox. It was unhealthy to be too attached to material things. She'd get Damien to rent a skip; John Paul or the bloody bank or the government – somebody who was at fault – could pay for it. She should throw it out, Rosie thought, carefully folding the drawing and placing it inside a shoebox.

Rosie sat down on the bed and sighed. She'd have a quick nap, she decided, necessary if she was going to make much headway. Her head flopped onto the pillow and she conked out and so that's where she was when John Paul broke into the garden.

11

Hopenhagen Poster (2009)

I have no choice but to resign …

Damien hesitated. It would be very easy to click 'send'; this, certainly, was what the voices outside Leinster House were clamouring for. Mark would be there, surely, taunting the Green traitors who had bailed out the banks and sold out their principles. Damien rubbed his temples and longed for a glass – a bottle – of red wine. It would be easy to press 'send'. He could walk away from the mess. He wouldn't have to listen to abuse on the phone or duck the path of pelted eggs or waste another day responding to crises, leaping from frying pan to fire and back again until his arse was hotter than J-Lo's, a joke that Mark might have made, if he were talking to Damien.

Damien walked over to the window and looked out at the crowd of protesters and cameras. It was hard to make out faces in the dark. Mark was surely there, *I told you so*s held back with great nobility, making Damien want to hug him or punch him, if they ever got close enough again. Mark had been right about Copenhagen too. If Damien were honest, Copenhagen was the real reason that he wanted to quit. He'd gone to the United Nations Climate Change Conference high on Obama's promise of climate action. Hopenhagen, the posters declared! Yes, we can take action, he allowed himself to hope, a binding international treaty on carbon emissions the only Christmas present he asked for. It had not happened. Damien had stared at his lanyard in the huge conference hall, aware of his insignificance. Ireland was a tiny piece in the

404

climate puzzle; whether or not the Greens managed to pass a climate change bill was irrelevant if meaningful international cooperation was not achieved. Damien stared at his lanyard and wondered what was the point of a Green Party or renewable energy initiatives or allowing same-sex partnerships if humans were incapable of doing anything to stop their imminent destruction. Damien believed in democracy and international treaties and friendly marches that would compel governments to act but then, there he was, staring at a plastic rectangle in an almost empty conference hall, hope as disposable as the coffee cups and abandoned folders that weary cleaners binned up.

Damien had started to write the email then, on the plane back from Copenhagen, though here he was a week later, the words awaiting the final click. *I quit.* I refuse to be part of this charade. I understand that the Green Party's legacy will now be irrevocably tarnished. I can no longer be part of a government where our only role is to play the conscience of Fianna Fáil. I see little to no hope that any of our bills will make it through to legislation in this charged political environment. *I quit.*

Damien sighed as he sat back in front of his desk, 'send' still impossible to click. That *little* in the *little to no hope* was what had them clinging on. There was still the chance that the Greens could push through some of their legislation, if they survived another few months. Including a bill regulating property development, Damien said to the protesters, when he wanted to prove that the Greens had nothing to do with this mess, had instead been Cassandraing against the property boom for years. Not to mention the civil partnership bill. The climate change bill. This would be a legacy worth holding out for; eggs splatting onto a suit nothing if a carbon tax could be passed.

Damien's finger moved to the backspace key. His impassioned arguments disappeared until all that was left of his resignation was a lonely *I* beside the flashing rectangle of the cursor.

The phone rang immediately, as if on cue.

Damien longed to pick up his coat and leave; it was too late to be dealing with another angry voice.

He answered the phone all the same.

'Hello?'

'Is that Damien Doyle?'

Damien clenched at the sound of an elderly lady; it was not too late to feign technological problems.

'It is.'

'It's Maureen McGinty.'

Damien pictured dark wine tumbling into an empty glass.

'Oh, hello. Mrs McGinty, I'm afraid that I'm about to head out the door so if you wanted to call about a government matter—'

'It isn't that …'

Unusual for Mrs McGinty to have any hesitation: Damien sensed the crisis in her pause.

'I wasn't sure if I should call the police …'

'What is it?'

Damien knew what words were coming before she sounded them.

'It's John Paul.'

12

Box of Matches (2009)

The trick was to keep moving. Don't dwell. Look to the future. Let the past go up in flames.

This was the brilliant idea, John Paul thought, breaking into the shed. His eyes rushed over the collection of mildewed books and gadgets he'd bought for Granny Doyle that she'd never managed to switch on. He would not dwell on the past. There was only one item John Paul was after and there it was by the rusted lawnmower that he hadn't used in years: the can of petrol. Enough in it to do the job.

John Paul lit a match and stared at the flame. He thrust his mouth towards it, cigarette reddening in time, match tossed out the shed door into the snow. Plenty of time for fireworks later, he thought, his knees knocking together, head buzzed from the coke. First, he'd have a fag and gather his thoughts; the box of matches slipped into his hoodie pocket as he slumped onto the floor. The plan was clear in his head. He'd pour the petrol over the armchairs and then he'd light the match and the pure fire would rip through the house and cleanse everything. The living room would disappear and with it, the last conversation he'd had with Granny Doyle, when he'd told her that the house was being seized and he finally did *it*, the thing to shatter all her delusions. He had recognized her shocked face; he'd seen her direct it to his father before, whose voice he heard in his own excuses, *don't worry* and *don't cry* and *I'll work something out*. He cried that day, messy, racking sobs that took the breath out of him, brought him red-faced to his knees as he gripped the living-room armchair and asked, with all his body, for a grand-mother to hold him, as she walked past him and stood with her hands on the sink waiting for the kettle to boil. For the first time, John Paul had felt the full force of Granny Doyle's back, immobile as he tried to talk to her before he left, his father's voice in his mouth, making him want to shove a penknife through his throat and slash out such a tongue.

He would not do that; he would fix things. He might have lost everything else – Popehood; Clodagh; the chance of Clo ever letting him see their daughter – but 7 Dunluce Crescent he could fix. Or burn. Or both. Burn the past to light up the future, a motto for his smartphone, were he still keeping track. He'd pour the petrol, light the match, leave. Ring the guards before it spread; much as they might deserve it, he wouldn't see the Donnellys cindered. Although maybe he shouldn't pour the petrol: there was a chance that a match on its own would do the trick, certainly enough shite inside to catch a flame. The petrol might be incrim-inating – he hadn't watched enough television to know if forensics could sniff it out and this was another thing to regret, the hours lost to *Jackass* and *Punk'd* when he could have been swotting up on *CSI*. John Paul felt his brilliant plan disintegrating, which was inconvenient as he'd come all the way and already ripped his jeans hopping over the back wall. He picked up the petrol can and stood with as much resolution as his traitorous legs, those wibbly wobblers, allowed; the trick was to keep moving. Don't dwell. Let the past go up in flames.

'What the fuck are you doing?'

John Paul's eyes wobbled: there was a guard at the back door, or a gargoyle; some shitebag in a suit blocking the brilliant plan, anyway.

'I should have known you'd be fucked.'

Disappointment as much as anger in the words; of course it was bloody Damien.

'Get out of my way,' John Paul said, though his legs moved side-ways instead of forwards, the bastards.

Damien had his patient face on, as bad as Clo's.

'You're drunk,' John Paul said, words clinging to the sight of the bottle in Damien's hand.

Damien sliced at him with his smile.

'Nearly.'

Damien was drunk, though: what else would have him gulping another glug straight from the bottle?

'So, you're planning a bonfire, are you?' Damien said, a nasty sliver of a smile on his face, another *I can't be fucked cleaning up your mess* swig straight from the bottle.

'Get out of my way,' John Paul said, remembering the brilliant plan, his legs finally obliging in a forward march.

You're not getting in, the fold of Damien's arms said.

Fucking joker, John Paul's laugh said.

The laugh was not enough to budge Damien.

'Go home,' Damien said. 'You've done enough damage here.'

Have I now? John Paul's laugh said.

'You're lucky Mrs McGinty didn't call the guards.'

'Sure I'll call them myself,' John Paul said. 'Tell them we've got one of the government fuckers who bailed out the banks here.'

I will not be taunted, the hardening of Damien's face said.

'You're lucky Gran can't see you like this.'

That wiped the smile from John Paul's face.

You'll not be slipping guilt on my shoulders, John Paul's gulp said.

'As if you ever gave a riddlers about her! How many times have *you* come here? You ever cleaned these windows or cut the grass for her? Sat with her on the porch? Get the fuck down from your high horse! You never did a thing for her!'

I never had the chance, the bob of Damien's Adam's apple said.

'At least I didn't kick her onto the street.'

Careful, boy, don't test me, the ball of John Paul's fist said.

409

You haven't changed a bit, the shake of Damien's head said.

'I'll call you a car,' Damien said.

I'm going to fix this, the whirl of John Paul's eyes said.

'This is my house!' John Paul shouted.

The curve of Damien's lips was cruel.

'Actually, it belongs to the bank now.'

'Bank sent you to do their dirty business, did they? Suppose you've gotten a lot of practice at that, haven't you?'

How dare you, Damien said, although the words didn't come out, his arms pushed forwards instead.

What the …? John Paul's gasp said as the back of his head dashed against the pebbles of the wall.

Oh shit, Damien's gulp said but then *finally* John Paul's smile said and *fuck you, you cocky shite* John Paul's glare said and *bring it on* Damien's headshake said and *fuck you* the lunge of their limbs said and that was that, the match sparked, the two of them tumbling onto the snow, the fight twenty-nine years in the making finally happening.

You brought this on yourself Damien's fist said and *you called me faggot* Damien's thump said and *you punched Rory* Damien's kick said as *you bailed out the banks* John Paul's push said and *you've never had an ounce of cop-on* John Paul's shove said and *you ratted me out* John Paul's roar said. Wine and petrol lay to the side as the pair of them flapped and flailed around the garden, fists and feet kicking up snow and curdled sentences: *you couldn't keep your gob shut* and *you broke her heart* and *you're pathetic* and *you fight like a girl* and *I've been gyming it up* and *I actually hate you* and *you represent everything that's wrong with the country* and *you never visited her* and *you haven't a clue* and *all I want is your respect* and *this is your fault, you fucker* batted forth and back, the two of them too fucked to break blood or bruise, the two of them rolling and raging on top of each other, knackered, the snow underneath them hard.

They were like that when Rosie woke up and came downstairs. Rosie stared at them for a moment but they were too absorbed in their own panting and punching to notice the arrival of their sister. It was their obliviousness to her existence that had Rosie scooping a handful of snow into her mitten, *I hate you equally* arcing through air.

Rosie gathered up quite a few handfuls of snow – *Why did I come here?* and *stop!* and *I am here* – before one of her missiles finally connected with John Paul's face. *What the...?* John Paul's laugh said and *Huh?* Damien's face said. The three of them looked at each other, John Paul and Damien, side by side on the ground, panting, while Rosie stood with a fistful of snow in her mitten.

And then, miraculously, the elastic band snapped back into place. *Bring it on* John Paul's laugh said and *fuck it* the whoosh of snow through the air said and who knew what the snow that scurried back and forth in the next minute said, there wasn't time to think; there were the triplets, ducking and diving around the tiny back garden of 7 Dunluce Crescent, which had once seemed as enormous as a universe. Damien aimed too far and a snowball whooshed over the back wall towards the Donnellys' house, prompting the twitch of a curtain and laughs from John Paul, who immediately scooped up a hard clump of snow and flung it towards 5 Dunluce Crescent, *fuck you* written in its arc, echoed by Damien's and Rosie's snowballs, *I want to smash something so it might as well be this* curved through the air, *thud thud thud* against the wall, prompting the opening of the window, the rare appearance of Mr Donnelly, whose face shouted *I'll call the police* as the triplets collapsed upon each other in fits.

Back in the day, this might have prompted a miracle from John Paul Doyle. Perhaps the triplets would have escaped together, dashing down Dunluce Crescent and sending snowballs and giggles into the air, the three of them thief-thick, united against the world, back on that day. Or, their small hands might have reached the ground together, three snowballs shooting through the Donnellys' open window, precise missiles that found their mark miraculously: the open mouth of Mrs Donnelly, about to exclaim that *mind you, I always said the Doyles had it coming.*

But John Paul had lost the knack of miracles. They did not skip through the streets, sending snowballs on perfect arcs as tensions melted underfoot. No snowball curved through the Donnellys' window. The elastic band broke; they barely even talked. Rosie and Damien got John Paul into a bed and Damien took a taxi home and Rosie smoked into the early hours, eventually falling into a shaky sleep in an armchair.

When John Paul awoke, dragged into the day by the hammering in his head, Rosie was asleep. Dunluce Crescent was coming to life. Mr Okorocho was heading out in his car, while Mrs Okorocho stood at the door of Mrs Nugent's house, shooing away the snow with her scowl. Two schoolbagged young things slouched out of Irene Hunter's house, disgusted at the melting snow. Curtains twitched in Mrs McGinty's window, though no figure appeared. Out in the back garden, the petrol can and empty wine bottle lay forlorn on scraps of grass, the brilliant plan evaporating too. John Paul had failed to burn the house down, just as he had failed to kill himself all those years ago: he couldn't even succeed at being a failure. This thought, coupled with the danger that Rosie might wake up – a look from her that morning would be enough to slay him, he was sure of it – sent John Paul out the front door, the memory of his coat only hitting him as he turned the corner, when it was impossible to go back, unnecessary too: the St Vincent de Paul would be glad to have it in one of their bags.

13

Brooklyn Botanic Garden
Annual Pass (2009)

Peg stood on Dev's balcony and took in an exhilarating breath of crisp, snowy air. She loved her fire escape but there was something luxurious about a balcony, especially with snowy-roofed houses laid out as if in a fairy tale. Only in Brooklyn, a place assuming a magical dimension for Peg, who imagined it as a Narnia without witches, every house festooned with wreaths, children bicycling by, every day a Saturday. Dev emerged from the shower, a different Dev; that was what moving to Brooklyn had achieved. Divorce had been the making of them, the grind of bills and bin-bags replaced with two available people in their lives' prime, cuddled under covers on a Saturday morning.

Peg handed him some fresh coffee.

'I should get going soon,' Dev said.

Peg pulled Dev into a kiss.

'Okay,' Peg said, followed by her new favourite word. 'Soon.'

Months passed but 'soon' hovered just outside of time, a word to swoon inside.

Soon, she would get dressed and go.

Soon, they would see each other again.

Soon, they would talk about whatever it was they were doing.

*

'Breakfast?' Dev said.

Peg nodded. They went inside, to Dev's kitchen, where Peg didn't mind that sometimes knives found their way to the fork compartment. He'd made eggs and pesto, this new Dev.

Soon, she would tell him how much she liked this.

Soon, she would say, why don't we walk to the Botanic Garden and sit in the warm greenhouses and hold hands.

Soon, she would tell him how much she loved him.

Dev checked the time on his phone. He had a meeting with some radical economics group he'd become part of, the world to be saved with meetings and mathematics and the overthrow of capitalism, soon.

Brooklyn had made a revolutionary of Dev, or the times had, more meetings and marches than ever necessary to put affairs to rights. Dev had been all in on Team Obama, the most enthusiastic canvasser in Brooklyn, but this was when they weren't talking, so Peg didn't know the new friends that Dev had amassed, his support group now that Obama had bailed out the banks and failed to pass a carbon tax and proved mortal, after all. Even so, Dev kept the Obama poster up in his kitchen; he would take it down, soon.

'There's a foreclosure protest tomorrow afternoon,' Dev said, some unpleasant questions from the past lurking underneath, *don't you want to come?* and *why can't you be the person I want?* there, even as Dev's voice was light.

'I have to work,' Peg lied.

Dev stabbed out a response to somebody on his phone. Peg tensed; she could still tell when Devansh Sabharwal was gearing up to something. She was worried it might have something to do with Rosie. Peg wasn't on Facebook, so she didn't know if Rosie had joined or poked at Dev's radical economics group. A Brooklyn kitchen was no place for the Doyles, so Peg nuzzled into Dev's chest and sipped her coffee.

Soon, there would be lovely heat in the greenhouses, where they would hold hands under brightly coloured vines.

Soon, there would be bluebells to walk through.

Soon, there would be pillows of cherry blossom under their heads.

Dev was happier now that he was teaching at a hippie school in Brooklyn where radical math was part of the curriculum. Peg had finished her Master's. She had her job in the library. She had the money from the house in Clougheally, enough to set them both up for a time. She had Robert and Tom and Enrique, for this was the twenty-first century, and here they were in New York, a city with all its secrets in plain view, and divorce had been the making of them, an open relationship the way they could stay together. Peg felt a sliver of longing for a world where people got to live more than one life; here she was at thirty-four, having only just figured some things out. What things she could do were she to go through it all again!

Dev looked at his phone; another text had arrived, but he didn't say from whom. He scrolled through his phone, working up to something. Peg drained her coffee and wondered if it was late enough to get away with mimosas (she would evaluate her behaviour and learn to love juice made from kale, soon).

'Peg ...'

She sensed them then, the words that Dev was collecting. He'd met somebody, somebody to be serious about, and the *soon we have to stop* had come now and Dev and Whoever would be wed within two years and have a baby within three and Peg wouldn't even get to read about it on Facebook.

'Peg ...'

Other words were coming first, unfortunately: she could tell the pause Devansh Sabharwal took before he broached the topic of the Doyles (who had no space in a Brooklyn kitchen). Peg looked out the window, where snow had started to fall again (perhaps they might be stuck in this apartment, for ever). She knew that things weren't going well in Ireland, everybody asked her about it, from the supervisor to the bodega clerk. She knew that things weren't going well for the Doyles. But what business did they have clambering onto this balcony, intruding upon this kitchen: couldn't they leave her be?

'Peg …'

She brought her eyes back to Dev. This was hard for him too, because he hated being the messenger and he didn't understand how she felt about her family, he never had, and he should have given up years ago, but here he was, one last time, a sentence he'd spoken before, though it had accumulated weight, tenderness too.

'I think you should call Rosie …'

Series X:
Last Rites

(2010–2011)

1

'What's the Craic, Barack?'
T-Shirt (2011)

It was May 2011 when Barack Obama brought hope to Ireland. For the first time in his life, John Paul longed to be in Moneygall. It looked brilliant on the TV: the Obamas stepping out of their limo onto Moneygall's main street, as cool as could be, babies lifted up and hands shaken and sweet shops strolled into. Obama demonstrated the best parts of his heritage: casually cracking jokes across pints like an Irishman; smiling until his teeth cracked like a good American, no crisis that optimism couldn't defeat.

John Paul might have been there. It was easy to imagine Pope John Paul III standing in the Moneygall drizzle and shaking hands with the President of the United States. No, Obama was too cool for that: fist-bumps and back-slaps it would have been. They would have clinked pints in the pub and John Paul would have made a brilliant video. Instead, he'd had the lunch-hour rush to get through and the hands that might have fist-bumped a president filled baguettes with sliced tomatoes and shredded cheese.

Not to worry: it would have been mad to trek to Moneygall, anyway. Obama was here in Dublin and John Paul was ready, his shift in Spar finished, Sophie with her legs around his shoulders, a giant shamrock hat on her head.

'That's the President, look!' John Paul said, as Sophie looked around the College Green crowd, more interested in another girl's Peppa Pig backpack than whatever it was the giant man on the screen was saying.

'That's President Obama!' John Paul said, sure that Sophie would wow the teachers at her playschool with her vocabulary.

He cast his eye around the crowd for the press. Other toddlers were also sporting shamrock hats, but none of them were as cute as Sophie; he could see her, beaming from the front page of the *Irish Independent*. He'd keep his head out of the frame, hoping that people wouldn't recognize him. He was glad of his beard and sunglasses and the thick of the crowd, not a space where Mrs Donnelly could squeeze through to say that she had a second cousin from Moneygall or, would you believe it, Jason had an invite to the dinner at the American ambassador's.

Sophie wanted her chocolate buttons.

'Don't tell your mammy,' John Paul said, finding the contraband.

Clodagh was fighting a daily battle with her mother about Sophie's sugar intake, the big house off the Coast Road too small for all of them. There they were, though, and whatever tensions Clodagh carried were stored in her shoulders; she did not complain about her mother to John Paul, because they didn't talk. They were in the civil stage; sentences were to be kept short and measured. They had done their fighting and crying and smashing. If Clodagh Reynolds felt any sadness as she looked at her reflection in the same mirror that she and John Paul Doyle had cracked when they were teenagers, she did not share it with John Paul. She kept her feelings stored in that small bedroom, let any tears fall on the same floorboards where once John Paul had taken off her bra and told her he'd love her for ever.

'... And, Ireland, as trying as these times are, I know our future is still as big and as bright as our children expect it to be.'

The crowd erupted in another cheer, Sophie joining in, sticky hands waving at the President.

'He's talking about you, so he is,' John Paul said.

'... And today, Ireland's youth, and those who've come back to build a new Ireland, are now among the best-educated, most entrepreneurial in the world. And I see those young people here today. And I know that Ireland will succeed.'

'Yeah, you will, won't you?' John Paul said.

Sophie would be up there one day, a president or a taoiseach, whatever she wanted.

She was the thing that that got him off the couch. It didn't matter how other people looked at him, or how he looked at himself: through Sophie's eyes he could rebuild himself. And they were great eyes, blue like her mother's, full of love and curiosity and wonder for the world, gawping at all the mad ones in College Green, taking it all in. He felt humbled that she even looked at him at all, with so many things to be stared at, and he cherished every glance and gaze, pocketed them like notes into a wallet.

'This little country, that inspires the biggest things – your best days are still ahead. Our greatest triumphs – in America and Ireland alike – are still to come.'

It was brilliant, Obama finding the words to lift a nation. Hard times always came, that was history. But up people got; on they went. That was the story of his ancestor, Falmouth Kearney, who had fled the Famine on a ship, looked across an empty American field and thought: *here I start*. Start he did, and look at where his great-great-great-grandson stood now, proof that sweat and tears could take you far, eventually. Obama was brilliant, John Paul thought, chorusing out 'Is Féidir Linn' with the rest of the crowd, encouraging Sophie to do the same; she'd be top of the class at Irish, a translator for the United Nations, an award-winning linguist.

2

Hospital Bracelet: 'Bridget Doyle' (2010)

A year before, John Paul held Sophie by the window and pointed towards the blank sky.

Ash hovered above, supposedly.

'That's Eyjafjallajökull,' he said, bouncing the word like a ball. Sophie gabbled something back and he could have sworn it bore a correspondence; she was a genius.

'And that's your great-grandmother,' he said, bringing her back over to the bed and holding her up, a shield or an offering, it wasn't clear which.

It wouldn't be long, the nurses said. The second stroke had taken it out of her. They could read death like a bird could read the clouds, the nurses. Granny Doyle looked at Sophie, who looked back at her, two dumb creatures. Sophie gabbled, and swatted her little hand through the air, the way she did, indiscriminately, but John Paul took it as a sign that she wanted to hold her great-grandmother, so he moved her closer.

'Yeah, that's your great-grandmother,' he said, talking to Sophie because it was easier, placing emphasis on the 'great', meaning it.

Sophie made a sound so John Paul said 'yeah' again, because it was nice to think of them in perpetual assent.

Granny Doyle looked at him. He felt everything inside him tighten. You were supposed to talk to her, the nurses said; she could probably hear. But you wouldn't know for sure. He saw some saps at it in other rooms: reading out the newspaper, story by story, or launching into a long account of their day. It was hard to keep such a monologue up, especially with people coming and going, and John Paul didn't have banter in him at the moment. Another thing that had gone. *No harm*, Granny Doyle might have said, in the days when she teased him gently, but that was gone from her too, and instead she made a sound that came from deep in the back of her throat and moved her fingers agitatedly. John Paul wanted to sing her a lullaby, one of the old country tunes that she'd sung to them as babies; that seemed the type of thing to do in this situation, but he couldn't remember the air of it and he couldn't be sure that it wouldn't upset her further so he looked at her and said again to Sophie, 'That's your great-grandmother.'

Later. He would talk to her later. John Paul reached out and held on to her hand, the good one. The bracelet was tight on her wrist and he tried to loosen it a little, failed. Another thing to atone for. He would find some way of making it right for her. There would be a tune to mend the broken string between them; he would find it.

She was a stubborn one, the nurses said. Oh yes, a former nurse, that explained it, they'd say, laughing. But she didn't have long; they could read it in the minutes now. She had a tear in one of her eyes and he wondered what this meant, if it was for him. Impossible to know where her mind was, how much of it she was taking in. His own eyes were full and he blinked, tried to clear his throat, but the words wouldn't come; there were too many things he had to say to her.

He looked into her eyes and rubbed her hand and hoped that she knew.

3

Climate Change and
Energy Bill (2011)

Damien took an experimental sip of coffee – terrible, he was spoiled by Brussels – and looked at Enda Bloody Kenny on the television in the bar.

He might have been there, although it was unlikely that an assistant to the Minister of the Environment would have much to do with Obama's visit. He would, at least, have been around Leinster House for the bustle; it would have been a welcome break from the other visitors, IMF men and their briefcases replaced by the man with the Hope. Ah well. Plenty of bustle in Brussels. Besides, Damien had been to the Climate Change Conference in Copenhagen: he had seen where Obama's hope could lead.

'They're saying he might not be able to stay the night in Dublin,' the bartender said. 'Another ash cloud, can you believe that? Ryanair will have to sue.'

Damien nodded along as the bartender talked, thinking instead about the time in Copenhagen when he'd seen Obama for a moment, striding through the conference centre, photographers and delegates swirling around, before Obama abandoned the whole affair, leaving Damien with his lanyard in the empty conference building, Obama ducking into a car and onto a plane, hope trailing after.

Damien decided to move on to a glass of the house red – horrible, why did he bother? – crinkling his nose as Obama quoted Yeats. Damien knew all about responsibility beginning in dreams. He could picture it in front of him, the climate change bill that would have been the Greens' legacy, the document to justify the compromises. Was there a word for bills that never got passed into law? Was this one lying in some vault in Leinster House, collecting dust as new governments chased new agendas?

Damien sighed. It was too soon to be visiting Dublin; his wounds felt less raw in Brussels, where, at least, there was more than one type of red wine to be found in a bar. And work, that too. He was lucky to have a job, European climate policy a thing to keep him going. On he went; on one went.

The bartender was enraptured with Obama's talk of dreams, so Damien let his mind wander, imagining what Mark might say.

Oh, not this American dream shite, Mark would say.

What the fuck use is a dream to pensioners without heat, or people sleeping on the streets, Mark would say.

And where does he get off, patting Ireland on the head and telling us we'll be grand, as if following the American fecking dream didn't lead us here in the first place, Mark would say.

And why is he going on about the bond between Ireland and America, not that strong a bond, when half the Yank companies fecked off without paying the taxes, Mark would say.

Give us some solutions, Mark would say; what are you going to do about the IMF, Mark would heckle.

Damien would smooth the edges of Mark's gruffness and say that Obama's hands were tied – they always had been – and that there wasn't much he could do to intervene in IMF policy. Damien would raise a hand to counter Mark's scoff and he would go on to defend Obama, arguing that policy was the place to balance the rhetoric of hope and the indignation of protest; Obama would find ways for his policies to catch up with his words, action on climate to be taken once he had secured a second term, Damien was sure. Defending Obama to Mark, Damien would find the qualities that he had admired in Obama in the first place; between the two of them they'd find the right balance, make space for the kind of hope that wouldn't give you a headache the next morning.

It wasn't Mark bounding in the door though, but Maxime.

A thing to love about Maxime: he wasn't like Mark, he always apologized when he was late.

'Sorry, babe, they've closed some of the streets and I couldn't find any WiFi; I don't know how anybody finds their way around this city.'

'You're grand,' Damien said, the truth, for who wouldn't find Maxime grand? Plenty of things to love about him, from his assurance at knowing the best bars in Brussels to his stellar vegetarian cooking, to the sight of his chest in a tank top.

'You okay, babe?'

A thing about Maxime: he wasn't Mark.

Damien gulped the last of his wine.

'I'm grand.'

4

Hospital Bracelet:
'Bridget Doyle' (2010)

A year before, Mark handed Damien a cup of coffee from the machine.

'Thanks,' Damien said.

Mark sat down on one of the plastic chairs behind him and took a gulp of his tea.

Damien sat down and sipped his coffee.

'She's doing well,' Mark said.

'She is,' Damien said.

It's great to see you, Damien didn't say

You too, Mark didn't say.

I hear you got a job at Focus, Damien didn't say.

Yeah, Mark didn't say.

And you're seeing someone, Damien didn't say.

Right, Mark didn't say.

And you got your ears pierced finally, Damien didn't say.

The earlobes of Mark Rafferty were once an area in which I could claim great expertise, Damien didn't say.

I never thought that would change, Damien didn't say.

'Thanks for coming,' Damien said.

'Of course,' Mark said.

They looked at their cups.

'She's a great old broad,' Mark said.

'She is,' Damien said.

They drank their drinks.

'You're doing all right?' Mark asked.

'You know,' Damien said.

You can't blame people after the bailout, Mark didn't say.

Let's not talk about the government, Damien didn't say.

'You?' Damien said.

'Ah, yeah,' Mark said. 'You know.'

Mark drank the rest of his tea in one go.

'I'll say goodbye,' Mark said.

'Yeah,' Damien said.

Mark and Damien stood. Mark threw his cup in the bin. Damien did the same, although he hadn't finished his coffee. They walked to the end of the corridor and took the lift up together. They walked down another corridor into the room where Granny Doyle was. She was sleeping, so they didn't disturb her. They stood, watching her sleep.

I love you, Damien didn't say.

I miss you, Mark didn't say.

I'm sorry, Damien didn't say.

Me too, Mark didn't say.

I thought I'd be by your side when you died, Damien didn't say.

You sick bastard, Mark didn't say.

I meant, Damien didn't say.

I know, Mark didn't say.

I always know what you mean, Mark didn't say.

I miss this, Damien didn't say.

I love you, Mark didn't say.

A nurse came in the door: 'Just checking in'. Mark unbundled his coat and put it on.

Mark moved to Granny Doyle's good side and squeezed her hand.

'Right,' Mark said.

'Thanks for coming,' Damien said.

'Of course,' Mark said.

The nurse wrote on the chart.

'Bye so,' Mark said.

'Bye,' Damien said.

Mark put his arms around Damien, patted his back three times.

Mark pulled away, touched Damien's cheek quickly with his thumb.

'Bye,' Mark said.

'Bye,' Damien said.

5

'Yes We Can Put People
Before Profit' Sign (2011)

Rosie held up her sign, pleased. She had managed to mimic some of the famous poster design and she'd found the right shade of red and blue for the words. Fionnuala had added a blob in the corner, an inadvertent result of her crawl through the kitchen, though Ciarán claimed she'd be a budding artist. She can do whatever she wants, Rosie said, smitten with the creature whose every gargle said *I love you!*

What Fionnuala wanted to do now was sleep, so Ciarán went on a walk with the baby sling, off to get photographed for Hot Dad of the Year, he joked.

Better not let them see the bald patch, Rosie said, for his fringe had gone; still, she loved him.

It was nice to have a babyless moment, Rosie thought, a chance to rediscover who she was. More or less the same person, it turned out. Certainly not somebody who would swoon in College Green at Obama's speech. She'd heard the reports of his earlier anecdote, shared as he supped a pint in Moneygall. The first time he'd had Irish Guinness had been in Shannon airport, en route to Afghanistan. A revelation, he said: the pints really were better in Ireland! Rosie had not thought it so cute, a story that blithely mentioned warplanes as vehicles for the stout education of a president.

So, it was good to have the protest to go to. A tiny thing, really, but Rosie felt the warmth of community, comrades from the Glen of the Downs there, including Conor, whose hair was brown and thinning too (they shared smiles and a smoke) and people she recognized from marches and new people too, students who wouldn't be lulled to sleep by some fine words. All the signs were home-made, her favourite kind. 'Close Guantanamo' they said and 'No War in Afghanistan!' and 'Free Private Manning!' Others shouted local concerns: 'No Bailout!'; 'No IMF Package!'; 'No to Austerity!' Rosie held her sign proudly; if people rather than profits could be considered, a lot of problems in Ireland and America might disappear, the pipe included.

Nice to have a pipeless moment too, that was the truth. They kept going, the coalition against the pipe, picking over small victories, proof that it had not been in vain. There was the fact that the gas wouldn't run at 345 bar, that was a solid achievement, Ciarán said, and Rosie said yes. There was the change in the pipe route, only a few metres, but significant, Ciarán said, and Rosie wanted to say yes but her mouth couldn't quite manage the shape. It was dispiriting – to see the refinery being constructed in Ballinaboy, to feel the wind pulled out of the campaign as Rosie had Fionnuala Brigid Doyle to look after and a life that had little space for the slog of a campaign. Shell's new tunnel-boring machine was to be named Fionnuala, a transformation unimagined by the Children of Lir, a detail that Rosie found particularly hard to take.

Still, on she went; there was a lot that one person could do with a square of cardboard. And she wasn't alone. There were her friends and comrades, her family! There were others, all around the world, occupying squares from Cairo to Madrid, thousands of people standing up for a better world. There were the ghosts, Rosie felt their aura, brushing through the streets, Aunty Mary among them, and Granny Doyle too – why not? – for plenty of people had shouted at stone buildings and died before the world had changed. They were here now, ghosts filling the streets, looking on at the world, which would change one day; it had to.

6

Hospital Bracelet:
'Bridget Doyle' (2010)

A year before, ash hovered in the air, falling like snow outside the hospital window; that was how Rosie imagined it, anyway. Rosie rubbed her eyes and wondered if she could take another cup of hospital coffee. It wouldn't be long, the nurses said. If there was anybody to call. Now was the time.

Rosie had rescued Granny Doyle's address book from a shoebox. It was a sad thing, half full, most of the names also present in the two boxes full of memorial cards that Rosie hadn't been able to throw away. Rosie had called everybody she thought she should and some she shouldn't. She imagined a string stretching across an ocean, two tin cans rattling on either side, *come home* vibrating across the waters. There was no tin can outside the window, of course, only ash falling, which she couldn't even see.

Rosie paced the room. Damien and John Paul avoided her gaze, because neither of them knew what to do. Ciarán appeared, conjuring up some chamomile tea and setting up a laptop in the room, so that some of the Clougheally crowd could Skype in for a moment.

There was a stream of visitors, then. Mrs McGinty came and said the rosary in a steady voice, giving a curt nod as she left. Sister Angela stopped by, and Mrs Fay's daughter, and some priest, and people totally out of the blue, like Mrs Nugent's granddaughter, who had *stopped that* years ago and was a pilot with three kids. They broke the rules about visiting hours but the nurses didn't say anything. It wouldn't be long, they said.

And then it was just the three of them, Ciarán taking a kip outside. The night dragged on and they rotated chairs, positions, trips to the coffee machine. Granny Doyle opened and closed her eyes and moved her hand and they took turns rubbing it.

The morning sun streaked in. Ash hovered outside the window. She would open the window a crack, later. She would light a stick of incense. She would close her eyelids. She would make the bed, tucking in the corners right, the way she would have wanted.

Granny Doyle made a sound. It might have been 'Danny' or 'John Paul' or 'Mary' or 'Peg'. It might have been nothing.

'I'm here,' Rosie said, putting her hand around Granny Doyle's good one and squeezing.

7

Ash (2010–2011)

Where was Peg Doyle in April 2010?

Peg packed a bag and took a taxi to JFK. But then there were no flights from JFK to anywhere in Europe, whatever the price.

Peg could understand a rational argument. She collected her suitcase, allowed herself the luxury of another cab back to Manhattan, watched the ash cloud on her television, pondered what she might do that evening, thinking she might read an Icelandic saga and meet up with the man who said his name was Luke and not answer the phone as it rang.

*

Or, ash hung over Europe and no planes were allowed in the sky, except one, which made its way through the fog of ash and unwanted things, flying over the Atlantic, over the West Coast of Ireland, crossing the country, sunlight illuminating all the dust in the air, which hovered over Ruadhan Kennedy-Carthy buying a *pain au chocolat* on his way to work, and over Clodagh Reynolds doing yoga in the morning sun, and over Denise Donnelly pushing her fist against a horn on a motorway, and over Jason Donnelly checking out his chest in the mirror of a gym, and over Irene Hunter squeezing a third use out of a teabag, and over Mrs Okorocho counting her blessings, and over Mr Okorocho counting his change, and over Mrs Fay running down the strand in her head as she sat in an armchair and talked to a window, and over Mrs McGinty walking to the morning Mass, and over Olly Edwards going down on Rory

O'Donoghue, and over Carl Brennan throwing a stone at a church window and crying, and over Father O'Shaughnessy taking a second helping of eggs, and over Kay Gallagher reviewing a brief, and over Mrs Donnelly bringing in the bins, and over Mr Geoghan heading out the door, so many lives like lint, that the cloud hung over, as the plane cycled round and round, unsure if it could ever land, for the ash cloud was getting thicker, wreathing its tentacles around all the other waste products in the air, all the gas and smoke from pipes and refineries, the snores and sighs, dreams and dandruff, until it was a giant cloud of all the unwanted things in the world and, wrapped in layers of metal, in the middle of it all, was Peg.

*

Or, Peg never got on board the plane, because why would somebody like Peg do something like that?

*

Or, Peg found a plane that would leave and made her way across the Atlantic. She landed in Dublin Airport and managed her way through customs. She adjusted to Terminal 2 and to the look of euros and to the half-light of a Dublin morning, as if the sun itself had a hangover. She found herself a taxi. She got dropped off at the hospital and threw an array of euros to the driver as a tip and got out of the car and stood there, with her suitcase by her side, watching the glass doors open and close, watching other people walk in and out, the doors opening and closing, other people walking in and out, until she turned round and waited for another taxi.

*

Or, Peg walked through the hospital doors and up the stairs until she found the corridor. She walked into the room. She looked at Granny Doyle and slapped her across the face.
  'Peg!'

But Peg would not be ssssssssh'd by John Paul.

'You turned your back on me. You kicked me out when I needed you most. I'll never forget that. That's not something that can ever be forgiven,' Peg said, walking out.

*

Or, she found the corridor but didn't walk into the room because Rosie was standing outside.

It was too late, Peg could tell from Rosie's face.

Rosie ran over and hugged her, sent tears streaming down the back of her cardigan, and, in the movement of their hands across each other's backs they both knew that it wasn't too late.

*

Or, she got on a plane and it touched down smoothly – a year later the skies were full of planes again and the President himself had made the journey only the day before. She got a taxi to a hotel. She slept for a few hours. She met the triplets in the afternoon, the four of them squeezing into the car that John Paul had rented and driving down the pier to the end of the Bull Wall, where they took out the urn and scattered the rest of its contents into the sea. It was a cold afternoon, but they stayed by the sea for some time. Peg imagined herself a great, feathered creature, swooping large wings around her siblings, shielding them from the wind with all its sorrows; this was what she imagined, as she stood behind them, watching.

*

She walked into the room and everybody turned to look at her.

Granny Doyle stirred.

She's a stubborn one, the nurse would say later, she was waiting for you.

Granny Doyle looked at Peg.

Peg looked at Granny Doyle.

They could see each other, all of their hurt and history, all of their secrets and lies, and in that look, Peg understood everything, saw a whole life unfurling before her.

Peg walked over to the bed, held Granny Doyle's hand. Rosie placed her hand on Peg's shoulder and John Paul held Granny Doyle's other hand and Damien held on to both Rosie and John Paul and in this way, they were all connected.

Granny Doyle died in the early morning, ash hovering outside the window, though you couldn't see it.

Before she passed, her eyes roamed the room, looked at each of them, pulsed with love.

Then she died and the four of them held each other and cried by the side of her bed.

That was the history that Peg told, searching for the right-shaped lid to close a box. It was the way she wanted it to happen. In the space between what had happened and what might have happened, there was room for all sorts of things: truth, lies, histories, heresies, even, surely, those elusive, shimmering things, miracles.

Acknowledgements

Thank you to everybody at 4th Estate and Harper Collins who helped bring this story to publication with pride and passion, including Jack Smyth, Mary Byrne, Matt Clacher, Paul Erdpresser, David Roth-Ey, Michelle Kane, Lottie Fyfe, and especially Anna Kelly, whose wise editing, sharp eye for detail, and brilliant ideas helped the book tremendously.

Thank you to everybody at The Bent Agency for guiding this story towards publication: to John Bowers and Victoria Cappello for believing in the story from the beginning; to the indomitable Louise Fury for representing me in the US; to the wonderful Nicola Barr for expertly guiding the book and me through publication in the UK.

Thank you to all my friends who read various rough drafts or sections of this project over the past six years. Thanks to Anisa, Ed, Chris, Mika, Ian, Daragh and Felix for their helpful encouragement and advice on everything from climate protests to correct archival procedure; to Hannah Fair and Juli for last minute advice on sentences and semi-colons; to Gillian, for being one of the first readers of everything I've written and giving me the confidence to write more; to Minou, for her brilliant advice and encouragement, reading multiple drafts, and being the best comrade through grad school that anybody could hope for; to Kevin, for believing in the project from the first time I nattered about it on a train to Montreal, being kind and supportive about the messy early drafts, and for being kind and supportive, always.

Thank you to all my friends and housemates who have listened to me talk about these ideas over the last six years and helped enormously by sharing advice on writing and the world. Special thanks to Sarah for embarking on an Erris trip; to Ed for the environmental politics chats; to Rachel Schragis for all the climate talk; to Hannah Temple for the Google alerts and conversations about Pride; to Jane for the local advice and being a fine friend across decades; to Peter, for the impromptu artistic residency in Melbourne and being a friend through procrastination; to Donncha and Giacomo for the pasta, friendship, and an Edinburgh room to finish a first draft; to Michael and Mary Carson for their inspiration and the room-with-a-view writing days in Milford; to Maggie Dear for the map mock-ups, emergency cake-tutorials and optimism.

Thank you to my family for all their support, fact-checking, and rooting out of old photographs. Mum, Dad, Aoife, Gillian, Caroline, Brendan, Yossa, Ryley, and Kyrah: you're all brilliant and I hope you'll believe that you're not in the novel now! Thank you to my grandmothers, Ellen Martin and Tess Garvey, who were wonderful mentors to me when I was younger. Some of the superficial details of Granny Doyle's life are drawn from observing my grandmothers but the character is very different from the warm and generous women I grew up with.

Thank you to the writing communities that helped make this novel possible: to the Blue Mountain Center for space to come up with ideas; to Michael Yates Crowley and the Hearthgods community for providing a place to test out words; to Pat and the LGBT's the Word creative writing group at 56 Dean Street for making space for queer stories; to Free Word, Tipping Point, and Durham University for hosting the Weatherfronts Conference and providing a regular space for writers to think about climate change; to Lola and all the Climate Writing group who provided advice on excerpts of this novel; to the First Story group at Chelsea Academy for their inspiration and advice on covers; to Aaron, Christine, Rachel Waldholz and many others for the chats about writing and the encouragement to keep going.

Thank you to the librarians of the British Library, the New York Public Library, the State Library of Victoria, the National Library of Scotland, the National Library of Ireland, Trinity College Library, Columbia University Library, Walthamstow Library, and Raheny Library. The majority of this novel was researched and written in different public libraries – thank you to everybody who keeps them running and funded.

Thank you to the writers of the following books, which helped to provide context for this story: *How Ireland Voted 2007: The Full Story of Ireland's General Election*; *Without Power or Glory: The Green Party in Government in Ireland*; *A Deal with the Devil: The Green Party in Government*; *Our Story: The Rossport Five*; *Once Upon a Time in the West: The Corrib Gas Controversy*; *The Irish Journey: Women's Stories of Abortion*; *Lesbian and Gay Visions of Ireland: Towards the Twenty-first Century*; Fintan O'Toole's *Ship of Fools*. I am indebted to the exhibitions, 'A History of the World in 100 Objects' and 'A History of Ireland in 100 Objects,' for the structure of this novel. I am also particularly grateful to the Irish Queer Archive and the papers of Charles Kerrigan; Risteard O Domhnaill's documentary *The Pipe*, Kathy Sheridan's 2012 feature article in *The Irish Times*, 'Stories of abortion: by people who have been through it' and to Betty Schult and Terence Conway in Erris. I should note here that both Clougheally and Dunluce Crescent are imagined places that I have located within Mayo and Dublin.

Finally, thank you to all the campaigners advocating for a fairer Ireland. In the six years since I started this novel, I've been heartened to see major shifts in Ireland for some of the movements that the characters in this novel engage with, including fossil fuel divestment and the Referendum votes in favour of gay marriage and repealing the Eighth Amendment. I wouldn't be able to write a story about fictional characters getting involved with campaigns for justice without the real people doing the work to make change happen; I'm grateful to them, especially.